Richard Doddridge B

Lorna Doone

Part II

Elibron Classics
www.elibron.com

CHAPTER XLI

Cold Comfort

All things being full of flaw, all things being full of holes, the strength of all things is in shortness. If Sir Ensor Doone had dwelled for half an hour upon himself, and an hour perhaps upon Lorna and me, we must both have wearied of him, and required change of air. But now I longed to see and know a great deal more about him, and hoped that he might not go to heaven, for at least a week or more. However he was too good for this world (as we say of all people who leave it); and I verily believe his heart was not a bad one, after all. Evil he had done, no doubt, as evil had been done to him; yet how many have done evil, while receiving only good! Be that as it may; nor further vexing of a question (settled for ever without our votes), let us own that he was, at least, a brave and courteous gentleman.

And his loss aroused great lamentation, not among the Doones alone, and the women they had carried off, but also of the general public, and many even of the magistrates, for several miles round Exmoor. All this, not only from fear lest one more wicked might succeed him (as appeared indeed too probable), but from true admiration of his strong will, and sympathy with his misfortunes.

I will not deceive anyone, by saying that Sir Ensor Doone gave (in so many words) his consent to my resolve about Lorna. This he never did, except by his speech last written down; from which, as he mentioned grandchildren, a lawyer perhaps might have argued it. Not but what he may have meant to bestow on us his blessing; only that he died next day, without taking the trouble to do it.

He called indeed for his box of snuff, which was a very high thing to take; and which he never took without being in very good humour, at least for him. And though it would not go up his nostrils, through the failure of his breath, he was pleased to have it there, and not to think of dying.

"Will your honour have it wiped?" I asked him very softly, for the brown appearance of it spoiled (to my idea) his white mostacchio; but he seemed to shake his head, and I thought it kept his spirits up. I had never before seen anyone do, what all of us have to do some day; and it greatly kept my spirits down, although it did not so very much frighten me. For it takes a man but a little while, his instinct being of death perhaps, at least as much as of life (which accounts for his slaying his fellow men so, and every other creature), it does not take a man very long to enter into another man's death, and bring his own mood to suit it. He knows that his own is sure to come; and nature is fond of practice. Hence it came to pass that I, after easing my mother's fears, and seeing a little to business, returned (as if drawn by a polar needle) to the death-bed of Sir Ensor.

There was some little confusion, people wanting to get away, and people trying to come in, from downright curiosity (of all things the most hateful), and others making great to-do, and talking of their own time to come, telling their own age, and so on. But every one seemed to think, or feel, that I had a right to be there; because the women took that view of it. As for Carver and Counsellor, they were minding their own affairs, so as to win the succession; and never found it in their business (at least so long as I was there) to come near the dying man.

He, for his part, never asked for anyone to come near him, not even a priest, nor a monk or friar; but seemed to be going his own way, peaceful, and well contented. Only the chief of the women said, that from his face she believed and knew, that he liked to have me at one side of his bed, and Lorna upon the other. An hour or two ere the old man died, when only we two were with him, he looked at us both very dimly and softly, as if he wished to do something for us, but had left it now too late. Lorna hoped that he wanted to bless us; but he only frowned at that, and let his hand drop downward, and crooked one knotted finger.

"He wants something out of the bed, dear," Lorna whispered to me; "see what it is, upon your side, there."

I followed the bent of his poor shrunken hand, and sought among the pilings; and there I felt something hard and sharp, and drew it forth and gave it to him. It flashed, like the spray of a fountain upon us, in the dark winter of the room. He could not take it in his hand, but let it hang, as daisies do; only making Lorna see that he meant her to have it.

"Why, it is my glass necklace!" Lorna cried, in great surprise; "my necklace he always promised me; and from which you have got the ring, John. But grandfather kept it, because the children wanted to pull it from my neck. May I have it now, dear grandfather? Not unless you wish, dear."

Darling Lorna wept again, because the old man could not tell her (except by one very feeble nod) that she was doing what he wished. Then she gave to me the trinket, for the sake of safety; and I stowed it in my breast. He seemed to me to follow this, and to be well content with it.

Before Sir Ensor Doone was buried, the greatest frost of the century had set in, with its iron hand, and step of stone, on everything. How it came is not my business, nor can I explain it; because I never have watched the skies; as people now begin to do, when the ground is not to their liking. Though of all this I know nothing, and less than nothing I may say (because I ought to know something); I can hear what people tell me; and I can see before my eyes.

The strong men broke three good pickaxes, ere they got through the hard brown sod, chequed with flakes of frosty white, where old Sir Ensor was to lie upon his back, awaiting the darkness of the Judgment-day. It was in the little chapel-yard; I will not tell the name of it; because we are now such Protestants, that I might do it an evil turn; only it was the little place where Lorna's Aunt Sabina lay.

Here was I, remaining long, with a little curiosity; because some people told me plainly, that I must be damned for ever by a Papist funeral; and here came Lorna; scarcely breathing through the thick of stuff around her, yet with all her little breath steaming on the air, like frost.

I stood apart from the ceremony, in which of course I was not entitled, either by birth or religion, to bear any portion; and indeed it would have been wiser in me to have kept away altogether; for now there was no one to protect me among those wild and lawless men; and both Carver and the Counsellor had vowed a fearful vengeance on me, as I heard from Gwenny. They had not dared to meddle with me, while the chief lay dying; nor was it in their policy, for a short time after that, to endanger their succession, by an open breach with Lorna, whose tender age and beauty held so many of the youths in thrall.

The ancient outlaw's funeral was a grand and moving sight; more perhaps from the sense of contrast, than from that of fitness. To see those dark and mighty men, inured to all of sin and crime, reckless both of man and God, yet now with heads devoutly bent, clasped hands, and downcast eyes, following the long black coffin of their common ancestor, to the place where they must join him, when their sum of ill was done; and to see the feeble priest chanting, over the dead form, words the living would have laughed at, sprinkling with his little broom drops that could not purify; while the children, robed in white, swung their smoking censers slowly over the cold and twilight grave: and after seeing all, to ask, with a shudder unexpressed, "Is this the end that God intended for a man so proud and strong?"

Not a tear was shed upon him, except from the sweetest of all sweet eyes; not a sigh pursued him home. Except in hot anger, his life had been very cold, and bitter, and distant; and now a week had exhausted all the sorrow of those around him, a grief flowing less from affection than fear. Aged men will show his tombstone; mothers haste with their infants by it; children shrink from the name upon it; until in time his history shall lapse, and be forgotten by all, except the great Judge and God.

After all was over, I strode across the moors very sadly; trying to keep the cold away, by virtue of quick movement. Not a flake of snow had fallen yet; all the earth was caked and hard, with a dry brown crust upon it; all the sky was banked with darkness, hard, austere, and frowning. The fog of the last three weeks was gone, neither did any rime remain; but all things had a look of sameness, and a kind of furzy colour. It was freezing hard and sharp, with a piercing wind to back it; and I had observed that the holy water froze upon Sir Ensor's coffin.

One thing struck me with some surprise, as I made off for our fireside (with a strong determination to heave an ash-tree up the chimney-place), and that was how the birds were going, rather than flying as they used to fly. All the birds were set in one direction, steadily journeying westward, not with any heat of speed, neither flying far at once; but all (as if on business bound), partly running, partly flying, partly fluttering along; silently, and without a voice, neither pricking head nor tail. This movement of the birds went on, even for a week or more; every kind of thrushes passed us, every kind of wild fowl, even plovers went away, and crows, and snipes, and woodcocks. And before half the frost was over, all we had in the snowy ditches were hares so tame that we could pat them; partridges that came to hand, with a dry noise in their crops; heath-poults, making cups of snow; and a few poor hopping redwings, flipping in and out the hedge, having lost the power to fly. And all the time, their great black eyes, set with gold around them, seemed to look at any man, for mercy and for comfort.

Annie took a many of them, all that she could find herself, and all the boys would bring her; and she made a great hutch near the fire, in the back-kitchen chimney-place. Here, in spite of our old Betty (who sadly wanted to roast them), Annie kept some fifty birds, with bread and milk, and raw chopped meat, and all the seed she could think of, and lumps of rotten apples, placed, to tempt them, in the corners. Some got on, and some died off; and Annie cried for all that died, and buried them under the wood-rick; but, I do assure you, it was a pretty thing to see, when she went to them in the morning. There was not a bird but knew her well, after one day of comforting; and some would come to her hand, and sit, and shut one eye, and look at her. Then she used to stroke their heads, and feel their breasts, and talk to them; and not a bird of them all was there, but liked to have it done to him. And I do believe they would eat from her hand things unnatural to them, lest she should be grieved and hurt, by not knowing what to do for them. One of them was a noble bird, such as I never had seen before, of very fine bright plumage, and larger than a missel-thrush. He was the hardest of all to please; and yet he tried to do his best. I have heard since then, from a man who knows all about birds, and beasts, and fishes, that he must have been a Norwegian bird, called in this country a "Roller," who never comes to England but in the most tremendous winters.

Another little bird there was, whom I longed to welcome home, and protect from enemies, a little bird no native to us, but than any native dearer. But lo, in the very night which followed old Sir Ensor's funeral, such a storm of snow began, as never have I heard nor read of, neither could have dreamed it. At what time of night it first began is more than I can say, at least from my own knowledge, for we all went to bed soon after supper, being cold, and not inclined to talk. At that time the wind was moaning sadly, and the sky as dark as a wood, and the straw in the yard swirling round and round, and the cows huddling into the great cowhouse, with their chins upon one another. But we, being blinder than they, I suppose, and not having had a great snow for years, made no preparation against the storm, except that the lambing ewes were in shelter.

It struck me, as I lay in bed, that we were acting foolishly; for an ancient shepherd had dropped in, and taken supper with us, and foretold a heavy fall, and great disaster to live stock. He said that he had known a frost beginning, just as this had done, with a black east wind, after days of raw cold fog, and then on the third night of the frost, at this very time of year (to wit on the 15th of December) such a snow set in as killed half of the sheep, and many even of the red deer, and the forest ponies. It was threescore years agone,[1] he said; and cause he had to remember it, inasmuch as two of his toes had been lost by frost nip, while he dug out his sheep, on the other side of the Dunkery. Hereupon mother nodded at him, having heard from her father about it, and how three men had been frozen to death, and how badly their stockings came off from them.

Remembering how the old man looked, and his manner of listening to the wind, and shaking his head very ominously (when Annie gave him a glass of schnapps), I grew quite uneasy in my bed, as the room got colder and colder; and I made up my mind, if it only pleased God not to send the snow till the morning, that every sheep, and horse, and cow, ay and even the jackass, should be brought in snug, and with plenty to eat, and fodder enough to roast them.

Alas, what use of man's resolves, when they come a day too late: even if they may avail a little, when they are most punctual!

In the bitter morning, I arose, to follow out my purpose, knowing the time from the force of habit, although the room was so dark and grey. An odd white light was on the rafters, such as I never had seen before; while all the length of the room was grisly, like the heart of a mouldy oat-rick. I went to the window, at once, of course; and at first I could not understand what was doing outside of it. It faced due east (as I may have said), with

---

[1] The frost of 1625.

the walnut-tree partly sheltering it; and generally I could see the yard, and the wood-rick, and even the church beyond.

But now, half the lattice was quite blocked up, as if plastered with grey lime; and little fringes, like ferns, came through, where the joining of the lead was; and in the only undarkened part, countless dots came swarming, clustering, beating with a soft low sound, then gliding down in a slippery manner, not as drops of rain do, but each distinct from his neighbour. Inside the iron frame (which fitted, not to say too comfortably, and went along the stone-work), at least a peck of snow had entered, following its own bend and fancy; light as any cobweb.

With some trouble, and great care, lest the ancient frame should yield, I spread the lattice open; and saw at once that not a moment must be lost, to save our stock. All the earth was flat with snow, all the air was thick with snow; more than this no man could see, for all the world was snowing.

I shut the window, and dressed in haste; and when I entered the kitchen, not even Betty, the earliest of all early birds, was there. I raked the ashes together a little, just to see a spark of warmth; and then set forth to find John Fry, Jem Slocomb, and Bill Dadds. But this was easier thought than done; for when I opened the court-yard door, I was taken up to my knees at once, and the power of the drifting cloud prevented sight of anything. However, I found my way to the wood-rick, and there got hold of a fine ash-stake, cut by myself not long ago. With this I ploughed along pretty well, and thundered so hard at John Fry's door, that he thought it was the Doones at least, and cocked his blunderbuss out of the window.

John was very loth to come down, when he saw the meaning of it; for he valued his life more than anything else, though he tried to make out that his wife was to blame. But I settled his doubts by telling him, that I would have him on my shoulder naked, unless he came in five minutes; not that he could do much good, but because the other men would be sure to skulk, if he set them the example. With spades, and shovels, and pitchforks, and a round of roping, we four set forth to dig out the sheep; and the poor things knew that it was high time.

CHAPTER XLII

The Great Winter

It must have snowed most wonderfully to have made that depth of covering in about eight hours. For one of Master Stickles' men, who had been out all night, said that no snow began to fall until nearly midnight. And here it was, blocking up the doors, stopping the ways, and the water-courses, and making it very much worse to walk than in a saw-pit newly used. However, we trudged along in a line; I first, and the other men after me; trying to keep my track, but finding legs and strength not up to it. Most of all, John Fry was groaning; certain that his time was come, and sending messages to his wife, and blessings to his children. For all this time it was snowing harder than it ever had snowed before, so far as a man might guess at it; and the leaden depth of the sky came down, like a mine, turned upside down on us. Not that the flakes were so very large; for I have seen much larger flakes in a shower of March, while sowing peas; but that there was no room between them, neither any relaxing, nor any change of direction.

Watch, like a good and faithful dog, followed us very cheerfully, leaping out of the depth, which took him over his back and ears already, even in the level places; while in the drifts he might have sunk to any distance out of sight, and never found his way up again. However, we helped him now and then, especially through the gaps and gateways; and so after a deal of floundering, some laughter and a little swearing, we came all safe to the lower meadow, where most of our flock was hurdled.

But behold, there was no flock at all! None, I mean, to be seen anywhere; only at one corner of the field, by the eastern end, where the snow drove in, a great white billow, as high as a barn and as broad as a house. This great drift was rolling and curdling beneath the violent blast, tufting and combing with rustling swirls, and carved (as in patterns of cornice) where the grooving chisel of the wind swept round. Ever and again, the tempest snatched little whiffs from the channelled edges, twirled them round, and made them dance over the chine of the monster pile, then let them lie like herring-bones, or the seams of sand where the tide had been. And all the while from the smothering sky, more and more fiercely at every blast, came the pelting pitiless arrows, winged with murky white, and pointed with the barbs of frost.

But although, for people who had no sheep, the sight was a very fine one (so far at least as the weather permitted any sight at all); yet for us, with our flock beneath it, this great mount had but little charm. Watch began to scratch at once, and to howl along the sides of it; he knew that his charge was buried there, and his business taken from him. But we four men set to in earnest, digging with all our might and main, shovelling away at the great white pile, and fetching it into the meadow. Each man made for himself a cave, scooping at the soft cold flux, which slid upon him at every stroke, and throwing it out behind him, in piles of castled fancy. At last we drove our tunnels in (for we worked indeed for the lives of us), and all converging towards the middle, held our tools and listened.

The other men heard nothing at all; or declared that they heard nothing, being anxious now to abandon the matter, because of the chill in their feet and knees. But I said, "Go, if you choose, all of you. I will work it out by myself, you piecrusts": and upon that they gripped their shovels, being more or less of Englishmen; and the least drop of English blood is worth the best of any other, when it comes to lasting out.

But before we began again, I laid my head well into the chamber; and there I heard a faint "ma-a-ah," coming through some ells of snow, like a plaintive buried hope, or a last appeal. I shouted aloud to cheer him up, for I knew what sheep it was, to wit the most valiant of all the wethers, who had met me when I came home from London, and been so glad to see me. And then we all fell to again; and very soon we hauled him out. Watch took charge of him at once, with an air of the noblest patronage, lying on his frozen fleece, and licking all his face and feet, to restore his warmth to him. Then fighting Tom jumped up at once and made a little butt at Watch, as if nothing had ever ailed him, and then set off to a shallow place, and looked for something to nibble at.

Further in, and close under the bank, where they had huddled themselves for warmth, we found all the rest of the poor sheep packed as closely as if they were in a great pie. It was strange to observe how their vapour, and breath, and the moisture exuding from their wool had scooped, as it were, a coved room for them, lined with a ribbing of deep yellow snow. Also the churned snow beneath their feet was as yellow as gamboge. Two or three of the weaklier hoggets were dead, from want of air, and from pressure; but more than threescore were as lively as ever, though cramped and stiff for a little while.

"However shall us get 'em home?" John Fry asked in great dismay, when he had cleared about a dozen of them; which we were forced to do very carefully, so as not to fetch the roof down. "No manner of maning to draive 'un, drough all they girt driftnesses."

"You see to this place, John," I replied, as we leaned on our shovels a moment, and the sheep came rubbing round us: "let no more of them out for the present; they are better where they be. Watch, here boy, keep them!"

Watch came, with his little scut of a tail cocked as sharp as duty; and I set him at the narrow mouth of the great snow antre. All the sheep sidled away, and got closer, that the other sheep might be bitten first, as the foolish things imagine: whereas no good sheep-dog even so much as lips a sheep to turn it.

Then of the outer sheep (all now snowed and frizzled like a lawyer's wig) I took the two finest and heaviest, and with one beneath my right arm, and the other beneath my left, I went straight home to the upper sheppey, and set them inside, and fastened them. Sixty and six I took home in that way, two at a time on each journey; and the work grew harder and harder each time, as the drifts of the snow were deepening. No other man should meddle with them: I was resolved to try my strength against the strength of the elements; and try it I did, ay and proved it. A certain fierce delight burned in me, as the struggle grew harder; but rather would I die than yield; and at last I finished it. People talk of it to this day: but none can tell what the labour was, who have not felt that snow and wind.

Of the sheep upon the mountain, and the sheep upon the western farm, and the cattle on the upper burrows, scarcely one in ten was saved; do what we would for them. And this was not through any neglect (now that our wits were sharpened), but from the pure impossibility of finding them at all. That great snow never ceased a moment for three days and nights; and then when all the earth was filled, and the topmost hedges were unseen, and the trees broke down with weight (wherever the wind had not lightened them), a brilliant sun broke forth and showed the loss of all our customs.

All our house was quite snowed up, except where we had purged a way, by dint of constant shovellings. The kitchen was as dark and darker than the cider-cellar, and long lines of furrowed scallops ran even up to the chimney-stacks. Several windows fell right inwards, through the weight of the snow against them; and the few that stood bulged in, and bent like an old bruised lanthorn. We were obliged to cook by candle-light; we were forced to read by candle-light; as for baking, we could not do it, because the oven was too chill; and a load of faggots only brought a little wet down the sides of it.

For when the sun burst forth at last upon that world of white, what he brought was neither warmth, nor cheer, nor hope of softening; only a clearer shaft of cold, from the violet depths of sky. Long-drawn alleys of white haze seemed to lead towards him, yet such as he could not come down, with any warmth remaining. Broad white curtains of the frost-fog looped around the lower sky, on the verge of hill and valley, and above the laden trees. Only round the sun himself, and the spot of heaven he claimed, clustered a bright purple-blue, clear, and calm, and deep.

That night, such a frost ensued as we had never dreamed of, neither read in ancient books, or histories of Frobisher. The kettle by the fire froze, and the crock upon the hearth-cheeks; many men were killed, and cattle rigid in their head-ropes. Then I heard that fearful sound, which never I had heard before, neither since have heard (except during that same winter), the sharp yet solemn sound of trees, burst open by the frost-blow. Our great walnut lost three branches, and has been dying ever since; though growing meanwhile, as the soul does. And the ancient oak at the cross was rent, and many score of ash-trees. But why should I tell all this? the people who have not seen it (as I have) will only make faces, and disbelieve; till such another frost comes; which perhaps may never be.

This terrible weather kept Tom Faggus from coming near our house for weeks; at which indeed I was not vexed a quarter so much as Annie was; for I had never half approved of him, as a husband for my sister; in spite of his purchase from Squire Bassett, and the grant of the Royal pardon. It may be however that Annie took the same view of my love for Lorna, and could not augur well of it; but if so, she held her peace, though I was not so sparing. For many things contributed to make me less good-humoured now than my real nature was; and the very least of all these things would have been enough to make some people cross, and rude, and fractious. I mean the red and painful chapping of my face and hands, from working in the snow all day, and lying in the frost all night. For being of a fair complexion, and a ruddy nature, and pretty plump withal, and fed on plenty of hot viktuals, and always forced by my mother to sit nearer the fire than I wished, it was wonderful to see how the cold ran revel on my cheeks and knuckles. And I feared that Lorna (if it should ever please God to stop the snowing) might take this for a proof of low and rustic blood and breeding.

And this I say was the smallest thing; for it was far more serious that we were losing half our stock, do all we would to shelter them. Even the horses in the stables (mustered altogether, for the sake of breath and steaming) had long icicles from their muzzles, almost every morning. But of all things the very gravest, to my apprehension, was the impossibility of hearing, or having any token, of or from my loved one. Not that those three days alone of snow (tremendous as it was) could have blocked the country so; but that the sky had never ceased, for more than two days at a time, for full three weeks thereafter, to pour fresh piles of fleecy mantle; neither had the wind relaxed a single day from shaking them. As a rule, it snowed all day, cleared up at night, and froze intensely, with the stars as bright as jewels, earth spread out in lustrous twilight, and the sounds in the air as sharp and crackling as artillery; then in the morning snow again, before the sun could come to help.

It mattered not what way the wind was. Often and often the vanes went round, and we hoped for change of weather: the only change was that it seemed (if possible) to grow colder. Indeed, after a week or so, the wind would regularly box the compass (as the sailors call it) in the course of every day, following where the sun should be, as if to make a mock of him. And this of course immensely added to the peril of the drifts; because they shifted every day; and no skill or care might learn them.

I believe it was on Epiphany morning, or somewhere about that period, when Lizzie ran into the kitchen to me, where I was thawing my goose-grease, with the dogs among the ashes — the live dogs, I mean, not the iron ones, for them we had given up long ago — and having caught me, by way of wonder (for generally I was out shovelling, long before my "young lady" had her night-cap off), she positively kissed me, for the sake of warming her lips perhaps, or because she had something proud to say.

"You great fool, John," said my lady, as Annie and I used to call her, on account of her airs and graces; "what a pity you never read, John!"

"Much use, I should think, in reading!" I answered, though pleased with her condescension; "read, I suppose, with roof coming in, and only this chimney left sticking out of the snow!"

"The very time to read, John," said Lizzie, looking grander; "our worst troubles are the need, whence knowledge can deliver us."

"Amen," I cried out; "are you parson or clerk? Whichever you are, good morning."

Thereupon I was bent on my usual round (a very small one nowadays), but Eliza took me with both hands, and I stopped of course; for I could not bear to shake the child, even in play, for a moment, because her back was tender. Then she looked up at me with her beautiful eyes, so large, unhealthy, and delicate, and strangely shadowing outward, as if to spread their meaning; and she said:

"Now, John, this is no time to joke. I was almost frozen in bed last night; and Annie like an icicle. Feel how cold my hands are. Now, will you listen to what I have read about climates ten times worse than this; and where none but clever men can live?"

"Impossible for me to listen now. I have hundreds of things to see to: but I will listen after breakfast to your foreign climates, child. Now attend to your mother's hot coffee."

She looked a little disappointed; but she knew what I had to do; and after all she was not so utterly unreasonable; although she did read books. And when I had done my morning's work, I listened to her patiently; and it was out of my power to think that all she said was foolish.

For I knew common sense pretty well, by this time, whether it happened to be my own, or any other person's, if clearly laid before me. And Lizzie had a particular way of setting forth very clearly whatever she wished to express and enforce. But the queerest part of it all was this, that if she could but have dreamed for a moment what would be the first application made by me of her lesson, she would rather have bitten her tongue off than help me to my purpose.

She told me that in the "Arctic Regions," as they call some places a long way north, where the Great Bear lies all across the heavens, and no sun is up, for whole months at a time, and yet where people will go exploring, out of pure contradiction, and for the sake of novelty, and love of being frozen — that here they always had such winters as we were having now. It never ceased to freeze, she said; and it never ceased to snow; except when it was too cold; and then, all the air was choked with glittering spikes; and a man's skin might come off of him, before he could ask the reason. Nevertheless the people there (although the snow was fifty feet deep, and all their breath fell behind them frozen, like a log of wood dropped from their shoulders), yet they managed to get along, and make the time of the year to each other, by a little cleverness. For seeing how the snow was spread, lightly over everything, covering up the hills and valleys, and the foreskin of the sea, they contrived a way to crown it, and to glide like a flake along. Through the sparkle of the whiteness, and the wreaths of windy tossings, and the ups and downs of cold, any man might get along with a boat on either foot, to prevent his sinking.

She told me how these boats were made; very strong and very light, of ribs with skin across them; five feet long, and one foot wide; and turned up at each end, even as a canoe is. But she did not tell me, nor did I give it a moment's thought myself, how hard it was to walk upon them, without early practice. Then she told me another thing equally useful to me; although I would not let her see how much I thought about it. And this concerned the use of sledges, and their power of gliding, and the lightness of their following; all of which I could see at once, through knowledge of our own farm-sleds; which we employ in lieu of wheels, used in flatter districts. When I had heard all this from her, a mere chit of a girl as she was, unfit to make a snowball even, or to fry snow-pancakes, I looked down on her with amazement, and began to wish a little that I had given more time to books.

But God shapes all our fitness, and gives each man his meaning, even as he guides the wavering lines of snow descending. Our Eliza was meant for books; our dear Annie for loving and cooking; I, John Ridd, for sheep, and wrestling, and the thought of Lorna; and mother to love all three of us, and to make the best of her children. And now, if I must tell the truth, as at every page I try to do (though God knows it is hard enough), I had felt through all this weather, though my life was Lorna's, something of a satisfaction in so doing duty to my kindest and best of mothers, and to none but her. For (if you come to think of it) a man's young love is very pleasant, very sweet, and tickling; and takes him through the core of heart; without his knowing how or why. Then he dwells upon it sideways, without people looking, and builds up all sorts of fancies, growing hot with working so at his own imaginings. So his love is a crystal Goddess, set upon an obelisk; and whoever will not bow the knee (yet without glancing at her), the lover makes it a sacred rite either to kick or to stick him. I am not speaking of me and Lorna, but of common people.

Then (if you come to think again) lo — or I will not say lo! for no one can behold it — only feel, or but remember, what a real mother is. Ever loving, ever soft, ever turning sin to goodness, vices into virtues; blind to all nine-tenths of wrong; through a telescope beholding (though herself so nigh to them) faintest decimal of promise, even in her vilest child. Ready to thank God again, as when her babe was born to her; leaping (as at kingdom-come) at a wandering syllable of Gospel for her lost one.

All this our mother was to us, and even more than all of this; and hence I felt a pride and joy in doing my sacred duty towards her, now that the weather compelled me. And she was as grateful, and delighted, as if she had no more claim upon me than a stranger's sheep might have. Yet from time to time I groaned within myself and by myself, at thinking of my sad debarment from the sight of Lorna, and of all that might have happened to her, now she had no protection.

Therefore I fell to at once, upon that hint from Lizzie, and being used to thatching work, and the making of traps, and so on, before very long I built myself a pair of strong and light snow-shoes, framed with ash and ribbed of withy, with half-tanned calf-skin stretched across, and an inner sole to support my feet. At first I could not walk at all, but floundered about most piteously, catching one shoe in the other, and both of them in the snow-drifts, to the great amusement of the maidens, who were come to look at me. But after a while I grew more expert, discovering what my errors were, and altering the inclination of the shoes themselves, according to a plan which Lizzie found in a book of old adventures. And this made such a difference, that I crossed the farm-yard and came back again (though turning was the worst thing of all) without so much as falling once, or getting my staff entangled.

But on the aching of my ankles, when I went to bed that night; I was forced to help myself upstairs with a couple of mop-sticks! and I rubbed the joints with neatsfoot oil, which comforted them greatly. And likely enough I would have abandoned any further trial, but for Lizzie's ridicule, and pretended sympathy; asking if the strong John Ridd would have old Betty to lean upon. Therefore I set to again, with a fixed resolve not to notice pain or stiffness, but to warm them out of me. And sure enough, before dark that day, I could get along pretty freely; especially improving every time, after leaving off and resting. The astonishment of poor John Fry, Bill Dadds, and Jem Slocomb, when they saw me coming down the hill upon them, in the twilight, where they were clearing the furze rick and trussing it for cattle, was more than I can tell you; because they did not let me see it, but ran away with one accord, and floundered into a snowdrift. They believed, and so did every one else (especially when I grew able to glide along pretty rapidly), that I had stolen Mother Melldrum's sieves, on which she was said to fly over the foreland at midnight every Saturday.

Upon the following day, I held some council with my mother; not liking to go without her permission, yet scarcely daring to ask for it. But here she disappointed me, on the right side of disappointment; saying that she had seen my pining (which she never could have done; because I had been too hard at work), and rather than watch me grieving so, for somebody or other, who now was all in all to me, I might go upon my course, and God's protection go with me! At this I was amazed, because it was not at all like mother; and knowing how well I had be-haved, ever since the time of our snowing up, I was a little moved to tell her that she could not understand me. However, my sense of duty kept me, and my knowledge of the catechism, from saying such a thing as that, or even thinking twice of it. And so I took her at her word, which she was not prepared for; and telling her how proud I was of her trust in Providence, and how I could run in my new snow-shoes, I took a short pipe in my mouth, and started forth accordingly.

CHAPTER XLIII

Not Too Soon

When I started on my road across the hills and valleys (which now were pretty much alike), the utmost I could hope to do was to gain the crest of hills, and look into the Doone Glen. Hence I might at least descry whether Lorna still was safe, by the six nests still remaining, and the view of the Captain's house. When I was come to the open country, far beyond the sheltered homestead, and in the full brunt of the wind, the keen blast of the cold broke on me, and the mighty breadth of snow. Moor and highland, field and common, cliff and vale, and water-course, over all the rolling folds of misty white were hovering. There was nothing square or jagged left, there was nothing perpendicular; all the rugged lines were eased, and all the breaches smoothly filled. Curves, and mounds, and rounded heavings took the place of rock and stump; and all the country looked as if a woman's hand had been on it.

Through the sparkling breadth of white, which seemed to glance my eyes away, and past the humps of laden trees, bowing their backs like a woodman, I contrived to get along, half sliding and half walking, in places where a plain-shodden man must have sunk, and waited freezing, till the thaw should come to him. For although there had been such violent frost, every night, upon the snow, the snow itself, having never thawed, even for an hour, had never coated over. Hence it was as soft and light, as if all had fallen yesterday. In places where no drift had been, but rather off than on to them, three feet was the least of depth: but where the wind had chased it round, or any draught led like a funnel, or anything opposed it, there you might very safely say that it ran up to twenty feet, or thirty, or even fifty, and I believe sometimes a hundred.

At last I got to my spy-hill (as I had begun to call it), although I never should have known it, but for what it looked on. And even to know this last again required all the eyes of love, soever sharp and vigilant. For all the beautiful Glen Doone (shaped from out the mountains, as if on purpose for the Doones, and looking in the summer-time like a sharp-cut vase of green) now was besnowed half up the sides, and at either end so, that it was more like the white basins wherein we boil plum-puddings. Not a patch of grass was there, not a black branch of a tree; all was white; and the little river flowed beneath an arch of snow; if it managed to flow at all.

Now this was a great surprise to me; not only because I believed Glen Doone to be a place outside all frost, but also because I thought perhaps that it was quite impossible to be cold near Lorna. And now it struck me all at once that perhaps her ewer was frozen (as mine had been for the last three weeks, requiring embers around it), and perhaps her window would not shut, any more than mine would; and perhaps she wanted blankets. This idea worked me up to such a chill of sympathy, and seeing no Doones now about, and doubting if any guns would go off, in this state of the weather, and knowing that no man could catch me up (except with shoes like mine), I even resolved to slide the cliffs, and bravely go to Lorna.

It helped me much in this resolve that the snow came on again, thick enough to blind a man who had not spent his time among it, as I had done now for days and days. Therefore I took my neatsfoot oil, which now was clogged like honey, and rubbed it hard into my leg-joints, so far as I could reach them. And then I set my back and elbows well against the snow-drift, hanging far adown the cliff, and saying some of the Lord's Prayer, threw myself on Providence. Before there was time to think or dream, I landed very beautifully upon a ridge of run-up snow in a quiet corner. My good shoes, or boots, preserved me from going far beneath it; though one of them was sadly strained, where a grub had gnawed the ash, in the early summer-time. Having set myself aright, and being in good spirits, I made boldly across the valley (where the snow was furrowed hard), being now afraid of nobody.

If Lorna had looked out of the window, she would not have known me, with those boots upon my feet, and a well-cleaned sheepskin over me, bearing my own (J.R.) in red, just between my shoulders, but covered now in snowflakes. The house was partly drifted up, though not so much as ours was; and I crossed the little stream almost without knowing that it was under me. At first, being pretty safe against interference from the other huts, by virtue of the blinding snow, and the difficulty of walking, I examined all the windows; but these were coated so with ice, like ferns and flowers and dazzling stars, that no one could so much as guess what might be inside of them. Moreover I was afraid of prying narrowly into them, as it was not a proper thing where a maiden might be: only I wanted to know just this, whether she were there, or not.

Taking nothing by this movement, I was forced, much against my will, to venture to the door and knock, in a hesitating manner, not being sure but what my answer might be the mouth of a carbine. However it was not so, for I heard a pattering of feet and a whispering going on, and then a shrill voice through the keyhole, asking, "Who's there?"

"Only me, John Ridd," I answered; upon which I heard a little laughter, and a little sobbing, or something that was like it; and then the door was opened about a couple of inches, with a bar behind it still; and then the little voice went on:

"Put thy finger in, young man, with the old ring on it. But mind thee, if it be the wrong one, thou shalt never draw it back again."

Laughing at Gwenny's mighty threat, I showed my finger in the opening: upon which she let me in, and barred the door again like lightning.

"What is the meaning of all this, Gwenny?" I asked, as I slipped about on the floor, for I could not stand there firmly with my great snow-shoes on.

"Maning enough, and bad maning too," the Cornish girl made answer. "Us be shut in here, and starving, and durstn't let anybody in upon us. I wish thou wer't good to ate, young man: I could manage most of thee."

I was so frightened by her eyes, full of wolfish hunger, that I could only say, "Good God!" having never seen the like before. Then drew I forth a large piece of bread, which I had brought in case of accidents, and placed it in her hands. She leaped at it, as a starving dog leaps at sight of his supper, and she set her teeth in it, and then withheld it from her lips, with something very like an oath at her own vile greediness; and then away round the corner with it, no doubt for her young mistress. I meanwhile was occupied, to the best of my ability, in taking my snow-shoes off, yet wondering much within myself, why Lorna did not come to me.

But presently I knew the cause; for Gwenny called me, and I ran, and found my darling quite unable to say so much as, "John, how are you?" Between the hunger, and the cold, and the excitement of my coming, she had fainted away, and lay back on a chair, as white as the snow around us. In betwixt her delicate lips, Gwenny was thrusting with all her strength the hard brown crust of the rye-bread, which she had snatched from me so.

"Get water, or get snow," I said; "don't you know what fainting is, you very stupid child?"

"Never heered on it, in Carnwall," she answered, trusting still to the bread: "be un the same as bleeding?"

"It will be directly, if you go on squeezing away with that crust so. Eat a piece: I have got some more. Leave my darling now to me."

Hearing that I had some more, the starving girl could resist no longer, but tore it in two, and had swallowed half before I had coaxed my Lorna back to sense, and hope, and joy, and love.

"I never expected to see you again. I had made up my mind to die, John; and to die without your knowing it."

As I repelled this fearful thought in a manner highly fortifying, the tender hue flowed back again into her famished cheeks and lips, and a softer brilliance glistened from the depth of her dark eyes. She gave me one little shrunken hand, and I could not help a tear for it.

"After all, Mistress Lorna," I said, pretending to be gay, for a smile might do her good; "you do not love me as Gwenny does; for she even wanted to eat me."

"And shall, afore I have done, young man," Gwenny answered, laughing; "you come in here with they red chakes, and make us think o' sirloin."

"Eat up your bit of brown bread, Gwenny. It is not good enough for your mistress. Bless her heart, I have something here such as she never tasted the like of, being in such appetite. Look here, Lorna; smell it first. I have had it ever since Twelfth-day, and kept it all the time for you. Annie made it. That is enough to warrant it good cooking."

And then I showed my great mince-pie in a bag of tissue paper, and I told them how the mince-meat was made of golden pippins finely shred, with the undercut of the sirloin, and spice and fruit accordingly and far beyond my knowledge. But Lorna would not touch a morsel, until she had thanked God for it, and given me the kindest kiss, and put a piece in Gwenny's mouth.

I have eaten many things myself, with very great enjoyment, and keen perception of their merits, and some thanks to God for them. But I never did enjoy a thing, that had found its way between my own lips, half or even a quarter as much as I now enjoyed beholding Lorna, sitting proudly upwards (to show that she was faint no more) entering into that mince-pie, and moving all her pearls of teeth (inside her little mouth-place) exactly as I told her. For I was afraid lest she should be too fast in going through it, and cause herself more damage so, than she got of nourishment. But I had no need to fear at all, and Lorna could not help laughing at me, for thinking that she had no self-control.

Some creatures require a deal of food (I myself among the number), and some can do with a very little; making, no doubt, the best of it. And I have often noticed, that the plumpest and most perfect women never eat so hard, and fast, as the skinny and three-cornered ones. These last be often ashamed of it, and eat most when the men be absent. Hence it came to pass that Lorna, being the loveliest of all maidens, had as much as she could do to finish her own half of pie; whereas Gwenny Carfax (though generous more than greedy) ate up hers without winking, after finishing the brown loaf; and then I begged to know the meaning of this state of things.

"The meaning is sad enough," said Lorna; "and I see no way out of it. We are both to be starved until I let them do what they like with me."

"That is to say, until you chose to marry Carver Doone, and be slowly killed by him."

"Slowly! No, John, quickly. I hate him with such bitterness, that less than a week would kill me."

"Not a doubt of that," said Gwenny: "oh, she hates him nicely then: but not half so much as I do."

I told them both that this state of things could be endured no longer: on which point they agreed with me, but saw no means to help it. For even if Lorna could make up her mind to come away with me, and live at Plover's Barrows farm, under my good mother's care, as I had urged so often, behold the snow was all around us, heaped as high as mountains, and how could any delicate maiden ever get across it?

Then I spoke, with a strange tingle upon both sides of my heart, knowing that this undertaking was a serious one for all, and might burn our farm down:

"If I warrant to take you safe, and without much fright or hardship, Lorna, will you come with me?"

"To be sure I will, dear," said my beauty with a smile, and a glance to follow it; "I have small alternative, to starve, or go with you, John."

"Gwenny, have you courage for it? Will you come with your young mistress?"

"Will I stay behind?" cried Gwenny, in a voice that settled it. And so we began to arrange about it; and I was much excited. It was useless now to leave it longer: if it could be done at all, it could not be too quickly done. It was the Counsellor who had ordered, after all other schemes had failed, that his niece should have no food until she would obey him. He had strictly watched the house, taking turns with Carver, to ensure that none came nigh it bearing food or comfort. But this evening, they had thought it needless to remain on guard; and it would have been impossible, because themselves were busy, offering high festival to all the valley, in right of their own commandership. And Gwenny said that nothing made her so nearly mad with appetite as the account she received, from a woman, of all the dishes preparing. Nevertheless she had answered bravely:

"Go and tell the Counsellor, and go and tell the Carver, who sent you to spy upon us, that we shall have a finer dish than any set before them." And so in truth they did, although so little dreaming it; for no Doone that was ever born, however much of a Carver, might vie with our Annie for mince-meat.

Now while we sat, reflecting much, and talking a good deal more, in spite of all the cold — for I never was in a hurry to go, when I had Lorna with me — she said, in her silvery voice, which always led me so along, as if I were slave to a beautiful bell:

"Now, John, we are wasting time, dear. You have praised my hair, till it curls with pride, and my eyes till you cannot see them, even if they are brown diamonds, which I have heard for the fiftieth time at least; though I never saw such a jewel. Don't you think that it is high time to put on your snow-shoes. John?"

"Certainly not," I answered, "till we have settled something more. I was so cold when I came in; and now I am as warm as a cricket. And so are you, you lively soul; though you are not upon my hearth yet."

"Remember, John," said Lorna, nestling for a moment to me; "the severity of the weather makes a great difference between us. And you must never take advantage."

"I quite understand all that, dear. And the harder it freezes the better, while that understanding continues. Now do try to be serious."

"I try to be serious! And I have been trying fifty times, and could not bring you to it, John! Although I am sure the situation, as the Counsellor always says, at the beginning of a speech, the situation, to say the least, is serious enough for anything. Come, Gwenny, imitate him.''

Gwenny was famed for her imitation of the Counsellor making a speech; and she began to shake her hair, and mount upon a footstool; but I really could not have this, though even Lorna ordered it. The truth was that my darling maiden was in such wild spirits, at seeing me so unexpected, and at the prospect of release, and of what she had never known, quiet life, and happiness, that like all warm and loving natures, she could scarce control herself.

"Come to this frozen window, John, and see them light the stack-fire. They will little know who looks at them. Now be very good, John. You stay in that corner, dear, and I will stand on this side; and try to breathe yourself a peep-hole through the lovely spears and banners. Oh, you don't know how to do it. I must do it for you. Breathe three times, like that, and that; and then you rub it with your fingers, before it has time to freeze again."

All this she did so beautifully, with her lips put up like cherries, and her fingers bent half back, as only girls can bend them, and her little waist thrown out against the white of the snowed-up window, that I made her do it three times over; and I stopped her every time, and let it freeze again, that so she might be the longer. Now I knew that all her love was mine, every bit as much as mine was hers; yet I must have her to show it, dwelling upon every proof, lengthening out all certainty. Perhaps the jealous heart is loth to own a life worth twice its own. Be that as it may, I know that we thawed the window nicely.

And then I saw, far down the stream (or rather down the bed of it, for there was no stream visible), a little form of fire arising, red, and dark, and flickering. Presently it caught on something, and went upward boldly; and then it struck into many forks, and then it fell, and rose again.

"Do you know what all that is, John?" asked Lorna, smiling cleverly at the manner of my staring.

"How on earth should I know? Papists burn Protestants in the flesh; and Protestants burn Papists in effigy, as we mock them. Lorna, are they going to burn anyone to-night?"

"No, you dear. I must rid you of these things. I see that you are bigoted. The Doones are firing Dunkery beacon, to celebrate their new captain."

"But how could they bring it here, through the snow? If they have sledges, I can do nothing."

"They brought it before the snow began. The moment poor grandfather was gone, even before his funeral, the young men, having none to check them, began at once upon it. They had always borne a grudge against it: not that it ever did them harm; but because it seemed so insolent. 'Can't a gentleman go home, without a smoke behind him?' I have often heard them saying. And though they have done it no great harm, since they threw the firemen on the fire, many, many years ago, they have often promised to bring it here for their candle; and now they have done it. Ah, now look! The tar is kindled."

Though Lorna took it so in joke, I looked upon it very gravely, knowing that this heavy outrage to the feelings of the neighbourhood would cause more stir than a hundred sheep stolen, or a score of houses sacked. Not of course that the beacon was of the smallest use to anyone, neither stopped anybody from stealing: nay, rather it was like the parish-knell, which begins when all is over, and depresses all the survivors; yet I knew that we valued it, and were proud, and spoke of it as a mighty institution; and even more than that, our vestry had voted, within the last two years, seven shillings and sixpence to pay for it, in proportion with other parishes. And one of the men who attended to it, or at least who was paid for doing so, was our Jem Slocomb's grandfather.

However, in spite of all my regrets, the fire went up very merrily, blazing red and white and yellow, as it leaped on different things. And the light danced on the snowdrifts with a misty lilac hue. I was astonished at its burning in such mighty depths of snow; but Gwenny said that the wicked men had been three days hard at work, clearing, as it were, a cockpit, for their fire to have its way. And now they had a mighty pile, which must have covered five landyards square, heaped up to a goodly height, and eager to take fire.

In this I saw great obstacle to what I wished to manage. For when this pyramid should be kindled thoroughly, and pouring light and blazes round, would not all the valley be like a white room full of candles? Thinking thus, I was half inclined to abide my time for another night; and then my second thoughts convinced me that I would be a fool in this. For lo, what an opportunity! All the Doones would be drunk of course, in about three hours' time, and getting more and more in drink, as the night went on. As for the fire, it must sink in about three hours or more, and only cast uncertain shadows friendly to my purpose. And then the outlaws must cower round it, as the cold increased on them, helping the weight of the liquor; and in their jollity any noise would be cheered as a false alarm. Most of all, and which decided once for all my action — when these wild and reckless villains should be hot with ardent spirits, what was door, or wall, to stand betwixt them and my Lorna?

This thought quickened me so much that I touched my darling reverently, and told her in a few short words how I hoped to manage it.

"Sweetest, in two hours' time I shall be again with you. Keep the bar up, and have Gwenny ready to answer anyone. You are safe while they are dining, dear, and drinking healths, and all that stuff; and before they have done with that, I shall be again with you. Have everything you care to take in a very little compass; and Gwenny must have no baggage. I shall knock loud, and then wait a little; and then knock twice, very softly."

With this, I folded her in my arms; and she looked frightened at me; not having perceived her danger: and then I told Gwenny over again what I had told her mistress; but she only nodded her head and said, "Young man, go and teach thy grandmother."

CHAPTER XLIV

Brought Home at Last

To my great delight, I found that the weather, not often friendly to lovers, and lately seeming so hostile, had in the most important matter done me a signal service. For when I had promised to take my love from the power of those wretches, the only way of escape apparent lay through the main Doone-gate. For though I might climb the cliffs myself, especially with the snow to aid me, I durst not try to fetch Lorna up them, even if she were not half-starved, as well as partly frozen; and as for Gwenny's door, as we called it (that is to say, the little entrance from the wooded hollow), it was snowed up long ago to the level of the hills around. Therefore I was at my wits' end, how to get them out; the passage by the Doone-gate being long, and dark, and difficult, and leading to such a weary circuit among the snowy moors and hills.

But now, being homeward bound by the shortest possible track, I slipped along between the bonfire and the boundary cliffs, where I found a caved way of snow behind a sort of avalanche: so that if the Doones had been keeping watch (which they were not doing, but revelling) they could scarcely have discovered me. And when I came to my old ascent, where I had often scaled the cliff and made across the mountains, it struck me that I would just have a look at my first and painful entrance, to wit, the water-slide. I never for a moment imagined that this could help me now; for I never had dared to descend it, even in the finest weather; still I had a curiosity to know what my old friend was like, with so much snow upon him. But, to my very great surprise, there was scarcely any snow there at all, though plenty curling high overhead from the cliff, like bolsters over it. Probably the sweeping of the north-east wind up the narrow chasm had kept the showers from blocking it, although the water had no power under the bitter grip of frost. All my water-slide was now less a slide than path of ice; furrowed where the waters ran over fluted ridges; seamed where wind had tossed and combed them, even while congealing; and crossed with little steps wherever the freezing torrent lingered. And here and there the ice was fibred with the trail of sludge-weed, slanting from the side, and matted, so as to make resting-place.

Lo, it was easy track and channel, as if for the very purpose made, down which I could guide my sledge, with Lorna sitting in it. There were only two things to be feared; one lest the rolls of snow above should fall in and bury us; the other lest we should rush too fast, and so be carried headlong into the black whirlpool at the bottom, the middle of which was still unfrozen, and looking more horrible by the contrast. Against this danger I made provision, by fixing a stout bar across; but of the other we must take our chance, and trust ourselves to Providence.

I hastened home at my utmost speed, and told my mother for God's sake to keep the house up till my return, and to have plenty of fire blazing, and plenty of water boiling, and food enough hot for a dozen people, and the best bed aired with the warming-pan. Dear mother smiled softly at my excitement, though her own was not much less, I am sure, and enhanced by sore anxiety. Then I gave very strict directions to Annie, and praised her a little, and kissed her; and I even endeavoured to flatter Eliza, lest she should be disagreeable.

After this I took some brandy, both within and about me; the former, because I had sharp work to do; and the latter in fear of whatever might happen, in such great cold, to my comrades. Also I carried some other provisions, grieving much at their coldness; and then I went to the upper linhay, and took our new light pony-sledd, which had been made almost as much for pleasure as for business; though God only knows how our girls could have found any pleasure in bumping along so. On the snow, however, it ran as sweetly as if it had been made for it; yet I durst not take the pony with it; in the first place, because his hoofs would break through the ever-shifting surface of the light and piling snow; and secondly, because those ponies, coming from the forest, have a dreadful trick of neighing, and most of all in frosty weather.

Therefore I girded my own body with a dozen turns of hay-rope, twisting both the ends in under at the bottom of my breast, and winding the hay on the skew a little, that the hempen thong might not slip between, and so cut me in the drawing. I put a good piece of spare rope in the sledd, and the cross-seat with the back to it, which was stuffed with our own wool, as well as two or three fur coats: and then, just as I was starting, out came Annie, in spite of the cold, panting for fear of missing me, and with nothing on her head, but a lanthorn in one hand. "Oh, John, here is the most wonderful thing! Mother has never shown it before; and I can't think how she could make up her mind. She had gotten it in a great well of a cupboard, with camphor, and spirits, and lavender. Lizzie says it is a most magnificent sealskin cloak, worth fifty pounds, or a farthing."

"At any rate it is soft and warm," said I, very calmly flinging it into the bottom of the sledd. "Tell mother I will put it over Lorna's feet."

"Lorna's feet! Oh, you great fool!" cried Annie, for the first time reviling me: "over her shoulders; and be proud, you very stupid John."

"It is not good enough for her feet," I answered, with strong emphasis; "but don't tell mother I said so, Annie. Only thank her very kindly."

With that I drew my traces hard, and set my ashen staff into the snow, and struck out with my best foot foremost (the best one at snow-shoes, I mean), and the sledd came after me as lightly as a dog might follow; and Annie with the lanthorn seemed to be left behind and waiting, like a pretty lamp-post.

The full moon rose as bright behind me as a patin of pure silver, casting on the snow long shadows of the few things left above, burdened rock, and shaggy foreland, and the labouring trees. In the great white desolation, distance was a mocking vision: hills looked nigh, and valleys far; when hills were far and valleys nigh. And the misty breath of frost, piercing through the ribs of rock, striking to the pith of trees, creeping to the heart of man, lay along the hollow places, like a serpent sloughing. Even as my own gaunt shadow (travestied as if I were the moonlight's daddy-longlegs) went before me down the slope; even I, the shadow's master, who had tried in vain to cough, when coughing brought good liquorice, felt a pressure on my bosom, and a husking in my throat.

However, I went on quietly, and at a very tidy speed; being only too thankful that the snow had ceased, and no wind as yet arisen. And from the ring of low white vapour girding all the verge of sky, and from the rosy blue above, and the shafts of starlight set upon a quivering bow, as well as from the moon itself, and the light behind it, having learned the signs of frost from its bitter twinges, I knew that we should have a night as keen as ever England felt. Nevertheless, I had work enough to keep me warm if I managed it. The question was, could I contrive to save my darling from it?

Daring not to risk my sledd by any fall from the valley-cliffs, I dragged it very carefully up the steep incline of ice, through the narrow chasm, and so to the very brink and verge where first I had seen my Lorna, in the fishing-days of boyhood. As then I had a trident fork, for sacking of the loaches, so now I had a strong ash stake, to lay across from rock to rock, and break the speed of descending. With this I moored the sledd quite safe, at the very lip of the chasm, where all was now substantial ice, green and black in the moonlight; and then I set off up the valley, skirting along one side of it.

The stack-fire still was burning strongly, but with more of heat than blaze; and many of the younger Doones were playing on the verge of it, the children making rings of fire, and their mothers watching them. All the grave and reverend warriors, having heard of rheumatism, were inside of log and stone, in the two lowest houses, with enough of candles burning to make our list of sheep come short.

All these I passed, without the smallest risk or difficulty, walking up the channel of drift which I spoke of once before. And then I crossed, with more of care, and to the door of Lorna's house, and made the sign, and listened, after taking my snow-shoes off.

But no one came, as I expected, neither could I espy a light. And I seemed to hear a faint low sound, like the moaning of the snow-wind. Then I knocked again more loudly, with a knocking at my heart; and receiving no answer, set all my power at once against the door. In a moment it flew inwards, and I glided along the passage with my feet still slippery. There in Lorna's room I saw, by the moonlight flowing in, a sight which drove me beyond sense.

Lorna was behind a chair, crouching in the corner, with her hands up, and a crucifix, or something that looked like it. In the middle of the room lay Gwenny Carfax, stupid, yet with one hand clutching the ankle of a struggling man. Another man stood above my Lorna, trying to draw the chair away. In a moment I had him round the waist, and he went out of the window with a mighty crash of glass; luckily for him that window had no bars like some of them. Then I took the other man by the neck; and he could not plead for mercy. I bore him out of the house as lightly as I would bear a baby, yet squeezing his throat a little more than I fain would do to an infant. By the bright moonlight I saw that I carried Marwood de Whichehalse. For his father's sake I spared him, and because he had been my schoolfellow: but with every muscle of my body strung with indignation, I cast him, like a skittle, from me into a snowdrift, which closed over him. Then I looked for the other fellow, tossed through Lorna's window; and found him lying stunned and bleeding, neither able to groan yet. Charleworth Doone, if his gushing blood did not much mislead me.

It was no time to linger now: I fastened my shoes in a moment, and caught up my own darling with her head upon my shoulder, where she whispered faintly; and telling Gwenny to follow me, or else I would come back for her, if she could not walk the snow, I ran the whole distance to my sledd, caring not who might follow me. Then by the time I had set up Lorna, beautiful and smiling, with the sealskin cloak all over her, sturdy Gwenny came along, having trudged in the track of my snow-shoes, although with two bags on her back. I set her in beside her mistress, to support her, and keep warm; and then with one look back at the glen, which had been so long my home of heart, I hung behind the sledd, and launched it down the steep and dangerous way.

Though the cliffs were black above us, and the road unseen in front, and a great white grave of snow might at a single word come down, Lorna was as calm and happy as an infant in its bed. She knew that I was with her; and when I told her not to speak, she touched my hand in silence. Gwenny was in a much greater fright, having never seen such a thing before, neither knowing what it is to yield to pure love's confidence. I could hardly keep her quiet, without making a noise myself. With my staff from rock to rock, and my weight thrown backward, I broke the sledd's too rapid way, and brought my grown love safely out, by the self-same road which first had led me to her girlish fancy, and my boyish slavery.

Unpursued, yet looking back as if some one must be after us, we skirted round the black whirling pool, and gained the meadows beyond it. Here there was hard collar work, the track being all uphill and rough; and Gwenny wanted to jump out, to lighten the sledd and to push behind. But I would not hear of it; because it was now so deadly cold, and I feared that Lorna might get frozen, without having Gwenny to keep her warm. And after all, it was the sweetest labour I had ever known in all my life, to be sure that I was pulling Lorna, and pulling her to our own farm-house.

Gwenny's nose was touched with frost, before we had gone much further, because she would not keep it quiet and snug beneath the sealskin. And here I had to stop in the moonlight (which was very dangerous) and rub it with a clove of snow, as Eliza had taught me; and Gwenny scolding all the time, as if myself had frozen it. Lorna was now so far oppressed with all the troubles of the evening, and the joy that followed them, as well as by the piercing cold and difficulty of breathing, that she lay quite motionless, like fairest wax in the moonlight — when we stole a glance at her, beneath the dark folds of the cloak; and I thought that she was falling into the heavy snow-sleep, whence there is no awaking.

Therefore I drew my traces tight, and set my whole strength to the business; and we slipped along at a merry pace, although with many joltings, which must have sent my darling out into the cold snow-drifts, but for the short strong arm of Gwenny. And so in about an hour's time, in spite of many hindrances, we came home to the old court-yard, and all the dogs saluted us. My heart was quivering, and my cheeks as hot as the Doone's bonfire, with wondering both what Lorna would think of our farmyard, and what my mother would think of her. Upon the former subject my anxiety was wasted, for Lorna neither saw a thing, nor even opened her heavy eyes. And as to what mother would think of her, she was certain not to think at all, until she had cried over her.

And so indeed it came to pass. Even at this length of time, I can hardly tell it, although so bright before my mind, because it moves my heart so. The sledd was at the open door, with only Lorna in it: for Gwenny Carfax had jumped out, and hung back in the clearing, giving any reason rather than the only true one —

that she would not be intruding. At the door were all our people; first of course Betty Muxworthy, teaching me how to draw the sledd, as if she had been born in it and flourishing with a great broom, wherever a speck of snow lay. Then dear Annie, and old Molly (who was very quiet, and counted almost for nobody), and behind them mother, looking as if she wanted to come first, but doubted how the manners lay. In the distance Lizzie stood, fearful of encouraging, but unable to keep out of it.

Betty was going to poke her broom right in under the sealskin cloak, where Lorna lay unconscious, and where her precious breath hung frozen, like a silver cobweb; but I caught up Betty's broom, and flung it clean away over the corn chamber; and then I put the others by, and fetched my mother forward.

"You shall see her first," I said; "is she not your daughter? Hold the light there, Annie."

Dear mother's hands were quick and trembling, as she opened the shining folds; and there she saw my Lorna sleeping, with her black hair all dishevelled, and she bent and kissed her forehead, and only said, "God bless her, John!" And then she was taken with violent weeping, and I was forced to hold her.

"Us may tich of her now, I rackon," said Betty in her most jealous way: "Annie, tak her by the head, and I'll tak her by the toesen. No taime to stand here like girt gawks. Don'ee tak on zo, missus. Ther be vainer vish in the zea — Lor, but her be a booty!"

With this, they carried her into the house, Betty chattering all the while, and going on now about Lorna's hands, and the others crowding round her, so that I thought I was not wanted among so many women, and should only get the worst of it, and perhaps do harm to my darling. Therefore I went and brought Gwenny in, and gave her a potful of bacon and peas, and an iron spoon to cat it with, which she did right heartily.

Then I asked her how she could have been such a fool as to let those two vile fellows enter the house where Lorna was; and she accounted for it so naturally, that I could only blame myself. For my agreement had been to give one loud knock (if you happen to remember) and after that two little knocks. Well, these two drunken rogues had come; and one, being very drunk indeed, had given a great thump; and then nothing more to do with it; and the other, being three-quarters drunk, had followed his leader (as one might say) but feebly, and making two of it. Whereupon up jumped Lorna, and declared that her John was there.

All this Gwenny told me shortly, between the whiles of eating, and even while she licked the spoon: and then there came a message for me, that my love was sensible, and was seeking all around for me. Then I told Gwenny to hold her tongue (whatever she did, among us), and not to trust to women's words; and she told me they all were liars, as she had found out long ago; and the only thing to believe in was an honest man, when found. Thereupon I could have kissed her, as a sort of tribute, liking to be appreciated; yet the peas upon her lips made me think about it; and thought is fatal to action. So I went to see my dear.

That sight I shall not forget; till my dying head falls back, and my breast can lift no more. I know not whether I were then more blessed, or harrowed by it. For in the settle was my Lorna, propped with pillows round her, and her clear hands spread sometimes to the blazing fireplace. In her eyes no knowledge was of anything around her, neither in her neck the sense of leaning towards anything. Only both her lovely hands were entreating something, to spare her or to love her; and the lines of supplication quivered in her sad white face.

"All go away except my mother," I said very quietly, but so that I would be obeyed; and everybody knew it. Then mother came to me alone; and she said, "The frost is in her brain: I have heard of this before, John." "Mother, I will have it out," was all that I could answer her; "leave her to me altogether: only you sit there and watch." For I felt that Lorna knew me, and no other soul but me; and that if not interfered with, she would soon come home to me. Therefore I sat gently by her, leaving nature, as it were, to her own good time and will. And presently the glance that watched me, as at distance and in doubt, began to flutter and to brighten, and to deepen into kindness, then to beam with trust and love, and then with gathering tears to falter, and in shame to turn away. But the small entreating hands found their way, as if by instinct, to my great protecting palms; and trembled there, and rested there.

For a little while we lingered thus, neither wishing to move away, neither caring to look beyond the presence of the other; both alike so full of hope, and comfort, and true happiness; if only the world would let us be. And then a little sob disturbed us, and mother tried to make believe that she was only coughing. But Lorna, guessing who she was, jumped up so very rashly that she almost set her frock on fire from the great ash-log; and away she ran to the old oak chair, where mother was by the clock-case pretending to be knitting, and she took the work from mothers hands, and laid them both upon her head, kneeling humbly, and looking up.

"God bless you, my fair mistress!" said mother, bending nearer; and then as Lorna's gaze prevailed, "God bless you, my sweet child!"

And so she went to mother's heart, by the very nearest road, even as she had come to mine; I mean the road of pity, smoothed by grace, and youth, and gentleness.

CHAPTER XLV

A Change Long Needed

Jeremy Stickles was gone south, ere ever the frost set in, for the purpose of mustering forces to attack the Doone Glen. But now this weather had put a stop to every kind of movement; for even if men could have borne the cold, they could scarcely be brought to face the perils of the snow-drifts. And to tell the truth, I cared not how long this weather lasted, so long as we had enough to eat, and could keep ourselves from freezing. Not only that I did not want Master Stickles back again, to make more disturbances; but also that the Doones could not come prowling after Lorna, while the snow lay piled between us, with the surface soft and dry. Of course, they would very soon discover where their lawful queen was, although the track of sledd and snow-shoes had been quite obliterated by another shower, before the revellers could have grown half as drunk as they intended. But Marwood de Whichehalse, who had been snowed up among them (as Gwenny said), after helping to strip the beacon, that young Squire was almost certain to have recognized me, and to have told vile Carver. And it gave me no little pleasure to think how mad that Carver must be with me, for robbing him of the lovely bride whom he was starving into matrimony. However, I was not pleased at all with the prospect of the consequences; but set all hands on to thresh the corn, ere the Doones could come and burn the ricks. For I knew that they could not come yet, inasmuch as even a forest pony could not traverse the country, much less the heavy horses needed to carry such men as they were. And hundreds of the forest ponies died in this hard weather, some being buried in the snow, and more of them starved for want of grass.

Going through this state of things, and laying down the law about it (subject to correction), I very soon persuaded Lorna that for the present she was safe, and (which made her still more happy) that she was not only welcome, but as gladdening to our eyes as the flowers of May. Truly, so far as regarded myself, this was not a hundredth part of the real truth; and even as regarded others, I might have said it ten times over. For Lorna had so won them all, by her kind and gentle ways, and her mode of hearkening to everybody's trouble, and replying without words, as well as by her beauty, and simple grace of all things, that I could almost wish sometimes the rest would leave her more to me. But mother could not do enough; and Annie almost worshipped her; and even Lizzie could not keep her bitterness towards her; especially when she found that Lorna knew as much of books as need be.

As for John Fry, and Betty, and Molly, they were a perfect plague, when Lorna came into the kitchen. For betwixt their curiosity to see a live Doone in the flesh (when certain not to eat them), and their high respect for birth (with or without honesty), and their intense desire to know all about Master John's sweetheart (dropped, as they said, from the snow-clouds), and most of their admiration of a beauty, such as never even their angels could have seen — betwixt and between all this, I say, there was no getting the dinner cooked, with Lorna in the kitchen.

And the worst of it was that Lorna took the strangest of all strange fancies for this very kitchen; and it was hard to keep her out of it. Not that she had any special bent for cooking, as our Annie had; rather indeed the contrary, for she liked to have her food ready cooked; but that she loved the look of the place, and the cheerful fire burning, and the racks of bacon to be seen, and the richness, and the homeliness, and the pleasant smell of everything. And who knows but what she may have liked (as the very best of maidens do) to be admired, now and then, between the times of business?

Therefore if you wanted Lorna (as I was always sure to do, God knows how many times a day) the very surest place to find her was our own old kitchen. Not gossiping, I mean, nor loitering, neither seeking into things; but seeming to be quite at home, as if she had known it from a child, and seeming (to my eyes at least) to light it up, and make life and colour out of all the dulness; as I have seen the breaking sun do among brown shocks of wheat.

But anyone who wished to learn whether girls can change or not, as the things around them change (while yet their hearts are steadfast, and for ever anchored), he should just have seen my Lorna, after a fortnight of our life, and freedom from anxiety. It is possible that my company — although I am accounted stu-

pid, by folk who do not know my way — may have had something to do with it; but upon this I will not say much, lest I lose
my character. And indeed, as regards company, I had all the
threshing to see to, and more than half to do myself (though any
stranger would have thought that even John Fry must work hard
this weather), else I could not hope at all, to get our corn into
such compass that a good gun might protect it.

But to come back to Lorna again (which I always longed
to do, and must long for ever), all the change between night and
day, all the shifts of cloud and sun, all the difference between
black death and brightsome liveliness, scarcely may suggest or
equal Lorna's transformation. Quick she had always been, and
"peart" (as we say on Exmoor) and gifted with a leap of thought
too swift for me to follow; and hence you may find fault with
much, when I report her sayings. But through the whole had always run, as a black string goes through pearls, something dark
and touched with shadow, coloured as with an early end.

But, now, behold, there was none of this! There was no
getting her, for a moment even, to be serious. All her bright
young wit was flashing, like a newly awakened flame, and all
her high young spirits leaped, as if dancing to its fire. And yet
she never spoke a word which gave more pain than pleasure.

And even in her outward look there was much of difference. Whether it was our warmth, and freedom, and our harmless
love of God, and trust in one another; or whether it were our air,
and water, and the pea-fed bacon; anyhow my Lorna grew richer
and more lovely, more perfect and more firm of figure, and more
light and buoyant, with every passing day that laid its tribute on
her cheeks and lips. I was allowed one kiss a day; only one for
manners' sake, because she was our visitor; and I might have it
before breakfast, or else when I came to say "good night!" according as I decided. And I decided, every night, not to take it in
the morning, but put it off till the evening time, and have the
pleasure to think about it, through all the day of working. But
when my darling came up to me in the early daylight, fresher
than the daystar, and with no one looking; only her bright eyes
smiling, and sweet lips quite ready, was it likely I could wait,
and think all day about it? For she wore a frock of Annie's,
nicely made to fit her, taken in at the waist and curved — I never

could explain it, not being a mantua-maker; but I know how her figure looked in it, and how it came towards me.

But this is neither here nor there; and I must on with my story. Those days are very sacred to me; and if I speak lightly of them, trust me, 'tis with lip alone; while from heart, reproach peeps sadly at the flippant tricks of mind.

Although it was the longest winter ever known in our parts (never having ceased to freeze for a single night, and scarcely for a single day, from the middle of December till the second week in March), to me it was the very shortest and the most delicious; and verily I do believe it was the same to Lorna. But when the Ides of March were come (of which I do remember something dim from school, and something clear from my favourite writer), lo there were increasing signals of a change of weather.

One leading feature of that long cold, and a thing re-marked by every one (however unobserved), had been the hollow moaning sound ever present in the air, morning, noon, and night-time, and especially at night, whether any wind were stirring, or whether it were a perfect calm. Our people said that it was a witch, cursing all the country from the caverns by the sea; and that frost and snow would last, until we could catch and drown her. But the land being thoroughly blocked with snow, and the inshore parts of the sea with ice (floating in great fields along). Mother Melldrum (if she it were) had the caverns all to herself, for there was no getting at her. And speaking of the sea reminds me of a thing reported to us, and on good authority; though people might be found hereafter who would not believe it, unless I told them that, from what I myself beheld of the channel, I place perfect faith in it; and this is, that a dozen sailors at the beginning of March crossed the ice, with the aid of poles, from Clevedon to Penarth, or where the Holm rocks barred the flotage.

But now, about the tenth of March, that miserable moan-ing noise, which had both foregone and accompanied the rigour, died away from out the air; and we, being now so used to it, thought at first that we must be deaf. And then the fog, which had hung about (even in full sunshine), vanished, and the shrouded hills shone forth with brightness manifold. And now the sky at length began to come to its true manner, which we had not seen for months, a mixture (if I so may speak) of various expressions. Whereas till now from Allhallows-tide, six weeks ere the great frost set in, the heavens had worn one heavy mask of ashen grey when clouded, or else one amethystine tinge with a hazy rim, when cloudless. So it was pleasant to behold, after that monotony, the fickle sky which suits our England, though abused by foreign folk.

And soon the dappled softening sky gave some earnest of its mood; for a brisk south wind arose, and the blessed rain came driving; cold indeed, yet most refreshing to the skin, all parched with snow, and the eyeballs so long dazzled. Neither was the heart more sluggish in its thankfulness to God. People had begun to think, and somebody had prophesied, that we should have no spring this year, no seed-time, and no harvest; for that the Lord had sent a judgment on this country of England, and the nation dwelling in it, because of the wickedness of the Court, and the encouragement shown to Papists. And this was proved, they said, by what had happened in the town of London; where, for more than a fortnight, such a chill of darkness lay, that no man might behold his neighbour, even across the narrowest street; and where the ice upon the Thames was more than four feet thick, and crushing London bridge in twain. Now to these prophets I paid no heed, believing not that Providence would freeze us for other people's sins; neither seeing how England could, for many generations, have enjoyed good sunshine, if Popery meant frosts and fogs. Besides, why could not Providence settle the business once for all, by freezing the Pope himself; even though (according to our view) he were destined to extremes of heat, together with all who followed him?

Not to meddle with that subject, being beyond my judgment, let me tell the things I saw, and then you must believe me. The wind, of course, I could not see, not having the powers of a pig; but I could see the laden branches of the great oaks moving, hoping to shake off the load packed and saddled on them. And hereby I may note a thing, which some one may explain perhaps in the after ages, when people come to look at things. This is, that in desperate cold, all the trees were pulled awry, even though the wind had scattered the snow burden from them. Of some sorts the branches bended downwards, like an archway; of other sorts the boughs curved upwards, like a red deer's frontlet. This I know no reason for; but am ready to swear that I saw it.

Now when the first of the rain began, and the old familiar softness spread upon the window glass, and ran a little way in channels (though from the coldness of the glass it froze before reaching the bottom), knowing at once the difference from the short sharp thud of snow, we all ran out, and filled our eyes, and filled our hearts, with gazing. True, the snow was piled up now all in mountains round us; true, the air was still so cold that our breath froze on the doorway, and the rain was turned to ice, wherever it struck anything: nevertheless that it was rain there was no denying, as we watched it across black doorways, and could see no sign of white. Mother, who had made up her mind that the farm was not worth having, after all those prophecies, and that all of us must starve, and holes be scratched in the snow for us, and no use to put up a tombstone (for our church had been shut up long ago), mother fell upon my breast, and sobbed that I was the cleverest fellow ever born of woman. And this because I had condemned the prophets for a pack of fools; not seeing how business could go on, if people stopped to hearken to them.

Then Lorna came, and glorified me, for I had predicted a change of weather, more to keep their spirits up, than with real hope of it; and then came Annie blushing shyly, as I looked at her, and told her that Winnie would soon have four legs now. This referred to some stupid joke made by John Fry or somebody, that in this weather a man had no legs, and a horse had only two.

But as the rain came down upon us, from the south-west wind, and we could not have enough of it, even putting our tongues to catch it, as little children might do, and beginning to talk of primroses, the very noblest thing of all was to hear, and see, the gratitude of the poor beasts yet remaining, and the few surviving birds. From the cowhouse lowing came, more than of fifty milking times; moo and moo, and a turn-up noise at the end of every bellow, as if from the very heart of kine. Then the horses in the stables, packed as closely as they could stick, at the risk of kicking, to keep the warmth in one another, and their spirits up by discoursing — these began with one accord to lift up their voices, snorting, snaffling, whinnying, and neighing, and trotting to the door to know when they should have work again. To whom, as if in answer, came the feeble bleating of the sheep, what few, by dint of greatest care, had kept their fleeces on their backs, and their four legs under them.

Neither was it a trifling thing, let whoso will say the contrary, to behold the ducks and geese marching forth, in handsome order, from their beds of fern and straw. What a goodly noise they kept, what a flapping of their wings, and a jerking of their tails, as they stood right up, and tried with a whistling in their throats to imitate a cockscrow! And then how daintily they took the wet upon their dusty plumes, and ducked their shoulders to it, and began to dress themselves, and laid their grooved bills on the snow, and dabbled for more ooziness!

Lorna had never seen, I dare say, anything like this before, and it was all that we could do to keep her from rushing forth, with only little lambswool shoes on, and kissing every one of them. "Oh the dear things, oh the dear things!" she kept saying continually, "how wonderfully clever they are! Only look at that one with his foot up, giving orders to the others, John!"

"And I must give orders to you, my darling," I answered, gazing on her face, so brilliant with excitement; "and that is, that you come in at once, with that worrisome cough of yours; and sit by the fire, and warm yourself."

"Oh no, John. Not for a minute, if you please, good John. I want to see the snow go away, and the green meadows coming forth. And here comes our favourite robin, who has lived in the oven so long, and sung us a song every morning. I must see what he thinks of it."

"You will do nothing of the sort," I answered very shortly, being only too glad of a cause for having her in my arms again. So I caught her up, and carried her in; and she looked and smiled so sweetly at me, instead of pouting (as I had feared), that I found myself unable to go very fast along the passage. And I set her there, in her favourite place, by the sweet-scented wood-fire; and she paid me porterage, without my even asking her; and for all the beauty of the rain, I was fain to stay with her; until our Annie came to say that my advice was wanted.

Now my advice was never much, as everybody knew quite well; but that was the way they always put it, when they wanted me to work for them. And in truth, it was time for me to work; not for others, but myself, and (as I always thought) for Lorna. For the rain was now coming down in earnest, and the top of the snow being frozen at last, and glazed as hard as a China cup, by means of the sun and frost afterwards, all the rain ran right away from the steep inclines, and all the outlets being blocked with ice set up like tables, it threatened to flood everything. Already it was ponding up, like a tide advancing, at the threshold of the door, from which we had watched the duck-birds; both because great piles of snow trended in that direction, in spite of all our scraping, and also that the gulley hole, where the water of the shoot went out (I mean when it was water), now was choked with lumps of ice, as big as a man's body. For the "shoot," as we called our little runnel of everlasting water, never known to freeze before, and always ready for any man either to wash his hands, or drink, where it spouted from a trough of bark, set among white flint-stones; this at last had given in, and its music ceased to lull us, as we lay in bed.

It was not long before I managed to drain off this threatening flood, by opening the old sluice-hole: but I had much harder work to keep the stables and cow-house, and the other sheds, from flooding. For we have a sapient practice (and I never saw the contrary, round about our parts, I mean) of keeping all rooms underground, so that you step down to them. We say that thus we keep them warmer, both for cattle and for men, in the time of winter, and cooler in the summer-time. This I will not contradict, though having my own opinion; but it seems to me to be a relic of the time, when people in the western countries lived in caves beneath the ground, and blocked the mouths with neat-skins.

Let that question still abide, for men who study ancient times to inform me, if they will: all I know is, that now we had no blessings for the system. If after all their cold and starving, our weak cattle now should have to stand up to their knees in water, it would be certain death to them; and we had lost enough already to make us poor for a long time; not to speak of our kind love for them. And I do assure you, I loved some horses, and even some cows for that matter, as if they had been my blood-relations; knowing as I did their virtues. And some of these were lost to us; and I could not bear to think of them. Therefore I worked hard all night, to try and save the rest of them.

CHAPTER XLVI

Squire Faggus makes Some Lucky Hits

Through that season of bitter frost, the red deer of the forest, having nothing to feed upon, and no shelter to rest in, had grown accustomed to our ricks of corn, and hay, and clover. There we might see a hundred of them, almost any morning, come for warmth, and food, and comfort, and scarce willing to move away. And many of them were so tame, that they quietly presented themselves at our back door, and stood there with their coats quite stiff, and their flanks drawn in and panting, and icicles sometimes on their chins, and their great eyes fastened wistfully upon any merciful person; craving for a bit of food, and a drink of water. I suppose that they had not sense enough to chew the snow and melt it; at any rate, all the springs being frozen, and rivers hidden out of sight, these poor things suffered even more from thirst than they did from hunger.

But now there was no fear of thirst, and more chance indeed of drowning; for a heavy gale of wind arose, with violent rain from the south-west, which lasted almost without pause, for three nights and two days. At first, the rain made no impression on the bulk of snow, but ran from every sloping surface, and froze on every flat one, through the coldness of the earth; and so it became impossible for any man to keep his legs, without the help of a shodden staff. After a good while, however, the air growing very much warmer, this state of things began to change, and a worse one to succeed it; for now the snow came thundering down from roof, and rock, and ivied tree, and floods began to roar and foam in every trough and gulley. The drifts, that had been so white and fair, looked yellow, and smirched, and muddy, and lost their graceful curves, and moulded lines and airiness. But the strangest sight of all to me was in the bed of streams, and brooks, and especially of the Lynn river. It was worth going miles to behold such a thing, for a man might never have the chance again.

Vast drifts of snow had filled the valley, and piled above the river-course, fifty feet high in many places, and in some as much as a hundred. These had frozen over the top, and glanced the rain away from them, and being sustained by rock, and tree, spanned the water mightily. But meanwhile the waxing flood, swollen from every moorland hollow, and from every spouting crag, had dashed away all icy fetters, and was rolling gloriously. Under white fantastic arches, and long tunnels freaked and fretted, and between pellucid pillars jagged with nodding architraves, the red impetuous torrent rushed, and the brown foam whirled and flashed. I was half inclined to jump in, and swim through such glorious scenery; for nothing used to please me more than swimming in a flooded river. But I thought of the rocks and I thought of the cramp, and more than all, of Lorna; and so, between one thing and another, I let it roll on without me.

It was now high time to work very hard; both to make up for the farm-work lost during the months of frost and snow, and also to be ready for a great and vicious attack from the Doones, who would burn us in our beds, at the earliest opportunity. Of farm-work there was little yet for even the most zealous man to begin to lay his hand to: because when the ground appeared through the crust of bubbled snow (as at last it did, though not as my Lorna had expected, at the first few drops of rain) it was all so soaked and sodden, and, as we call it, "mucksy," that to meddle with it in any way was to do more harm than good. Nevertheless, there was yard-work, and house-work, and tendance of stock, enough to save any man from idleness.

As for Lorna, she would come out. There was no keeping her in the house. She had taken up some peculiar notion, that we were doing more for her than she had any right to, and that she must earn her living by the hard work of her hands. It was quite in vain to tell her that she was expected to do nothing, and far worse than vain (for it made her cry sadly) if anyone assured her that she could do no good at all. She even began upon mother's garden, before the snow was clean gone from it, and sowed a beautiful row of peas, every one of which the mice ate.

But though it was very pretty to watch her working for her very life, as if the maintenance of the household hung upon her labours, yet I was grieved for many reasons, and so was mother also. In the first place, she was too fair and dainty for this rough, rude work; and though it made her cheeks so bright, it surely must be bad for her, to get her little feet so wet. Moreover, we could not bear the idea that she should labour for her keep; and again (which was the worst of all things), mother's garden lay exposed to a dark deceitful coppice, where a man might lurk, and watch all the fair gardener's doings. It was true that none could get at her thence, while the brook which ran between poured so great a torrent. Still the distance was but little for a gun to carry, if anyone could be brutal enough to point a gun at Lorna. I thought that none could be found to do it; but mother, having more, experience, was not so certain of mankind.

Now in spite of the floods, and the sloughs being out, and the state of the roads most perilous. Squire Faggus came at last, riding his famous strawberry mare. There was a great ado between him and Annie, as you may well suppose, after some four months of parting. And so we left them alone awhile, to coddle over their raptures. But when they were tired of that, or at least had time enough to be so, mother and I went in, to know what news Tom had brought with him. Though he did not seem to want us yet, he made himself agreeable, and so we sent Annie to cook the dinner while her sweetheart should tell us everything.

Tom Faggus had very good news to tell, and he told it with such force of expression as made us laugh very heartily. He had taken up his purchase from old Sir Roger Bassett of a nice bit of land, to the south of the moors, and in the parish of Molland. When the lawyers knew thoroughly who he was, and how he had made his money, they behaved uncommonly well to him, and showed great sympathy with his pursuits. He put them up to a thing or two; and they poked him in the ribs, and laughed, and said that he was quite a boy: but of the right sort none the less. And so they made old Squire Bassett pay the bill for both sides; and all he got for three hundred acres was a hundred and twenty pounds; though Tom had paid five hundred. But lawyers know that this must be so, in spite of all their endeavours; and the old gentleman, who now expected to find a bill for him to pay, almost thought himself a rogue for getting anything out of them.

It is true that the land was poor and wild, and the soil exceeding shallow; lying on the slope of rock, and burned up in hot summers. But with us, hot summers are things known by tradition only (as this great winter may be); we generally have more moisture, especially in July, than we well know what to do with. I have known a fog for a fortnight, at the summer solstice, and farmers talking in church about it, when they ought to be praying. But it always contrives to come right in the end, as other visitations do, if we take them as true visits, and receive them kindly.

Now this farm of Squire Faggus (as he truly now had a right to be called) was of the very finest pasture, when it got good store of rain. And Tom, who had ridden the Devonshire roads with many a reeking jacket, knew right well that he might trust the climate for that matter. The herbage was of the very sweetest, and the shortest, and the closest, having perhaps from ten to eighteen inches of wholesome soil between it and the solid rock. Tom saw at once what it was fit for — the breeding of fine cattle.

Being such a hand as he was, at making the most of everything, both his own and other people's (although so free in scattering, when the humour lay upon him), he had actually turned to his own advantage that extraordinary weather, which had so impoverished every one around him. For he taught his Winnie (who knew his meaning as well as any child could, and obeyed not only his word of mouth, but every glance he gave her) to go forth in the snowy evenings, when horses are seeking everywhere (be they wild or tame) for fodder and for shelter; and to whinny to the forest ponies, miles away from home perhaps, and lead them all, with rare appetite and promise of abundance, to her master's homestead. He shod good Winnie in such a manner, that she could not sink in the snow; and he clad her over the loins with a sheep-skin dyed to her own colour, which the wild horses were never tired of coming up and sniffing at; taking it for an especial gift, and proof of inspiration. And Winnie never came home at night without at least a score of ponies trotting shyly after her, tossing their heads and their tails in turn, and making believe to be very wild, although hard pinched by famine. Of course, Tom would get them all into his pound in about five minutes: for he himself could neigh in a manner which went to the heart of the wildest horse. And then he fed them well, and turned them into his great cattle-pen, to abide their time for breaking, when the snow and frost should be over.

He had gotten more than three hundred now, in this sagacious manner; and he said it was the finest sight to see their mode of carrying on. How they would snort, and stamp, and fume, and prick their ears, and rush backwards, and lash themselves with their long rough tails, and shake their jagged manes, and scream, and fall upon one another, if a strange man came anigh them. But as for feeding time, Tom said it was better than fifty plays to watch them, and the tricks they were up to, to cheat their feeders, and one another. I asked him how on earth he had managed to get fodder, in such impassable weather, for such a herd of horses; but he said that they lived upon straw and sawdust; and he knew that I did not believe him, any more than about his star-shavings. And this was just the thing he loved — to mystify honest people, and be a great deal too knowing. However, I may judge him harshly, because I myself tell everything.

I asked him what he meant to do with all that enormous lot of horses, and why he had not exerted his wits to catch the red deer as well. He said that the latter would have been against the laws of venery, and might have brought him into trouble; but as for disposing of his stud, it would give him little difficulty. He would break them, when the spring weather came on, and deal with them as they required, and keep the handsomest for breeding. The rest he would despatch to London, where he knew plenty of horse-dealers; and he doubted not that they would fetch him as much as ten pounds apiece all round, being now in great demand. I told him I wished that he might get it: but as it proved afterwards, he did.

Then he pressed us both on another point, the time for his marriage to Annie: and mother looked at me to say when, and I looked back at mother. However, knowing something of the world, and unable to make any further objection, by reason of his prosperity, I said that we must even do as the fashionable people did, and allow the maid herself to settle, when she would leave home and all. And this I spoke with a very bad grace, being perhaps of an ancient cast, and over fond of honesty — I mean, of course, among lower people.

But Tom paid little heed to this, knowing the world a great deal better than ever I could pretend to do; and being ready to take a thing, upon which he had set his mind, whether it came with a good grace, or whether it came with a bad one. And seeing that it would be awkward to provoke my anger, he left the room before more words, to submit himself to Annie.

Upon this I went in search of Lorna, to tell her of our cousin's arrival, and to ask whether she would think fit to see him, or to dine by herself that day; for she should do exactly as it pleased her in everything, while remaining still our guest. But I rather wished that she might choose not to sit in Tom's company, though she might be introduced to him. Not but what he could behave quite as well as I could, and much better as regarded elegance and assurance, only that his honesty had not been as one might desire. But Lorna had some curiosity to know what this famous man was like, and declared that she would by all means have the pleasure of dining with him, if he did not object to her company, on the ground of the Doones' dishonesty; moreover, she said that it would seem a most foolish air on her part, and one which would cause the greatest pain to Annie, who had been so good to her, if she should refuse to sit at table with a man who held the King's pardon, and was now a pattern of honesty.

Against this I had not a word to say; and could not help acknowledging in my heart that she was right, as well as wise, in her decision. And afterwards I discovered that mother would have been much displeased if she had decided otherwise.

Accordingly she turned away, with one of her very sweetest smiles (whose beauty none can describe), saying that she must not meet a man of such fashion and renown, in her common gardening frock; but must try to look as nice as she could, if only in honour of dear Annie. And truth to tell, when she came to dinner, everything about her was the neatest, and the prettiest, that can possibly be imagined. She contrived to match the colours so, to suit one another and her own, and yet with a certain delicate harmony of contrast, and the shape of everything was so nice, that when she came into the room, with a crown of winning modesty upon the consciousness of beauty, I was quite as proud as if the Queen of England entered.

My mother could not help remarking, though she knew that it was not mannerly, how like a princess Lorna looked, now she had her best things on; but two things caught Squire Faggus' eyes, after he had made a most gallant bow, and received a most graceful courtesy; and he kept his bright bold gaze upon them, first on one and then on the other, until my darling was hot with blushes, and I was ready to knock him down, if he had not been our visitor. But here again I should have been wrong, as I was apt to be in those days; for Tom intended no harm whatever, and his gaze was of pure curiosity; though Annie herself was vexed with it. The two objects of his close regard were, first, and most worthily, Lorna's face, and secondly, the ancient necklace restored to her by Sir Ensor Doone.

Now wishing to save my darling's comfort, and to keep things quiet, I shouted out that dinner was ready, so that half the parish could hear me; upon which my mother laughed, and chid me, and despatched her guest before her. And a very good dinner we made, I remember, and a very happy one; attending to the women first, as now is the manner of eating; except among the workmen. With them, of course, it is needful that the man (who has his hours fixed) should be served first, and make the utmost of his time for feeding; while the women may go on, as much as ever they please, afterwards. But with us, who are not bound to time, there is no such reason to be quoted; and the women being the weaker vessels, should be the first to begin to fill. And so we always arranged it.

Now though our Annie was a graceful maid, and Lizzie a very learned one, you should have seen how differently Lorna managed her dining: she never took more than about a quarter of a mouthful at a time, and she never appeared to be chewing that, although she must have done so. Indeed she appeared to dine, as if it were a matter of no consequence, and as if she could think of other things more than of her business. All this, and her own manner of eating, I described to Eliza once, when I wanted to vex her for something very spiteful that she had said; and I never succeeded so well before, for the girl was quite outrageous, having her own perception of it, which made my observation ten times as bitter to her. And I am not sure but what she ceased to like poor Lorna from that day; and if so, I was quite paid out, as I well deserved, for my bit of satire.

For it strikes me that of all human dealings, satire is the very lowest, and most mean and common. It is the equivalent in words, for what bullying is in deeds; and no more bespeaks a clever man, than the other does a brave one. These two wretched tricks exalt a fool in his own low esteem, but never in his neighbour's; for the deep common sense of our nature tells that no man of a genial heart, or of any spread of mind, can take pride in either. And though a good man may commit the one fault or the other, now and then, by way of outlet, he is sure to have compunctions soon, and to scorn himself more than the sufferer.

Now when the young maidens were gone — for we had quite a high dinner of fashion that day, with Betty Muxworthy waiting, and Gwenny Carfax at the gravy — and only mother, and Tom, and I remained at the white deal table, with brandy, and schnapps, and hot water jugs; Squire Faggus said quite suddenly, and perhaps on purpose to take us aback, in case of our hiding anything:

"What do you know of the history of that beautiful maiden, good mother?"

"Not half so much as my son does," mother answered, with a soft smile at me: "and when John does not choose to tell a thing, wild horses will not pull it out of him."

"That is not at all like me, mother," I replied rather sadly; "you know almost every word about Lorna, quite as well as I do."

"Almost every word, I believe, John; for you never tell a falsehood. But the few unknown may be of all the most important to me."

To this I made no answer, for fear of going beyond the truth, or else of making mischief. Not that I had, or wished to have, any mystery with mother; neither was there, in purest truth, any mystery in the matter; to the utmost of my knowledge. And the only things that I had kept back, solely for mother's comfort, were the death of poor Lord Alan Brandir (if indeed he were dead) and the connection of Marwood de Whichehalse with the dealings of the Doones, and the threats of Carver Doone against my own prosperity; and, may be, one or two little things, harrowing more than edifying.

"Come, come," said Master Faggus, smiling very pleasantly, "you two understand each other, if any two on earth do. Ah, if I had only had a mother, how different I might have been!" And with that he sighed, in the tone which always overcame mother upon that subject, and had something to do with his getting Annie; and then he produced his pretty box, full of rolled tobacco, and offered me one, as I now had joined the goodly company of smokers. So I took it, and watched what he did with his own, lest I might go wrong about mine.

But when our cylinders were both lighted, and I enjoying mine wonderfully, and astonishing mother by my skill, Tom Faggus told us that he was sure he had seen my Lorna's face before, many and many years ago, when she was quite a little child, but he could not remember where it was, or anything more about it at present; though he would try to do so afterwards. He could not be mistaken, he said, for he had noticed her eyes especially; and had never seen such eyes before, neither again, until this day. I asked him if he had ever ventured into the Doone-valley; but he shook his head, and replied that he valued his life a deal too much for that. Then we put it to him, whether anything might assist his memory; but he said that he knew not of aught to do so, unless it were another glass of schnapps.

This being provided, he grew very wise, and told us clearly and candidly that we were both very foolish. For he said that we were keeping Lorna, at the risk not only of our stock, and the house above our heads, but also of our precious lives; and after all was she worth it, although so very beautiful? Upon which I told him, with indignation, that her beauty was the least part of her goodness, and that I would thank him for his opinion, when I had requested it.

"Bravo, our John Ridd!" he answered: "fools will be fools till the end of the chapter: and I might be as big a one, if I were in thy shoes, John. Nevertheless, in the name of God, don't let that helpless child go about, with a thing worth half the county on her."

"She is worth all the county herself," said I, "and all England put together: but she has nothing worth half a rick of hay upon her; for the ring I gave her cost only —— " and here I stopped, for mother was looking, and I never would tell her how much it had cost me; though she had tried fifty times to find out.

"Tush, the ring!" Tom Faggus cried, with a contempt that moved me; "I would never have stopped a man for that. But the necklace, you great oaf, the necklace is worth all your farm put together, and your Uncle Ben's fortune to the back of it; ay, and all the town of Dulverton."

"What," said I, "that common glass thing, which she has had from her childhood!"

"Glass indeed! They are the finest brilliants ever I set eyes on; and I have handled a good many."

"Surely," cried mother, now flushing as red as Tom's own cheeks, with excitement, "you must be wrong, or the young mistress would herself have known it."

I was greatly pleased with my mother, for calling Lorna "the young mistress": it was not done for the sake of her diamonds, whether they were glass or not; but because she felt, as I had done, that Tom Faggus, a man of no birth whatever, was speaking beyond his mark, in calling a lady like Lorna a "helpless child"; as well as in his general tone, which displayed no deference. He might have been used to the quality, in the way of stopping their coaches, or roystering at hotels with them; but he never had met a high lady before, in equality, and upon virtue; and we both felt that he ought to have known it, and to have thanked us for the opportunity; in a word, to have behaved a great deal more humbly than he had even tried to do.

"Trust me," answered Tom, in his loftiest manner, which Annie said was "so noble," but which seemed to me rather flashy, "trust me, good mother, and simple John, for knowing brilliants, when I see them. I would have stopped an eight-horse coach, with four carabined outriders, for such a booty as that. But alas, those days are over: those were days worth living in. Ah, I never shall know the like again. How fine it was by moonlight!"

"Master Faggus," began my mother, with a manner of some dignity, such as she could sometimes use, by right of her integrity, and thorough kindness to every one, "this is not the tone in which you have hitherto spoken to me about your former pursuits and life. I fear that the spirits" — but here she stopped, because the spirits were her own, and Tom was our visitor — "what I mean, Master Faggus, is this: you have won my daughter's heart somehow; and you won my consent to the matter, through your honest sorrow, and manly undertaking to lead a different life, and touch no property but your own. Annie is my eldest daughter, and the child of a most upright man. I love her best of all on earth, next to my boy John here" — here mother gave me a mighty squeeze, to be sure that she would have me at least — "and I will not risk my Annie's life, with a man who yearns for the highway."

Having made this very long speech (for her), mother came home upon my shoulder, and wept so that (but for heeding her) I would have taken Tom by the nose, and thrown him, and Winnie after him, over our farm-yard gate. For I am violent when roused; and freely hereby acknowledge it; though even my enemies will own that it takes a great deal to rouse me. But I do consider the grief, and tears (when justly caused), of my dearest friends, to be a great deal to rouse me.

CHAPTER XLVII
Jeremy in Danger

Nothing very long abides; as the greatest of all writers (in whose extent I am for ever lost in raptured wonder, and yet for ever quite at home, as if his heart were mine, although his brains so different), in a word, as Mr. William Shakespeare, in every one of his works insists, with a humoured melancholy. And if my journey to London led to nothing else of advancement, it took me a hundred years in front of what I might else have been, by the most simple accident.

Two women were scolding one another across the road, very violently, both from upstair windows; and I in my hurry for quiet life and not knowing what might come down upon me, quickened my step for the nearest corner. But suddenly something fell on my head; and at first I was afraid to look, especially as it weighed heavily. But hearing no breakage of ware, and only the other scold laughing heartily, I turned me about and espied a book, which one had cast at the other, hoping to break her window. So I took the book, and tendered it at the door of the house from which it had fallen; but the watchman came along just then, and the man at the door declared that it never came from their house, and begged me to say no more. This I promised readily, never wishing to make mischief; and I said, "Good sir, now take the book; and I will go on to my business." But he answered that he would do no such thing; for the book alone, being hurled so hard, would convict his people of a lewd assault, and he begged me, if I would do a good turn, to put the book under my coat and go. And so I did; in part at least. For I did not put the book under my coat, but went along with it openly, looking for any to challenge it. Now this book, so acquired, has been not only the joy of my younger days, and main delight of my manhood, but also the comfort, and even the hope, of my now declining years. In a word, it is next to my Bible to me, and written in equal English; and if you espy any goodness whatever in my own loose style of writing, you must not thank me, John Ridd, for it, but the writer who holds the champion's belt in wit, as I once did in wrestling.

Now as nothing very long abides, it cannot be expected that a woman's anger should last very long, if she be at all of the proper sort. And my mother, being one of the very best, could not long retain her wrath against the Squire Faggus; especially when she came to reflect, upon Annie's suggestion, how natural, and one might say, how inevitable it was, that a young man fond of adventure and change, and winning good profits by jeopardy, should not settle down without some regret to a fixed abode, and a life of sameness, however safe and respectable. And even as Annie put the case, Tom deserved the greater credit for vanquishing so nobly these yearnings of his nature; and it seemed very hard to upbraid him, considering how good his motives were; neither could Annie understand how mother could reconcile it with her knowledge of the Bible, and the one sheep that was lost, and the hundredth piece of silver, and the man that went down to Jericho.

Whether Annie's logic was good and sound, I am sure I cannot tell; but it seemed to me that she ought to have left the Jericho traveller alone, inasmuch as he rather fell among Tom Fagguses, than resembled them. However, her reasoning was too much for mother to hold out against; and Tom was replaced, and more than that, being regarded now as an injured man. But how my mother contrived to know, that because she had been too hard upon Tom, he must be right about the necklace, is a point which I never could clearly perceive, though no doubt she could explain it.

To prove herself right in that conclusion, she went herself to fetch Lorna, that the trinket might be examined, before the day grew dark. My darling came in, with a very quick glance and smile at my cigarro (for I was having the third by this time, to keep things in amity); and I waved it towards her, as much as to say, "you see that I can do it." And then mother led her up to the light, for Tom to examine her necklace.

On the shapely curve of her neck it hung like dewdrops upon a white hyacinth; and I was vexed that Tom should have the chance to see it there. But even as if she had read my thoughts, or outrun them with her own, Lorna turned away, and softly took the jewels from the place which so much adorned them. And as she turned away, they sparkled through the rich dark waves of hair. Then she laid the glittering circlet in my mother's hands; and Tom Faggus took it eagerly, and bore it to the window.

"Don't you go out of sight," I said; "you cannot resist such things as those, if they be what you think them."

"Jack, I shall have to trounce you yet. I am now a man of honour, and entitled to the duello. What will you take for it, Mistress Lorna? At a hazard, say now."

"I am not accustomed to sell things, sir," replied Lorna, who did not like him much, else she would have answered sportively, "What is it worth, in your opinion?"

"Do you think it is worth five pounds, now?"

"Oh no! I never had so much money as that in all my life. It is very bright and very pretty; but it cannot be worth five pounds, I am sure."

"What a chance for a bargain! Oh, if it were not for Annie, I could make my fortune."

"But, sir, I would not sell it to you, not for twenty times five pounds. My grandfather was so kind about it; and I think it belonged to my mother."

"There are twenty-five rose diamonds in it, and twenty-five large brilliants that cannot be matched in London. How say you, Mistress Lorna, to a hundred thousand pounds?"

My darling's eyes so flashed at this, brighter than any diamonds, that I said to myself, "Well, all have faults; and now I have found out Lorna's — she is fond of money!" And then I sighed rather heavily; for of all faults this seems to me one of the worst in a woman. But even before my sigh was finished, I had cause to condemn myself. For Lorna took the necklace very quietly from the hand of Squire Faggus, who had not half done with admiring it, and she went up to my mother, with the sweetest smile I ever saw.

"Dear, kind mother, I am so glad," she said in a whisper, coaxing mother out of sight of all but me; "now you will have it, won't you, dear? And I shall be so happy; for a thousandth part of your kindness to me no jewels in the world can match."

I cannot lay before you the grace with which she did it, all the air of seeking favour, rather than conferring it, and the high-bred fear of giving offence, which is of all fears the noblest. Mother knew not what to say. Of course she would never dream of taking such a gift as that; and yet she saw how sadly Lorna would be disappointed. Therefore mother did, from habit, what she almost always did, she called me to help her. But knowing that my eyes were full — for anything noble moves me so, quite as rashly as things pitiful — I pretended not to hear my mother, but to see a wild cat in the dairy.

Therefore I cannot tell what mother said in reply to Lorna; for when I came back, quite eager to let my love know how I worshipped her, and how deeply I was ashamed of myself, for meanly wronging her in my heart, behold Tom Faggus had gotten again the necklace which had such charms for him, and was delivering all around (but especially to Annie, who was wondering at his learning), a dissertation on precious stones, and his sentiments about those in his hand. He said that the work was very ancient, but undoubtedly very good; the cutting of every line was true, and every angle was in its place. And this, he said, made all the difference in the lustre of the stone, and therefore in its value. For if the facets were ill-matched, and the points of light soever little out of perfect harmony, all the lustre of the jewel would be loose and wavering, and the central fire dulled; instead of answering, as it should, to all possibilities of gaze, and overpowering any eye intent on its deep mysteries. We laughed at the Squire's dissertation; for how should he know all these things, being nothing better, and indeed much worse, than a mere Northmolton blacksmith? He took our laughter with much good nature; having Annie to squeeze his hand and convey her grief at our ignorance; but he said that of one thing he was quite certain, and therein I believed him. To wit, that a trinket of this kind never could have belonged to any ignoble family, but to one of the very highest and most wealthy in England. And looking at Lorna, I felt sure that she must have come from a higher source than the very best of diamonds.

Tom Faggus said that the necklace was made, he would answer for it, in Amsterdam, two or three hundred years ago, long before London jewellers had begun to meddle with diamonds; and on the gold clasp he found some letters, done in some inverted way, the meaning of which was beyond him; also a bearing of some kind, which he believed was a mountain-cat. And thereupon he declared that now he had earned another glass of schnapps, and would Mistress Lorna mix it for him?

I was amazed at his impudence; and Annie, who thought this her business, did not look best pleased; and I hoped that Lorna would tell him at once to go and do it for himself. But instead of that she rose to do it, with a soft humility, which went direct to the heart of Tom; and he leaped up with a curse at himself, and took the hot water from her, and would not allow her to do anything except to put the sugar in; and then he bowed to her grandly. I knew what Lorna was thinking of; she was thinking all the time that her necklace had been taken by the Doones with violence upon some great robbery; and that Squire Faggus knew it, though he would not show his knowledge; and that this was perhaps the reason why mother had refused it so.

We said no more about the necklace, for a long time afterwards; neither did my darling wear it, now that she knew its value, but did not know its history. She came to me the very next day, trying to look cheerful, and begged me if I loved her (never mind how little) to take charge of it again, as I once had done before, and not even to let her know in what place I stored it. I told her that this last request I could not comply with; for having been round her neck so often, it was now a sacred thing, more than a million pounds could be. Therefore it should dwell for the present in the neighbourhood of my heart; and so could not be far from her. At this she smiled her own sweet smile, and touched my forehead with her lips, and wished that she could only learn how to deserve such love as mine.

Tom Faggus took his good departure, which was a kind farewell to me, on the very day I am speaking of, the day after his arrival. Tom was a thoroughly upright man, according to his own standard; and you might rely upon him always, up to a certain point I mean, to be there or thereabouts. But sometimes things were too many for Tom, especially with ardent spirits, and then he judged, perhaps too much, with only himself for the jury. At any rate, I would trust him fully, for candour and for honesty, in almost every case in which he himself could have no interest. And so we got on very well together; and he thought me a fool; and I tried my best not to think anything worse of him.

Scarcely was Tom clean out of sight, and Annie's tears not dry yet (for she always made a point of crying upon his departure), when in came Master Jeremy Stickles, splashed with mud from head to foot, and not in the very best of humours, though happy to get back again.

"Curse those fellows!" he cried, with a stamp which sent the water hissing from his boot among the embers; "a pretty plight you may call this, for His Majesty's Commissioner to return to his headquarters in! Annie, my dear," for he was always very affable with Annie, "will you help me off with my overalls, and then turn your pretty hand to the gridiron? Not a blessed morsel have I touched for more than twenty-four hours."

"Surely then you must be quite starving, sir," my sister replied with the greatest zeal; for she did love a man with an appetite; "how glad I am that the fire is clear!" But Lizzie, who happened to be there, said with her peculiar smile:

"Master Stickles must be used to it; for he never comes back without telling us that."

"Hush!" cried Annie, quite shocked with her; "how would you like to be used to it? Now, Betty, be quick with the things for me. Pork, or mutton, or deer's meat, sir? We have some cured since the autumn."

"Oh, deer's meat, by all means," Jeremy Stickles answered; "I have tasted none since I left you, though dreaming of it often. Well, this is better than being chased over the moors for one's life, John. All the way from Landacre Bridge, I have ridden a race for my precious life, at the peril of my limbs and neck. Three great Doones galloping after me, and a good job for me that they were so big, or they must have overtaken me. Just go and see to my horse, John, that's an excellent lad. He deserves a good turn, this day, from me; and I will render it to him."

However he left me to do it, while he made himself comfortable: and in truth the horse required care; he was blown so that he could hardly stand, and plastered with mud, and steaming so that the stable was quite full of it. By the time I had put the poor fellow to rights, his master had finished dinner, and was in a more pleasant humour, having even offered to kiss Annie, out of pure gratitude, as he said; but Annie answered with spirit, that gratitude must not be shown by increasing the obligation. Jeremy made reply to this, that his only way to be grateful then was to tell us his story; and so he did, at greater length than I can here repeat it; for it does not bear particularly upon Lorna's fortunes.

It appears that as he was riding towards us, from the town of Southmolton in Devonshire, he found the roads very soft and heavy, and the floods out in all directions; but met with no other difficulty until he came to Landacre Bridge. He had only a single trooper with him, a man not of the militia, but of the King's army, whom Jeremy had brought from Exeter. As these two descended towards the bridge, they observed that both the Kensford water and the River Barle were pouring down in mighty floods, from the melting of the snow. So great indeed was the torrent, after they united, that only the parapets of the bridge could be seen above the water, the road across either bank being covered and very deep on the hither side. The trooper did not like the look of it, and proposed to ride back again, and round by way of Simonsbath, where the stream is smaller. But Stickles would not have it so, and, dashing into the river, swam his horse for the bridge, and gained it with some little trouble; and there he found the water not more than up to his horse's knees perhaps. On the crown of the bridge he turned his horse to watch the trooper's passage, and to help him with directions; when suddenly he saw him fall headlong into the torrent, and heard the report of a gun from behind, and felt a shock to his own body, such as lifted him out of the saddle. Turning round he beheld three men, risen up from behind the hedge on one side of his onward road, two of them ready to load again, and one with his gun unfired, waiting to get good aim at him. Then Jeremy did a gallant thing, for which I doubt whether I should have had the presence of mind in the danger. He saw that to swim his horse back again would be almost certain death; as affording such a target, where even a wound must be fatal. Therefore he struck the spurs into the nag, and rode through the water straight at the man who was pointing the long gun at him. If the horse had been carried off his legs, there must have been an end of Jeremy; for the other men were getting ready to have another shot at him. But luckily the horse galloped right on without any need for swimming, being himself excited, no doubt, by all he had seen and heard of it. And Jeremy lay almost flat on his neck, so as to give little space for good aim, with the mane tossing wildly in front of him. Now if that young fellow with the gun had his brains as ready as his flint was, he would have shot the horse at once, and then had Stickles at his mercy; but instead of that he let fly at the man, and missed him altogether, being scared perhaps by the pistol which Jeremy showed him the mouth of. And galloping by at full speed, Master Stickles tried to leave his mark behind him, for he changed the aim of his pistol to the biggest man, who was loading his gun and cursing like ten cannons. But the pistol missed fire, no doubt from the flood which had gurgled in over the holsters; and Jeremy seeing three horses tethered at a gate just up the hill, knew that he had not yet escaped, but had more of danger behind him. He tried his other great pistol at one of the horses tethered there, so as to lessen (if possible) the number of his pursuers. But the powder again failed him; and he durst not stop to cut the bridles, hearing the men coming up the hill. So he even made the most of his start, thanking God that his weight was light, compared at least to what theirs was.

And another thing he had noticed which gave him some hope of escaping, to wit, that the horses of the Doones, although very handsome animals, were suffering still from the bitter effects of the late long frost, and the scarcity of fodder. "If they do not catch me up, or shoot me, in the course of the first two miles, I may see my home again;" this was what he said to himself, as he turned to mark what they were about, from the brow of the steep hill. He saw the flooded valley shining with the breadth of water, and the trooper's horse on the other side, shaking his drenched flanks and neighing; and half-way down the hill he saw the three Doones mounting hastily. And then he knew that his only chance lay in the stoutness of his steed.

The horse was in pretty good condition; and the rider knew him thoroughly, and how to make the most of him; and though they had travelled some miles that day through very heavy ground, the bath in the river had washed the mud off, and been some refreshment. Therefore Stickles encouraged his nag, and put him into a good hand gallop, heading away towards Withycombe. At first he had thought of turning to the right, and making off for Withypool, a mile or so down the valley; but his good sense told him that no one there would dare to protect him against the Doones, so he resolved to go on his way; yet faster than he had intended.

The three villains came after him, with all the speed they could muster, making sure from the badness of the road that he must stick fast ere long, and so be at their mercy. And this was

Jeremy's chiefest fear, for the ground being soft, and thoroughly rotten, after so much frost and snow, the poor horse had terrible work of it, with no time to pick the way; and even more good luck than skill was needed to keep him from foundering. How Jeremy prayed for an Exmoor fog (such as he had often sworn at), that he might turn aside and lurk, while his pursuers went past him! But no fog came, nor even a storm to damp the priming of their guns; neither was wood or coppice nigh, nor any place to hide in; only hills, and moor, and valleys; with flying shadows over them, and great banks of snow in the corners. At one time poor Stickles was quite in despair, for after leaping a little brook which crosses the track at Newland, he stuck fast in a "dancing-bog," as we call them upon Exmoor. The horse had broken through the crust of moss and sedge and marish-weed, and could do nothing but wallow and sink, with the black water spirting over him. And Jeremy, struggling with all his might, saw the three villains now topping the crest, less than a furlong behind him; and heard them shout in their savage delight. With the calmness of despair, he yet resolved to have one more try for it; and scrambling over the horse's head, gained firm land, and tugged at the bridle. The poor nag replied with all his power to the call upon his courage, and reared his forefeet out of the slough, and with straining eyeballs gazed at him. "Now," said Jeremy, "now, my fine fellow!" lifting him with the bridle; and the brave beast gathered the roll of his loins, and sprang from his quagmired haunches. One more spring, and he was on earth again, instead of being under it; and Jeremy leaped on his back, and stooped, for he knew that they would fire. Two bullets whistled over him, as the horse, mad with fright, dashed forward; and in five minutes more he had come to the Exe, and the pursuers had fallen behind him. The Exe, though a much smaller stream than the Barle, now ran in a foaming torrent, unbridged, and too wide for leaping. But Jeremy's horse took the water well; and both he and his rider were lightened, as well as comforted by it. And as they passed towards Lucott hill, and struck upon the founts of Lynn, the horses of the three pursuers began to tire under them. Then Jeremy Stickles knew that if he could only escape the sloughs, he was safe for the present; and so he stood up in his stirrups, and gave them a loud hallo, as if they had been so many foxes.

Their only answer was to fire the remaining charge at him; but the distance was too great for any aim from horseback; and the dropping bullet idly ploughed the sod upon one side of him. He acknowledged it with a wave of his hat, and laid one thumb to his nose, in the manner fashionable in London for expression of contempt. However, they followed him yet further, hoping to make him pay out dearly, if he should only miss the track, or fall upon morasses. But the neighbourhood of our Lynn stream is not so very boggy; and the King's messenger now knew his way as well as any of his chasers did; and so he arrived at Plover's Barrows, thankful, and in rare appetite.

"But was the poor soldier drowned?" asked Annie; "and you never went to look for him! Oh, how very dreadful!"

"Shot, or drowned; I know not which. Thank God it was only a trooper. But they shall pay for it, as dearly as if it had been a captain."

"And how was it you were struck by a bullet, and only shaken in your saddle? Had you a coat of mail on, or of Milanese chain armour? Now, Master Stickles, had you?"

"No, Mistress Lizzie; we do not wear things of that kind nowadays. You are apt, I perceive, at romances. But I happened to have a little flat bottle of the best stoneware slung beneath my saddle-cloak, and filled with the very best *eau de vie,* from the George Hotel, at Southmolton. The brand of it now is upon my back. Oh, the murderous scoundrels, what a brave spirit they have spilled!"

"You had better set to and thank God," said I, "that they have not spilled a braver one."

CHAPTER XLVIII
Every Man must defend Himself

It was only right in Jeremy Stickles, and of the simplest common sense, that he would not tell, before our girls, what the result of his journey was. But he led me aside in the course of the evening, and told me all about it; saying that I knew, as well as he did, that it was not woman's business. This I took, as it was meant, for a gentle caution that Lorna (whom he had not seen as yet) must not be informed of any of his doings. Herein I quite agreed with him; not only for his furtherance, but because I always think that women, of whatever mind, are best when least they meddle with the things that appertain to men.

Master Stickles complained that the weather had been against him bitterly, closing all the roads around him; even as it had done with us. It had taken him eight days, he said, to get from Exeter to Plymouth; whither he found that most of the troops had been drafted off from Exeter. When all were told, there was but a battalion of one of the King's horse regiments, and two companies of foot soldiers; and their commanders had orders, later than the date of Jeremy's commission, on no account to quit the southern coast and march inland. Therefore, although they would gladly have come for a brush with the celebrated Doones, it was more than they durst attempt, in the face of their instructions. However, they spared him a single trooper, as a companion of the road, and to prove to the justices of the county, and the lord lieutenant, that he had their approval.

To these authorities Master Stickles now was forced to address himself, although he would rather have had one trooper than a score from the very best trained bands. For these trained bands had afforded very good soldiers, in the time of the civil wars, and for some years afterwards; but now their discipline was gone; and the younger generation had seen no real fighting. Each would have his own opinion, and would want to argue it; and if this were not allowed, he went about his duty in such a temper as to prove that his own way was the best.

Neither was this the worst of it; for Jeremy made no doubt but what (if he could only get the militia to turn out in force) he might manage, with the help of his own men, to force the stronghold of the enemy; but the truth was that the officers, knowing how hard it would be to collect their men at that time of the year, and in that state of the weather, began with one accord to make every possible excuse. And especially they pressed this point, that Bagworthy was not in their county; the Devonshire people affirming vehemently that it lay in the county of Somerset, and the Somerset folk averring, even with imprecations, that it lay in Devonshire. Now I believe the truth to be that the boundary of the two counties, as well as of Oare and Brendon parishes, is defined by the Bagworthy river; so that the disputants, on both sides, were both right and wrong.

Upon this, Master Stickles suggested, and as I thought very sensibly, that the two counties should unite, and equally contribute to the extirpation of this pest, which shamed and injured them both alike. But hence arose another difficulty; for the men of Devon said they would march when Somerset had taken the field; and the sons of Somerset replied, that indeed they were quite ready, but what were their cousins of Devonshire doing? And so it came to pass that the King's Commissioner returned, without any army whatever; but with promise of two hundred men when the roads should be more passable. And meanwhile, what were we to do, abandoned as we were to the mercies of the Doones, with only our own hands to help us? And herein I grieved at my own folly, in having let Tom Faggus go, whose wit and courage would have been worth at least half a dozen men to us. Upon this matter I held long council with my good friend Stickles; telling him all about Lorna's presence, and what I knew of her history. He agreed with me, that we could not hope to escape an attack from the outlaws, and the more especially now that they knew himself to be returned to us. Also he praised me for my forethought, in having threshed out all our corn, and hidden the produce in such a manner that they were not likely to find it. Furthermore, he recommended that all the entrances to the house should at once be strengthened, and a watch must be maintained at night; and he thought it wiser that I should go (late as it was) to Lynmouth, if a horse could pass the valley, and fetch every one of his mounted troopers, who might now be quartered there. Also if any men of courage, though capable only of handling a pitchfork, could be found in the neighbourhood, I was to try to summon them. But our district is so thinly peopled, that I had little faith in this; however, my errand was given me, and I set forth upon it; for John Fry was afraid of the waters.

Knowing how fiercely the floods were out, I resolved to travel the higher road, by Cosgate and through Countisbury; therefore I swam my horse through the Lynn, at the ford below our house (where sometimes you may step across), and thence galloped up and along the hills. I could see all the inland valleys ribbon'd with broad waters; and in every winding crook, the banks of snow that fed them; while on my right the turbid sea was flaked with April showers. But when I descended the hill towards Lynmouth, I feared that my journey was all in vain.

For the East Lynn (which is our river) was ramping and roaring frightfully, lashing whole trunks of trees on the rocks, and rending them, and grinding them. And into it rushed, from the opposite side, a torrent even madder; upsetting what it came to aid; shattering wave with boiling billow, and scattering wrath with fury. It was certain death to attempt the passage; and the little wooden footbridge had been carried away long ago. And the men I was seeking must have their dwelling on the other side of this deluge, for on my side there was not a single house.

I followed the bank of the flood to the beach, some two or three hundred yards below; and there had the luck to see Will Watcombe on the opposite side, caulking an old boat. Though I could not make him hear a word, from the deafening roar of the torrent, I got him to understand at last that I wanted to cross over. Upon this he fetched another man, and the two of them launched a boat; and paddling well out to sea, fetched round the mouth of the frantic river. The other man proved to be Stickles' chief mate; and so he went back, and fetched his comrades, bringing their weapons, but leaving their horses behind. As it happened there were but four of them; however, to have even these was a help; and I started again at full speed for my home; for the men must follow afoot, and cross our river high up on the moorland.

This took them a long way round, and the track was rather bad to find, and the sky already darkening; so that I arrived at Plover's Barrows more than two hours before them. But they had done a sagacious thing, which was well worth the delay; for by hoisting their flag upon the hill, they fetched the two watchmen from the Foreland, and added them to their number.

It was lucky that I came home so soon; for I found the house in a great commotion, and all the women trembling. When I asked what the matter was, Lorna, who seemed the most self-possessed, answered, that it was all her fault, for she alone had frightened them. And this in the following manner. She had stolen out to the garden towards dusk, to watch some favourite hyacinths just pushing up, like a baby's teeth, and just attracting the fatal notice of a great house-snail at night-time. Lorna at last had discovered the glutton, and was bearing him off in triumph to the tribunal of the ducks, when she descried two glittering eyes glaring at her steadfastly, from the elder bush beyond the stream. The elder was smoothing its wrinkled leaves, being at least two months behind time; and among them this calm cruel face appeared; and she knew it was the face of Carver Doone.

The maiden, although so used to terror (as she told me once before), lost all presence of mind hereat, and could neither shriek nor fly, but only gaze, as if bewitched. Then Carver Doone, with his deadly smile, gloating upon her horror, lifted his long gun, and pointed full at Lornas heart. In vain she strove to turn away; fright had stricken her stiff as stone. With the inborn love of life, she tried to cover the vital part wherein the winged death must lodge — for she knew Carver's certain aim — but her hands hung numbed, and heavy: in nothing but her eyes was life.

With no sign of pity in his face, no quiver of relenting, but a well-pleased grin at all the charming palsy of his victim, Carver Doone lowered, inch by inch, the muzzle of his gun. When it pointed to the ground, between her delicate arched insteps, he pulled the trigger, and the bullet flung the mould all over her. It was a refinement of bullying, for which I swore to God that night, upon my knees, in secret, that I would smite down Carver Doone; or else he should smite me down. Base beast! what largest humanity, or what dreams of divinity, could make a man put up with this?

My darling (the loveliest, and most harmless, in the world of maidens) fell away on a bank of grass, and wept at her own cowardice; and trembled, and wondered where I was; and what I would think of this. Good God! What could I think of it? She overrated my slow nature, to admit the question.

While she leaned there, quite unable yet to save herself, Carver came to the brink of the flood, which alone was between them; and then he stroked his jet-black beard, and waited for Lorna to begin. Very likely, he thought that she would thank him for his kindness to her. But she was now recovering the power of her nimble limbs; and ready to be off like hope and wonder at her own cowardice.

"I have spared you this time," he said, in his deep, calm voice, "only because it suits my plans; and I never yield to temper. But unless you come back to-morrow, pure, and with all you took away, and teach me to destroy that fool, who has destroyed himself for you, your death is here, your death is here, where it has long been waiting."

Although his gun was empty, he struck the breech of it with his finger; and then he turned away, not deigning even once to look back again; and Lorna saw his giant figure striding across the meadow-land, as if the Ridds were nobodies, and he the proper owner. Both mother and I were greatly hurt at hearing of this insolence; for we had owned that meadow from the time of the great Alfred; and even when that good king lay in the Isle of Athelney, he had a Ridd along with him.

Now I spoke to Lorna gently, seeing how much she had been tried: and I praised her for her courage, in not having run away, when she was so unable; and my darling was pleased with this, and smiled upon me for saying it; though she knew right well that, in this matter, my judgment was not impartial. But you may take this as a general rule, that a woman likes praise from the man whom she loves, and cannot stop always to balance it.

Now, expecting a sharp attack that night — which Jeremy Stickles the more expected, after the words of Carver, which seemed to be meant to mislead us — we prepared a great quantity of knuckles of pork, and a ham in full cut, and a fillet of hung mutton. For we would almost surrender, rather than keep our garrison hungry. And all our men were exceedingly brave; and counted their rounds of the house in half-pints.

Before the maidens went to bed, Lorna made a remark which seemed to me a very clever one, and then I wondered how on earth it had never occurred to me before. But first she had done a thing which I could not in the least approve of; for she had gone up to my mother, and thrown herself into her arms, and begged to be allowed to return to Glen Doone.

"My child, are you unhappy here?" mother asked her, very gently, for she had begun to regard her now as a daughter of her own.

"Oh no! Too happy, by far too happy, Mrs. Ridd. I never knew rest or peace before, or met with real kindness. But I cannot be so ungrateful, I cannot be so wicked, as to bring you all into deadly peril, for my sake alone. Let me go; you must not pay this great price for my happiness."

"Dear child, we are paying no price at all," replied my mother, embracing her; "we are not threatened for your sake only. Ask John, he will tell you. He knows every bit about politics, and this is a political matter."

Dear mother was rather proud in her heart, as well as terribly frightened, at the importance now accruing to Plover's Barrows farm; and she often declared that it would be as famous in history as the Rye House, or the meal-tub, or even the great black box, in which she was a firm believer; and even my knowledge of politics could not move her upon that matter. "Such things had happened before," she would say, shaking her head with its wisdom, "and why might they not happen again? Women would be women, and men would be men, to the end of the chapter; and if she had been in Lucy Walter's place, she would keep it quiet, as she had done"; and then she would look round, for fear, lest either of her daughters had heard her; "but now, can you give me any reason, why it may not have been so? You are so fearfully positive, John; just as men always are." "No," I used to say; "I can give you no reason why it may not have been so, mother. But the question is, if it was so, or not; rather than what it might have been. And, I think, it is pretty good proof against it, that what nine men of every ten in England would only too gladly believe, if true, is nevertheless kept dark from them." "There you are again, John," mother would reply, "all about men, and not a single word about women. If you had any argument at all, you would own that marriage is a question upon which women are the best judges." "Oh!" I would groan in my spirit, and go; leaving my dearest mother quite sure, that now at last she must have convinced me. But if mother had known that Jeremy Stickles was working against the black box, and its issue, I doubt whether he would have fared so well, even though he was a visitor. However, she knew that something was doing, and something of importance; and she trusted in God for the rest of it. Only she used to tell me, very seriously, of an evening, "The very least they can give you, dear John, is a coat of arms. Be sure you take nothing less, dear; and the farm can well support it."

But lo! I have left Lorna ever so long, anxious to consult me upon political matters. She came to me, and her eyes alone asked a hundred questions, which I rather had answered upon her lips, than troubled her pretty ears with them. Therefore I told her nothing at all, save that the attack (if any should be) would not be made on her account; and that if she should hear, by any chance, a trifle of a noise in the night, she was to wrap the clothes around her, and shut her beautiful eyes again. On no account, whatever she did, was she to go to the window. She liked my expression about her eyes, and promised to do the very best she could; and then she crept so very close, that I needs must have her closer; and with her head on my breast she asked:

"Can't you keep out of this fight, John?"

"My own one," I answered, gazing through the long black lashes, at the depths of radiant love; "I believe there will be nothing; but what there is, I must see out."

"Shall I tell you what I think, John? It is only a fancy of mine, and perhaps it is not worth telling."

"Let us have it, dear, by all means. You know so much about their ways."

"What I believe is this, John. You know how high the rivers are, higher than ever they were before, and twice as high, you have told me. I believe that Glen Doone is flooded, and all the houses under water."

"You little witch," I answered; "what a fool I must be not to think of it! Of course it is; it must be. The torrent from all the Bagworthy forest, and all the valleys above it, and the great drifts in the glen itself, never could have outlet down my famous water-slide. The valley must be under water twenty feet at least. Well, if ever there was a fool, I am he, for not having thought of it."

"I remember once before," said Lorna, reckoning on her fingers, "when there was very heavy rain, all through the autumn and winter, five or it may be six years ago, the river came down with such a rush that the water was two feet deep in our rooms, and we all had to camp by the cliff-edge. But you think that the floods are higher now, I believe I heard you say, John."

"I don't think about it, my treasure," I answered; "you may trust me for understanding floods, after our work at Tiverton. And I know that the deluge in all our valleys is such as no living man can remember, neither will ever behold again. Consider three months of snow, snow, snow, and a fortnight of rain on the top of it, and all to be drained in a few days away! And great barricades of ice still in the rivers blocking them up, and ponding them. You may take my word for it, Mistress Lorna, that your pretty bower is six feet deep."

"Well, my bower has served its time," said Lorna, blushing as she remembered all that had happened there; "and my bower now is here, John. But I am so sorry to think of all the poor women flooded out of their houses, and sheltering in the snowdrifts. However, there is one good of it; they cannot send many men against us, with all this trouble upon them."

"You are right" I replied; "how clever you are! and that is why there were only three to cut off Master Stickles. And now we shall beat them, I make no doubt, even if they come at all. And I defy them to fire the house; the thatch is too wet for burning."

We sent all the women to bed quite early, except Gwenny Carfax and our old Betty. These two we allowed to stay up, because they might be useful to us, if they could keep from quarrelling. For my part, I had little fear, after what Lorna had told me, as to the result of the combat. It was not likely that the Doones could bring more than eight or ten men against us, while their homes were in such danger; and to meet these we had eight good men, including Jeremy, and myself, all well armed, and resolute, besides our three farm-servants, and the parish clerk, and the shoemaker. These five could not be trusted much for any valiant conduct, although they spoke very confidently over their cans of cider. Neither were their weapons fitted for much execution, unless it were at close quarters, which they would be likely to avoid. Bill Dadds had a sickle, Jim Slocomb a flail, the cobbler had borrowed the constable's staff (for the constable would not attend, because there was no warrant), and the parish clerk had brought his pitch-pipe, which was enough to break any man's head. But John Fry, of course, had his blunderbuss, loaded with tin-tacks and marbles, and more likely to kill the man who discharged it than any other person; but we knew that John had it only for show, and to describe its qualities.

Now it was my great desire, and my chiefest hope, to come across Carver Doone that night, and settle the score between us; not by any shot in the dark, but by a conflict man to man. As yet, since I came to full-grown power, I had never met anyone whom I could not play tee-totum with; but now at last I had found a man whose strength was not to be laughed at. I could guess it in his face, I could tell it in his arms, I could see it in his stride and gait, which more than all the rest betray the substance of a man. And being so well used to wrestling, and to judge antagonists, I felt that here (if anywhere) I had found my match.

Therefore I was not content to abide within the house, or go the rounds with the troopers; but betook myself to the rick-yard, knowing that the Doones were likely to begin their onset there. For they had a pleasant custom, when they visited farm-houses, of lighting themselves towards picking up anything they wanted, or stabbing the inhabitants, by first creating a blaze in the rick-yard. And though our ricks were all now of mere straw (except indeed two of prime clover hay), and although on the top they were so wet that no firebrands might hurt them, I was both unwilling to have them burned, and fearful that they might kindle, if well roused up with fire upon the windward side.

By the by, these Doones had got the worst of this pleasant trick one time. For happening to fire the ricks of a lonely farm called Yeanworthy, not far above Glenthorne, they approached the house to get people's goods, and to enjoy their terror. The master of the farm was lately dead, and had left, inside the clockcase, loaded, the great long gun, wherewith he had used to sport at the ducks and the geese on the shore. Now Widow Fisher took out this gun, and not caring much what became of her (for she had loved her husband dearly) she laid it upon the window-sill, which looked upon the rick-yard; and she backed up the butt with a chest of oak drawers, and she opened the window a little back, and let the muzzle out on the slope. Presently five or six fine young Doones came dancing a reel (as their manner was) be-twixt her and the flaming rick. Upon which she pulled the trigger with all the force of her thumb, and a quarter of a pound of duck-shot went out with a blaze on the dancers. You may suppose what their dancing was, and their reeling how changed to staggering, and their music none of the sweetest. One of them fell into the rick, and was burned, and buried in a ditch next day; but the others were set upon their horses, and carried home on a path of blood. And strange to say, they never avenged this very dreadful injury; but having heard that a woman had fired this desperate shot among them, they said that she ought to be a Doone, and inquired how old she was.

Now I had not been so very long waiting in our mow-yard, with my best gun ready, and a big club by me, before a heaviness of sleep began to creep upon me. The flow of water was in my ears, and in my eyes a hazy spreading, and upon my brain a closure, as a cobbler sews a vamp up. So I leaned back in the clover-rick, and the dust of the seed, and the smell came round me, without any trouble; and I dozed about Lorna, just once or twice, and what she had said about new-mown hay; and then back went my head, and my chin went up; and if ever a man was blest with slumber, down it came upon me, and away went I into it.

Now this was very vile of me, and against all good resolutions, even such as I would have sworn to an hour ago or less. But if you had been in the water as I had, ay, and had long fight with it, after a good day's work, and then great anxiety afterwards, and brain-work (which is not fair for me), and upon that a stout supper, mayhap you would not be so hard on my sleep; though you felt it your duty to wake me.

CHAPTER XLIX

Maiden Sentinels are Best

It was not likely that the outlaws would attack our premises, until some time after the moon was risen; because it would be too dangerous to cross the flooded valleys in the darkness of the night. And but for this consideration, I must have striven harder against the stealthy approach of slumber. But even so, it was very foolish to abandon watch, especially in such as I, who sleep like any dormouse. Moreover I had chosen the very worst place in the world for such employment, with a goodly chance of awaking in a bed of solid fire.

And so it might have been, nay, it must have been, but for Lorna's vigilance. Her light hand upon my arm awoke me, not too readily; and leaping up, I seized my club, and prepared to knock down somebody.

"Who's that?" I cried; "stand back, I say, and let me have fair chance at you."

"Are you going to knock me down, dear John?" replied the voice I loved so well; "I am sure I should never get up again, after one blow from you, John."

"My darling, is it you?" I cried; "and breaking all your orders! Come back into the house at once; and nothing on your head, dear!"

"How could I sleep, while at any moment you might be killed beneath my window? And now is the time of real danger; for men can see to travel."

I saw at once the truth of this. The moon was high and clearly lighting all the watered valleys. To sleep any longer might be death, not only to myself, but all.

"The man on guard at the back of the house is fast asleep," she continued; "Gwenny, who let me out, and came with me; has heard him snoring for two hours. I think the women ought to be the watch, because they have had no travelling. Where do you suppose little Gwenny is?"

"Surely not gone to Glen Doone?" I was not sure, however: for I could believe almost anything of the Cornish maiden's hardihood.

"No," replied Lorna, "although she wanted even to do that. But of course I would not hear of it, on account of the swollen waters. But she is perched in yonder tree, which commands the Barrow valley. She says that they are almost sure to cross the streamlet there; and now it is so wide and large, that she can trace it in the moonlight, half a mile beyond her. If they cross, she is sure to see them, and in good time to let us know."

"What a shame," I cried, "that the men should sleep, and the maidens be the soldiers! I will sit in that tree myself, and send little Gwenny back to you. Go to bed, my best and dearest; I will take good care not to sleep again."

"Please not to send me away, dear John," she answered very mournfully. "You and I have been together through perils worse than this. I shall only be more timid, and more miserable, indoors."

"I cannot let you stay here," I said; "it is altogether impossible. Do you suppose that I can fight, with you among the bullets, Lorna? If this is the way you mean to take it, we had better go both to the apple-room, and lock ourselves in, and hide under the tiles, and let them burn all the rest of the premises."

At this idea Lorna laughed, as I could see by the moonlight; and then she said:

"You are right, John. I should only do more harm than good; and of all things I hate fighting most, and disobedience next to it. Therefore I will go indoors, although I cannot go to bed. But promise me one thing, dearest John. You will keep yourself out of the way, now won't you, as much as you can, for my sake?"

"Of that you may be quite certain, Lorna. I will shoot them all through the hay-ricks."

"That is right, dear," she answered, never doubting but what I could do it; "and then they cannot see you, you know. But don't think of climbing that tree, John; it is a great deal too dangerous. It is all very well for Gwenny; she has no bones to break."

"None worth breaking, you mean, I suppose. Very well; I will not climb the tree, for I should defeat my own purpose, I fear; being easier to be seen than see. Now go indoors, darling, without more words. The more you linger, the more I shall keep you."

She laughed her own bright laugh at this, and only said, "God keep you, love!" and then away she tripped across the yard, with the step I loved to watch so. And thereupon I shouldered arms, and resolved to tramp till morning. For I was vexed at my own neglect, and that Lorna should have to right it.

But before I had been long on duty, making the round of the ricks and stables, and hailing Gwenny now and then from the bottom of her tree, a short wide figure stole towards me, in and out the shadows, and I saw that it was no other than the little maid herself, and that she bore some tidings.

"Ten on 'em crossed the water down yonder," said Gwenny, putting her hand to her mouth, and seeming to regard it as good news rather than otherwise; "be arl craping up by the hedgerow now. I could shutt dree on 'em from the bar of the gate, if so be I had your goon, young man."

"There is no time to lose, Gwenny. Run to the house, and fetch Master Stickles, and all the men; while I stay here, and watch the rick-yard."

Perhaps I was wrong in heeding the ricks, at such a time as that; especially as only the clover was of much importance. But it seemed to me like a sort of triumph that they should even be able to boast of having fired our mow-yard. Therefore I stood in a nick of the clover, whence we had cut some trusses, with my club in hand, and gun close by.

The robbers rode into our yard as coolly as if they had been invited, having lifted the gate from the hinges first, on account of its being fastened. Then they actually opened our stable-doors, and turned our honest horses out, and put their own rogues in the place of them. At this my breath was quite taken away, for we think so much of our horses. By this time I could see our troopers, waiting in the shadow of the house, round the corner from where the Doones were, and expecting the order to fire. But Jeremy Stickles very wisely kept them in readiness, until the enemy should advance upon them.

"Two of you lazy fellows go," it was the deep voice of Carver Doone, "and make us a light to cut their throats by. Only one thing, once again. If any man touches Lorna, I will stab him where he stands. She belongs to me. There are two other young damsels here, whom you may take away if you please. And the mother, I hear, is still comely. Now for our rights. We have borne too long the insolence of these yokels. Kill every man, and every child, and burn the cursed place down."

As he spoke thus blasphemously, I set my gun against his breast; and by the light buckled from his belt, I saw the little "sight" of brass gleaming alike upon either side, and the sleek round barrel glimmering. The aim was sure as death itself. If I only drew the trigger (which went very lightly) Carver Doone would breathe no more. And yet — will you believe me? — I could not pull the trigger. Would to God that I had done so!

For I never had taken human life, neither done bodily harm to man; beyond the little bruises, and the trifling aches and pains, which follow a good and honest bout in the wrestling ring. Therefore I dropped my carbine, and grasped again my club, which seemed a more straightforward implement.

Presently two young men came towards me, bearing brands of resined hemp kindled from Carver's lamp. The foremost of them set his torch to the rick within a yard of me, the smoke concealing me from him. I struck him with a back-handed blow on the elbow, as he bent it; and I heard the bone of his arm break, as clearly as ever I heard a twig snap. With a roar of pain he fell on the ground and his torch dropped there, and singed him. The other man stood amazed at this, not having yet gained sight of me; till I caught his firebrand from his hand, and struck it into his countenance. With that he leaped at me; but I caught him, in a manner learned from early wrestling, and snapped his collar-bone, as I laid him upon the top of his comrade.

This little success so encouraged me, that I was half inclined to advance, and challenge Carver Doone to meet me; but I bore in mind that he would be apt to shoot me without ceremony; and what is the utmost of human strength against the power of powder? Moreover, I remembered my promise to sweet Lorna; and who would be left to defend her, if the rogues got rid of me?

While I was hesitating thus (for I always continue to hesitate except in actual conflict) a blaze of fire lit up the house, and brown smoke hung around it. Six of our men had let go at the Doones, by Jeremy Stickles' order, as the villains came swaggering down in the moonlight, ready for rape or murder. Two of them fell, and the rest hung back, to think at their leisure what this was. They were not used to this sort of thing: it was neither just nor courteous.

Being unable any longer to contain myself, as I thought of Lorna's excitement at all this noise of firing, I came across the yard, expecting whether they would shoot at me. However, no one shot at me; and I went up to Carver Doone, whom I knew by his size in the moonlight, and I took him by the beard, and said, "Do you call yourself a man?"

For a moment, he was so astonished that he could not answer. None had ever dared, I suppose, to look at him in that way; and he saw that he had met his equal, or perhaps his master. And then he tried a pistol at me; but I was too quick for him.

"Now, Carver Doone, take warning," I said to him, very soberly; "you have shown yourself a fool by your contempt of me. I may not be your match in craft; but I am in manhood. You are a despicable villain. Lie low in your native muck."

And with that word, I laid him flat upon his back in our straw-yard, by a trick of the inner heel which he could not have resisted (though his strength had been twice as great as mine), unless he were a wrestler. Seeing him down, the others ran, though one of them made a shot at me, and some of them got their horses, before our men came up: and some went away without them. And among these last was Captain Carver, who arose, while I was feeling myself (for I had a little wound), and strode away with a train of curses, enough to poison the light of the moon.

We gained six very good horses, by this attempted rapine, as well as two young prisoners, whom I had smitten by the clover-rick. And two dead Doones were left behind; whom (as we buried them in the churchyard, without, any service over them) I for my part was most thankful that I had not killed. For to have the life of a fellow-man laid upon one's conscience — deserved he his death; or deserved it not — is to my sense of right and wrong the heaviest of all burdens; and the one that wears most deeply inwards, with the dwelling of the mind on this view and on that of it.

I was inclined to pursue the enemy, and try to capture more of them; but Jeremy Stickles would not allow it, for he said that all the advantage would be upon their side, if we went hurrying after them, with only the moon to guide us. And who could tell but what there might be another band of them ready to fall upon the house, and burn it, and seize the women, if we left them unprotected? When he put the case thus, I was glad enough to abide by his decision. And one thing was quite certain, that the Doones had never before received so rude a shock, and so violent a blow to their supremacy, since first they had built up their power, and become the Lords of Exmoor. I knew that Carver Doone would gnash those mighty teeth of his, and curse the men around him, for the blunder (which was in truth his own) of over confidence and carelessness. And at the same time, all the rest would feel that such a thing had never happened, while old Sir Ensor was alive; and that it was caused by nothing short of gross mismanagement.

I scarcely know who made the greatest fuss about my little wound, mother, or Annie, or Lorna. I was heartily ashamed to be so treated like a milksop; but most unluckily it had been impossible to hide it. For the ball had cut along my temple, just above the eye-brow; and being fired so near at hand, the powder too had scarred me. Therefore it seemed a great deal worse than it really was; and the sponging, and the plaistering, and the sobbing, and the moaning, made me quite ashamed to look Master Stickles in the face.

However, at last I persuaded them that I had no intention of giving up the ghost that night; and then they all fell to, and thanked God, with an emphasis quite unknown in church. And hereupon Master Stickles said, in his free and easy manner (for no one courted his observation), that I was the luckiest of all mortals in having a mother, and a sister, and a sweetheart, to make much of me. For his part, he said, he was just as well off, in not having any to care for him. For now he might go and get shot, or stabbed, or knocked on the head, at his pleasure, without anyone being offended. I made bold, upon this, to ask him what was become of his wife; for I had heard him speak of having one. He said that he neither knew nor cared; and perhaps I should be like him some day. That Lorna should hear such sentiments was grievous to me. But she looked at me with a smile, which proved her contempt for all such ideas; and lest anything still more unfit might be said, I dismissed the question.

But Master Stickles told me afterwards, when there was no one with us, to have no faith in any woman, whatever she might seem to be. For he assured me that now he possessed very large experience, for so small a matter; being thoroughly acquainted with women of every class, from ladies of the highest blood, to Bonarobas, and peasants' wives: and that they might all be divided into three heads and no more; that is to say as follows. First, the very hot and passionate, who were only contemptible; second, the cold and indifferent, who were simply odious; and third, the mixture of the other two, who had the bad qualities of both. As for reason, none of them had it: it was like a sealed book to them, which if they ever tried to open, they began at the back of the cover.

Now I did not like to hear such things; and to me they appeared to be insolent, as well as narrow-minded. For if you came to that, why might not men, as well as women, be divided into the same three classes, and be pronounced upon by women, as being even more devoid than their gentle judges of reason? Moreover I knew, both from my own sense, and from the greatest of all great poets, that there are, and always have been, plenty of women, good and gentle, warm-hearted, loving, and lovable, very keen, moreover, at seeing the right, be it by reason, or otherwise. And upon the whole, I prefer them much to the people of my own sex, as goodness of heart is more important than to show good reason for having it. And so I said to Jeremy:

"You have been ill-treated, perhaps. Master Stickles, by some woman or other?"

"Ay, that have I," he replied with an oath; "and the last on earth who should serve me so, the woman who was my wife. A woman whom I never struck, never wronged in any way, never even let her know that I liked another better. And yet when I was at Berwick last, with the regiment on guard there against those vile moss-troopers, what does that woman do but fly in the face of all authority, and of my especial business, by running away herself with the biggest of all moss-troopers! Not that I cared a groat about her; and I wish the fool well rid of her: but the insolence of the thing was such that everybody laughed at me; and back I went to London, losing a far better and safer job than this; and all through her. Come, let's have another onion."

Master Stickles' view of the matter was so entirely unromantic, that I scarcely wondered at Mistress Stickles for having run away from him to an adventurous moss-trooper. For nine women out of ten must have some kind of romance or other, to make their lives endurable; and when their love has lost this attractive element, this soft dew-fog (if such it be), the love itself is apt to languish; unless its bloom be well replaced by the budding hopes of children. Now Master Stickles neither had, nor wished to have, any children.

Without waiting for any warrant, only saying something about *"captus in flagrante delicto"* — if that be the way to spell it — Stickles sent our prisoners off, bound and looking miserable, to the jail at Taunton. I was desirous to let them go free, if they would promise amendment; but although I had taken them, and surely therefore had every right to let them go again. Master Stickles said, "Not so." He assured me that it was a matter of public polity; and of course, not knowing what he meant, I could not contradict him; but thought that surely my private rights ought to be respected. For if I throw a man in wrestling, I expect to get his stakes; and if I take a man prisoner — why, he ought, in common justice, to belong to me, and I have a good right to let him go, if I think proper to do so. However Master Stickles said that I was quite benighted, and knew nothing of the Constitution; which was the very thing I knew, beyond any man in our parish!

Nevertheless, it was not for me to contradict a commissioner; and therefore I let my prisoners go, and wished them a happy deliverance. Stickles replied, with a merry grin, that if they ever got it, it would be a jail deliverance, and the bliss of dancing; and he laid his hand to his throat in a manner which seemed to me most uncourteous. However his foresight proved too correct; for both those poor fellows were executed, soon after the next assizes. Lorna had done her very best to earn another chance for them; even going down on her knees to that common Jeremy, and pleading with great tears for them. However, although much moved by her, he vowed that he durst do nothing else. To set them free was more than his own life was worth; for all the country knew, by this time, that two captive Doones were roped to the cider-press at Plover's Barrows. Annie bound the broken arm of the one whom I had knocked down with the club, and I myself supported it; and then she washed and rubbed with lard the face of the other poor fellow, whom the torch had injured; and I fetched back his collar-bone to the best of my ability. For before any surgeon could arrive, they were off with a well-armed escort. That day we were reinforced so strongly from the stations along the coast, even as far as Minehead, that we not only feared no further attack, but even talked of assaulting Glen Doone, without waiting for the train-bands. However, I thought that it would be mean to take advantage of the enemy in the thick of the floods and confusion; and several of the others thought so too, and did not like fighting in water. Therefore it was resolved to wait, and keep a watch upon the valley, and let the floods go down again.

CHAPTER L

A Merry Meeting a Sad One

Now the business I had most at heart (as every one knows by this time) was to marry Lorna as soon as might be, if she had no objection, and then to work the farm so well, as to nourish all our family. And herein I saw no difficulty; for Annie would soon be off our hands, and somebody might come and take a fancy to little Lizzie (who was growing up very nicely now, though not so fine as Annie); moreover, we were almost sure to have great store of hay and corn after so much snow, if there be any truth in the old saying:

> A foot deep of rain
> Will kill hay and grain;
> But three feet of snow
> Will make them come mo'.

And although it was too true that we had lost a many cattle, yet even so we had not lost money, for the few remaining fetched such prices as were never known before. And though we grumbled with all our hearts, and really believed, at one time, that starvation was upon us, I doubt whether, on the whole, we were not the fatter, and the richer, and the wiser for that winter. And I might have said the happier, except for the sorrow which we felt at the failures among our neighbours. The Snowes lost every sheep they had, and nine out of ten horned cattle; and poor Jasper Kebby would have been forced to throw up the lease of his farm, and perhaps to go to prison, but for the help we gave him.

However, my dear mother would have it that Lorna was too young, as yet, to think of being married: and indeed I myself was compelled to admit that her form was becoming more perfect and lovely; though I had not thought it possible. And another difficulty was, that as we had all been Protestants from the time of Queen Elizabeth, the maiden must be converted first, and taught to hate all Papists. Now Lorna had not the smallest idea of ever being converted. She said that she loved me truly, but wanted not to convert me; and if I loved her equally, why should I wish to convert her? With this I was tolerably content, not seeing so very much difference between a creed and a credo, and believing God to be our Father, in Latin as well as English. Moreover my darling knew but little of the Popish ways — whether excellent or otherwise — inasmuch as the Doones, though they stole their houses, or at least the joiner's work, had never been tempted enough by the devil, to steal either church or chapel.

Lorna came to our little church, when Parson Bowden reappeared after the snow was over; and she said that all was very nice, and very like what she had seen in the time of her Aunt Sabina, when they went far away to the little chapel, with a shilling in their gloves. It made the tears come into her eyes, by the force of memory, when Parson Bowden did the things, not so gracefully nor so well, yet with pleasant imitation of her old priest's sacred rites.

"He is a worthy man," she said, being used to talk in the service time, and my mother was obliged to cough: "I like him very much indeed: but I wish he would let me put his things the right way on his shoulders."

Everybody in our parish, who could walk at all, or hire a boy and a wheelbarrow, ay and half the folk from Countisbury, Brendon, and even Lynmouth, was and were to be found that Sunday in our little church of Oare. People who would not come anigh us when the Doones were threatening with carbine and with firebrand, flocked in their very best clothes, to see a lady Doone go to church. Now all this came of that vile John Fry; I knew it as well as possible; his tongue was worse than the clacker of a charity school-bell, or the ladle in the frying-pan, when the bees are swarming.

However, Lorna was not troubled; partly because of her natural dignity and gentleness; partly because she never dreamed that the people were come to look at her. But when we came to the Psalms of the day, with some vague sense of being stared at more than ought to be, she dropped the heavy black lace fringing of the velvet hat she wore, and concealed from the congregation all except her bright red lips, and the oval snowdrift of her chin. I touched her hand, and she pressed mine; and we felt that we were close together, and God saw no harm in it.

As for Parson Bowden (as worthy a man as ever lived, and one who could shoot flying) he scarcely knew what he was doing, without the clerk to help him. He had borne it very well indeed, when I returned from London: but to see a live Doone in his church, and a lady Doone, and a lovely Doone, moreover one engaged to me, upon whom he almost looked as the Squire of his parish (although not rightly an Armiger), and to feel that this lovely Doone was a Papist, and therefore of higher religion — as all our parsons think — and that she knew exactly how he ought to do all the service, of which he himself knew little; I wish to express my firm belief that all these things together turned Parson Bowden's head a little, and made him look to me for orders.

My mother, the very best of women, was (as I could well perceive) a little annoyed and vexed with things. For this particular occasion, she had procured from Dulverton, by special message to Ruth Huckaback (whereof more anon), a head dress with a feather never seen before upon Exmoor, to the best of every one's knowledge. It came from a bird called a flaming something — a flaming oh, or a flaming ah, I will not be positive — but I can assure you that it did flame! and dear mother had no other thought but that all the congregation would neither see nor think of any other mortal thing, or immortal even, to the very end of the sermon.

Herein she was so disappointed, that no sooner did she get home, but upstairs she went at speed, not even stopping at the mirror in our little parlour, and flung the whole thing into a cupboard, as I knew by the bang of the door, having eased the lock for her lately. Lorna saw there was something wrong; and she looked at Annie and Lizzie (as more likely to understand it) with her former timid glance; which I knew so well, and which had first enslaved me.

"I know not what ails mother," said Annie, who looked very beautiful, with lilac lutestring ribbons, which I saw the Snowe girls envying; "but she has not attended to one of the prayers, nor said 'Amen,' all the morning. Never fear, darling Lorna, it is nothing about you. It is something about our John, I am sure; for she never worries herself very much about anybody but him." And here Annie made a look at me, such as I had had five hundred of.

"You keep your opinions to yourself," I replied; because I knew the dear, and her little bits of jealousy; "it happens that you are quite wrong, this time. Lorna, come with me, my darling."

"Oh yes, Lorna; go with him," cried Lizzie, dropping her lip, in a way which you must see to know its meaning; "John wants nobody now but you; and none can find fault with his taste, dear."

"You little fool, I should think not," I answered very rudely; for, betwixt the lot of them, my Lorna's eyelashes were quivering; "now, dearest angel, come with me; and snap your hands at the whole of them."

My angel did come, with a sigh, and then with a smile, when we were alone; but without any unangelic attempt at snapping her sweet white fingers.

These little things are enough to show, that while every one so admired Lorna, and so kindly took to her, still there would, just now and then, be petty and paltry flashes of jealousy concerning her; and perhaps it could not be otherwise among so many women. However, we were always doubly kind to her afterwards; and although her mind was so sensitive and quick, that she must have suffered, she never allowed us to perceive it, nor lowered herself by resenting it.

Possibly I may have mentioned that little Ruth Huckaback had been asked, and had promised, to spend her Christmas with us; and this was more desirable, because she had left us through some offence, or sorrow, about things said of her. Now my dear mother, being the kindest and best-hearted of all women, could not bear that poor dear Ruth (who would some day have such a fortune) should be entirely lost to us. "It is our duty, my dear children," she said more than once about it, "to forgive and forget, as freely as we hope to have it done to us. If dear little Ruth has not behaved quite as we might have expected, great allowance should be made for a girl with so much money. Designing people get hold of her, and flatter her, and coax her, to obtain a base influence over her; so that when she falls among simple folk, who speak the honest truth of her, no wonder the poor child is vexed, and gives herself airs, and so on. Ruth can be very useful to us, in a number of little ways; and I consider it quite a duty to pardon her freak of petulance."

Now one of the little ways in which Ruth had been very useful, was the purchase of the scarlet feathers of the flaming bird; and now that the house was quite safe from attack, and the mark on my forehead was healing, I was begged, over and over again, to go and see Ruth, and make all things, straight, and pay for the gorgeous plumage. This last I was very desirous to do, that I might know the price of it, having made a small bet on the subject with Annie; and having held council with myself, whether or not it were possible to get something of the kind for Lorna, of still more distinguished appearance. Of course she could not wear scarlet as yet, even, if I had wished it; but I believe that people of fashion often wore purple for mourning; purple too was the royal colour, and Lorna was by right a queen; therefore I was quite resolved to ransack Uncle Reuben's stores, in search of some bright purple bird, if nature had kindly provided one.

All this however I kept to myself, intending to trust Ruth Huckaback, and no one else in the matter. And so, one beautifull spring morning, when all the earth was kissed with scent, and all the air caressed with song, up the lane I stoutly rode, well armed, and well provided.

Now though it is part of my life to heed, it is not part of my tale to tell, how the wheat was coming on. I reckon that you, who read this story, after I am dead and gone (and before that none shall read it), will say, "Tush! What is his wheat to us? We are not wheat: we are human beings: and all we care for is human doings." This may be very good argument and in the main, I believe that it is so. Nevertheless, if a man is to tell only what he thought and did, and not what came around him, he must not mention his own clothes, which his father and mother bought for him. And more than my own clothes to me, ay and as much as my own skin, are the works of nature round about, whereof a man is the smallest.

And now I will tell you, although most likely only to be laughed at, because I cannot put it in the style of Mr. Dryden — whom to compare to Shakespeare! but if once I begin upon that, you will never hear the last of me — nevertheless, I will tell you this; not wishing to be rude; but only just because I know it; the mote a man can fling his arms (so to gay) round nature's neck, the more he can upon her bosom, like an infant, lie and suck —

the more that man shall earn the trust, and love, of all his fellow-men. In this matter is no jealousy (when the man is dead); because thereafter all others know how much of the milk he had; and he can suck no longer; and they value him accordingly, for the nourishment he is to them. Even as when we keep a roaster of the sucking pigs, we choose, and praise at table most, the favourite of its mother. Fifty times have I seen this, and smiled, and praised our people's taste, and offered them more of the vitals.

Now here am I upon Shakespeare (who died, of his own fruition, at the age of fifty-two, yet lived more than fifty thousand men, within his little span of life), when all the while I ought to be riding as hard as I can to Dulverton. But, to tell the truth, I could not ride hard, being held at every turn, and often without any turn at all, by the beauty of things around me. These things grow upon a man, if once he stops to notice them.

It wanted yet two hours of noon, when I came to Master Huckaback's door, and struck the panels smartly. Knowing nothing of their manners, only that people in a town could not be expected to entertain (as we do in farm-houses), having, moreover, keen expectation of Master Huckaback's avarice, I had brought some stuff to eat, made by Annie, and packed by Lorna, and requiring no thinking about it.

Ruth herself came and let me in, blushing very heartily; for which colour I praised her health, and my praises heightened it. That little thing had lovely eyes, and could be trusted thoroughly. I do like an obstinate little woman, when she is sure that she is right. And indeed if love never sped me straight to the heart of Lorna (compared to whom, Ruth was no more than the thief is to the candle), who knows but what I might have yielded to the law of nature, that thorough trimmer of balances, and verified the proverb that the giant loves the dwarf?

"I take the privilege, Mistress Ruth, of saluting you according to kinship, and the ordering of the Canons." And therewith I bussed her well, and put my arm around her waist, being so terribly restricted in the matter of Lorna, and knowing the use of practice. Not that I had any warmth — all that was darling Lorna's — only out of pure gallantry, and my knowledge of London fashions. Ruth blushed to such a pitch at this, and looked up at me with such a gleam, as if I must have my own way; that all my love of kissing sank, and I felt that I was wronging her. Only my mother had told me, when the girls were out of the way, to do all I could to please darling Ruth, and I had gone about it accordingly.

Now Ruth as yet had never heard a word about dear Lorna; and when she led me into the kitchen (where everything looked beautiful), and told me not to mind, for a moment, about the scrubbing of my boots, because she would only be too glad to clean it all up after me, and told me how glad she was to see me, blushing more at every word, and recalling some of them, and stooping down for pots and pans, when I looked at her too ruddily — all these things came upon me so, without any legal notice, that I could only look at Ruth, and think how very good she was, and how bright her handles were; and wonder if I had wronged her. Once or twice I began — this I say upon my honour — to endeavour to explain exactly, how we were at Plover's Barrows; how we all had been bound to fight, and had defeated the enemy, keeping their queen amongst us. But Ruth would make some great mistake between Lorna and Gwenny Carfax, and gave me no chance to set her aright, and cared about nothing much, except some news of Sally Snowe.

What could I do with this little thing? All my sense of modesty, and value for my dinner, were against my over pressing all the graceful hints I had given about Lorna. Ruth was just a girl of that sort, who will not believe one word, except from her own seeing; not so much from any doubt, as from the practice of using eyes which have been in business.

I asked Cousin Ruth (as we used to call her, though the cousinship was distant) what was become of Uncle Ben, and how it was that we never heard anything of, or from, him now. She replied that she hardly knew what to make of her grandfather's manner of carrying on, for the last half-year or more. He was apt to leave his home, she said, at any hour of the day or night; going none knew whither, and returning no one might say when. And his dress, in her opinion, was enough to frighten a hodman, or a scavenger of the roads, instead of the decent suit of kersey, or of Sabbath doe-skin, such as had won the respect and reverence of his fellow-townsmen. But the worst of all things was, as she confessed, with tears in her eyes, that the poor old gentleman had something weighing heavily on his mind.

"It will shorten his days, Cousin Ridd," she said, for she never would call me Cousin John; "he has no enjoyment of anything that he eats or drinks, nor even in counting his money, as he used to do all Sunday; indeed no pleasure in anything, unless it be smoking his pipe, and thinking and staring, at bits of brown stone, which he pulls, every now and then, out of his pockets. And the business, he used to take such pride in, is now left almost entirely to the foreman, and to me."

"And what will become of you, dear Ruth, if anything happens to the old man?"

"I am sure I know not," she answered simply; "and I cannot bear to think of it. It must depend, I suppose, upon dear grandfather's pleasure about me."

"It must rather depend," said I, though having no business to say it, "upon your own good pleasure, Ruth; for all the world will pay court to you."

"That is the very thing which I never could endure. I have begged dear grandfather to leave no chance of that. When he has threatened me with poverty, as he does sometimes, I have always met him truly, with the answer, that I feared one thing a great deal worse than poverty; namely, to be an heiress. But I cannot make him believe it. Only think how strange, Cousin Ridd, I cannot make him believe it!"

"It is not strange at all," I answered; "considering how he values money. Neither would anyone else believe you, except by looking into your true, and very pretty eyes, dear."

Now I beg that no one will suspect for a single moment either that I did not mean exactly what I said, or meant a single atom more, or would not have said the same, if Lorna had been standing by. What I had always liked in Ruth, was the calm straightforward gaze, and beauty of her large brown eyes. Indeed I had spoken of them to Lorna, as the only ones to be compared (though not for more than a moment) to her own, for truth and light, but never for depth and softness. But now the little maiden dropped them, and turned away without reply.

"I will go and see to my horse," I said; "the boy that has taken him seemed surprised at his having no horns on his forehead. Perhaps he will lead him into the shop, and feed him upon broadcloth."

"Oh he is such a stupid boy," Ruth answered with great sympathy; "how quick of you to observe that now: and you call yourself 'Slow John Ridd!' I never did see such a stupid boy; sometimes he spoils my temper. But you must be back in half an hour, at the latest, Cousin Ridd. You see I remember what you are; when once you get among horses, or cows, or things of that sort."

"Things of that sort! Well done, Ruth! One would think you were quite a Cockney."

Uncle Reuben did not come home to his dinner; and his granddaughter said she had strictest orders never to expect him. Therefore we had none to dine with us, except the foreman of the shop, a worthy man, named Thomas Cockram, fifty years of age or so. He seemed to me to have strong intentions of his own about little Ruth; and on that account to regard me with a wholly undue malevolence. And perhaps, in order to justify him, I may have been more attentive to her than otherwise need have been; at any rate, Ruth and I were pleasant; and he the very opposite.

"My dear Cousin Ruth," I said, on purpose to vex Master Cockram, because he eyed us so heavily, and squinted so un-luckily, "we have long been looking for you, at our Plover's Bar-rows farm. You remember how you used to love hunting for eggs in the morning, and hiding up in the tallat with Lizzie, for me to seek you among the hay, when the sun was down. Ah, Master Cockram, those are the things young people find their pleasure in, not in selling a yard of serge, and giving twopence-halfpenny change, and writing 'settled' at the bottom, with a pencil that has blacked their teeth. Now, Master Cockram, you ought to come as far as our good farm, at once, and eat two new-laid eggs for breakfast, and be made to look quite young again. Our good Annie would cook for you; and you should have the hot new milk, and the pope's eye from the mutton; and every foot of you would become a yard in about a fortnight." And hereupon, I spread my chest, to show him an example. Ruth could not keep her countenance; but I saw that she thought it wrong of me; and would scold me, if ever I gave her the chance of taking those little liberties. However, he deserved it all, according to my young ideas, for his great impertinence in aiming at my cousin.

But what I said was far less grievous, to a man of honest mind, than little Ruth's own behaviour. I could hardly have believed that so thoroughly true a girl, and one so proud and upright, could have got rid of any man so cleverly as she got rid of Master Thomas Cockram. She gave him not even a glass of wine, but commended to his notice, with a sweet and thoughtful gravity, some invoice which must be corrected, before her dear grandfather should return; and to amend which, three great ledgers must be searched from first to last. Thomas Cockram winked at me, with the worst of his two wrong eyes; as much as to say "I understand it; but I cannot help myself. Only you look out, if ever —— " and before he had finished winking, the door was shut behind him. Then Ruth said to me in the simplest manner, "You have ridden far to-day, Cousin Ridd; and have far to ride to get home again. What will dear Aunt Ridd say, if we send you away without nourishment? All the keys are in my keeping; and dear grandfather has the finest wine; not to be matched in the west of England, as I have heard good judges say; though I know not wine from cider. Do you like the wine of Oporto, or the wine of Xeres?"

"I know not one from the other, fair cousin, except by the colour," I answered; "but the sound of Oporto is nobler, and richer. Suppose we try wine of Oporto."

The good little creature went and fetched a black bottle of an ancient cast, covered with dust and cobwebs. These I was anxious to shake aside; and indeed I thought that the wine would be better for being roused up a little. Ruth, however, would not hear a single word to that purport; and seeing that she knew more about it, I left her to manage it. And the result was very fine indeed, to wit, a sparkling rosy liquor, dancing with little flakes of light, and scented like new violets. With this I was so pleased and gay, and Ruth so glad to see me gay, that we quite forgot how the time went on; and though my fair cousin would not be persuaded to take a second glass herself, she kept on filling mine so fast that it was never empty, though I did my best to keep it so.

"What is a little drop like this to a man of your size and strength, Cousin Ridd?" she said, with her cheeks just brushed with rose, which made her look very beautiful; "I have heard you say that your head is so thick — or rather so clear you ought to say — that no liquor ever moves it."

"That is right enough," I answered; "what a witch you must be, dear Ruth, to have remembered that now!"

"Oh, I remember every word I have ever heard you say, Cousin Ridd; because your voice is so deep, you know, and you talk so little. Now it is useless to say 'no.' These bottles hold almost nothing. Dear grandfather will not come home, I fear, until long after you are gone. What will Aunt Ridd think of me, I am sure? You are all so dreadfully hospitable. Now not another 'no,' Cousin Ridd. We must have another bottle."

"Well, must is must," I answered with a certain resignation. "I cannot bear bad manners, dear; and how old are you next birthday?"

"Eighteen, dear John," said Ruth, coming over with the empty bottle; and I was pleased at her calling me "John," and had a great mind to kiss her. However, I thought of my Lorna suddenly, and of the anger I should feel if a man went on with her so; therefore I lay back in my chair, to wait for the other bottle.

"Do you remember how we danced that night?" I asked, while she was opening it; "and how you were afraid of me first, because I looked so tall, dear?"

"Yes, and so very broad, Cousin Ridd. I thought that you would eat me. But I have come to know, since then, how very kind and good you are."

"And will you come and dance again, at my wedding, Cousin Ruth?"

She nearly let the bottle fall, the last of which she was sloping carefully into a vessel of bright glass; and then she raised her hand again, and finished it judiciously. And after that, she took the window, to see that all her work was clear; and then she poured me out a glass, and said with very pale cheeks, but else no sign or meaning about her, "What did you ask me, Cousin Ridd?"

"Nothing of any importance, Ruth; only we are so fond of you. I mean to be married as soon as I can. Will you come and help us?"

"To be sure I will, Cousin Ridd — unless, unless, dear grandfather cannot spare me from the business." She went away: and her breast was heaving, like a rick of under-carried hay. And she stood at the window long, trying to make yawns of sighs.

For my part, I knew not what to do. And yet I could think about it, as I never could with Lorna; with whom I was always in a whirl, from the power of my love. So I thought some time about it; and perceived that it was the manliest way, just to tell her everything; except that I feared she liked me. But it seemed to me unaccountable, that she did not even ask the name of my intended wife. Perhaps she thought it must be Sally; or perhaps she feared to trust her voice.

"Come and sit by me, dear Ruth; and listen to a long, long story, how things have come about with me."

"No, thank you, Cousin Ridd," she answered; "at least I mean that I shall be happy — that I shall be ready to hear you — to listen to you, I mean of course. But I would rather stay where I am, and have the air — or rather be able to watch for dear grandfather coming home. He is so kind and good to me. What should I do without him?"

Then I told her how, for years and years, I had been in love with Lorna, and all the dangers and difficulties which had so long beset us, and how I hoped that these were passing, and no other might come between us, except on the score of religion; upon which point I trusted soon to overcome my mother's objections. And then I told her how poor, and helpless, and alone in the world, my Lorna was; and how sad all her youth had been until I brought her away at last. And many other little things I mentioned, which there is no need for me again to dwell upon. Ruth heard it all without a word, and without once looking at me; and only by her attitude could I guess that she was weeping. Then when all my tale was told, she asked me in a low and gentle voice, but still without showing her face to me:

"And does she love you, Cousin Ridd? Does she say that she loves you, with — with all her heart?"

"Certainly, she does," I answered. "Do you think it impossible for one like her to do so?"

She said no more; but crossed the room before I had time to look at her, and came behind my chair, and kissed me gently on the forehead.

I hope you may be very happy, with — I mean in your new life," she whispered very softly; "as happy as you deserve to be, and as happy as you can make others be. Now how I have been neglecting you! I am quite ashamed of myself, for thinking only of grandfather: and it makes me so low-spirited. You have told me a very nice romance, and I have never even helped you to a glass of wine. Here, pour it for yourself, dear cousin; I shall be back again directly."

With that she was out of the door in a moment: and when she came back, you would not have thought that a tear had dimmed those large bright eyes, or wandered down those pale clear cheeks. Only her hands were cold and trembling: and she made me help myself.

Uncle Reuben did not appear at all; and Ruth, who had promised to come and see us, and stay for a fortnight at our house (if her grandfather could spare her), now discovered, before I left, that she must not think of doing so. Perhaps she was right in deciding thus; at any rate it had now become improper for me to press her. And yet I now desired tenfold that she should consent to come, thinking that Lorna herself would work the speediest cure of her passing whim.

For such, I tried to persuade myself, was the nature of Ruth's regard for me: and upon looking back I could not charge myself with any misconduct towards the little maiden. I had never sought her company, I had never trifled with her (at least until that very day), and being so engrossed with my own love, I had scarcely even thought of her. And the maiden would never have thought of me, except as a clumsy yokel, but for my mother's and sister's meddling, and their wily suggestions. I believe they had told the little soul that I was deeply in love with her; although they both stoutly denied it. But who can place trust in a woman's word, when it comes to a question of match-making?

CHAPTER LI

A Visit from the Counsellor

Now while I was riding home that evening, with a tender conscience about Ruth, although not a wounded one, I guessed but little that all my thoughts were needed much for my own affairs. So however it proved to be; for as I came in, soon after dark, my sister Eliza met me at the corner of the cheese-room, and she said, "Don't go in there, John," pointing to mother's room, "until I have had a talk with you."

"In the name of Moses," I inquired, having picked up that phrase at Dulvenon; "what are you at, about me now? There is no peace for a quiet fellow."

"It is nothing we are at," she answered; "neither may you make light of it. It is something very important about Mistress Lorna Doone."

"Let us have it at once," I cried: "I can bear anything about Lorna, except that she does not care for me."

"It has nothing to do with that, John. And I am quite sure that you never need fear anything of that sort. She perfectly wearies me sometimes, although her voice is so soft and sweet, about your endless perfections."

"Bless her little heart!" I said: "the subject is inexhaustible."

"No doubt!" replied Lizzie, in the driest manner; "especially to your sisters. However, this is no time to joke. I fear you will get the worst of it, John. Do you know a man of about Gwenn's shape, nearly as broad as he is long, but about six times the size of Gwenny, and with a length of snow-white hair, and a thickness also; as the copses were last winter? He never can comb it, that is quite certain, with any comb yet invented."

"Then go you and offer your services. There are few things you cannot scarify. I know the man from your description, although I have never seen him. Now where is my Lorna?"

"Your Lorna is with Annie, having a good cry, I believe; and Annie too glad to second her. She knows that this great man is here, and knows that he wants to see her. But she begged to defer the interview, until dear John's return."

"What a nasty way you have of telling the very common-est piece of news!" I said on purpose to pay her out. "What man will ever fancy you, you unlucky little snapper? Now, no more nursery talk for me. I will go and settle this business. You had better go and dress your dolls; if you can give them clothes unpoisoned." Hereupon Lizzie burst into a perfect roar of tears; feeling that she had the worst of it. And I took her in my arms, and begged her pardon; although she scarcely deserved it: for she knew that I was out of luck, and she might have spared her satire.

I was almost sure that the man who was come must be the Counsellor himself; of whom I felt much keener fear than of his son Carver. And knowing that his visit boded ill to me and Lorna, I went and sought my dear; and led her with a heavy heart, from the maiden's room to mother's, to meet our dreadful visitor.

Mother was standing by the door, making courtesies now and then, and listening to a long harangue upon the rights of state and land, which the Counsellor (having found that she was the owner of her property, and knew nothing of her title to it) was encouraged to deliver. My dear mother stood gazing at him, spell-bound by his eloquence, and only hoping that he would stop. He was shaking his hair upon his shoulders, in the power of his words, and his wrath at some little thing she had suffered, which he declared to be quite illegal.

Then I ventured to show myself, in the flesh, before him; although he feigned not to see me: but he advanced with zeal to Lorna; holding out both hands at once.

"My darling child, my dearest niece; how wonderfully well you look! Mistress Ridd, I give you credit. This is the country of good things. I never would have believed our Queen could have looked so Royal. Surely of all virtues, hospitality is the finest, and the most romantic. Dearest Lorna, kiss your uncle; it is quite a privilege."

"Perhaps it is to you, sir," said Lorna, who could never quite check her sense of oddity; "but I fear that you have smoked tobacco, which spoils reciprocity."

"You are right, my child. How keen your scent is. It is always so with us. Your grandfather was noted for his olfactory powers. Ah, a great loss, dear Mrs. Ridd, a terrible loss to this neighbourhood! As one of our great writers says — I think it must be Milton — 'We ne'er shall look upon his like again.' "

"With your good leave, sir," I broke in, "Master Milton could never have written so sweet and simple a line as that. It is one of the great Shakespeare."

"Woe is me for my neglect!" said the Counsellor, bowing airily; "this must be your son, Mistress Ridd, the great John, the wrestler. And one who meddles with the Muses! Ah, since I was young, how everything is changed, madam! Except indeed the beauty of women, which seems to me to increase every year." Here the old villain bowed to my mother; and she blushed, and made another courtesy, and really did look very nice.

"Now though I have quoted the poets amiss, as your son informs me (for which I tender my best thanks, and must amend my reading), I can hardly be wrong in assuming that this young armiger must be the too attractive cynosure to our poor little maiden. And for my part, she is welcome to him. I have never been one of those who dwell upon distinctions of rank, and birth, and such like; as if they were in the heart of nature, and must be eternal. In early youth, I may have thought so, and been full of that little pride. But now I have long accounted it one of the first axioms of political economy — you are following me, Mistress Ridd?"

"Well, sir, I am doing my best; but I cannot quite keep up with you."

"Never mind, madam; I will be slower. But your son's intelligence is so quick —— "

"I see, sir; you thought that mine must be. But no; it all comes from his father, sir. His father was that quick and clever —— "

"Ah, I can well suppose it, madam. And a credit he is to both of you. Now to return to our muttons — a figure which you will appreciate — I may now be regarded, I think, as this young lady's legal guardian; although I have not had the honour of being formally appointed such. Her father was the eldest son of Sir Ensor Doone; and I happened to be the second son; and as young maidens cannot be baronets, I suppose I am 'Sir Counsellor.' Is it so, Mistress Ridd, according to your theory of genealogy?"

"I am sure I don't know, sir," my mother answered carefully: "I know not anything of that name, sir, except in the Gospel of Matthew: but I see not why it should be otherwise."

"Good, madam! I may look upon that as your sanction and approval: and the college of heralds shall hear of it. And in return, as Lorna's guardian, I give my full and ready consent to her marriage with your son, madam."

"O how good of you, sir, how kind! Well, I always did say, that the learnedest people were, almost always, the best and kindest, and the most simple-hearted."

"Madam, that is a great sentiment. What a goodly couple they will be! and if we can add him to our strength —— "

"Oh no, sir, oh no!" cried mother: "you really must not think of it. He has always been brought up so honest —— "

"Hem! that makes a difference. A decided disqualification for domestic life among the Doones. But, surely, he might get over those prejudices, madam?"

"Oh no, sir! he never can: he never can indeed. When he was only that high, sir, he could not steal even an apple, when some wicked boys tried to mislead him."

"Ah," replied the Counsellor, shaking his white head gravely; "then I greatly fear that his case is quite incurable. I have known such cases; violent prejudice, bred entirely of education, and anti-economical to the last degree. And when it is so, it is desperate: no man after imbibing ideas of that sort, can in any way be useful."

"Oh yes, sir, John is very useful. He can do as much work as three other men; and you should see him load a sledd, sir."

"I was speaking, madam, of higher usefulness — power of the brain and heart. The main thing for us upon earth is to take a large view of things. But while we talk of the heart, what is my niece Lorna doing, that she does not come and thank me, for my perhaps too prompt concession to her youthful fancies? Ah, if I had wanted thanks, I should have been more stubborn."

Lorna, being challenged thus, came up and looked at her uncle, with her noble eyes fixed full upon his, which beneath his white eyebrows glistened, like dormer windows piled with snow.

"For what am I to thank you, uncle?"

"My dear niece, I have told you. For removing the heaviest obstacle, which to a mind so well regulated could possibly have existed, between your dutiful self and the object of your affections."

"Well, uncle, I should be very grateful, if I thought that you did so from love of me; or if I did not know that you have something yet concealed from me."

"And my consent," said the Counsellor, "is the more meritorious, the more liberal, frank, and candid, in the face of an existing fact, and a very clearly established one; which might have appeared to weaker minds in the light of an impediment; but to my loftier view of matrimony seems quite a recommendation."

"What fact do you mean, sir? Is it one that I ought to know?"

"In my opinion it is, good niece. It forms, to my mind, so fine a basis for the invariable harmony of the matrimonial state. To be brief — as I always endeavour to be without becoming obscure — you two young people (ah, what a gift is youth! one can never be too thankful for it) you will have the rare advantage of commencing married life, with a subject of common interest to discuss, whenever you weary of — well, say of one another; if you can now, by any means, conceive such a possibility. And perfect justice meted out: mutual good-will resulting, from the sense of reciprocity."

"I do not understand you, sir. Why can you not say what you mean, at once?"

"My dear child, I prolong your suspense. Curiosity is the most powerful of all feminine instincts; and therefore the most delightful, when not prematurely satisfied. However, if you must have my strong realities, here they are. Your father slew dear John's father, and dear John's father slew yours."

Having said thus much, the Counsellor leaned back upon his chair, and shaded his calm white-bearded eyes from the rays of our tallow-candles. He was a man who liked to look rather than to be looked at. But Lorna came to me for aid; and I went up to Lorna; and mother looked at both of us.

Then feeling that I must speak first (as no one would begin it) I took my darling round the waist, and led her up to the Counsellor; while she tried to bear it bravely: yet must lean on me, or did.

"Now, Sir Counsellor Doone," I said, with Lorna squeezing both my hands, I never yet knew how (considering that she was walking all the time, or something like it); "you know right well, Sir Counsellor, that Sir Ensor Doone gave approval." I cannot tell what made me think of this: but so it came upon me.

"Approval to what, good rustic John? To the slaughter so reciprocal?"

"No, sir, not to that; even if it ever happened; which I do not believe. But to the love betwixt me and Lorna; which your story shall not break, without more evidence than your word. And even so, shall never break; if Lorna thinks as I do."

The maiden gave me a little touch, as much as to say, "you are right, darling; give it to him, again, like that." However, I held my peace, well knowing that too many words do mischief.

Then mother looked at me with wonder, being herself too amazed to speak; and the Counsellor looked with great wrath in his eyes, which he tried to keep from burning.

"How say you then, John Ridd," he cried, stretching out one hand, like Elijah, "is this a thing of the sort you love? Is this what you are used to?"

"So please your worship," I answered; "no kind of violence can surprise us, since first came Doones upon Exmoor. Up to that time none heard of harm; except of taking a purse, may be, or cutting a strange sheep's throat. And the poor folk who did this were hanged, with some benefit of clergy. But ever since the Doones came first, we are used to anything."

"Thou varlet," cried the Counsellor, with the colour of his eyes quite changed with the sparkles of his fury; "is this the way we are to deal with such a low-bred clod as thou? To question the doings of our people, and to talk of clergy! What, dream you not that we could have clergy, and of the right sort too, if only we cared to have them? Tush! Am I to spend my time, arguing with a plough-tail Bob?"

"If your worship will hearken to me," I answered very modestly, not wishing to speak harshly, with Lorna looking up at me; "there are many things that might be said, without any kind of argument, which I would never wish to try with one of your worship's learning. And in the first place it seems to me that if our fathers hated one another bitterly, yet neither won the victory, only mutual discomfiture; surely that is but a reason why we should be wiser than they, and make it up in this generation by goodwill and loving —— "

"Oh, John, you wiser than your father!" mother broke upon me here: "not but what you might be as wise, when you come to be old enough."

"Young people of the present age," said the Counsellor severely, "have no right feeling of any sort, upon the simplest matter. Lorna Doone, stand forth from contact with that heir of parricide; and state in your own mellifluous voice, whether you regard this slaughter as a pleasant trifle."

"You know without any words of mine," she answered very softly, yet not withdrawing from my hand, "that although I have been seasoned well to every kind of outrage, among my gentle relatives, I have not yet so purely lost all sense of right and wrong, as to receive what you have said, as lightly as you declared it. You think it a happy basis for our future concord. I do not quite think that, my uncle; neither do I quite believe that a word of it is true. In our happy valley, nine-tenths of what is said is false; and you were always wont to argue, that true and false are but a blind turned upon a pivot. Without any failure of respect for your character, good uncle, I decline politely to believe a word of what you have told me. And even if it were proved to me, all I can say is this, if my John will have me, I am his for ever."

This long speech was too much for her; and she had overrated her strength about it, which had long been waiting for her; and there she lay with no other sound, except a gurgling in her throat.

"You old villain," cried my mother, shaking her fist at the Counsellor, while I could do nothing else but hold, and bend across, my darling, and whisper to deaf ears. "What is the good of the Quality, if this is all that comes of it? Out of the way! You know the words that make the deadly mischief; but not the ways that heal them. Give me that bottle, if hands you have; what is the use of Counsellors?"

I saw that dear mother was carried away; and indeed I myself was something like it; with the pale face upon my bosom, and the heaving of the heart, and the heat and cold all through me, as my darling breathed or lay. Meanwhile the Counsellor stood back, and seemed a little sorry; although of course it was not in his power to be at all ashamed of himself.

"My sweet love, my darling child," our mother went on to Lorna, in a way that I shall never forget, though I live to be a hundred; "pretty pet, not a word of it is true, upon that old liar's oath: and if every word were true, poor chick, you should have our John all the more for it. You, and John, were made by God and meant for one another, whatever falls between you. Little lamb, look up and speak: here is your own John, and I; and the devil take the Counsellor."

I was amazed at mother's words, being so unlike her; while I loved her all the more because she forgot herself so. In another moment in ran Annie, ay and Lizzie also, knowing by some mystic sense (which I have often noticed, but never could explain) that something was astir, belonging to the world of women, yet foreign to the eyes of men. And now the Counsellor, being well-born, although such a heartless miscreant, beckoned to me to come away; which I, being smothered with women, was only too glad to do, as soon as my own love would let go of me.

"That is the worst of them," said the old man, when I had led him into our kitchen, with an apology at every step, and given him hot schnapps and water, and a cigarro of brave Tom Faggus: "you never can say much, sir, in the way of reasoning (however gently meant and put) but what these women will fly out. It is wiser to put a wild bird in a cage, and expect him to sit and look at you, and chirp without a feather rumpled, than it is to expect a woman to answer reason reasonably." Saying this, he looked at his puff of smoke as if it contained more reason.

"I am sure I do not know, sir," I answered according to a phrase which has always been my favourite, on account of its general truth: moreover, he was now our guest, and had right to be treated accordingly: "I am, as you see, not acquainted with the ways of women, except my mother and sisters."

"Except not even them, my son," said the Counsellor, now having finished his glass, without much consultation about it; "if you once understand your mother and sisters — why you understand the lot of them."

He made a twist in his cloud of smoke, and dashed his finger through it, so that I could not follow his meaning, and in manners liked not to press him.

"Now of this business, John," he said, after getting to the bottom of the second glass, and having a trifle or so to eat, and praising our chimney-corner; "taking you on the whole, you know, you are wonderfully good people: and instead of giving me up to the soldiers, as you might have done, you are doing your best to make me drunk."

"Not at all, sir," I answered; "not at all, your worship. Let me mix you another glass. We rarely have a great gentleman by the side of our embers and oven. I only beg your pardon, sir, that my sister Annie (who knows where to find all the good pans and the lard) could not wait upon you this evening; and I fear they have done it with dripping instead, and in a pan with the bottom burned. But old Betty quite loses her head sometimes, by dint of over-scolding."

"My son," replied the Counsellor, standing across the front of the fire, to prove his strict sobriety: "I meant to come down upon you to-night; but you have turned the tables upon me. Not through any skill on your part, nor through any paltry weakness as to love (and all that stuff, which boys and girls spin tops at, or knock dolls' noses together), but through your simple way of taking me, as a man to be believed: combined with the comfort of this place, and the choice tobacco, and cordials. I have not enjoyed an evening so much: God bless me if I know when!"

"Your worship," said I, "makes me more proud than I well know what to do with. Of all the things that please and lead us into happy sleep at night, the first and chiefest is to think that we have pleased a visitor."

"Then, John, thou hast deserved good sleep; for I am not pleased easily. But although our family is not so high now as it hath been, I have enough of the gentleman left to be pleased when good people try me. My father, Sir Ensor, was better than I in this great element of birth, and my son Carver is far worse. *Ætas parentum,* what is it, my boy? I hear that you have been at a grammar-school."

"So I have, your worship, and at a very good one; but I only got far enough to make more tail than head of Latin."

"Let that pass," said the Counsellor: "John, thou art all the wiser." And the old man shook his hoary locks, as if Latin had been his ruin. I looked at him sadly, and wondered whether it might have so ruined me, but for God's mercy in stopping it.

CHAPTER LII

The Way to make the Cream Rise

That night the reverend Counsellor, not being in such state of mind as ought to go alone, kindly took our best old bedstead, carved in panels, well enough, with the woman of Samaria. I set him up, both straight and heavy, so that he need but close both eyes, and keep his mouth just open; and in the morning he was thankful for all that he could remember.

I, for my part, scarcely knew whether he really had begun to feel good-will towards us, and to see that nothing else could be of any use to him; or whether he was merely acting, so as to deceive us. And it had struck me, several times, that he had made a great deal more of the spirit he had taken than the quantity would warrant, with a man so wise and solid. Neither did I quite understand a little story which Lorna told me, how that in the night awaking, she had heard, or seemed to hear, a sound of feeling in her room; as if there had been some one groping carefully among the things within her drawers or wardrobe-closet. But the noise had ceased at once, she said, when she sat up in bed and listened; and knowing how many mice we had, she took courage, and fell asleep again.

After breakfast, the Counsellor (who looked no whit the worse for schnapps, but even more grave and venerable) followed our Annie into the dairy, to see how we managed the clotted cream, of which he had eaten a basinful. And thereupon they talked a little; and Annie thought him a fine old gentleman, and a very just one; for he had nobly condemned the people who spoke against Tom Faggus.

"Your honour must plainly understand," said Annie, being now alone with him, and spreading out her light quick hands over the pans, like butterflies, "that they are brought in here to cool, after being set in the basin-holes, with the wood ash under them, which I showed you in the back-kitchen. And they must have very little heat, not enough to simmer even; only just to make the bubbles rise, and the scum upon the top set thick: and after that, it clots as firm — oh, as firm as my two hands be."

"Have you ever heard," asked the Counsellor, who enjoyed this talk with Annie, "that if you pass across the top, without breaking the surface, a string of beads, or polished glass, or anything of that kind, the cream will set three times as solid, and in thrice the quantity?"

"No, sir; I have never heard that," said Annie, staring with all her simple eyes; "what a thing it is to read books, and grow learned! But it is very easy to try it: I will get my coral necklace; it will not be witchcraft, will it, sir?"

"Certainly not," the old man replied: "I will make the experiment myself, and you may trust me not to be hurt, my dear. But coral will not do, my child, neither will anything coloured. The beads must be of plain common glass; but the brighter they are the better."

"Then I know the very thing," cried Annie; "as bright as bright can be, and without any colour in it, except in the sun or candle-light. Dearest Lorna has the very thing, a necklace of some old glass-beads, or I think they called them jewels: she will be too glad to lend it to us. I will go for it, in a moment."

"My dear, it cannot be half so bright as your own pretty eyes. But remember one thing, Annie, you must not say what it is for; or even that I am going to use it, or anything at all about it; else the charm will be broken. Bring it here, without a word; if you know where she keeps it."

"To be sure I do," she answered; "John used to keep it for her. But she took it away from him last week, and she wore it when — I mean when somebody was here; and he said it was very valuable, and spoke with great learning about it, and called it by some particular name, which I forget at this moment. But valuable, or not, we cannot hurt it, can we, sir, by passing it over the cream-pan?"

"Hurt it!" cried the Counsellor: "nay, we shall do it good, my dear. It will help to raise the cream: and you may take my word for it, young maiden, none can do good in this world, without in turn receiving it." Pronouncing this great sentiment, he looked so grand and benevolent, that Annie (as she said afterwards) could scarce forbear from kissing him, yet feared to take the liberty. Therefore, she only ran away, to fetch my Lorna's necklace.

Now as luck would have it — whether good luck, or otherwise, you must not judge too hastily — my darling had taken it into her head, only a day or two before, that I was far too valuable to be trusted with her necklace. Now that she had some idea of its price and quality, she had begun to fear that some one, perhaps even Squire Faggus (in whom her faith was illiberal), might form designs against my health, to win the bauble from me. So, with many pretty coaxings, she had led me to give it up; which, except for her own sake, I was glad enough to do, misliking a charge of such importance.

Therefore Annie found it sparkling in the little secret hole, near the head of Lorna's bed, which she herself had recommended for its safer custody; and without a word to anyone she brought it down, and danced it in the air before the Counsellor, for him to admire its lustre.

"Oh, that old thing!" said the gentleman, in a tone of some contempt; "I remember that old thing well enough. However, for want of a better, no doubt it will answer our purpose. Three times three, I pass it over. Crinkleum, crankum, grass and clover! What are you feared of, you silly child?"

"Good sir, it is perfect witchcraft! I am sure of that, because it rhymes. Oh, what would mother say to me? Shall I ever go to heaven again? Oh, I see the cream already!"

"To be sure you do; but you must not look, or the whole charm will be broken, and the devil fly away with the pan, and drown every cow you have got in it."

"Oh, sir, it is too horrible. How could you lead me to such a sin? Away with thee, witch of Endor!"

For the door began to creak, and a broom appeared suddenly in the opening with our Betty, no doubt, behind it. But Annie, in the greatest terror, slammed the door, and bolted it, and then turned again to the Counsellor, yet looking at his face, had not the courage to reproach him. For his eyes rolled like two blazing barrels, and his white shagged brows were knit across them, and his forehead scowled in black furrows, so that Annie said that if she ever saw the devil, she saw him then, and no mistake. Whether the old man wished to scare her, or whether he was trying not to laugh, is more than I can tell you.

"Now," he said, in a deep stern whisper; "not a word of this to living soul: neither must you, nor any other enter this place for three hours at least. By that time the charm will have done its work: the pan will be cream to the bottom; and you will bless me for a secret which will make your fortune. Put the bauble under this pannikin; which none must lift for a day and a night. Have no fear, my simple wench; not a breath of harm shall come to you, if you obey my orders."

"Oh, that I will, sir, that I will; if you only tell me what to do."

"Go to your room, without so much as a single word to anyone. Bolt yourself in, and for three hours now, read the Lord's Prayer backwards."

Poor Annie was only too glad to escape, upon these conditions; and the Counsellor kissed her upon the forehead, and told her not to make her eyes red, because they were much too sweet and pretty. She dropped them at this, with a sob and a courtesy, and ran away to her bedroom: but as for reading the Lord's Prayer backwards, that was much beyond her; and she had not done three words quite right, before the three hours expired.

Meanwhile the Counsellor was gone. He bade our mother adieu, with so much dignity of bearing, and such warmth and gratitude, and the high-bred courtesy of the old school (now fast disappearing), that when he was gone, dear mother fell back on the chair which he had used last night; as if it would teach her the graces. And for more than an hour, she made believe not to know what there was for dinner.

"Oh the wickedness of the world! Oh the lies that are told of people — or rather I mean the falsehoods — because a man is better born, and has better manners! Why, Lorna, how is it that you never speak about your charming uncle? Did you notice, Lizzie, how his silver hair was waving upon his velvet collar, and how white his hands were, and every nail like an acorn; only pink, like shell-fish, or at least like shells? And the way he bowed, and dropped his eyes, from his pure respect for me! And then, that he would not even speak, on account of his emotion; but pressed my hand in silence! Oh Lizzie, you have read me beautiful things about Sir Gallyhead, and the rest; but nothing to equal Sir Counsellor."

"You had better marry him, madam," said I, coming in very sternly; though I knew I ought not to say it: "he can repay your adoration. He has stolen a hundred thousand pounds."

" John," cried my mother, "you are mad!" And yet she turned as pale as death; for women are so quick at turning; and she inkled what it was.

"Of course, I am, mother; mad about the marvels of Sir Galahad. He has gone off with my Lorna's necklace. Fifty farms like ours can never make it good to Lorna."

Hereupon ensued grim silence. Mother looked at Lizzie's face, for she could not look at me; and Lizzie looked at me, to know; and as for me, I could have stamped almost on the heart of anyone. It was not the value of the necklace — I am not so low a hound as that — nor was it even the damned folly shown by every one of us — it was the thought of Lorna's sorrow for her ancient plaything; and even more, my fury at the breach of hospitality.

But Lorna came up to me softly, as a woman should always come; and she laid one hand upon my shoulder; and she only looked at me. She even seemed to fear to look, and dropped her eyes, and sighed at me. Without a word, I knew by that, how I must have looked like Satan; and the evil spirit left my heart; when she had made me think of it.

"Darling John, did you want me to think that you cared for my money, more than for me?"

I led her away from the rest of them, being desirous of explaining things, when I saw the depth of her nature opened, like an everlasting well, to me. But she would not let me say a word, or do anything by ourselves, as it were: she said, "Your duty is to your mother: this blow is on her, and not on me."

I saw that she was right; though how she knew it is beyond me; and I asked her just to go in front, and bring my mother round a little. For I must let my passion pass: it may drop its weapons quickly; but it cannot come and go, before a man has time to think.

Then Lorna went up to my mother, who was still in the chair of elegance; and she took her by both hands, and said:

"Dearest mother, I shall fret so, if I see you fretting. And to fret will kill me, mother. They have always told me so."

Poor mother bent on Lorna's shoulder, without thought of attitude, and laid her cheek on Lorna's breast, and sobbed till Lizzie was jealous, and came with two pocket handkerchiefs. As for me, my heart was lighter (if they would only dry their eyes, and come round by dinner-time) than it had been since the day on which Tom Faggus discovered the value of that blessed and cursed necklace. None could say that I wanted Lorna for her money now. And perhaps the Doones would let me have her; now that her property was gone.

But who shall tell of Annie's grief? The poor little thing would have staked her life upon finding the trinket, in all its beauty, lying under the pannikin. She proudly challenged me to lift it — which I had done, long ere that, of course — if only I would take the risk of the spell for my incredulity. I told her not to talk of spells, until she could spell a word backwards; and then to look into the pan where the charmed cream should be. She would not acknowledge that the cream was the same as all the rest was; and indeed it was not quite the same, for the points of poor Lorna's diamonds had made a few star-rays across the rich firm crust of yellow.

But when we raised the pannikin, and there was nothing under it, poor Annie fell against the wall, which had been whitened lately; and her face put all the white to scorn. My love, who was as fond of her, as if she had known her for fifty years, hereupon ran up and caught her, and abused all diamonds. I will dwell no more upon Annie's grief, because we felt it all so much. But I could not help telling her, if she wanted a witch, to seek good Mother Melldrum, a legitimate performer.

That same night Master Jeremy Stickles (of whose absence the Counsellor must have known) came back, with all equipment ready for the grand attack. Now the Doones knew, quite as well as we did, that this attack was threatening; and that, but for the wonderful weather, it would have been made long ago. Therefore we, or at least our people (for I was doubtful about going), were sure to meet with a good resistance, and due preparation.

It was very strange to hear and see, and quite impossible to account for, that now some hundreds of country people (who feared to whisper so much as a word against the Doones a year ago, and would sooner have thought of attacking a church, in service time, than Glen Doone) sharpened their old cutlasses, and laid pitchforks on the grindstone, and bragged at every village cross, as if each would kill ten Doones himself, neither care to wipe his hands afterwards. And this fierce bravery, and tall contempt, had been growing ever since the news of the attack upon our premises had taken good people by surprise; at least as concerned the issue.

Jeremy Stickles laughed heartily about Annie's new manner of charming the cream; but he looked very grave at the loss of the jewels, so soon as he knew their value.

"My son," he exclaimed, "this is very heavy. It will go ill with all of you to make good this loss, as I fear that you will have to do."

"What!" cried I, with my blood running cold. "We make good the loss, Master Stickles! Every farthing we have in the world, and the labour of our lives to boot, will never make good the tenth of it."

"It would cut me to the heart," he answered, laying his hand on mine, "to hear of such a deadly blow to you, and your good mother. And this farm; how long, John, has it been in your family?"

"For at least six hundred years," I said, with a foolish pride that was only too like to end in groans; "and some people say, by a Royal grant, in the time of the great King Alfred. At any rate, a Ridd was with him, throughout all his hiding-time. We have always held by the King and Crown: surely none will turn us out, unless we are guilty of treason?"

"My son," replied Jeremy very gently, so that I could love him for it, "not a word to your good mother of this unlucky matter. Keep it to yourself, my boy, and try to think but little of it. After all, I may be wrong: at any rate, least said best mended."

"But Jeremy, dear Jeremy, how can I bear to leave it so? Do you suppose that I can sleep, and eat my food and go about, and look at other people, as if nothing at all had happened? And all the time have it on my mind, that not an acre of all the land, nor even our old sheep-dog, belongs to us of right at all! It is more than I can do, Jeremy. Let me talk, and know the worst of it."

"Very well," replied Master Stickles, seeing that both the doors were closed; "I thought that nothing could move you,

John; or I never would have told you. Likely enough I am quite wrong; and God send that I be so. But what I guessed at some time back seems more than a guess, now that you have told me about those wondrous jewels. Now will you keep as close as death every word I tell you?"

"By the honour of a man, I will. Until you yourself release me."

"That is quite enough, John. From you I want no oath; which, according to my experience, tempts a bad man to lie the more, by making it more important. I know you now too well to swear you, though I have the power. Now, my lad, what I have to say will scare your mind in one way, and ease it in another. I think that you have been hard pressed — I can read you like a book, John — by something which that old villain said before he stole the necklace. You have tried not to dwell upon it; you have even tried to make light of it for the sake of the women: but on the whole it has grieved you more than even this dastard robbery."

"It would have done so, Jeremy Stickles, if I could once have believed it. And even without much belief, it is so against our manners, that it makes me miserable. Only think of loving Lorna, only think of kissing her; and then remembering that her father had destroyed the life of mine!"

"Only think," said Master Stickles, imitating my very voice, "of Lorna loving you, John, of Lorna kissing you, John; and all the while saying to herself, 'this man's father murdered mine.' Now look at it in Lorna's way, as well as in your own way. How one-sided all men are!"

"I may look at it in fifty ways, and yet no good will come of it. Jeremy, I confess to you, that I tried to make the best of it; partly to baffle the Counsellor, and partly because my darling needed my help, and bore it so, and behaved to me so nobly. But to you in secret, I am not ashamed to say that a woman may look over this, easier than a man may."

"Because her nature is larger, my son, when she truly loves; although her mind be smaller. Now if I can ease you from this secret burden, will you bear, with strength and courage, the other which I plant on you?"

"I will do my best," said I.

"No man can do more," said he; and so began his story.

CHAPTER LIII
Jeremy finds out Something

" You know, my son," said Jeremy Stickles, with a good pull at his pipe, because he was going to talk so much, and putting his legs well along in the settle; "it has been my duty, for a wearier time than I care to think of (and which would have been unbearable, except for your great kindness), to search this neighbourhood narrowly, and learn everything about everybody. Now the neighbourhood itself is queer; and people have different ways of thinking from what we are used to in London. For instance now, among your folk, when any piece of news is told, or any man's conduct spoken of, the very first question that arises in your minds is this: 'Was this action kind and good?' Long after that you say to yourselves, 'does the law enjoin or forbid this thing?' Now here is your fundamental error: for among all truly civilized people the foremost of all questions is, 'how stands the law herein?' And if the law approve, no need for any further questioning. That this is so, you may take my word: for I know the law pretty thoroughly.

"Very well: I need not say any more about that, for I have shown that you are all quite wrong. I only speak of this savage tendency, because it explains so many things which have puzzled me among you, and most of all your kindness to men whom you never saw before; which is an utterly illegal thing. It also explains your toleration of these outlaw Doones so long. If your views of law had been correct, and law an element of your lives, these robbers could never have been indulged for so many years amongst you: but you must have abated the nuisance."

"Now, Stickles," I cried, "this is too bad!" he was delivering himself so grandly. "Why you yourself have been amongst us, as the balance, and sceptre, and sword of law, for nigh upon a twelvemonth; and have you abated the nuisance, or even cared to do it, until they began to shoot at you?"

"My son," he replied, "your argument is quite beside the purpose, and only tends to prove more clearly that which I have said of you. However, if you wish to hear my story, no more interruptions. I may not have a chance to tell you, perhaps for weeks, or I know not when; if once those yellows and reds arrive, and be blessed to them, the lubbers! Well, it may be six months ago, or it may be seven, at any rate a good while before that cursed frost began, the mere name of which sends a shiver down every bone of my body, when I was riding one afternoon from Dulverton to Watchett —— "

"Dulverton to Watchett!" I cried. "Now what does that remind me of? I am sure, I remember something —— "

"Remember this, John, if anything — that another word from thee, and thou hast no more of mine. Well, I was a little weary perhaps, having been plagued at Dulverton with the grossness of the people. For they would tell me nothing at all about their fellow townsman, your worthy Uncle Huckaback, except that he was a God-fearing man, and they only wished I was like him. I blessed myself for a stupid fool, in thinking to have pumped them: for by this time I might have known that, through your Western homeliness, every man in his own country is something more than a prophet. And I felt, of course, that I had done more harm than good by questioning; inasmuch as every soul in the place would run straightway, and inform him that the King's man, from the other side of the forest, had been sifting out his ways and works."

"Ah," I cried, for I could not help it; "you begin to understand us at last, that we are not quite such a set of oafs, as you at first believed us."

"I was riding on from Dulverton," he resumed with great severity, yet threatening me no more, which checked me more than fifty threats; "and it was late in the afternoon, and I was growing weary. The road (if road it could be called) turned suddenly down from the higher land to the very brink of the sea; and rounding a little jut of cliff I met the roar of the breakers. My horse was scared, and leaped aside; for a northerly wind was piping, and driving hunks of foam across, as children scatter snow-balls. But he only sank to his fetlocks in the dry sand, piled with pop-weed; and I tried to make him face the waves; and then I looked about me.

"Watchett town was not to be seen, on account of a little foreland, a mile or more upon my course, and standing to the right of me. There was room enough below the cliffs (which are nothing there to yours, John) for horse and man to get along, although the tide was running high with a northerly gale to back it. But close at hand and in the corner, drawn above the yellow sands and long eyebrows of wrack-weed, as snug a little house blinked on me as ever I saw, or wished to see.

"You know that I am not luxurious, neither in any way given to the common lusts of the flesh, John. My father never allowed his hair to grow a fourth part of an inch in length, and he was a thoroughly godly man; and I try to follow in his footsteps, whenever I think about it. Nevertheless I do assure you that my view of that little house, and the way the lights were twinkling, so different from the cold and darkness of the rolling sea, moved the ancient Adam in me, if he could be found to move. I love not a house with too many windows: being out of house and doors some three-quarters of my time, when I get inside a house I like to feel the difference. Air and light are good for people who have any lack of them; and if a man once talks about them, 'tis enough to prove his need of them. But, as you know, John Ridd, the horse who has been at work all day, with the sunshine on his eyes, sleeps better in dark stable, and needs no moon to help him.

"Seeing therefore that this same inn had four windows, and no more, I thought to myself how snug it was, and how beautifully I could sleep there. And so I made the old horse draw hand, which he was only too glad to do, and we clomb above the spring-tide mark, and over a little piece of turf, and struck the door of the hostelry. Some one came, and peeped at me through the lattice overhead, which was full of bulls eyes; and then the bolt was drawn back, and a woman met me very courteously. A dark and foreign-looking woman, very hot of blood, I doubt, but not altogether a bad one. And she waited for me to be first to speak, which an Englishwoman would not have done.

" 'Can I rest here for the night?' I asked, with a lift of my hat to her; for she was no provincial dame, who would stare at me for the courtesy; 'my horse is weary from the sloughs, and myself but little better: besides that, we are both famished.'

" 'Yes, sir, you can rest and welcome. But of food, I fear, there is but little, unless of the common order. Our fishers would have drawn the nets, but the waves were violent. However, we have — what you call it? I never can remember, it is so hard to say — the flesh of the hog salted.'

" 'Bacon!' said I; 'what can be better? And half a dozen eggs with it, and a quart of fresh-drawn ale. You make me rage with hunger, madam. Is it cruelty, or hospitality?'

" 'Ah, good!' she replied with a merry smile, full of southern sunshine: 'you are not of the men round here: you can think, and you can laugh!'

" 'And most of all, I can eat, good madam. In that way I shall astonish you: even more than by my intellect.'

"She laughed aloud, and swung her shoulders, as your natives cannot do; and then she called a little maid, to lead my horse to stable. However I preferred to see that matter done myself, and told her to send the little maid for the frying-pan and the egg-box.

"Whether it were my natural wit and elegance of manner; or whether it were my London freedom and knowledge of the world; or (which is perhaps the most probable, because the least pleasing supposition) my ready and permanent appetite, and appreciation of garlic — I leave you to decide, John; but perhaps all three combined to recommend me to the graces of my charming hostess. When I say 'charming,' I mean of course by manners and by intelligence, and most of all by cooking; for as regards external charms (most fleeting and fallacious) hers had ceased to cause distress, for I cannot say how many years. She said that it was the climate — for even upon that subject she requested my opinion — and I answered, 'if there be a change, let madam blame the seasons.'

"However, not to dwell too much upon our little pleasantries (for I always get on with these foreign women, better than with your Molls and Pegs), I became not inquisitive, but reasonably desirous to know, by what strange hap or hazard a clever and a handsome woman, as she must have been some day, a woman moreover with great contempt for the rustic minds around her, could have settled here in this lonely inn, with only the waves for company, and a boorish husband who slaved all day in turning a potter's wheel at Watchett. And what was the meaning of the emblem set above her doorway, a very unattractive cat sitting in a ruined tree?

"However, I had not very long to strain my curiosity; for when she found out who I was, and how I held the King's commission, and might be called an officer, her desire to tell me all was more than equal to mine of hearing it. Many and many a day, she had longed for some one both skilful and trustworthy, most of all for some one bearing warrant from a court of justice. But the magistrates of the neighbourhood would have nothing to say to her, declaring that she was a crack-brained woman, and a wicked, and even a foreign one.

"With many grimaces, she assured me that never by her own free will would she have lived so many years in that hateful country, where the sky for half the year was fog, and rain for nearly the other half. It was so the very night when first her evil fortune brought her there; and so no doubt it would be, long after it had killed her. But if I wished to know the reason of her being there, she would tell me in few words, which I will repeat as briefly.

"By birth she was an Italian, from the mountains of Apulia, who had gone to Rome to seek her fortunes, after being badly treated in some love affair. Her Christian name was Benita; as for her surname, that could make no difference to anyone. Being a quick and active girl, and resolved to work down her troubles, she found employment in a large hotel; and rising gradually, began to send money to her parents. And here she might have thriven well, and married well under sunny skies, and been a happy woman, but that some black day sent thither a rich and noble English family, eager to behold the Pope. It was not however their fervent longing for the Holy Father which had brought them to St Peter's roof; but rather their own bad luck in making their home too hot to hold them. For although in the main good Catholics, and pleasant receivers of anything, one of their number had given offence, by the folly of trying to think for himself. Some bitter feud had been among them, Benita knew not how it was; and the sister of the nobleman who had died quite lately was married to the rival claimant whom they all detested. It was something about dividing land; Benita knew not what it was.

"But this Benita did know, that they were all great people, and rich, and very liberal; so that when they offered to take her, to attend to the children, and to speak the language for them, and to comfort the lady, she was only too glad to go, little foreseeing the end of it. Moreover she loved the children so, from their pretty ways and that, and the things they gave her, and the style of their dresses, that it would have broken her heart almost never to see the dears again.

"And so, in a very evil hour, she accepted the service of the noble Englishman, and sent her father an old shoe filled to the tongue with money, and trusted herself to fortune. But even before she went, she knew that it could not turn out well; for the laurel leaf which she threw on the fire would not crackle even once, and the horn of the goat came wrong in the twist, and the heel of her foot was shining. This made her sigh at the starting-time; and after that, what could you hope for?

"However, at first all things went well. My lord was as gay as gay could be; and never would come inside the carriage, when a decent horse could be got to ride. He would gallop in front, at a reckless pace, without a weapon of any kind, delighted with the pure blue air, and throwing his heart around him. Benita had never seen any man so admirable, and so childish. As inno-cent as an infant; and not only contented, but noisily happy with anything. Only other people must share his joy; and the shadow of sorrow scattered it, though it were but the shade of poverty.

"Here Benita wept a little; and I liked her none the less, and believed her ten times more; in virtue of a tear or two.

"And so they travelled through Northern Italy, and throughout the south of France, making their way anyhow; sometimes in coaches, sometimes in carts, sometimes upon mule-back, sometimes even a-foot and weary; but always as happy as could be. The children laughed, and grew, and throve (especially the young lady, the elder of the two), and Benita be-gan to think that omens must not be relied upon. But suddenly her faith in omens was confirmed for ever.

"My Lord, who was quite a young man still, and laughed at English arrogance, rode on in front of his wife and friends, to catch the first of a famous view, on the French side of the Py-renee hills. He kissed his hand to his wife, and said that he would save her the trouble of coming. For those two were so one in one, that they could make each other know, whatever he, or she, had felt. And so my Lord went round the corner, with a fine young horse leaping up at every step.

"They waited for him, long and long; but he never came again; and within a week, his mangled body lay in a little chapel-yard; and if the priests only said a quarter of the prayers they took the money for, God knows they can have no throats left; only a relaxation.

"My Lady dwelled for six months more — it is a melancholy tale (what true tale is not so?) — scarcely able to believe that all her fright was not a dream. She would not wear a piece, or shape, of any mourning-clothes; she would not have a person cry, or any sorrow among us. She simply disbelieved the thing, and trusted God to right it. The Protestants, who have no faith, cannot understand this feeling. Enough that so it was; and so my Lady went to heaven.

"For when the snow came down in autumn on the roots of the Pyrenees, and the chapel-yard was white with it, many people told the lady that it was time for her to go. And the strongest plea of all was this, that now she bore another hope of repeating her husband's virtues. So at the end of October, when wolves came down to the farm-lands, the little English family went home towards their England.

"They landed somewhere on the Devonshire coast, ten or eleven years agone, and stayed some days at Exeter; and set out thence in a hired coach, without any proper attendance, for Watchett, in the north of Somerset. For the lady owned a quiet mansion in the neighbourhood of that town, and her one desire was to find refuge there, and to meet her lord, who was sure to come (she said) when he heard of his new infant. Therefore, with only two serving-men and two maids (including Benita) the party set forth from Exeter, and lay the first night at Bampton.

"On the following morn they started bravely, with earnest hope of arriving at their journey's end by daylight. But the roads were soft and very deep, and the sloughs were out in places; and the heavy coach broke down in the axle, and needed mending at Dulverton; and so they lost three hours or more, and would have been wiser to sleep there. But her ladyship would not hear of it; she must be home that night, she said, and her husband would be waiting. How could she keep him waiting now, after such a long, long time?

"Therefore, although it was afternoon, and the year now come to December, the horses were put to again, and the heavy coach went up the hill, with the lady and her two children, and Benita, sitting inside of it; the other maid, and two serving-men (each man with a great blunderbuss) mounted upon the outside;

and upon the horses three Exeter postilions. Much had been said at Dulverton, and even back at Bampton, about some great freebooters, to whom all Exmoor owed suit and service, and paid them very punctually. Both the serving-men were scared, even over their ale, by this. But the lady only said, 'Drive on; I know a little of highwaymen; they never rob a lady.'

"Through the fog, and through the muck, the coach went on, as best it might; sometimes foundering in a slough, with half of the horses splashing it, and sometimes knuckled up on a bank, and straining across the middle, while all the horses kicked at it. However, they went on till dark, as well as might be expected. But when they came, all thanking God, to the pitch and slope of the sea-bank, leading on towards Watchett town, and where my horse had shied so, there the little boy jumped up, and clapped his hands at the water; and there (as Benita said) they met their fate, and could not fly it.

"Although it was past the dusk of day, the silver light from the sea flowed in, and showed the cliffs, and the grey sand-line, and the drifts of wreck, and wrack-weed. It showed them also a troop of horsemen, waiting under a rock hard by, and ready to dash upon them. The postilions lashed towards the sea, and the horses strove in the depth of sand, and the serving-men cocked their blunderbusses, and cowered away behind them; but the lady stood up in the carriage bravely, and neither screamed nor spoke, but hid her son behind her. Meanwhile the drivers drove into the sea, till the leading horses were swimming.

"But before the waves came into the coach, a score of fierce men were round it. They cursed the postilions for mad cowards, and cut the traces, and seized the wheel-horses, all wild with dismay in the wet and the dark. Then, while the carriage was heeling over, and well-nigh upset in the water, the lady exclaimed, 'I know that man! He is our ancient enemy;' and Benita (foreseeing that all their boxes would be turned inside out, or carried away) snatched the most valuable of the jewels, a magnificent necklace of diamonds, and cast it over the little girl's head, and buried it under her travelling-cloak, hoping so to save it. Then a great wave, crested with foam, rolfed in, and the coach was thrown on its side, and the sea rushed in at the top and the windows, upon shrieking, and clashing, and fainting away.

"What followed Benita knew not, as one might well suppose, herself being stunned by a blow on the head, beside being palsied with terror. 'See, I have the mark now,' she said; 'where the jamb of the door came down on me!' But when she recovered her senses, she found herself upon the sand, the robbers were out of sight, and one of the serving-men was bathing her forehead with sea water. For this she rated him well, having taken already too much of that article; and then she arose and ran to her mistress, who was sitting upright on a little rock, with her dead boy's face to her bosom, sometimes gazing upon him, and sometimes questing round for the other one.

"Although there were torches and links around, and she looked at her child by the light of them, no one dared to approach the lady, or speak, or try to help her. Each man whispered his fellow to go, but each hung back himself, and muttered that it was too awful to meddle with. And there she would have sat all night, with the fine little fellow stone dead in her arms, and her tearless eyes dwelling upon him, and her heart but not her mind thinking, only that the Italian woman stole up softly to her side, and whispered, 'It is the will of God.'

" 'So it always seems to be,' were all the words the mother answered; and then she fell on Benita's neck; and the men were ashamed to be near her weeping; and a sailor lay down and bellowed. Surely these men are the best.

"Before the light of the morning came along the tide to Watchett my Lady had met her husband. They took her into the town that night, but not to her own castle; and so the power of womanhood (which is itself maternity) came over swiftly upon her. The lady, whom all people loved (though at certain times, particular), lies in Watchett little churchyard, with son and heir at her right hand, and a little babe, of sex unknown, sleeping on her bosom.

"This is a miserable tale," said Jeremy Stickles brightly; "hand me over the schnapps, my boy. What fools we are to spoil our eyes for other people's troubles! Enough of our own to keep them clean, although we all were chimney-sweeps. There is nothing like good hollands, when a man becomes too sensitive. Restore the action of the glands; that is my rule, after weeping. Let me make you another, John. You are quite low-spirited."

But although Master Jeremy carried on so (as became his manhood), and laughed at the sailor's bellowing, bless his heart, I knew as well that tears were in his brave keen eyes, as if I had dared to look for them, or show mine own against them.

"And what was the lady's name?" I asked; "and what became of the little girl? And why did the woman stay there?"

"Well!" cried Jeremy Stickles, only too glad to be cheerful again; "talk of a woman after that! As we used to say at school — 'Who dragged whom, how many times, in what manner round the wall of what?' But to begin, last first, my John (as becomes a woman): Benita stayed in that blessed place, because she could not get away from it. The Doones — if Doones indeed they were, about which you of course know best — took every stiver out of the carriage: wet or dry they took it. And Benita could never get her wages; for the whole affair is in Chancery, and they have appointed a receiver."

"Whew!" said I, knowing something of London, and sorry for Benita's chance.

"So the poor thing was compelled to drop all thought of Apulia, and settle down on the brink of Exmoor, where you get all its evils, without the good to balance them. She married a man who turned a wheel for making the blue Watchett ware, partly because he could give her a house, and partly because he proved himself a good soul towards my Lady. There they are, and have three children; and there you may go and visit them."

"I understand all that, Jeremy, though you do tell things too quickly, and I would rather have John Fry's style; for he leaves one time for his words to melt. Now for my second question. What became of the little maid?"

"You great oaf!" cried Jeremy Stickles; "you are rather more likely to know, I should think, than anyone else in all the kingdoms."

"If I knew, I should not ask you. Jeremy Stickles, do try to be neither conceited, nor thick-headed."

"I will when you are neither," answered Master Jeremy; "but you occupy all the room, John. No one else can get in with you there."

"Very well then, let me out. Take me down in both ways."

"If ever you were taken down; you must have your double joints ready now. And yet in other ways you will be as proud and set up as Lucifer. As certain sure as I stand here, that little maid is Lorna Doone."

CHAPTER LIV
Mutual Discomfiture

It must not be supposed that I was altogether so thick-headed as Jeremy would have made me out. But it is part of my character that I like other people to think me slow, and to labour hard to enlighten me, while all the time I can say to myself, "This man is shallower than I am; it is pleasant to see his shoals come up, while he is sounding mine so!" Not that I would so behave, God forbid, with anybody (be it man or woman) who in simple heart approached me, with no gauge of intellect. But when the upper hand is taken, upon the faith of one's patience, by a man of even smaller wits (not that Jeremy was that, neither could he have lived to be thought so), why, it naturally happens, that we knuckle under, with an ounce of indignation.

Jeremy's tale would have moved me greatly, both with sorrow and anger, even without my guess at first, and now my firm belief, that the child of those unlucky parents was indeed my Lorna. And as I thought of the lady's troubles, and her faith in Providence, and her cruel, childless death, and then imagined how my darling would be overcome to hear it, you may well believe that my quick replies to Jeremy Stickles' banter were but as the flourish of a drum to cover the sounds of pain.

For when he described the heavy coach, and the persons in and upon it, and the breaking down at Dulverton, and the place of their destination, as well as the time and the weather, and the season of the year, my heart began to burn within me, and my mind replaced the pictures, first of the foreign lady's-maid by the pump caressing me, and then of the coach struggling up the hill, and the beautiful dame, and the fine little boy, with the white cockade in his hat; but most of all the little girl, dark-haired and very lovely, and having even in those days the rich soft look of Lorna.

But when he spoke of the necklace thrown over the head of the little maiden, and of her disappearance, before my eyes arose at once the flashing of the beacon-fire, the lonely moors embrowned with light, the tramp of the outlaw cavalcade, and the helpless child head downward lying across the robber's sad-

dle-bow. Then I remembered my own mad shout of boyish indignation, and marvelled at the strange long way by which the
events of life come round. And while I thought of my own return, and childish attempt to hide myself from sorrow in the saw-
pit, and the agony of my mother's tears, it did not fail to strike
me as a thing of omen, that the self-same day should be, both to
my darling and myself, the blackest and most miserable of all
youthful days.

The King's Commissioner thought it wise, for some good
reason of his own, to conceal from me, for the present, the name
of the poor lady supposed to be Lorna's mother; and knowing
that I could easily now discover it, without him, I let that question abide awhile. Indeed I was half afraid to hear it, remembering that the nobler and the wealthier she proved to be, the
smaller was my chance of winning such a wife for plain John
Ridd. Not that she would give me up; that I never dreamed of.
But that others would interfere; or indeed I myself might find it
only honest to relinquish her. That last thought was a dreadful
blow, and took my breath away from me.

Jeremy Stickles was quite decided — and of course the
discovery being his, he had a right to be so — that not a word of
all these things must be imparted to Lorna herself, or even to my
mother, or anyone whatever. "Keep it tight as wax, my lad," he
cried, with a wink of great expression; "this belongs to me,
mind; and the credit, ay, and the premium, and the right of dis-
count, are altogether mine. It would have taken you fifty years to
put two and two together so, as I did, like a clap of thunder. Ah,
God has given some men brains; and others have good farms and
money, and a certain skill in the lower beasts. Each must use his
special talent. You work your farm: I work my brains. In the end,
my lad, I shall beat you."

"Then, Jeremy, what a fool you must be, if you cudgel
your brains to make money of this, to open the barn-door to me,
and show me all your threshing."

"Not a whit, my son. Quite the opposite. Two men always
thresh better than one. And here I have you bound to use your
flail, one two, with mine, and yet in strictest honour bound not to
bushel up, till I tell you."

"But," said I, being much amused by a Londoner's brave,
yet uncertain, use of simplest rural metaphors, for he had wholly

forgotten the winnowing: "surely if I bushel up, even when you tell me, I must take half-measure."

"So you shall, my boy," he answered, "if we can only cheat those confounded knaves of Equity. You shall take the beauty, my son, and the elegance and the love, and all that — and, my boy, I will take the money."

This he said in a way so dry, and yet so richly unctuous, that being gifted somehow by God, with a kind of sense of queerness, I fell back in my chair, and laughed, though the underside of my laugh was tears.

"Now, Jeremy, how if I refuse to keep this half as tight as wax? You bound me to no such partnership, before you told the story; and I am not sure, by any means, of your right to do so afterwards."

"Tush!" he replied; "I know you too well, to look for meanness in you. If from pure good-will, John Ridd, and anxiety to relieve you, I made no condition precedent, you are not the man to take advantage, as a lawyer might. I do not even want your promise. As sure as I hold this glass, and drink your health and love, in another drop (forced on me by pathetic words), so surely will you be bound to me until I do release you. Tush! I know men well by this time: a mere look of trust from one is worth another's ten thousand oaths."

"Jeremy, you are right," I answered; "at least as regards the issue. Although perhaps you were not right in leading me into a bargain like this, without my own consent or knowledge. But supposing that we should both be shot in this grand attack on the valley (for I mean to go with you now, heart and soul), is Lorna to remain untold of that which changes all her life?"

"Both shot!" cried Jeremy Stickles: "my goodness, boy, talk not like that! And those Doones are cursed good shots too. Nay, nay, the yellows shall go in front; we attack on the Somerset side, I think. I from a hill will reconnoitre, as behoves a general, you shall stick behind a tree, if we can only find one big enough to hide you. You and I to be shot, John Ridd, with all this inferior food for powder anxious to be devoured?"

I laughed, for I knew his cool hardihood, and never-flinching courage; and sooth to say no coward would have dared to talk like that.

"But when one comes to think of it," he continued, smiling at himself," some provision should be made for even that unpleasant chance. I will leave the whole in writing, with orders to be opened, etc., etc. — Now no more of that, my boy; a cigarro after schnapps, and go to meet my yellow boys."

His "yellow boys," as he called the Somersetshire trained bands, were even now coming down the valley from the "London-road," as every one since I went up to town, grandly entitled the lane to the moors. There was one good point about these men, that having no discipline at all, they made pretence to none whatever. Nay, rather they ridiculed the thing, as below men of any spirit. On the other hand, Master Stickles' troopers looked down on these native fellows from a height which I hope they may never tumble, for it would break the necks of all of them.

Now these fine natives came along, singing for their very lives, a song the like of which set down here would oust my book from modest people, and make everybody say, "this man never can have loved Lorna." Therefore the less of that the better; only I thought, "what a difference from the goodly psalms of the ale-house!"

Having finished their canticle, which contained more mirth than melody, they drew themselves up, in a sort of way supposed by them to be military, each man with heel and elbow struck into those of his neighbour, and saluted the King's Commissioner. "Why, where are your officers?" asked Master Stickles; "how is it that you have no officers?" Upon this there arose a general grin, and a knowing look passed along their faces, even up to the man by the gatepost. "Are you going to tell me, or not," said Jeremy, "what is become of your officers?"

"Plaise zur," said one little fellow at last, being nodded at by the rest to speak, in right of his known eloquence; "hus tould Harfizers, as a wor no nade of un, now King's man hiszel wor coom, a puppose vor to command us laike."

"And do you mean to say, you villains," cried Jeremy, scarce knowing whether to laugh, or to swear, or what to do; "that your officers took their dismissal thus, and let you come on without them?"

"What could 'em do?" asked the little man, with reason certainly on his side: "hus zent 'em about their business, and they was glad enough to goo."

"Well!" said poor Jeremy, turning to me; "a pretty state of things, John! Threescore cobblers, and farming men, plaisterers, tailors, and kettles-to-mend; and not a man to keep order among them, except my blessed self, John! And I trow there is not one among them could hit a barn-door flying. The Doones will make riddles of all of us."

However, he had better hopes, when the sons of Devon appeared, as they did in about an hour's time; fine fellows, and eager to prove themselves. These had not discarded their officers, but marched in good obedience to them, and were quite prepared to fight the men of Somerset (if need be) in addition to the Doones. And there was scarcely a man among them but could have trounced three of the yellow men, and would have done it gladly too, in honour of the red facings.

"Do you mean to suppose, Master Jeremy Stickles," said I, looking on with amazement, beholding also all our maidens at the upstair windows wondering; "that we, my mother, a widow woman, and I a young man of small estate, can keep and support all these precious fellows, both yellow ones, and red ones, until they have taken the Doone Glen?"

"God forbid it, my son!" he replied, laying a finger upon his lip. "Nay, nay, I am not of the shabby order, when I have the strings of government. Kill your sheep at famine prices, and knead your bread at a figure expressing the rigours of last winter. Let Annie make out the bill every day, and I at night will double it. You may take my word for it, Master John, this spring-harvest shall bring you in three times as much as last autumn's did. If they cheated you in town, my lad, you shall have your change in the country. Take thy bill, and write down quickly."

However, this did not meet my views of what an honest man should do; and I went to consult my mother about it, as all the accounts would be made in her name.

Dear mother thought that if the King paid only half again as much as other people would have to pay, it would be perhaps the proper thing; the half being due for loyalty; and here she quoted an ancient saying:

"The King and his staff
Be a man and a half;"

which, according to her judgment, ruled beyond dispute
the law of the present question. To argue with her after that
(which she brought up with such triumph) would have been
worse than useless. Therefore I just told Annie to make the bills
at a third below the current market prices; so that the upshot
would be fair. She promised me honestly that she would; but
with a twinkle in her bright blue eyes, which she must have
caught from Tom Faggus. It always has appeared to me, that
stern and downright honesty upon money matters is a thing not
understood of women; be they as good as good can be.

The yellows and the reds together numbered a hundred
and twenty men, most of whom slept in our barns and stacks;
and besides these we had fifteen troopers of the regular army.
You may suppose that all the country was turned upside down
about it; and the folk who came to see them drill — by no means
a needless exercise — were a greater plague than the soldiers.
The officers too of the Devonshire band were such a torment to
us, that we almost wished their men had dismissed them, as the
Somerset troop had done with theirs. For we could not keep them
out of our house, being all young men of good family, and therefore not to be met with bars. And having now three lovely maidens (for even Lizzie might be called so, when she cared to
please), mother and I were at wits' ends, on account of those
blessed officers. I never got a wink of sleep, they came whistling
under the window so; and directly I went out to chase them,
there was nothing but a cat to see.

Therefore all of us were right glad (except perhaps Farmer
Snowe, from whom we had bought some victuals at rare price)
when Jeremy Stickles gave orders to march, and we began to try
to do it. A good deal of boasting went overhead, as our men de-
filed along the lane; and the thick broad patins of pennywort
jutted out between the stones, ready to heal their bruises. The
parish choir came part of the way, and the singing-loft from
Countisbury; and they kept our soldiers' spirits up, with some of
the most pugnacious Psalms. Parson Bowden marched ahead,
leading all our van and file, as against the Papists; and promising
to go with us, till we came to bullet distance. Therefore we
marched bravely on, and children came to look at us. And I

wondered where Uncle Reuben was, who ought to have led the culverins (whereof we had no less than three) if Stickles could only have found him; and then I thought of little Ruth; and without any fault on my part, my heart went down within me.

The culverins were laid on bark; and all our horses pulling them, and looking round every now and then, with their ears curved up like a squirrel'd nut, and their noses tossing anxiously, to know what sort of plough it was man had been pleased to put behind them — man, whose endless whims and wildness they could never understand, any more than they could satisfy. However, they pulled their very best — as all our horses always do — and the culverins went up the hill, without smack of whip, or swearing. It had been arranged, very justly no doubt, and quite in keeping with the spirit of the Constitution, but as it proved not too wisely, that either body of men should act in its own county only. So when we reached the top of the hill, the sons of Devon marched on, and across the track leading into Doone-gate, so as to fetch round the western side, and attack with their culverin from the cliffs, whence the sentry had challenged me on the night of my passing the entrance. Meanwhile the yellow lads were to stay upon the eastern highland, whence Uncle Reuben and myself had reconnoitred so long ago; and whence I had leaped into the valley at the time of the great snowdrifts. And here they were not to show themselves; but keep their culverin in the woods, until their cousins of Devon appeared on the opposite parapet of the glen.

The third culverin was entrusted to the fifteen troopers; who with ten picked soldiers from either trained band, making in all five-and-thirty men, were to assault the Doone-gate itself, while the outlaws were placed between two fires from the eastern cliff and the western. And with this force went Jeremy Stickles, and with it went myself, as knowing more about the passage than any other stranger did. Therefore, if I have put it clearly, as I strive to do, you will see that the Doones must repulse at once three simultaneous attacks, from an army numbering in the whole one hundred and thirty-five men, not including the Devonshire officers; fifty men on each side I mean, and thirty-five at the head of the valley.

The tactics of this grand campaign appeared to me so clever, and beautifully ordered, that I commended "Colonel

Stickles," as everybody now called him, for his great ability and mastery of the art of war. He admitted that he deserved high praise; but said that he was not by any means equally certain of success, so large a proportion of his forces being only a raw militia, brave enough no doubt for anything, when they saw their way to it; but knowing little of gunnery, and wholly unused to be shot at. Whereas all the Doones were practised marksmen, being compelled when lads (like the Balearic slingers) to strike down their meals before tasting them. And then Colonel Stickles asked me, whether I myself could stand fire; he knew that I was not a coward, but this was a different question. I told him that I had been shot at, once or twice before; but nevertheless disliked it, as much as almost anything. Upon that, he said that I would do; for that when a man got over the first blush of diffidence, he soon began to look upon it as a puff of destiny.

I wish I could only tell what happened, in the battle of that day, especially as nearly all the people round these parts, who never saw gun-fire in it, have gotten the tale so much amiss; and some of them will even stand in front of my own hearth, and contradict me to the teeth; although at the time they were not born, nor their fathers put into breeches. But in truth, I cannot tell, exactly, even the part in which I helped; how then can I be expected, time by time, to lay before you, all the little ins and outs of places, where I myself was not? Only I can contradict things, which I know could not have been; and what I plainly saw should not be controverted in my own house.

Now we five-and-thirty men lay back, a little way round the corner, in the hollow of the track which leads to the strong Doone-gate. Our culverin was in amongst us, loaded now to the muzzle, and it was not comfortable to know that it might go off at any time. Although the yeomanry were not come (according to arrangement), some of us had horses there; besides the horses who dragged the cannon, and now were sniffing at it. And there were plenty of spectators to mind these horses for us, as soon as we should charge; inasmuch as all our friends and neighbours, who had so keenly prepared for the battle, now resolved to take no part, but look on, and praise the winners.

At last, we heard the loud bang-bang, which proved that Devon and Somerset were pouring their indignation hot into the den of malefactors, or at least so we supposed; therefore at double quick march we advanced round the bend of the cliff which had hidden us, hoping to find the gate undefended, and to blow down all barriers with the fire of our cannon. And indeed it seemed likely at first to be so, for the wild and mountainous gorge of rock appeared to be all in pure loneliness, except where the coloured coats of our soldiers, and their metal trappings, shone with the sun behind them. Therefore we shouted a loud hurrah, as for an easy victory.

But while the sound of our cheer ran back among the crags above us, a shrill clear whistle cleft the air for a single moment, and then a dozen carbines bellowed, and all among us flew murderous lead. Several of our men rolled over, but the rest rushed on like Britons, Jeremy and myself in front, while we heard the horses plunging at the loaded gun behind us. "Now, my lads," cried Jeremy, "one dash, and we are beyond them!" For he saw that the foe was overhead in the gallery of brush-wood.

Our men with a brave shout answered him, for his courage was fine example; and we leaped in under the feet of the foe, before they could load their guns again. But here, when the foremost among us were past, an awful crash rang behind us, with the shrieks of men, and the din of metal, and the horrible screaming of horses. The trunk of the tree had been launched overhead, and crashed into the very midst of us. Our cannon was under it, so were two men and a horse with his poor back broken. Another horse vainly struggled to rise with his thighbone smashed and protruding.

Now I lost all presence of mind at this, for I loved both those good horses, and shouting for any to follow me, dashed headlong into the cavern. Some five or six men came after me, the foremost of whom was Jeremy, when a storm of shots whis-tled and pattered around me, with a blaze of light and a thunder-ous roar. On I leaped, like a madman, and pounced on one gun-ner, and hurled him across his culverin; but the others had fled, and a heavy oak door fell to with a bang, behind them. So utterly were my senses gone, and nought but strength remaining, that I caught up the Doone cannon with both hands, and dashed it, breech first, at the doorway. The solid oak burst with the blow, and the gun stuck fast, like a builder's putlog.

But here I looked round in vain, for any to come and follow up my success. The scanty light showed me no figure moving through the length of the tunnel behind me; only a heavy groan or two went to my heart, and chilled it. So I hurried back to seek Jeremy, fearing that he must be smitten down.

And so indeed I found him, as well as three other poor fellows, struck by the charge of the culverin, which had passed so close beside me. Two of the four were as dead as stones, and growing cold already, but Jeremy and the other could manage to groan, just now and then. So I turned my attention to them, and thought no more of fighting.

Having so many wounded men, and so many dead among us, we loitered at the cavern's mouth, and looked at one another, wishing only for somebody to come and take command of us. But no one came; and I was grieved so much about poor Jeremy, besides being wholly unused to any violence of bloodshed, that I could only keep his head up, and try to stop him from bleeding. And he looked at me pitifully, being perhaps in a haze of thought, as a calf looks at a butcher.

The shot had taken him in the mouth; about that no doubt could be, for two of his teeth were in his beard, and one of his lips was wanting. I laid his shattered face on my breast, and nursed him, as a woman might. But he looked at me with a jerk at this; and I saw that he wanted coolness.

While here we stayed, quite out of danger (for the fellows from the gallery could by no means shoot us, even if they remained there, and the oaken door whence the others fled was blocked up by the culverin), a boy who had no business there (being in fact our clerk's apprentice to the art of shoe-making) came round the corner upon us, in the manner which boys, and only boys, can use with grace and freedom; that is to say, with a sudden rush, and a sidelong step, and an impudence:

"Got the worst of it!" cried the boy: "better be off all of you. Zomerzett and Devon a vighting; and the Doones have drashed 'em both. Maister Ridd, even thee be drashed."

We few, who yet remained of the force which was to have won the Doone-gate, gazed at one another, like so many fools, and nothing more. For we still had some faint hopes of winning the day, and recovering our reputation, by means of what the other men might have done without us. And we could not understand at all how Devonshire and Somerset, being embarked in the same cause, should be fighting with one another.

Finding nothing more to be done in the way of carrying on the war, we laid poor Master Stickles and two more of the wounded upon the carriage of bark and hurdles, whereon our gun had laid; and we rolled the gun into the river, and harnessed the horses yet alive, and put the others out of their pain, and sadly wended homewards, feeling ourselves to be thoroughly beaten, yet ready to maintain that it was no fault of ours whatever. And in this opinion the women joined, being only too glad and thankful to see us come home alive again.

Now this enterprise having failed so, I prefer not to dwell too long upon it; only just to show the mischief which lay at the root of the failure. And this mischief was the vile jealousy betwixt red and yellow uniform. Now I try to speak impartially, belonging no more to Somerset than I do to Devonshire, living upon the borders, and born of either county. The tale was told me by one side first; and then quite to a different tune by the other; and then by both together, with very hot words of reviling, and a desire to fight it out again. And putting this with that, the truth appears to be as follows:

The men of Devon, who bore red facings, had a long way to go round the hills, before they could get into due position on the western side of the Doone Glen. And knowing that their cousins in yellow would claim the whole of the glory, if allowed to be first with the firing, these worthy fellows waited not to take good aim with their cannon, seeing the others about to shoot; but fettled it anyhow on the slope, pointing in a general direction; and trusting in God for aim-worthiness, laid the rope to the breech, and fired. Now as Providence ordained it, the shot, which was a casual mixture of anything considered hard — for instance jug-bottoms and knobs of doors — the whole of this pernicious dose came scattering and shattering among the unfortunate yellow men upon the opposite cliff, killing one and wounding two.

Now what did the men of Somerset do, but instead of waiting for their friends to send round and beg pardon, train their gun full mouth upon them, and with a vicious meaning shoot? Nor only this, but they loudly cheered, when they saw four or five red coats lie low; for which savage feeling not even the remarks of the Devonshire men concerning their coats could entirely excuse them. Now I need not tell the rest of it; for the tale makes a man discontented. Enough that both sides waxed hotter and hotter with the fire of destruction. And but that the gorge of the cliffs lay between, very few would have lived to tell of it; for our western blood becomes stiff and firm, when churned with the sense of wrong in it.

At last the Doones (who must have laughed at the thunder passing overhead) recalling their men from the gallery, issued out of Gwenny's gate (which had been wholly overlooked) and fell on the rear of the Somerset men, and slew four beside their cannon. Then while the survivors ran away, the outlaws took the hot culverin, and rolled it down into their valley. Thus of three cannons set forth that morning, only one ever came home again, and that was the gun of the Devonshire men, who dragged it home themselves, with the view of making a boast about it.

This was a melancholy end of our brave setting out: and everybody blamed every one else: and several of us wanted to have the whole thing over again, as then we must have righted it. But upon one point all agreed, by some reasoning not clear to me, that the root of the evil was to be found in the way Parson Bowden went up the hill, with his hat on, and no cassock.

CHAPTER LV
Getting into Chancery

Two of the Devonshire officers (Captains Pyke and Dallan) now took command of the men who were left, and ordered all to go home again, commending much the bravery which had been displayed on all sides, and the loyalty to the King, and the English Constitution. This last word always seems to me to settle everything when said, because nobody understands it, and yet all can puzzle their neighbours. So the Devonshire men, having beans to sow (which they ought to have done on Good Friday), went home: and our Somerset friends only stayed for two days more, to backbite them.

To me the whole thing was purely grievous; not from any sense of defeat (though that was bad enough), but from the pain and anguish caused by death, and wounds, and mourning. "Surely we have woes enough," I used to think of an evening, when the poor fellows could not sleep, or rest, or let others rest around them; "surely all this smell of wounds is not incense men should pay to the God who made them. Death, when it comes and is done with, may be a bliss to anyone; but the doubt of life or death, when a man lies, as it were, like a trunk upon a saw-pit, and a grisly head looks up at him, and the groans of pain are cleaving him, this would be beyond all bearing, but for Nature's sap — sweet hope."

Jeremy Stickles lay and tossed, and thrust up his feet in agony, and bit with his lipless mouth the clothes, and was proud to see blood upon them. He looked at us ever so many times, as much as to say, "Fools, let me die; then I shall have some comfort;" but we nodded at him sagely, especially the women, trying to convey to him, on no account to die yet. And then we talked to one another (on purpose for him to hear us), how brave he was, and not the man to knock under in a hurry, and how he should have the victory yet; and how well he looked, considering.

These things cheered him, a little now, and a little more next time; and every time we went on so, he took it with less impatience. Then once when he had been very quiet, and not even tried to frown at us, Annie leaned over, and kissed his forehead, and spread the pillows, and sheet, with a curve as delicate as his own white ears, and then he feebly lifted hands, and prayed to God to bless her. And after that he came round gently; though never to the man he had been, and never to speak loud again.

For a time (as I may have implied before) Master Stickles' authority, and manner of levying duties, had not been taken kindly by the people round our neighbourhood. The manners of East Lynn, and West Lynn, and even that of Woolhanger — although just then all three were at issue about some rights of wreck, and the hanging of a sheep-stealer (a man of no great eminence, yet claimed by each, for the sake of his clothes) — these three, having their rights impugned, or even superseded, as they declared, by the quartering of soldiers in their neighbourhood, united very kindly to oppose the King's Commissioner. However, Jeremy had contrived to conciliate the whole of them, not so much by anything engaging in his deportment, or delicate address, as by holding out bright hopes that the plunder of the Doone Glen might become divisible among the adjoining manors. Now I have never discovered a thing which the lords of manors (at least in our part of the world) do not believe to belong to themselves, if only they could get their rights. And it did seem natural enough that if the Doones were ousted, and a nice collection of prey remained, this should be parted among the people having elder rights of plunder. Nevertheless Master Jeremy knew that the soldiers would have the first of it, and the King what they could not carry.

And perhaps he was punished justly for language so misleading, by the general indignation of the people all around us, not at his failure, but at himself for that which he could in no wise prevent. And the stewards of the manors rode up to our house, on purpose to reproach him, and were greatly vexed with all of us, because he was too ill to see them.

To myself (though by rights the last to be thought of among so much pain and trouble) Jeremy's wound was a great misfortune, in more ways than one. In the first place, it deferred my chance of imparting either to my mother or to Mistress Lorna my firm belief that the maid I loved was not sprung from the race which had slain my father; neither could he in any way have offended against her family. And this discovery I was yearning more and more to declare to them; being forced to see (even in the midst of all warlike troubles) that a certain difference was growing betwixt them both, and betwixt them and me. For although the words of the Counsellor had seemed to fail among us, being bravely met and scattered, yet our courage was but as wind flinging wide the tare-seeds, when the sower casts them from his bag. The crop may not come evenly, many places may long lie bare, and the field be all in patches; yet almost every vetch will spring, and tiller out, and stretch across the scatterings where the wind puffed.

And so dear mother, and darling Lorna now had been for many a day thinking worrying, and wearing about the matter between us. Neither liked to look at the other, as they used to do; with mother admiring Lorna's eyes, and grace, and form of breeding; and Lorna loving mother's goodness, softness, and simplicity. And the saddest, and most hurtful thing, was that neither could ask the other of the shadow falling between them. And so it went on, and deepened.

In the next place Colonel Stickles' illness was a grievous thing to us, in that we had no one now to command the troopers. Ten of these were still alive, and so well approved to us, that they could never fancy aught, whether for dinner or supper, without its being forthcoming. If they wanted trout, they should have it; if colloped venison, or broiled ham, or salmon from Lynmouth and Trentisoe, or truffles from the woodside; all these were at the warriors' service, until they lusted for something else. Even the wounded men ate nobly; all except poor Jeremy, who was forced to have a young elder shoot, with the pith drawn, for to feed him. And once, when they wanted pickled loach[2] (from my description of it), I took up my boyish sport again, and pronged them a good jarful. Therefore none of them could complain: and yet they were not satisfied, perhaps for want of complaining.

Be that as it might, we knew that if they once resolved to go (as they might do at any time, with only a corporal over them), all our house, and all our goods, ay, and our own precious lives, would and must be at the mercy of embittered enemies. For now the Doones, having driven back, as every one said, five

---

[2] There are said to be no loach now in the Lynn. This proves that John Ridd caught all of them.

hundred men — though not thirty had ever fought with them — were in such feather all round the country, that nothing was too good for them. Offerings poured in at the Doone-gate, faster than Doones could away with them; and the sympathy both of Devon and Somerset became almost oppressive. And perhaps this wealth and congratulation, and mutual good feeling between plunderer and victim, saved us from any piece of spite; kindliness having won the day, and every one loving every one.

But yet another cause arose, and this the strongest one of all, to prove the need of Stickles' aid, and calamity of his illness. And this came to our knowledge first, without much time to think of it. For two men appeared at our gate one day, stripped to their shirts, and void of horses, and looking very sorrowful. Now having some fear of attack from the Doones, and scarce knowing what their tricks might be, we received these strangers cautiously, desiring to know who they were, before we let them see all our premises.

However it soon became plain to us that although they might not be honest fellows, at any rate they were not Doones; and so we took them in, and fed, and left them to tell their business. And this they were glad enough to do; as men who have been maltreated almost always are. And it was not for us to contradict them, lest our victuals should go amiss.

These two very worthy fellows — nay, more than that by their own account, being downright martyrs — were come, for the public benefit, from the Court of Chancery, sitting for everybody's good, and boldly redressing evil. This Court has a power of scent unknown to the Common-law practitioners, and slowly, yet surely, tracks its game; even as the great lumbering dogs, now introduced from Spain, and called by some people "pointers," differ from the swift gaze-hound, who sees his prey and runs him down, in the manner of the common lawyers. If a man's ill fate should drive him to make choice between these two, let him rather be chased by the hounds of law, than tracked by the pointers of Equity.

Now, as it fell in a very black day (for all except the lawyers), His Majesty's Court of Chancery, if that be what it called itself, gained scent of poor Lorna's life, and of all that might be made of it. Whether through that brave young lord who ran into such peril, or through any of his friends; or whether through that deep old Counsellor, whose game none might penetrate; or through any disclosures of the Italian woman, or even of Jeremy himself; none just now could tell us: only this truth was too clear — Chancery had heard of Lorna, and then had seen how rich she was; and never delaying in one thing, had opened mouth, and swallowed her.

The Doones, with a share of that dry humour which was in them hereditary, had welcomed the two apparitors (if that be the proper name for them) and led them kindly down the valley, and told them then to serve their writ. Misliking the look of things, these poor men began to fumble among their clothes; upon which the Doones cried, "Off with them! Let us see if your message be on your skins." And with no more manners than that, they stripped, and lashed them out of the valley; only bidding them come to us, if they wanted Lorna Doone: and to us they came accordingly. Neither were they sure at first but that we should treat them so; for they had no knowledge of west country, and thought it quite a godless place, wherein no writ was holy.

We however comforted and cheered them so considerably that, in gratitude, they showed their writs, to which they had stuck like leeches. And these were twofold: one addressed to Mistress Lorna Doone, so called, and bidding her keep in readiness to travel whenever called upon, and commit herself to nobody, except the accredited messengers of the right honourable Court; while the other was addressed to all subjects of His Majesty, having custody of Lorna Doone, or any power over her. And this last both threatened, and exhorted, and held out hopes of recompense, if she were rendered truly. My mother and I held consultation over both these documents, with a mixture of some wrath and fear, and a fork of great sorrow to stir them. And now having Jeremy Stickles' leave, which he gave with a nod when I told him all, and at last made him understand it, I laid bare to my mother as well what I knew, as what I merely surmised, or guessed, concerning Lorna's parentage. All this she received with great tears, and wonder, and fervent thanks to God, and still more fervent praise of her son, who had nothing whatever to do with it. However, now the question was, how to act about these writs. And herein it was most unlucky, that we could not have Master Stickles, with his knowledge of the world, and especially of the law-courts, to advise us what to do, and to help in doing it.

And firstly of the first, I said, "We have rogues to deal with: but try we not to rogue them."

To this, in some measure, dear mother agreed, though she could not see the justice of it, yet thought that it might be wiser, because of our want of practice. And then I said, "Now, we are bound to tell Lorna, and to serve her citation upon her, which these good fellows have given us."

"Then go, and do it thyself, my son," mother replied with a mournful smile, misdoubting what the end might be. So I took the slip of brown parchment, and went to seek my darling.

Lorna was in her favourite place, the little garden which she tended with such care and diligence. Seeing how the maiden loved it, and was happy there, I had laboured hard to fence it from the dangers of the wood. And here she had corrected me, with better taste, and sense of pleasure, and the joys of musing. For I meant to shut out the brook, and build my fence inside of it; but Lorna said no; if we must have a fence, which could not but be injury, at any rate leave the stream inside, and a pleasant bank beyond it. And soon I perceived that she was right, though not so much as afterwards; for the fairest of all things in a garden, and in summer-time most useful, is a brook of crystal water; where a man may come and meditate, and the flowers may lean and see themselves, and the rays of the sun are purified. Now partly with her own white hands, and partly with Gwenny's red ones, Lorna had made of this sunny spot a haven of beauty to dwell in. It was not only that colours lay in the harmony we would seek of them; neither was it the height of plants, sloping to one another; nor even the delicate tone of foliage following suit, and neighbouring. Even the breathing of the wind, soft and gentle in and out, moving things that need not move, and passing longer-stalked ones, even this was not enough among the flush of fragrance, to tell a man the reason of his quiet satisfaction. But so it shall for ever be. As the river we float upon (with wine, and flowers, and music) is nothing at the well-spring but a bubble without reason.

Feeling many things, but thinking without much to guide me, over the grass-plats laid between, I went up to Lorna. She in a shower of damask roses, raised her eyes, and looked at me. And even now, in those sweet eyes, so deep with lovingness and soft maiden dreamings, there seemed to be a slight unwilling, half-confessed withdrawal; overcome by love and duty, yet a painful thing to see.

"Darling," I said, "are your spirits good? Are you strong enough to-day, to bear a tale of cruel sorrow; but which perhaps, when your tears are shed, will leave you all the happier?"

"What can you mean?" she answered trembling, not having been very strong of late, and now surprised at my manner: "are you come to give me up, John?"

"Not very likely," I replied; "neither do I hope such a thing would leave you all the happier. Oh, Lorna, if you can think that, so quickly as you seem to have done; now you have every prospect, and strong temptation to it. You are far, far above me in the world; and I have no right to claim you. Perhaps, when you have heard these tidings, you will say, 'John Ridd, begone; your life and mine are parted.' "

"Will I?" cried Lorna, with all the brightness of her playful ways returning: "you very foolish and jealous John, how shall I punish you for this? Am I to forsake every flower I have, and not even know that the world goes round, while I look up at you the whole day long, and say, 'John, I love, love, love you'?"

During these words, she leaned upon me, half in gay imitation of what I so often made her do, and half in depth of earnestness as the thrice-repeated word grew stronger, and grew warmer, with and to her heart. And as she looked up at the finish, saying, "you," so musically, I was much inclined to clasp her round; but remembering who she was, forbore; at which she seemed surprised with me.

"Mistress Lorna," I replied, with I know not what temptation, making little of her caresses, though more than all my heart to me; "Mistress Lorna, you must keep your rank and proper dignity. You must never look at me with anything but pity now."

"I shall look at you with pity, John," said Lorna, trying to laugh it off, yet not knowing what to make of me, "if you talk any more of this nonsense, knowing me as you ought to do. I shall even begin to think that you, and your friends, are weary of me, and of so long supporting me; and are only seeking cause to send me back to my old misery. If it be so, I will go. My life matters little to anyone." Here the great bright tears arose; but the maiden was too proud to sob.

"Sweetest of all sweet loves," I cried, for the sign of a tear defeated me; "what possibility could make me ever give up Lorna?"

"Dearest of all dears," she answered; "if you dearly love me, what possibility could make me ever give you up, dear?"

Upon that there was no more forbearing; but I kissed, and clasped her, whether she were Countess, or whether Queen of England; mine she was, at least in heart; and mine she should be wholly. And she being of the same opinion, nothing was said between us.

"Now, Lorna," said I, as she hung on my arm, willing to trust me anywhere, "come to your little plant-house, and hear my moving story."

"No story can move me much, dear," she answered rather faintly, for any excitement stayed with her; "since I know your strength of kindness, scarcely any tale can move me, unless it be of yourself, love; or of my poor mother."

"It is of your poor mother, darling. Can you bear to hear it?" And yet I wondered why she did not say as much of her father.

"Yes, I can hear anything. But although I cannot see her, and have long forgotten, I could not bear to hear ill of her."

"There is no ill to hear, sweet child, except of evil done to her. Lorna, you are of an ill-starred race."

"Better that than a wicked race," she answered with her usual quickness, leaping at conclusion: "tell me I am not a Doone, and I will — but I cannot love you more."

"You are not a Doone, my Lorna, for that, at least, I can answer; though I know not what your name is."

"And my father — your father — what I mean is —— "

"Your father and mine never met one another. Your father was killed by an accident in the Pyrenean mountains, and your mother by the Doones; or at least they caused her death, and carried you away from her."

All this, coming as in one breath upon the sensitive maiden, was more than she could bear all at once; as any but a fool like me must of course have known. She lay back on the garden bench, with her black hair shed on the oaken bark, while her colour went and came; and only by that, and her quivering breast, could anyone say that she lived and thought. And yet she pressed my hand with hers, that now I might tell her all of it.

CHAPTER LVI

John becomes Too Popular

No flower that I have ever seen, either in shifting of light and shade, or in the pearly morning, may vie with a fair young woman's face when tender thought and quick emotion vary, enrich, and beautify it. Thus my Lorna hearkened softly, almost without word or gesture, yet with sighs and glances telling, and the pressure of my hand, how each word was moving her.

When at last my tale was done, she turned away and wept bitterly for the sad fate of her parents. But to my surprise, she spoke not even a word of wrath or rancour. She seemed to take it all as fate.

"Lorna, darling," I said at length, for men are more impatient in trials of time than women are, "do you not even wish to know what your proper name is?"

"How can it matter to me, John?" she answered, with a depth of grief which made me seem a trifler. "It can never matter now, when there are none to share it."

"Poor little soul!" was all I said, in a tone of purest pity; and to my surprise she turned upon me, caught me in her arms, and loved me, as she never had done before.

"Dearest, I have you," she cried; "you, and only you, love. Having you, I want no other. All my life is one with yours. Oh, John, how can I treat you so?"

Blushing through the wet of weeping, and the gloom of pondering, yet she would not hide her eyes, but folded me, and dwelled on me.

"I cannot believe," in the pride of my joy, I whispered into one little ear, "that you could ever so love me, beauty, as to give up the world for me."

"Would you give up your farm for me, John?" cried Lorna, leaping back and looking, with her wondrous power of light, at me; "would you give up your mother, your sisters, your home, and all that you have in the world, and every hope of your life, John?"

"Of course I would. Without two thoughts. You know it; you know it, Lorna."

"It is true that I do," she answered, in a tone of deepest sadness; "and it is this power of your love which has made me love you so. No good can come of it; no good. God's face is set against selfishness."

As she spoke in that low tone, I gazed at the clear lines of her face (where every curve was perfect), not with love and wonder only, but with a strange new sense of awe.

"Darling," I said, "come nearer to me. Give me surety against that. For God's sake never frighten me, with the thought that He would part us."

"Does it, then, so frighten you?" she whispered, coming close to me; "I know it, dear; I have known it long; but it never frightens me. It makes me sad, and very lonely, till I can remember!"

"Till you can remember what?" I asked with a long, deep shudder; for we are so superstitious.

"Until I do remember, love, that you will soon come back to me, and be my own for ever. This is what I always think of; this is what I hope for."

Although her eyes were so glorious, and beaming with eternity, this distant sort of beatitude was not much to my liking. I wanted to have my love on earth; and my dear wife in my own home; and children in good time, if God should please to send us any. And then I would be to them exactly what my father was to me. And besides all this, I doubted much about being fit for heaven, where no ploughs are, and no cattle; unless sacrificed bulls went thither.

Therefore I said, "Now kiss me, Lorna; and don't talk any nonsense." And the darling came and did it; being kindly obedient, as the other world often makes us.

"You sweet love," I said at this, being slave to her soft obedience; "do you suppose I should be content to leave you until Elysium?"

"How on earth can I tell, dear John, what you will be content with?"

"You and only you," said I; "the whole of it lies in a syllable. Now you know my entire want: and want must be my comfort."

"But surely if I have money, sir, and birth, and rank, and all sorts of grandeur, you never would dare to think of me?"

She drew herself up with an air of pride, as she gravely pronounced these words, and gave me a scornful glance, or tried; and turned away as if to enter some grand coach or palace; while I was so amazed, and grieved, in my raw simplicity, especially after the way in which she had first received my news (so loving and warm-hearted), that I never said a word, but stared and thought, "How does she mean it?"

She saw the pain upon my forehead, and the wonder in my eyes, and leaving coach and palace too, back she flew to me in a moment, as simple as simplest milkmaid.

"Oh, you fearfully stupid John, you inexpressibly stupid John," she cried, with both arms round my neck, and her lips upon my forehead; "you have called yourself thick-headed, John; and I never would believe it. But now I do with all my heart. Will you never know what I am, love?"

"No, Lorna, that I never shall. I can understand my mother well, and one at least of my sisters, and both the Snowe girls very easily; but you I never understand, only love you all the more for it."

"Then never try to understand me, if the result is that, dear John. And yet I am the very simplest of all foolish simple creatures. Nay, I am wrong; therein I yield the palm to you, my dear. To think that I can act so! No wonder they want me in London, as an ornament for the stage, John."

Now in after days, when I heard of Lorna, as the richest, and noblest, and loveliest lady to be found in London, I often remembered that little scene, and recalled every word and gesture, wondering what lay under it. Even now, while it was quite impossible once to doubt those clear deep eyes, and the bright lips trembling so; nevertheless I felt how much the world would have to do with it; and that the best and truest people cannot shake themselves quite free. However, for the moment, I was very proud, and showed it.

And herein differs fact from fancy, things as they befall us from things as we would have them, human ends from human will; that the first are moved by a thousand, and the last on two wheels only, which (being named) are — desire, and fear. Hope, for instance, is nothing more than desire with a telescope, magnifying distant matters, overlooking near ones; opening one eye on the objects, closing the other to all objections. And if hope be the future tense of desire, the future of fear is religion — at least with too many of us.

Whether I am right, or wrong, in these small moralities, one thing is sure enough, to wit, that hope is the fastest traveller, at any rate in the time of youth. And so I hoped that Lorna might be proved of blameless family, and honourable rank and fortune; and yet none the less for that, love me, and belong to me. So I led her into the house, and she fell into my mother's arms; and I left them to have a good cry of it, with Annie ready to help them.

If Master Stickles should not mend enough to gain his speech a little, and declare to us all he knew, I was to set out for Watchett, riding upon horseback, and there to hire a cart with wheels, such as we had not begun as yet to use on Exmoor. For all our work went on broad wood, with runners and with earth boards; and many of us still looked upon wheels (though mentioned in the Bible) as the invention of the Evil One, and Pharaoh's especial property.

Now instead of getting better, Colonel Stickles grew worse and worse, in spite of all our tendance of him, with simples and with nourishment, and no poisonous medicines, such as doctors would have given him. And the fault of this lay not with us, but purely with himself, and his unquiet constitution. For he roused himself up to a perfect fever, when through Lizzie's giddiness, he learned the very things which mother and Annie were hiding from him with the utmost care: namely, that Serjeant Bloxham had taken upon himself to send direct to London, by the Chancery officers, a full report of what had happened, and of the illness of his chief, together with an urgent prayer for a full battalion of King's troops, and a plenary commander.

This Serjeant Bloxham, being senior of the surviving soldiers, and a very worthy man in his way, but a trifle over zealous, had succeeded to the captaincy upon his master's disablement. Then, with desire to serve his country and show his education, he sat up most part of three nights, and wrote this wonderful report by the aid of our stable lanthorn. It was a very fine piece of work, as three men to whom he read it (but only one at a time) pronounced, being under seal of secrecy. And all might have gone well with it, if the author could only have held his tongue, when near the ears of women. But this was beyond his sense, as it seems, although so good a writer. For having heard that our Lizzie was a famous judge of literature (as indeed she told almost every one) he could not contain himself, but must have her opinion upon his work.

Lizzie sat on a log of wood, and listened with all her ears up, having made proviso that no one else should be there to interrupt her. And she put in a syllable here and there, and many a time she took out one (for the Serjeant overloaded his gun, more often than undercharged it; like a liberal man of fetters), and then she declared the result so good, and the style to be so elegant, so chaste, and yet so fervent, that the Serjeant broke his pipe in three, and fell in love with her on the spot. Now this has led me out of my way; as things are always doing, partly through their own perverseness, partly through my kind desire to give fair turn to all of them, and to all the people who do them. If anyone expects of me a strict and well-drilled story, standing "at attention" all the time, with hands at the side like two wens on my trunk, and eyes going neither right nor left; I trow that man has been disappointed many a page ago, and has left me to my evil ways; and if not, I love his charity. Therefore let me seek his grace, and get back, and just begin again.

That great despatch was sent to London by the Chancery officers, whom we fitted up with clothes, and for three days fattened them; which in strict justice they needed much, as well as in point of equity. They were kind enough to be pleased with us, and accepted my new shirts generously: and urgent as their business was, another week (as they both declared) could do no harm to nobody, and might set them upon their legs again. And knowing, although they were London-men, that fish do live in water, these two fellows went fishing all day, but never landed anything. However their holiday was cut short; for the Serjeant, having finished now his narrative of proceedings, was not the man to let it hang fire, and be quenched perhaps by Stickles.

Therefore, having done their business, and served both citations, these two good men had a pannier of victuals put up by dear Annie, and borrowing two of our horses, rode to Dunster, where they left them, and hired on towards London. We had not time to like them much, and so we did not miss them, especially in our great anxiety about poor Master Stickles.

Jeremy lay between life and death, for at least a fortnight. If the link of chain had flown upwards (for half a link of chain it was which took him in the mouth so), even one inch upwards, the poor man could have needed no one except Parson Bowden; for the bottom of his skull, which holds the brain as in an egg-cup, must have clean gone from him. But striking him horizontally, and a little upon the skew, the metal came out at the back of the neck, and (the powder not being strong, I suppose) it lodged in his leather collar.

Now the rust of this iron hung in the wound, or at least we thought so; though since I have talked with a man of medicine, I am not so sure of it. And our chief aim was to purge this rust; when rather we should have stopped the hole, and let the oxide do its worst, with a plug of new flesh on both sides of it.

At last I prevailed upon him, by argument, that he must get better, to save himself from being ignobly and unjustly superseded; and hereupon I reviled Serjeant Bloxham more fiercely than Jeremy's self could have done, and indeed to such a pitch that Jeremy almost forgave him, and became much milder. And after that his fever, and the inflammation of his wound, diminished very rapidly.

However, not knowing what might happen, or even how soon poor Lorna might be taken from our power, and, falling into lawyer's hands, have cause to wish herself most heartily back among robbers, I set forth one day for Watchett, taking advantage of the visit of some troopers from an outpost, who would make our house quite safe. I rode alone, being fully primed, and having no misgivings. For it was said that even the Doones had begun to fear me, since I cast their culverin through the door, as above related; and they could not but believe, from my being still untouched (although so large an object) in the thickest of their fire, both of gun and cannon, that I must bear a charmed life, proof against ball and bullet. However, I knew that Carver Doone was not a likely man to hold any superstitious opinions; and of him I had an unshapen dread, although quite ready to face him.

Riding along, I meditated upon Lorna's history; how many things were now beginning to unfold themselves, which had been obscure and dark! For instance, Sir Ensor Doone's consent, or to say the least his indifference, to her marriage with a yeoman; which in a man so proud (though dying) had greatly puzzled both of us. But now, if she not only proved to be no grandchild of the Doone, but even descended from his enemy, it was natural enough that he should feel no great repugnance to her humiliation. And that Lorna's father had been a foe to the house of Doone, I gathered from her mother's cry when she beheld their leader. Moreover that fact would supply their motive in carrying off the unfortunate little creature, and yet hiding her true birth from her. She was a "great card," as we say, when playing All-fours at Christmas-time; and if one of them could marry her, before she learned of right and wrong, vast property, enough to buy pardons for a thousand Doones, would be at their mercy. And since I was come to know Lorna better, and she to know me thoroughly — many things had been outspoken, which her early bashfulness had kept covered from me. Attempts I mean to pledge her love to this one, or that other; some of which perhaps might have been successful, if there had not been too many.

And then, as her beauty grew richer and brighter, Carver Doone was smitten strongly, and would hear of no one else as a suitor for her; and by the terror of his claim drove off all the others. Here too lay the explanation of a thing which seemed to be against the laws of human nature, and upon which I longed, but dared not, to cross-question Lorna. How could such a lovely maid, although so young, and brave, and distant, have escaped the vile affections of a lawless company?

But now it was as clear as need be. For any proven violence would have utterly vitiated all claim upon her grand estates; at least as those claims must be urged before a court of equity. And therefore all the elders (with views upon her real estate) kept strict watch on the youngers, who confined their views to her personality.

Now I do not mean to say that all this, or the hundred other things which came, crowding consideration, were half as plain to me at the time, as I have set them down above. Far be it from me to deceive you so. No doubt my thoughts were then dark and hazy, like an oil-lamp full of fungus; and I have trimmed them, as though at the time, with scissors sharpened long afterwards. All I mean to say is this, that jogging along to a certain tune of the horse's feet, which we call "three halfpence and two pence," I saw my way a little into some things which had puzzled me.

When I knocked at the little door, whose sill was gritty and grimed with sand, no one came for a very long time to answer me, or to let me in. Not wishing to be unmannerly, I waited a long time, and watched the sea, from which the wind was blowing; and whose many lips of waves — though the tide was halfway out — spoke to and refreshed me. After a while I knocked again, for my horse was becoming hungry; and a good while after that again, a voice came through the keyhole:

"Who is that wishes to enter?"

"The boy who was at the pump," said I, "when the carriage broke down at Dulverton. The boy that lives at Oh — ah; and some day you would come seek for him.''

"Oh yes, I remember certainly. My leetle boy, with the fair white skin. I have desired to see him, oh many, yes, many times."

She was opening the door, while saying this; and then she started back in affright, that the little boy should have grown so.

"You cannot be that leetle boy. It is quite impossible. Why do you impose on me?"

"Not only am I that little boy, who made the water to flow for you, till the nebule came upon the glass; but also I am come to tell you all about your little girl."

"Come in, you very great leetle boy," she answered, with her dark eyes brightened. And I went in, and looked at her. She was altered by time, as much as I was. The slight and graceful shape was gone; not that I remembered anything of her figure, if you please; for boys of twelve are not yet prone to note the shapes of women; but that her lithe straight gait had struck me as being so unlike our people. Now her time for walking so was past, and transmitted to her children. Yet her face was comely still, and full of strong intelligence. I gazed at her, and she at me; and we were sure of one another.

"Now what will ye please to eat?" she asked, with a lively glance at the size of my mouth: "that is always the first thing you people ask, in these barbarous places."

"I will tell you by and by," I answered, misliking this satire upon us: "but I might begin with a quart of ale, to enable me to speak, madam."

"Very well. One quevart of be-or," she called out to a little maid, who was her eldest child, no doubt. "It is to be expected, sir. Be-or, be-or, be-or, all day long, with you Englishmen!"

"Nay," I replied; "not all day long, if madam will excuse me. Only a pint at breakfast-time, and a pint and a half at eleven o'clock, and a quart or so at dinner. And then no more till the afternoon; and half a gallon at supper-time. No one can object to that."

"Well, I suppose it is right," she said, with an air of resignation; "God knows. But I do not understand it. It is 'good for business,' as you say, to preclude everything."

"And it is good for us, madam," I answered with indignation, for beer is my favourite beverage; "and I am a credit to beer, madam; and so are all who trust to it."

"At any rate you are, young man. If beer has made you grow so large, I will put my children upon it; it is too late for me to begin. The smell to me is hateful."

Now I only set down that to show how perverse those foreign people are. They will drink their wretched heartless stuff, such as they call claret, or wine of Medoc, or Bordeaux, or what not, with no more meaning than sour rennet, stirred with the pulp from the cider press, and strained through the cap of our Betty. This is very well for them; and as good as they deserve, no doubt; and meant perhaps by the will of God for those unhappy natives. But to bring it over to England, and set it against our home-brewed ale (not to speak of wines from Portugal), and sell it at ten times the price, as a cure for British bile, and a great enlightenment; this I say is the vilest feature of the age we live in.

Madame Benita Odam — for the name of the man who turned the wheel proved to be John Odam — showed me into a little room containing two chairs and a fir-wood table, and sat down on a three-legged seat and studied me very stead-fastly. This she had a right to do; and I, having all my clothes on now, was not disconcerted. It would not become me to repeat her judgment upon my appearance, which she delivered as calmly as if I were a pig at market, and as proudly as if her own pig. And she asked me whether I had ever got rid of the black marks on my breast.

Not wanting to talk about myself (though very fond of doing so, when time and season favour), I led her back to that fearful night of the day when first I had seen her. She was not desirous to speak of it, because of her own little children: however, I drew her gradually to recollection of Lorna, and then of the little boy who died, and the poor mother buried with him. And her strong hot nature kindled, as she dwelled upon these things: and my wrath waxed within me; and we forgot reserve and prudence under the sense of so vile a wrong. She told me (as nearly as might be) the very same story which she had told to Master Jeremy Stickles; only she dwelled upon it more, because of my knowing the outset. And being a woman, with an inkling of my situation, she enlarged upon the little maid, more than to dry Jeremy.

"Would you know her again?" I asked, being stirred by these accounts of Lorna, when she was five years old: "would you know her as a full-grown maiden?"

"I think I should," she answered; "it is not possible to say, until one sees the person: but from the eyes of the little girl, I think that I must know her. Oh, the poor young creature! Is it to be believed that the cannibals devoured her? What a people you are in this country! Meat, meat, meat!"

As she raised her hands and eyes in horror at our carnivorous propensities, to which she clearly attributed the disappearance of Lorna, I could scarce help laughing, even after that sad story. For though it is said at the present day, and will doubtless be said hereafter, that the Doones had devoured a baby once, as they came up Porlock hill, after fighting hard in the marketplace, I knew that the tale was utterly false: for cruel and brutal as they were, their taste was very correct and choice, and indeed one might say fastidious. Nevertheless, I could not stop to argue that matter with her.

"The little maid has not been devoured," I said to Mistress Odam: "and now she is a tall young lady, and as beautiful as can be. If I sleep in your good hostel to-night after going to Watchett town, will you come with me to Oare to-morrow, and see your little maiden?"

"I would like — and yet I fear. This country is so barbarous. And I am good to eat — my God, there is much picking on my bones!"

She surveyed herself with a glance so mingled of pity and admiration, and the truth of her words was so apparent (only that it would have taken a week to get at the bones, before picking), that I nearly lost good manners; for she really seemed to suspect even me of cannibal inclinations. However, at last I made her promise to come with me on the morrow, presuming that Master Odam could by any means be persuaded to keep her company in the cart, as propriety demanded. Having little doubt that Master Odam was entirely at his wife's command, I looked upon that matter as settled, and set off for Watchett, to see the grave of Lorna's poor mother, and to hire a cart for the morrow.

And here (as so often happens with men) I succeeded without any trouble or hindrance, where I had looked for both of them, namely in finding a suitable cart; whereas the other matter, in which I could have expected no difficulty, came very near to defeat me. For when I heard that Lorna's father was the Earl of Dugal — as Benita impressed upon me with a strong enforcement, as much as to say, "Who are you, young man, to come even asking about her?" — then I never thought but that everybody in Watchett town must know all about the tombstone of the Countess of Dugal.

This however proved otherwise. For Lord Dugal had never lived at Watchett Grange, as their place was called; neither had his name become familiar as its owner. Because the Grange had only devolved to him by will, at the end of a long entail, when the last of the Fitz-Pains died out; and though he liked the idea of it, he had gone abroad, without taking seisin. And upon news of his death, John Jones, a rich gentleman from Llandaff, had taken possession, as next of right, and hushed up all the story. And though, even at the worst of times, a lady of high rank and wealth could not be robbed, and as bad as murdered, and then buried in a little place, without moving some excitement; yet it had been given out, on purpose and with diligence, that this was only a foreign lady, travelling for her health and pleasure, along the sea-coast of England. And as the poor thing never spoke, and several of her servants and her baggage looked so foreign, and she herself died in a collar of lace unlike any made in England, all Watchett, without hesitation, pronounced her to be a foreigner. And the English serving-man and maid, who might have cleared up everything, either were bribed by Master Jones, or else decamped of their own accord with the relics of the baggage. So the poor Countess of Dugal, almost in sight of her own grand house, was buried in an unknown grave, together with her pair of infants, without a plate, without a tombstone (worse than all), without a tear, except from the hired Italian woman. Surely my poor Lorna came of an ill-starred family.

Now in spite of all this, if I had only taken Benita with me, or even told her what I wished, and craved her directions, there could have been no trouble. But I do assure you that among the stupid people of Watchett (compared with whom our folk of Oare, exceeding dense though being, are as Hamlet against Dogberry), what with one of them and another, and the firm conviction of all the town that I could be come only to wrestle, I do assure you (as I said before) that my wits almost went out of me. And what vexed me yet more about it was, that I saw my own mistake, in coming myself to seek out the matter, instead of sending some unknown person. For my face and form were known at that time (and still are so) to nine people out of every ten living in forty miles of me. Not through any excellence, or anything of good desert, in either the one or the other, but simply because folk will be fools, on the rivalry of wrestling. The art is a fine one in itself, and demands a little wit of brain, as well as strength of body; it binds the man who studies it to temperance, and chastity, to self-respect, and most of all to an even and sweet temper; for I have thrown stronger men than myself (when I was a mere sapling, and before my strength grew hard on me) through their loss of temper. But though the art is an honest one, surely they who excel therein have a right (like all the rest of mankind) to their own private life.

Be that either way — and I will not speak too strongly for fear of indulging my own annoyance — any how, all Watchett town cared ten times as much to see John Ridd, as to show him what he wanted. I was led to every public-house, instead of to the churchyard; and twenty tables were ready for me, in lieu of a single gravestone. "Zummerzett thou bee'st, Jan Ridd, and Zummerzett thou shalt be. Thee carl theezell a Davonshire man! Whoy, thee lives in Zummerzett; and in Zummerzett thee wast barn, lad." And so it went on, till I was weary; though very much obliged to them.

Steadfast and solid as I am, and with a wild duck waiting for me at good Mistress Odam's, I saw that there was nothing for it but to yield to these good people, and prove me a man of Somerset by eating a dinner at their expense. As for the churchyard, none would hear of it; and I grieved for broaching the matter.

But how was I to meet Lorna again without having done the thing of all things which I had promised to see to? It would never do to tell her, that so great was my popularity, and so strong the desire to feed me, that I could not attend to her mother. Least of all could I say that every one in Watchett knew John Ridd; while none had heard of the Countess of Dugal. And yet that was about the truth, as I hinted very delicately to Mistress Odam that evening. But she (being vexed about her wild duck, and not having English ideas on the matter of sports, and so on) made a poor unwitting face at me. Nevertheless Master Odam restored me to my self-respect; for he stared at me till I went to bed; and he broke his hose with excitement. For being in the leg-line myself, I wanted to know what the muscles were of a man who turned a wheel all day. I had never seen a treadmill (though they have one now at Exeter), and it touched me much to learn whether it were good exercise. And herein, from what I saw of Odam, I incline to think that it does great harm; as moving the muscles too much in a line, and without variety.

CHAPTER LVII

Lorna knows Her Nurse

Having obtained from Benita Odam a very close and full description of the place where her poor mistress lay, and the marks whereby to know it, I hastened to Watchett the following morning, before the sun was up, or any people were about. And so, without interruption, I was in the churchyard at sunrise.

In the furthest and darkest nook, overgrown with grass, and overhung by a weeping tree, a little bank of earth betokened the rounding off of a hapless life. There was nothing to tell of rank, or wealth, of love, or even pity; nameless as a peasant lay the last (as supposed) of a mighty race. Only some unskilful hand, probably Master Odam's under his wife's teaching, had carved a rude L., and a ruder D., upon a large pebble from the beach, and set it up as a headstone.

I gathered a little grass for Lorna, and a sprig of the weeping tree, and then returned to the "Forest Cat," as Benita's lonely inn was called. For the way is long from Watchett to Oare; and though you may ride it rapidly, as the Doones had done on that fatal night, to travel on wheels, with one horse only, is a matter of time and of prudence. Therefore we set out pretty early, three of us, and a baby, who could not well be left behind. The wife of the man who owned the cart had undertaken to mind the business and the other babies upon condition of having the keys of all the taps left with her.

As the manner of journeying over the moor has been described oft enough already, I will say no more, except that we all arrived, before dusk of the summer's day, safe at Plover's Barrows. Mistress Benita was delighted with the change from her dull hard life; and she made many excellent observations, such as seem natural to a foreigner looking at our country.

As luck would have it, the first who came to meet us at the gate was Lorna, with nothing whatever upon her head (the weather being summerly), but her beautiful hair shed round her; and wearing a sweet white frock tucked in, and showing her figure perfectly. In her joy she ran straight up to the cart; and then stopped and gazed at Benita. At one glance her old nurse knew her: "Oh the eyes, the eyes!" she cried, and was over the rail of the cart in a moment, in spite of all her substance. Lorna, on the other hand, looked at her with some doubt and wonder; as though having right to know much about her, and yet unable to do so. But when the foreign woman said something in Roman language, and flung new hay from the cart upon her, as if in a romp of childhood, the young maid cried, "Oh, Nita, Nita!" and fell upon her breast, and wept; and after that looked round at us.

This being so, there could be no doubt as to the power of proving Lady Lorna's birth, and rights, both by evidence and token. For though we had not the necklace now — thanks to Annie's wisdom — we had the ring of heavy gold, a very ancient relic, with which my maid (in her simple way) had pledged herself to me. And Benita knew this ring as well as she knew her own fingers, having heard a long history about it; and the effigy on it of the wild cat was the bearing of the house of Lorne.

For though Lorna's father was a nobleman of high and goodly lineage, her mother was of yet more ancient and renowned descent, being the last in line direct from the great and kingly chiefs of Lorne. A wild and headstrong race they were, and must have everything their own way. Hot blood was ever among them, even of one household; and their sovereignty (which more than once had defied the King of Scotland) waned and fell among themselves, by continual quarrelling. And it was of a piece with this, that the Doones (who were an offset, by the mother's side, holding in co-partnership some large property, which had come by the spindle, as we say) should fall out with the Earl of Lorne, the last but one of that title.

The daughter of this nobleman had married Sir Ensor Doone; but this, instead of healing matters, led to fiercer conflict. I never could quite understand all the ins and outs of it; which none but a lawyer may go through, and keep his head at the end of it. The motives of mankind are plainer than the motions they produce. Especially when charity (such as found among us) sits to judge the former, and is never weary of it: while reason does not care to trace the latter complications, except for fee or title.

Therefore it is enough to say, that knowing Lorna to be direct in heirship to vast property, and bearing especial spite against the house of which she was the last, me Doones had brought her up with full intention of lawful marriage; and had

168

carefully secluded her from the wildest of their young gallants. Of course, if they had been next in succession, the child would have gone down the waterfall to save any further trouble; but there was an intercepting branch of some honest family; and they being outlaws, would have a poor chance (though the law loves outlaws) against them. Only Lorna was of the stock; and Lorna they must marry. And what a triumph against the old Earl, for a cursed Doone to succeed him!

As for their outlawry, great robberies, and grand murders, the veriest child, nowadays, must know that money heals the whole of that. Even if they had murdered people of a good position, it would only cost about twice as much to prove their motives loyal. But they had never slain any man above, the rank of yeoman; and folk even said that my father was the highest of their victims; for the death of Lorna's mother, and brother, was never set to their account.

Pure pleasure it is to any man, to reflect upon all these things. How truly we discern clear justice, and how well we deal it! If any poor man steals a sheep, having ten children starving, and regarding it as mountain game (as a rich man does a hare), to the gallows with him. If a man of rank beats down a door, smites the owner upon the head, and honours the wife with attention, it is a thing to be grateful for, and to slouch smitten head the lower.

While we were full of all these things, and wondering what would happen next, or what we ought ourselves to do, another very important matter called for our attention. This was no less than Annie's marriage to the Squire Faggus. We had tried to put it off again; for in spite of all advantages, neither my mother, nor myself, had any real heart for it. Not that we dwelled upon Tom's short-comings, or rather perhaps his going too far, at the time when he worked the road so. All that was covered by the King's pardon, and universal respect of the neighbourhood. But our scruple was this — and the more we talked the more it grew upon us — that we both had great misgivings as to his future steadiness.

For it would be a thousand pities, we said, for a fine, well grown, and pretty maiden (such as our Annie was), useful too in so many ways, and lively, and warm-hearted, and mistress of £500, to throw herself away on a man with a kind of a turn for drinking. If that last were ever hinted, Annie would be most indignant, and ask, with cheeks as red as roses, who had ever seen Master Faggus any the worse for liquor indeed? Her own opinion was, in truth, that he took a great deal too little, after all his hard work, and hard riding, and coming over the hills to be insulted! And if ever it lay in her power, and with no one to grudge him his trumpery glass, she would see that poor Tom had the nourishment which his cough and his lungs required.

His lungs being quite as sound as mine, this matter was out of all argument; so mother and I looked at one another, as much as to say, "Let her go upstairs; she will cry, and come down more reasonable." And while she was gone, we used to say the same thing over and over again; but without perceiving a cure for it. And we almost always finished up with the following reflection, which sometimes came from mother's lips, and sometimes from my own: "Well, well, there is no telling. None can say how a man may alter, when he takes to matrimony. But if we could only make Annie promise to be a little firm with him!"

I fear that all this talk on our part only hurried matters forward, Annie being more determined every time we pitied her. And at last Tom Faggus came, and spoke, as if he were on the King's highroad, with a pistol at my head, and one at mother's. "No more fast and loose," he cried, "either one thing or the other. I love the maid, and she loves me; and we will have one another, either with your leave or without it. How many more times am I to dance over these vile hills, and leave my business, and get nothing more than a sigh or a kiss, and 'Tom, I must wait for mother'? You are famous for being straightforward, you Ridds. Just treat me as I would treat you, now."

I looked at my mother; for a glance from her would have sent Tom out of the window; but she checked me with her hand, and said, "You have some ground of complaint, sir; I will not deny it. Now I will be as straightforward with you as even a Ridd is supposed to be. My son and myself have all along disliked your marriage with Annie. Not for what you have been, so much as for what we fear you will be. Have patience, one moment, if you please. We do not fear your taking to the highway life again; for that you are too clever, no doubt, now that you have property. But we fear that you will take to drinking, and to squandering money. There are many examples of this around us; and we know what the fate of the wife is. It has been hard to tell you this, under our own roof, and with our own —— " Here mother hesitated.

"Spirits, and cider, and beer," I broke in; "out with it, like a Ridd, mother; as he will have all of it."

"Spirits, and cider, and beer," said mother very firmly after me; and then she gave way and said, "You know, Tom, you are welcome to every drop, and more of it."

Now Tom must have had a far sweeter temper than ever I could claim; for I should have thrust my glass away, and never taken another drop in the house where such a check had met me. But instead of that, Master Faggus replied with a pleasant smile:

"I know that I am welcome, good mother; and to prove it, I will have some more."

And thereupon he mixed himself another glass of hollands, with lemon and hot water, yet pouring it very delicately.

"Oh, I have been so miserable! — take a little more, Tom," said mother, handing the bottle.

"Yes, take a little more," I said; "you have mixed it over weak, Tom."

"If ever there was a sober man," cried Tom, complying with our request; "if ever there was in Christendom a man of perfect sobriety, that man is now before you. Shall we say tomorrow week, mother? It will suit your washing-day."

"How very thoughtful you are, Tom! Now John would never have thought of that, in spite of all his steadiness."

"Certainly not," I answered proudly; "when my time comes for Lorna, I shall not study Betty Muxworthy."

In this way the Squire got over us; and Farmer Nicholas Snowe was sent for, to counsel with mother about the matter, and to set his two daughters sewing.

When the time for the wedding came, there was such a stir and commotion as had never been known in the parish of Oare since my father's marriage. For Annie's beauty and kindliness had made her the pride of the neighbourhood; and the presents sent her, from all around, were enough to stock a shop with. Master Stickles, who now could walk, and who certainly owed his recovery, with the blessing of God, to Annie, presented her with a mighty Bible, silver-clasped, and very handsome, beating the parson's out and out, and for which he had sent to Taunton.

Even the common troopers, having tasted her cookery many times (to help out their poor rations), clubbed together, and must have given at least a week's pay apiece, to have turned out what they did for her. This was no less than a silver pot, well designed, but suited surely rather to the bridegroom's taste than bride's. In a word, everybody gave her things.

And now my Lorna came to me, with a spring of tears in appealing eyes — for she was still somewhat childish, or rather, I should say, more childish now than when she lived in misery — and she placed her little hands in mine, and she was half afraid to speak, and dropped her eyes for me to ask.

"What is it, little darling?" I asked, as I saw her breath come fast; for the smallest excitement moved her form.

"You don't think, John, you don't think, dear, that you could lend me any money?"

"All I have got," I answered; "how much do you want, dear heart?"

"I have been calculating; and I fear that I cannot do any good with less than ten pounds, John."

Here she looked up at me, with horror at the grandeur of the sum, and not knowing what I could think of it. But I kept my eyes from hers. "Ten pounds!" I said, in my deepest voice, on purpose to have it out in comfort, when she should be frightened; "what can you want with ten pounds, child?"

"That is my concern," said Lorna, plucking up her spirit at this; "when a lady asks for a loan, no gentleman pries into the cause of her asking it."

"That may be, as may be," I answered in a judicial manner: "ten pounds, or twenty, you shall have. But I must know the purport."

"Then that you never shall know, John. I am very sorry for asking you. It is not of the smallest consequence. Oh dear, no!" Herewith she was running away.

"Oh dear, yes!" I replied; "it is of very great consequence; and I understand the whole of it. You want to give that stupid Annie, who has lost you a hundred thousand pounds, and who is going to be married before us, dear — God only can tell why, being my younger sister — you want to give her a wedding present. And you shall do it, darling; because it is so good of you. Don't you know your title, love? How humble you are with us humble folk. You are Lady Lorna something, so far as I can make out yet; and you ought not even to speak to us. You will go away, and disdain us."

"If you please, talk not like that, John. I will have nothing to do with it, if it comes between you and me, John."

"You cannot help yourself," said I. And then she vowed that she could and would. And rank and birth were banished from between our lips in no time.

"What can I get her good enough? I am sure I do not know," she asked: "she has been so kind and good to me, and she is such a darling. How I shall miss her, to be sure! By the by, you seem to think, John, that I shall be rich some day."

"Of course you will. As rich as the French King who keeps ours. Would the Lord Chancellor trouble himself about you, if you were poor?"

"Then if I am rich, perhaps you would lend me twenty pounds, dear John. Ten pounds would be very mean for a wealthy person to give her."

To this I agreed, upon condition that I should make the purchase myself, whatever it might be. For nothing could be easier than to cheat Lorna about the cost, until time should come for her paying me. And this was better than to cheat her for the benefit of our family. For this end, and for many others, I set off to Dulverton, bearing more commissions, more messages, and more questions, than a man of thrice my memory might carry so far as the corner where the saw-pit is. And to make things worse, one girl, or other, would keep on running up to me, or even after me (when started), with something or other she had just thought of, which she could not possibly do without, and which I must be sure to remember, as the most important of the whole.

To my dear mother, who had partly outlived the exceeding value of trifles, the most important matter seemed to ensure Uncle Reuben's countenance and presence at the marriage. And if I succeeded in this, I might well forget all the maidens' trumpery. This she would have been wiser to tell me when they were out of hearing; for I left her to fight her own battle with them; and laughing at her predicament, promised to do the best I could for all, so far as my wits would go.

Uncle Reuben was not at home; but Ruth, who received me very kindly, although without any expressions of joy, was sure of his return in the afternoon, and persuaded me to wait for him. And by the time that I had finished all I could recollect of my orders, even with paper to help me, the old gentleman rode into the yard, and was more surprised than pleased to see me. But if he was surprised, I was more than that — I was utterly astonished at the change in his appearance since the last time I had seen him. From a hale, and rather heavy man, grey-haired, but plump, and ruddy, he was altered to a shrunken, wizened, trembling, and almost decrepit figure. Instead of curly and comely locks, grizzled indeed, but plentiful, he had only a few lank white hairs scattered and flattened upon his forehead. But the greatest change of all was in the expression of his eyes, which had been so keen, and restless, and bright, and a little sarcastic. Bright indeed they still were, but with a slow unhealthy lustre; their keenness was turned to perpetual outlook, their restlessness to a haggard want. As for the humour which once gleamed there (which people who fear it call sarcasm), it had been succeeded by stares of terror, and then mistrust, and shrinking. There was none of the interest in mankind, which is needful even for satire.

"Now what can this be!" thought I to myself: "has the old man lost all his property, or taken top much to strong waters?"

"Come inside, John Ridd," he said; "I will have a talk with you. It is cold out here: and it is too light. Come inside, John Ridd, boy."

I followed him into a little dark room, quite different from Ruth Huckaback's. It was closed from the shop by an old division of boarding, hung with tanned canvas; and the smell was very close and faint. Here there was a ledger-desk, and a couple of chairs, and a long-legged stool.

"Take the stool," said Uncle Reuben, showing me in very quietly; "it is fitter for your height, John, Wait a moment: there is no hurry."

Then he slipped out by another-door, and closing it quickly after him, told the foreman, and waiting-men, that the business of the day was done. They had better all go home at once; and he would see to the fastenings. Of course they were only too glad to go; but I wondered at his sending them, with at least two hours of daylight left.

However, that was no business of mine; and I waited and pondered whether fair Ruth ever came into this dirty room; and if so, how she kept her hands from it. For Annie would have had it upside down in about two minutes, and scrubbed, and brushed, and dusted, until it looked quite another place; and yet all this done without scolding and crossness; which are the curse of clean women, and ten times worse than the dustiest dust.

Uncle Ben came reeling in, not from any power of liquor, but because he was stiff from horse-back, and weak from work and worry.

"Let me be, John, let me be," he said, as I went to help him; "this is an unkid dreary place; but many a hundred of good gold Carolus has been turned in this place, John."

"Not a doubt about it, sir," I answered, in my loud and cheerful manner; "and many another hundred, sir; and may you long enjoy them!"

"My boy, do you wish me to die?" he asked, coming up close to my stool, and regarding me with a shrewd, though blear-eyed gaze; "many do. Do you, John?"

"Come," said I, "don't ask such nonsense. You know better than that, Uncle Ben. Or else, I am sorry for you. I want you to live as long as possible, for the sake of —— " Here I stopped.

"For the sake of what, John? I know it is not for my own sake. For the sake of what, my boy?"

"For the sake of Ruth," I answered; "if you must have all the truth. Who is to mind her when you are gone?"

"But if you knew that I had gold, or a manner of getting gold, far more than ever the sailors got out of the Spanish galleons, far more than ever was heard of; and the secret was to be yours, John; yours after me, and no other soul's; then you would wish me dead, John." Here he eyed me, as if a speck of dust in my eyes should not escape him.

"You are wrong, Uncle Ben; altogether wrong. For all the gold ever heard or dreamed of, not a wish would cross my heart to rob you of one day of life."

At last he moved his eyes from mine; but without any word, or sign, to show whether he believed or disbelieved. Then he went to a chair, and sat with his chin upon the ledger-desk; as if the effort of probing me had been too much for his weary brain. "Dreamed of? All the gold ever dreamed of! As if it were but a dream!" he muttered; and then he closed his eyes, to think.

"Good Uncle Reuben," I said to him, "you have been a long way to-day, sir. Let me go and get you a glass of good wine. Cousin Ruth knows where to find it."

"How do you know how far I have been?" he asked, with a vicious look at me. "And Cousin Ruth! You are very pat with my granddaughter's name, young man!"

"It would be hard upon me, sir, not to know my own cousin's name."

"Very well. Let that go by. You have behaved very badly to Ruth. She loves you; and you love her not."

At this I was so wholly amazed — not at the thing itself, I mean, but at his knowledge of it — that I could not say a single word; but looked, no doubt, very foolish.

"You may well be ashamed, young man," he cried, with some triumph over me; "you are the biggest of all fools, as well as a conceited coxcomb. What can you want more than Ruth? She is a little damsel truly; but finer men than you, John Ridd, with all your boasted strength and wrestling, have wedded smaller maidens. And as for quality, and value — bots! one inch of Ruth is worth all your seven feet put together."

Now I am not seven feet high; nor ever was six feet eight inches, in my very prime of life; and nothing vexes me so much as to make me out a giant, and above human sympathy, and human scale of weakness. It cost me hard to hold my tongue; which luckily is not in proportion to my stature. And only for Ruth's sake I held it. But Uncle Ben (being old and worn) was vexed by not having any answer, almost as much as a woman is.

"You want me to go on," he continued, with a look of spite at me," about my poor Ruth's love for you, to feed your cursed vanity. Because a set of asses call you the finest man in England; there is no maid (I suppose) who is not in love with you. I believe you are as deep as you are long, John Ridd. Shall I ever get to the bottom of your character?"

This was a little too much for me. Any insult I could take (with good will) from a white-haired man, and one who was my relative; unless it touched my love for Lorna, or my conscious modesty. Now both of these were touched to the quick by the sentences of the old gentleman. Therefore, without a word, I went; only making a bow to him.

But women, who are (beyond all doubt) the mothers of all mischief, also nurse that babe to sleep, when he is too noisy. And there was Ruth, as I took my horse (with a trunk of frippery on him), poor little Ruth was at the bridle, and rusting all the knops of our town-going harness with tears.

"Good-bye, dear," I said, as she bent her head away from me; "shall I put you up on the saddle, dear?"

"Cousin Ridd, you may take it lightly," said Ruth, turning full upon me, "and very likely you are right, according to your nature" — this was the only cutting thing the little soul ever said to me — "but oh, Cousin Ridd, you have no idea of the pain you will leave behind you."

"How can that be so, Ruth, when I am as good as ordered to be off the premises?"

"In the first place, Cousin Ridd, grandfather will be angry with himself, for having so ill-used you. And now he is so weak and poorly, that he is always repenting. In the next place, I shall scold him first, until he admits his sorrow; and when he has admitted it, I shall scold myself for scolding him. And then he will come round again, and think that I was hard on him; and end perhaps by hating you; for he is like a woman now, John."

That last little touch of self-knowledge in Ruth, which she delivered with a gleam of some secret pleasantry, made me stop and look closely at her; but she pretended not to know it. "There is something in this child," I thought, "very different from other girls. What it is I cannot tell; for one very seldom gets at it."

At any rate the upshot was that the good horse went back to stable, and had another feed of corn; while my wrath sank within me. There are two things, according to my experience (which may not hold with another man), fitted beyond any others to take hot tempers out of us. The first is to see our favourite creatures feeding, and licking up their food, and happily snuffling over it, yet sparing time to be grateful, and showing taste and perception; the other is to go gardening boldly, in the spring of the year, without any misgiving about it, and hoping the utmost of everything. If there be a third anodyne, approaching these two in power, it is to smoke good tobacco well, and watch the setting of the moon; and if this should only be over the sea, the result is irresistible.

Master Huckaback showed no especial signs of joy at my return; but received me with a little grunt, which appeared to me to mean, "Ah, I thought he would hardly be fool enough to go." I told him how sorry I was for having in some way offended him; and he answered that I did well to grieve for one at least of my offences. To this I made no reply, as behoves a man dealing with cross and fractious people: and presently he became better-tempered, and sent little Ruth for a bottle of wine. She gave me a beautiful smile of thanks for my forbearance, as she passed; and I knew by her manner that she would bring the best bottle in all the cellar.

As I had but little time to spare (although the days were long and light), we were forced to take our wine with promptitude and rapidity; and whether this loosened my uncle's tongue, or whether he meant beforehand to speak, is now almost uncertain. But true it is that he brought his chair very near to mine, after three or four glasses, and sent Ruth away upon some errand which seemed of small importance. At this I was vexed; for the room always looked so different without her.

"Come, Jack," he said, "here's your health, young fellow, and a good and obedient wife to you. Not that your wife will ever obey you, though; you are much too easy-tempered. Even a bitter and stormy woman might live in peace with you, Jack. But never you give her the chance to try. Marry some sweet little thing if you can. If not, don't marry any. Ah, we have the maid to suit you, my lad, in this old town of Dulverton."

"Have you so, sir? but perhaps the maid might have no desire to suit me."

"That you may take my word she has. The colour of this wine will prove it. The sly little hussy has been to the cobwebbed arch of the cellar, where she has no right to go, for anyone under a magistrate. However, I am glad to see it; and we will not spare it, John. After my time, somebody, whoever marries little Ruth, will find some rare wine there, I trow, and perhaps not know the difference."

Thinking of this, the old man sighed, and expected me to sigh after him. But a sigh is not (like a yawn) infectious; and we are all more prone to be sent to sleep, than to sorrow, by one another. Not but what a sigh sometimes may make us think of sighing.

"Well, sir," cried I, in my sprightliest manner, which rouses up most people, "here's to your health and dear little Ruth's; and may you live to knock off the cobwebs from every bottle in under the arch! Uncle Reuben, your life and health, sir!"

With that, I took my glass thoughtfully, for it was wondrous good; and Uncle Ben was pleased to see me dwelling pleasantly on the subject, with parenthesis, and self-commune, and oral judgment unpronounced, though smacking of fine decision. "Curia vult advisari," as the lawyers say; which means, "Let us have another glass, and then we can think about it."

"Come now, John," said Uncle Ben, laying his wrinkled hand on my knee, when he saw that none could heed us, "I know that you have a sneaking fondness for my grandchild Ruth. Don't interrupt me now; you have; and to deny it will only provoke me."

"I do like Ruth, sir," I said boldly, for fear of misunderstanding; "but I do not love her."

"Very well; that makes no difference. Liking may very soon be loving (as some people call it), when the maid has money to help her."

"But if there be, as there is in my case ―― "

"Once for all, John, not a word. I do not attempt to lead you into any engagement with little Ruth; neither will I blame you (though I may be disappointed) if no such engagement should ever be. But whether you will have my grandchild, or whether you will not ― and such a chance is rarely offered to a fellow of your standing" ― Uncle Ben despised all farmers ― "in any case I have at last resolved to let you know my secret; and for two good reasons. The first is, that it wears me out to dwell upon it, all alone: and the second is, that I can trust you to fulfil a promise. Moreover you are my next of kin, except among the womenkind; and you are just the man I want to help me in my enterprise."

"And I will help you, sir," I answered, fearing some conspiracy, "in anything that is true, and loyal, and according to the laws of the realm."

"Ha, ha!" cried the old man, laughing until his eyes ran over, and spreading out his skinny hands upon his shining breeches, "thou hast gone the same fool's track as the rest; even as spy Stickles went, and all his precious troopers. Landing of arms at Glenthorne and Lynmouth, waggons escorted across the moor, sounds of metal, and booming noises! Ah, but we managed it cleverly, to cheat even those so near to us. Disaffection at Taunton, signs of insurrection at Dulverton, revolutionary tanner at Dunster! We set it all abroad, right well! And not even you to suspect our work; though we thought at one time that you watched us. Now who, do you suppose, is at the bottom of all this Exmoor insurgency, all this western rebellion — not that I say there is none, mind — but who is at the bottom of it?"

"Either Mother Melldrum," said I, being now a little angry, "or else old Nick himself."

"Nay, old Uncle Reuben!" Saying this, Master Huckaback cast back his coat, and stood up, and made the most of himself.

"Well!" cried I, being now quite come to the limits of my intellect, "then after all Captain Stickles was right in calling you a rebel, sir!"

"Of course he was: could so keen a man be wrong, about an old fool like me? But come, and see our rebellion, John. I will trust you now with everything. I will take no oath from you; only your word to keep silence; and most of all from your mother."

"I will give you my word," I said, although liking not such pledges; which make a man think before he speaks in ordinary company, against his usual practice. However, I was now so curious, that I thought of nothing else; and scarcely could believe at all that Uncle Ben was quite right in his head.

"Take another glass of wine, my son," he cried, with a cheerful countenance, which made him look more than ten years younger; "you shall come into partnership with me; your strength will save us two horses, and we always fear the horse work. Come and see our rebellion, my boy! you are a made man from to-night."

"But where am I to come in, and see it? Where am I to find it, sir?"

"Meet me," he answered, yet closing his hands and wrinkling with doubt his forehead; "come alone, of course; and meet me at the Wizard's Slough, at ten to-morrow morning."

CHAPTER LVIII

Master Huckaback's Secret

Knowing Master Huckaback to be a man of his word, as well as one who would have others so, I was careful to be in good time the next morning, by the side of the Wizard's Slough. I am free to admit that the name of the place bore a feeling of uneasiness, and a love of distance, in some measure to my heart. But I did my best not to think of this: only I thought it a wise precaution, and due for the sake of my mother and Lorna, to load my gun with a dozen slugs made from the lead of the old church-porch, laid by, long since, against witchcraft.

I am well aware that some people now begin to doubt about witchcraft; or at any rate feign to do so, being desirous to disbelieve whatever they are afraid of. This spirit is growing too common among us, and will end (unless we put a stop to it) in the destruction of all religion. And as regards witchcraft, a man is bound either to believe in it, or to disbelieve the Bible. For even in the New Testament, discarding many things of the Old, such as sacrifices, and sabbath, and fasting, and other miseries, witchcraft is clearly spoken of as a thing that must continue; that the Evil One be not utterly robbed of his vested interests. Hence let no one tell me that witchcraft is done away with; for I will meet him with St Paul, than whom no more religious man, and few less superstitious, can be found in all the Bible.

Feeling these things more in those days than I feel them now, I fetched a goodish compass round, by the way of the Cloven rocks, rather than cross Black Barrow Down, in a reckless and unholy manner. There were several spots, upon that Down, cursed, and smitten, and blasted, as if thunderbolts had fallen there, and Satan sat to keep them warm. At any rate, it was good (as every one acknowledged) not to wander there too much: even with a doctor of divinity upon one arm, and of medicine upon the other.

Therefore I, being all alone, and on foot (as seemed the wisest), preferred a course of roundabout; and starting about eight o'clock, without mentioning my business, arrived at the mouth of the deep descent, such as John Fry described it. Now this (though I have not spoken of it) was not my first time of being there. For, although I could not bring myself to spy upon Uncle Reuben, as John Fry had done, yet I thought it no ill manners, after he had left our house, to have a look at the famous place, where the malefactor came to life, at least in John's opinion. At that time, however, I saw nothing, except the great ugly black morass, with the grisly reeds around it; and I did not care to go very near it, much less to pry on the further side.

Now, on the other hand, I was bent to get at the very bottom of this mystery (if there were any), having less fear of witch or wizard, with a man of Uncle Reuben's wealth to take my part, and see me through. So I rattled the ramrod down my gun, just to know if the charge were right, after so much walking; and finding it full six inches deep, as I like to have it, went boldly down the steep gorge of rock, with a firm resolve to shoot any witch, unless it were good Mother Melldrum. Nevertheless, to my surprise, all was quiet, and fair to look at, in the decline of the narrow way; with great stalked ferns coming forth, like trees, yet hanging like cobwebs over one. And along one side, a little spring was getting rid of its waters. Any man might stop and think; or he might go on and think; and in either case, there was none to say that he was making a fool of himself.

When I came to the foot of this ravine, and over against the great black slough, there was no sign of Master Huckaback, nor of any other living man, except myself, in the silence. Therefore I sat in a niche of rock, gazing at the slough, and pondering the old tradition about it.

They say that, in the ancient times, a mighty necromancer lived in the wilderness of Exmoor. Here, by spell and incantation, he built himself a strong high palace, eight-sided like a spider's web, and standing on a central steep; so that neither man nor beast could cross the moor without his knowledge. If he wished to rob and slay a traveller, or to have wild ox, or stag for food, he had nothing more to do than sit at one of his eight windows, and point his unholy book at him. Any moving creature, at which that book was pointed, must obey the call, and come from whatever distance, if sighted once by the wizard.

This was a bad condition of things, and all the country groaned under it; and Exmoor (although the most honest place that a man could wish to live in) was beginning to get a bad reputation, and all through that vile wizard. No man durst even go to steal a sheep, or a pony, or so much as a deer for dinner, lest he should be brought to book by a far bigger rogue than he was. And this went on for many years; though they prayed to God to abate it. But at last, when the wizard was getting fat, and haughty upon his high stomach, a mighty deliverance came to Exmoor, and a warning, and a memory. For one day the sorcerer gazed from his window facing the south-east of the compass; and he yawned, having killed so many men, that now he was weary of it.

" 'Ifackins," he cried, or some such oath, both profane and uncomely, "I see a man on the verge of the sky-line, going along laboriously. A pilgrim, I trow, or some such fool, with the nails of his boots inside them. Too thin to be worth eating: but I will have him for the fun of the thing: and most of those saints have got money."

With these words, he stretched forth his legs on a stool, and pointed the book of heathenish spells, back upwards, at the pilgrim. Now this good pilgrim was plodding along, soberly and religiously, with a pound of flints in either boot, and not an ounce of meat inside him. He felt the spell of the wicked book, but only as a horse might feel a "gee-wug!" addressed to him. It was in the power of this good man, either to go on, or turn aside, and see out the wizard's meaning. And for a moment he halted and stood, like one in two minds about a thing. Then the wizard clapped one cover to, in a jocular and insulting manner; and the sound of it came to the pilgrim's ear, about five miles in the distance, like a great gun fired at him.

"By our Lady," he cried, "I must see to this; although my poor feet have no skin below them. I will teach this heathen miscreant, how to scoff at Glastonbury."

Thereupon he turned his course, and ploughed along through the moors and bogs, towards the eight-sided palace. The wizard sat on his chair of comfort; and with the rankest contempt observed the holy man ploughing towards him. "He has something good in his wallet, I trow," said the black thief to himself; "these fellows get always the pick of the wine, and the best of a woman's money." Then he cried, "Come in, come in, good sir," as he always did to every one.

"Bad sir, I will not come in," said the pilgrim; "neither shall you come out again. Here are the bones of all you have slain; and here shall your own bones be."

"Hurry me not," cried the sorcerer; "that is a thing to think about. How many miles hast thou travelled this day?"

But the pilgrim was too wide awake; for if he had spoken of any number bearing no cross upon it, the necromancer would have had him, like a ball at bando-play. Therefore he answered, as truly as need be, "By the grace of our Lady, nine."

Now nine is the crossest of all cross numbers, and full to the lip of all crotchets. So the wizard staggered back, and thought, and inquired again with bravery, "Where can you find a man and wife, one going up-hill, and one going down, and not a word spoken between them?"

"In a cucumber plant," said the modest saint; blushing even to think of it, and the wizard knew he was done for.

"You have tried me with ungodly questions," continued the honest pilgrim, with one hand still over his eyes, as he thought of the feminine cucumber; "and now I will ask you a pure one: To whom of mankind have you ever done good, since God saw fit to make you?"

The wizard thought, but could quote no one: and he looked at the saint, and the saint at him: and both their hearts were trembling. "Can you tell of only one?" asked the saint, pointing a piece of the true cross at him, hoping he might cling to it: "even a little child will do: try to think of some one."

The earth was rocking beneath their feet, and the palace windows darkened on them, with a tint of blood; for now the saint was come inside, hoping to save the wizard.

"If I must tell the pure truth," said the wizard, looking up at the arches of his windows, "I can tell of only one to whom I ever have done good."

"One will do; one is quite enough: be quick before the ground opens. The name of one — and this cross will save you. Lay your thumb on the end of it."

"Nay, that I cannot do, great saint. The devil have mercy upon me!"

All this while the palace was sinking, and blackness coming over them.

"Thou hast all but done for thyself," said the saint, with a glory burning round his head; "by that last invocation. Yet give us the name of the one, my friend; if one there be, it will save thee, with the cross upon thy breast. All is crashing round us; dear brother, who is that one?"

"My own self," cried the wretched wizard.

"Then there is no help for thee." And with that, the honest saint went upward, and the wizard, and all his palace, and even the crag that bore it, sank to the bowels of the earth; and over them was nothing left, except a black bog fringed with reed of the tint of the wizard's whiskers. The saint, however, was all right, after sleeping off the excitement; and he founded a chapel some three miles westward; and there he lies with his holy relic; and thither in after ages came (as we all come home at last) both my Lorna's Aunt Sabina, and her guardian, Sir Ensor Doone.

While yet I dwelled upon this strange story, wondering if it all were true, and why such things do not happen now, a man on horseback appeared as suddenly as if he had risen out of the earth, on the other side of the great black slough. At first I was a little scared, my mind being in the tune for wonders; but presently the white hair, whiter from the blackness of the bog between us, showed me that it was Uncle Reuben come to look for me, that way. Then I left my chair of rock, and waved my hat, and shouted to him, and the sound of my voice among the crags and lonely corners frightened me.

Old Master Huckaback made no answer, but (so far as I could guess) beckoned me to come to him. There was just room between the fringe of reed and the belt of rock around it, for a man going very carefully to escape that horrible pit-hole. And so I went round to the other side, and there found open space enough, with stunted bushes, and starveling trees, and straggling tufts of rushes.

"You fool, you are frightened," said Uncle Ben, as he looked in my face after shaking hands: "I want a young man of steadfast courage, as well as of strength and silence. And after what I heard of the battle at Glen Doone, I thought I might trust you for courage."

"So you may," said I, "wherever I see mine enemy; but not where witch and wizard be."

"Tush, great fool!" cried Master Huckaback; "the only witch, or wizard, here is the one that bewitcheth all men. Now fasten up my horse, John Ridd, and not too near the slough, lad. Ah, we have chosen our entrance wisely. Two good horsemen, and their horses, coming hither to spy us out, are gone mining on their own account (and their last account it is) down this good wizard's bog-hole."

With these words Uncle Reuben clutched the mane of his horse, and came down, as a man does when his legs are old; and as I myself begin to do, at this time of writing. I offered a hand, but he was vexed, and would have nought to do with it.

"Now follow me, step for step," he said, when I had tethered his horse to a tree; "the ground is not death (like the wizard's hole), but many parts are treacherous. I know it well by this time."

Without any more ado, he led me, in and out the marshy places, to a great round hole or shaft, bratticed up with timber. I never had seen the like before, and wondered how they could want a well, with so much water on every side. Around the mouth were a few little heaps of stuff unused to the daylight; and I thought at once of the tales I had heard concerning mines in Cornwall, and the silver cup at Combe-Martin, sent to the Queen Elizabeth.

"We had a tree across it, John," said Uncle Reuben, smiling grimly at my sudden shrink from it: "but some rogue came spying here, just as one of our men went up. He was frightened half out of his life, I believe, and never ventured to come again. But we put the blame of that upon you. And I see that we were wrong, John." Here he looked at me with keen eyes, though weak.

"You were altogether wrong," I answered. "Am I mean enough to spy upon anyone dwelling with us? And more than that, Uncle Reuben, it was mean of you to suppose it."

"All ideas are different," replied the old man to my heat, like a little worn-out rill running down a smithy; "you with your strength and youth, and all that, are inclined to be romantic. I take things as I have known them, going on for seventy years. Now will you come and meet the wizard, or does your courage fail you?"

"My courage must be none," said I, "if I would not go where you go, sir."

He said no more, but signed to me to lift a heavy wooden corb, with an iron loop across it, and sunk in a little pit of earth, a yard or so from the mouth of the shaft. I raised it, and by his direction dropped it into the throat of the shaft, where it hung and shook from a great cross-beam laid at the level of the earth. A very stout thick rope was fastened to the handle of the corb, and ran across a pulley hanging from the centre of the beam, and thence out of sight in the nether places.

"I will first descend," he said; "your weight is too great for safety. When the bucket comes up again, follow me, if your heart is good."

Then he whistled down, with a quick sharp noise, and a whistle from below replied; and he clomb into the vehicle, and the rope ran through the pulley, and Uncle Ben went merrily down, and was out of sight before I had time to think of him.

Now being left on the bank like that, and in full sight of the goodly heaven, I wrestled hard with my flesh and blood, about going down into the pit-hole. And but for the pale shame of the thing, that a white-headed man should adventure so, and green youth doubt about it, never could I have made up my mind; for I do love air and heaven. However, at last up came the bucket; and with a short sad prayer, I went into whatever might happen.

My teeth would chatter, do all I could; but the strength of my arms was with me; and by them I held on the grimy rope, and so eased the foot of the corb, which threatened to go away fathoms under me. Of course I should still have been safe enough, being like an egg in an egg-cup, too big to care for the bottom; still I wished that all should be done in good order, without excitement.

The scoopings of the side grew black, and the patch of sky above more blue, as, with many thoughts of Lorna, a long way underground I sank. Then I was fetched up at the bottom, with a jerk and rattle; and but for holding by the rope so, must have tumbled over. Two great torches of bale-resin showed me all the darkness, one being held by Uncle Ben and the other by a short square man with a face which seemed well known to me.

"Hail to the world of gold, John Ridd," said Master Huckaback, smiling in the old dry manner: "bigger coward never came down the shaft, now did he, Carfax?"

"They be all alike," said the short square man, "fust time as they doos it."

"May I go to heaven," I cried, "which is a thing quite out of sight" — for I always have a vein of humour, too small to be followed by anyone — "if ever again of my own accord I go so far away from it!" Uncle Ben grinned less at this than at the way I knocked my shin in getting out of the bucket; and as for Master Carfax, he would not even deign to smile. And he seemed to look upon my entrance as an interloping.

For my part, I had nought to do, after rubbing my bruised leg, except to look about me, so far as the dulness of light would help. And herein I seemed, like a mouse in a trap, able no more than to run to and fro, and knock himself, and stare at things. For here was a little channel grooved with posts on either side of it, and ending with a heap of darkness, whence the sight came back again; and there was a scooped place, like a funnel, but pouring only to darkness. So I waited for somebody to speak first, not seeing my way to anything.

"You seem to be disappointed, John," said Uncle Reuben, looking blue by the light of the flambeaux: "did you expect to see the roof of gold, and the sides of gold, and the floor of gold, John Ridd?"

"Ha, ha!" cried Master Carfax: "I reckon her did; no doubt her did."

"You are wrong," I replied: "but I did expect to see something better than dirt and darkness."

"Come on then, my lad; and we will show you something better. We want your great arm on here, for a job that has beaten the whole of us."

With these words, Uncle Ben led the way along a narrow passage, roofed with rock, and floored with slate-coloured shale and shingle, and winding in and out, until we stopped at a great stone block or boulder, lying across the floor, and as large as my mother's best oaken wardrobe. Beside it were several sledge-hammers, some battered, and some with broken helves.

"Thou great villain!" cried Uncle Ben, giving the boulder a little kick; "I believe thy time has come at last. Now, John, give us a sample of the things they tell of thee. Take the biggest of them sledge-hammers and crack this rogue in two for us. We have tried at him for a fortnight, and he is a nut worth cracking. But we have no man who can swing that hammer, though all in the mine have handled it."

"I will do my very best," said I, pulling on my coat and waistcoat, as if I were going to wrestle: "but I fear he will prove too tough for me."

"Ay, that her wull," grunted Master Carfax; "lack'th a Carnishman, and a beg one too, not a little charp such as I be. There be no man outside Carnwall, as can crack that boolder."

"Bless my heart," I answered; "but I know something of you, my friend, or at any rate of your family. Well, I have beaten most of your Cornish men, though not my place to talk of it. But mind, if I crack this rock for you, I must have some of the gold inside it."

"Dost think to see the gold come tumbling out, like the kernel of a nut, thou zany?" asked Uncle Reuben pettishly: "now wilt thou crack it, or wilt thou not? For I believe thou canst do it, though only a lad of Somerset."

Uncle Reuben showed, by saying this, and by a glance at Carfax, that he was proud of his county, and would be disappointed for it, if I failed to crack the boulder. So I begged him to stoop his torch a little, that I might examine my subject. To me there appeared to be nothing at all remarkable about it, except that it sparkled here and there, when the flash of the flame fell upon it. A great obstinate, oblong, sullen stone: how could it be worth the breaking, except for making roads with?

Nevertheless I took up the hammer, and swinging it far behind my head, fetched it down, with all my power, upon the middle of the rock. The roof above rang mightily, and the echo went down delven galleries, so that all the miners flocked to know what might be doing. But Master Carfax only smiled, although the blow shook him where he stood, for behold the stone was still unbroken, and as firm as ever. Then I smote it again, with no better fortune, and Uncle Ben looked vexed and angry, but all the miners grinned with triumph.

"This little tool is too light," I cried; "one of you give me a piece of strong cord."

Then I took two more of the weightiest hammers, and lashed them fast to the back of mine, not so as to strike, but to burden the fall. Having made this firm, and with room to grasp the handle of the largest one only — for the helves of the others were shorter — I smiled at Uncle Ben, and whirled the mighty implement round my head, just to try whether I could manage it. Upon that, the miners gave a cheer, being honest men, and desirous of seeing fair play between this "shameless stone" (as Dan Homer calls it) and me with my hammer hammering.

Then I swung me on high, to the swing of the sledge, as a thresher bends back to the rise of his flail, and with all my power descending delivered the ponderous onset. Crashing and crushed the great stone fell over, and threads of sparkling gold appeared in the jagged sides of the breakage.

"How now, Simon Carfax?" cried Uncle Ben triumphantly; "wilt thou find a man in Cornwall can do the like of that?"

"Ay, and more," he answered: "however, it be pretty fair for a lad of these outlandish parts. Get your rollers, my lads, and lead it to the crushing engine."

I was glad to have been of some service to them: for it seems that this great boulder had been too large to be drawn along the gallery, and too hard to crack. But now they moved it very easily, taking piece by piece, and carefully picking up the fragments.

"Thou hast done us a good turn, my lad," said Uncle Reuben, as the others passed out of sight at the corner; "and now I will show thee the bottom of a very wondrous mystery. But we must not do it more than once, for the time of day is the wrong one."

The whole affair being a mystery to me, and far beyond my understanding, I followed him softly, without a word, yet thinking very heavily, and longing to be above ground again. He led me through small passages, to a hollow place near the descending-shaft, where I saw a most extraordinary monster fitted up. In form it was like a great coffee-mill, such as I had seen in London, only a thousand times larger, and with a heavy windlass to work it.

"Put in a barrow-load of the smoulder," said Uncle Ben to Carfax; "and let them work the crank, for John to understand a thing or two."

"At this time of day!" cried Simon Carfax; "and the watching as has been o' late!"

However, he did it without more remonstrance; pouring into the scuttle at the top of the machine about a basketful of broken rock; and then a dozen men went to the wheel, and forced it round, as sailors do. Upon that such a hideous noise arose, as I never should have believed any creature capable of making: and I ran to the well of the mine for air, and to ease my ears, if possible.

"Enough, enough!" shouted Uncle Ben, by the time I was nearly deafened; "we will digest our goodly boulder, after the devil is come abroad for his evening work. Now, John, not a word about what you have learned; but henceforth you will not be frightened by the noise we make at dusk."

I could not deny but what this was very clever management. If they could not keep the echoes of the upper air from moving, the wisest plan was to open their valves during the discouragement of the falling evening; when folk would rather be driven away, than drawn into the wilds and quagmires, by a sound so deep and awful coming through the darkness.

CHAPTER LIX

Lorna Gone Away

Although there are very ancient tales of gold being found upon Exmoor, in lumps and solid hummocks, and of men who slew one another for it, this deep digging and great labour seemed to me a dangerous and unholy enterprise. And Master Huckaback confessed that, up to the present time, his two partners and himself (for they proved to be three adventurers) had put into the earth more gold than they had taken out of it. Nevertheless he felt quite sure that it must in a very short time succeed, and pay them back an hundredfold; and he pressed me with great earnestness to join them, and work there as much as I could, without moving my mother's suspicions. I asked him how they had managed so long to carry on, without discovery; and he said that this was partly through the wildness of the neighbourhood, and the legends that frightened people of a superstitious turn; partly through their own great caution, and manner of fetching both supplies and implements by night; but most of all, they had to thank the troubles of the period, the suspicions of rebellion, and the terror of the Doones, which (like the wizard I was speaking of) kept folk from being too inquisitive where they had no business. The slough, moreover, had helped them well, both by making their access dark, and yet more by swallowing up and concealing all that was cast from the mouth of the pit. Once, before the attack on Glen Doone, they had a narrow escape from the King's Commissioner: for Captain Stickles, having heard no doubt the story of John Fry, went with half a dozen troopers, on purpose to search the neighbourhood. Now if he had ridden alone, most likely he would have discovered everything; but he feared to venture so, having suspicion of a trap. Coming as they did in company, all mounted and conspicuous, the watchman (who was posted now on the top of the hill, almost every day, since John Fry's appearance) could not help espying them, miles distant, over the moorland. He watched them under the shade of his hand, and presently ran down the hill, and raised a great commotion. Then Simon Carfax and all his men came up and made things natural, removing every sign of work; and finally, sinking underground, drew across the mouth of the pit a hurdle thatched with sedge and heather. Only Simon himself was left behind, ensconced in a hole of the crags, to observe the doings of the enemy.

Captain Stickles rode very bravely, with all his men clattering after him, down the rocky pass, and even to the margin of the slough. And there they stopped, and held council; for it was a perilous thing to risk the passage upon horseback between the treacherous brink and the cliff, unless one knew it thoroughly. Stickles, however, and one follower, carefully felt their way along, having their horses well in hand, and bearing a rope to draw them out, in case of being foundered. Then they spurred across the rough boggy land further away than the shaft was. Here the ground lay jagged and shaggy, wrought up with high tufts of reed, or scragged with stunted brushwood. And between the ups and downs (which met anybody anyhow) green covered places tempted the foot, and black bog-holes discouraged it. It is not to be marvelled at that amid such place as this, for the first time visited, the horses were a little skeary; and their riders partook of the feeling as all good riders do. In and out the tufts they went, with their eyes dilating; wishing to be out of harm, if conscience were but satisfied. And of this tufty flaggy ground, pocked with bogs and boglets, one especial nature is that it will not hold impressions.

Seeing thus no track of men, nor anything but marshwork, and stormwork, and of the seasons, these two honest men rode back, and were glad to do so. For above them hung the mountains, cowled with fog, and seamed with storm; and around them desolation; and below their feet the grave. Hence they went with all good will; and vowed for ever afterwards that fear of a simple place like that was only too ridiculous. So they all rode home with mutual praises, and their courage well-approved; and the only result of the expedition was to confirm John Fry's repute as a bigger liar than ever.

Now I had enough of that underground work, as before related, to last me for a year to come; neither would I, for sake of gold, have ever stepped into that bucket of my own good will again. But when I told Lorna — whom I could trust in any matter of secrecy, as if she had never been a woman — all about my great descent, and the honeycombing of the earth, and the mournful noise at eventide, when the gold was under the crusher, and bewailing the mischief it must do, then Lorna's chief desire was to know more about Simon Carfax.

"It must be our Gwenny's father," she cried; "the man who disappeared underground, and whom she has ever been seeking. How grieved the poor little thing will be, if it should turn out, after all, that he left his child on purpose! I can hardly believe it; can you, John?"

"Well," I replied; "all men are wicked, more or less, to some extent: and no man may say otherwise."

For I did not wish to commit myself to an opinion about Simon, lest I might be wrong, and Lorna think less of my judgment.

But being resolved to seek this out, and do a good turn, if I could, to Gwenny, who had done me many a good one, I begged my Lorna to say not a word of this matter to the handmaiden, until I had further searched it out. And to carry out this resolve, I went again to the place of business, where they were grinding gold as freely as an apothecary at his pills.

Having now true right of entrance, and being known to the watchman, and regarded (since I cracked the boulder) as one who could pay his footing, and perhaps would be the master, when Uncle Ben should be choked with money, I found the corb sent up for me rather sooner than I wished it. For the smell of the places underground, and the way men's eyes come out of them, with links and brands, and flambeaux, instead of God's light to look at, were to me a point of caution, rather than of pleasure.

No doubt but that some men enjoy it, being born, like worms, to dig and to live in their own scoopings. Yet even the worms come up sometimes, after a good soft shower of rain, and hold discourse with one another; whereas these men, and the horses let down, come above ground never.

And the changing of the sky is half the change our nature calls for. Earth we have, and all its produce (moving from the first appearance, and the hope with infant's eyes, through the bloom of beauty's promise, to the rich and bright fulfilment, and the falling back to rest); sea we have (with all its wonder shed on eyes, and ears, and heart; and the thought of something more) — but without the sky to look at, what would earth, and sea, and even our own selves, be to us?

Do we look at earth with hope? Yes, for victuals only. Do we look at sea with hope? Yes, that we may escape it. At the sky alone (though questioned with the doubts of sunshine, or scattered with uncertain stars), at the sky alone we look, with pure hope, and with memory.

Hence it always hurt my feelings when I got into that bucket, with my small clothes turned up over, and a kerchief round my hat. But knowing that my purpose was sound, and my motives pure, I let the sky grow to a little blue hole, and then to nothing over me. At the bottom Master Carfax met me, being captain of the mine, and desirous to know my business. He wore a loose sack round his shoulders, and his beard was two feet long.

"My business is to speak with you," I answered rather sternly; for this man, who was nothing more than Uncle Reuben's servant, had carried things too far with me, showing no respect whatever; and though I do not care for much, I liked to receive a little, even in my early days.

"Coom into the muck-hole, then," was his gracious answer; and he led me into a filthy cell, where the miners changed their jackets.

"Simon Carfax," I began, with a manner to discourage him; "I fear you are a shallow fellow, and not worth my trouble."

"Then don't take it," he replied; "I want no man's trouble."

"For your sake I would not," I answered; "but for your daughter's sake I will: the daughter whom you left to starve so pitifully in the wilderness."

The man stared at me with his pale grey eyes, whose colour was lost from candle-light; and his voice as well as his body shook, while he cried:

"It is a lie, man. No daughter and no son have I. Nor was ever child of mine left to starve in the wilderness. You are too big for me to tackle, and that makes you a coward for saying it." His hands were playing with a pickaxe-helve, as if he longed to have me under it.

"Perhaps I have wronged you, Simon," I answered very softly; for the sweat upon his forehead shone in the smoky torchlight: "if I have, I crave your pardon. But did you not bring up from Cornwall a little maid named 'Gwenny,' and supposed to be your daughter?"

"Ay, and she was my daughter, my last and only child of five; and for her I would give this mine, and all the gold will ever come from it."

"You shall have her, without either mine or gold; if you only prove to me that you did not abandon her."

"Abandon her! I abandon Gwenny!" he cried, with such a rage of scorn, that I at once believed him. "They told me she was dead, and crushed, and buried in the drift here; and half my heart died with her. The Almighty blast their mining-work, if the scoundrels lied to me!"

"The scoundrels must have lied to you," I answered, with a spirit fired by his heat and fury: "the maid is living, and with us. Come up; and you shall see her."

"Rig the bucket," he shouted out along the echoing gallery; and then he fell against the wall, and through the grimy sack I saw the heaving of his breast, as I have seen my opponent's chest, in a long hard bout of wrestling. For my part, I could do no more than hold my tongue, and look at him.

Without another word, we rose to the level of the moors and mires; neither would Master Carfax speak, as I led him across the barrows. In this he was welcome to his own way, for I do love silence; so little harm can come of it. And though Gwenny was no beauty, her father might be fond of her.

So I put him in the cow-house (not to frighten the little maid), and the folding shutters over him, such as we used at the beestings; and he listened to my voice outside, and held on, and preserved himself. For now he would have scooped the earth, as cattle do at yearning-time, and as meekly and as patiently, to have his child restored to him. Not to make long tale of it — for this thing is beyond me, through want of true experience — I went and fetched his Gwenny forth from the back kitchen, where she was fighting, as usual, with our Betty.

"Come along, you little Vick," I said, for so we called her; "I have a message to you, Gwenny, from the Lord in heaven."

"Don't 'ee talk about He," she answered: "Her have long forgotten me."

"That He has never done, you stupid. Come, and see who is in the cow-house."

Gwenny knew; she knew in a moment. Looking into my eyes, she knew; and hanging back from me to sigh, she knew it even better.

She had not much elegance of emotion, being flat and square all over; but none the less for that her heart came quick, and her words came slowly.

"Oh, Jan, you are too good to cheat me. Is it joke you are putting upon me?"

I answered her with a gaze alone; and she tucked up her clothes and followed me, because the road was dirty. Then I opened the door just wide enough for the child to go to her father; and left those two to have it out, as might be most natural. And they took a long time about it.

Meanwhile I needs must go and tell my Lorna all the matter; and her joy was almost as great as if she herself had found a father. And the wonder of the whole was this, that I got all the credit; of which not a thousandth part belonged by right and reason to me. Yet so it almost always is. If I work for good desert, and slave, and lie awake at night, and spend my unborn life in dreams, not a blink, nor wink, nor inkling of my labour ever tells. It would have been better to leave unburned, and to keep undevoured, the fuel and the food of life. But if I have laboured not, only acted by some impulse, whim, caprice, or anything; or even acting not at all, have floated upon fortune's haul — piled upon me commendations, bravoes, and applauses, almost work me up to tempt once again (though sick of it) the ill-luck of deserving.

Without intending any harm, and meaning only good indeed, I had now done serious wrong to Uncle Reuben's prospects. For Captain Carfax was full as angry at the trick played on him, as he was happy in discovering the falsehood and the fraud of it. Nor could I help agreeing with him, when he told me all of it, as with tears in his eyes he did, and ready to be my slave henceforth. I could not forbear from owning that it was a low and heartless trick, unworthy of men who had families; and the recoil whereof was well deserved, what ever it might end in.

For when this poor man left his daughter (asleep as he supposed, and having his food, and change of clothes, and Sunday hat to see to), he meant to return in an hour or so, and settle about her sustenance in some house of the neighbourhood. But this was the very thing of all things which the leaders of the enterprise, who had brought him up from Cornwall, for his noted skill in metals, were determined, whether by fair means or foul, to stop at the very outset. Secrecy being their main object, what chance could there be of it, if the miners were allowed to keep their children in the neighbourhood? Hence, on the plea of feasting Simon, they kept him drunk for three days and three nights, assuring him (whenever he had gleams enough to ask for her) that his daughter was as well as could be, and enjoying herself with the children. Not wishing the maid to see him tipsy, he pressed the matter no further; but applied himself to the bottle again, and drank her health with pleasure.

However, after three days of this, his constitution rose against it, and he became quite sober; with a certain lowness of heart moreover, and a sense of error. And his first desire to right himself, and easiest way to do it, was by exerting parental authority upon Gwenny. Possessed with this intention (for he was not a sweet-tempered man, and his head was aching sadly), he sought for Gwenny high and low; first with threats, and then with fears, and then with tears and wailing. And so he became to the other men a warning and great annoyance. Therefore they combined to swear what seemed a very likely thing, and might be true for all they knew; to wit, that Gwenny had come to seek for her father down the shaft-hole, and peering too eagerly into the dark, had toppled forward, and gone down, and lain at the bottom as dead as a stone.

"And thou being so happy with drink," the villains finished up to him, "and getting drunker every day, we thought it shame to trouble thee, and we buried the wench in the lower drift; and no use to think more of her; but come and have a glass, Sim."

But Simon Carfax swore that drink had lost him his wife, and now had lost him the last of his five children, and would lose him his own soul, if further he went on with it; and from that day to his death he never touched strong drink again. Nor only this; but being soon appointed captain of the mine, he allowed no man on any pretext to bring cordials thither; and to this and his stern hard rule, and stealthy secret management (as much as to good luck and place) might it be attributed that scarcely any but themselves had dreamed about this Exmoor mine.

As for me, I had no ambition to become a miner; and the state to which gold-seeking had brought poor Uncle Ben was not at all encouraging. My business was to till the ground, and tend the growth that came of it, and store the fruit in Heaven's good time, rather than to scoop and burrow, like a weasel or a rat, for the yellow root of evil. Moreover, I was led from home, between the hay and corn harvests (when we often have a week to spare), by a call there was no resisting; unless I gave up all regard for wrestling, and for my county.

Now here many persons may take me amiss, and there always has been some confusion; which people who ought to have known better have wrought into subject of quarrelling. By birth, it is true, and cannot be denied, that I am a man of Somerset; nevertheless by breed I am, as well as by education, a son of Devon also. And just as both our two counties vowed that Glen Doone was none of theirs, but belonged to the other one; so now, each with hot claim and jangling (leading even to blows sometimes), asserted and would swear to it (as I became more famous) that John Ridd was of its own producing, bred of its own true blood, and basely stolen by the other.

Now I have not judged it in any way needful, or even becoming and delicate, to enter into my wrestling adventures, or describe my progress. The whole thing is so different from Lorna, and her gentle manners, and her style of walking; moreover I must seem (even to kind people) to magnify myself so much, or at least attempt to do it, that I have scratched out written pages, through my better taste and sense.

Neither will I, upon this head, make any difference even now; being simply betrayed into mentioning the matter, because bare truth requires it, in the tale of Lorna's fortunes.

For a mighty giant had arisen in a part of Cornwall; and his calf was twenty-five inches round, and the breadth of his shoulders two feet and a quarter; and his stature seven feet and three-quarters. Round the chest he was seventy inches, and his hand a foot across, and there were no scales strong enough to judge of his weight in the market-place. Now this man — or I should say, his backers and his boasters, for the giant himself was modest — sent me a brave and haughty challenge, to meet him in the ring at Bodmin-town, on the first day of August, or else to return my champion's belt to them by the messenger.

It is no use to deny that I was greatly dashed and scared at first. For my part, I was only, when measured without clothes on, sixty inches round the breast, and round the calf scarce twenty-one, only two feet across the shoulders, and in height not six and three-quarters. However, my mother would never believe that this man could beat me; and Lorna being of the same mind, I resolved to go and try him, as they would pay all expenses, and a hundred pounds, if I conquered him; so confident were those Cornishmen.

Now this story is too well-known for me to go through it again and again. Every child in Devonshire knows, and his grandson will know, the song which some clever man made of it, after I had treated him to water, and to lemon, and a little sugar, and a drop of eau-de-vie. Enough that I had found the giant quite as big as they had described him, and enough to terrify anyone. But trusting in my practice and study of the art, I resolved to try a back with him; and when my arms were round him once, the giant was but a farthingale put into the vice of a blacksmith. The man had no bones; his frame sank in, and I was afraid of crushing him. He lay on his back, and smiled at me; and I begged his pardon.

Now this affair made a noise at the time, and redounded so much to my credit, that I was deeply grieved at it, because deserving none. For I do like a good strife and struggle; and the doubt makes the joy of victory; whereas in this case I might as well have been sent for a match with a haymow. However, I got my hundred pounds, and made up my mind to spend every farthing in presents for mother and Lorna.

For Annie was married by this time, and long before I went away; as need scarcely be said perhaps, if anyone follows the weeks and the months. The wedding was quiet enough, except for everybody's good wishes; and I desire not to dwell upon it, because it grieved me in many ways.

But now that I had tried to hope the very best for dear Annie, a deeper blow than could have come, even through her, awaited me. For after that visit to Cornwall, and with my prize-money about me, I came on foot from Okehampton to Oare, so as to save a little sum towards my time of marrying. For Lorna's fortune I would not have; small or great I would not have it; only if there were no denying, we would devote the whole of it to charitable uses, as Master Peter Blundell had done; and perhaps the future ages would endeavour to be grateful. Lorna and I had settled this question, at least twice a day, on the average; and each time with more satisfaction. Now coming into the kitchen, with all my cash in my breeches pocket (golden guineas, with an elephant on them, for the stamp of the guinea company), I found dear mother most heartily glad to see me safe and sound again — for she had dreaded that giant, and dreamed of him — and she never asked me about the money. Lizzie also was softer, and more gracious than usual; especially when she saw me pour guineas, like pepper-corns, into the pudding-basin. But by the way they hung about, I knew that something was gone wrong.

"Where is Lorna?" I asked at length, after trying not to ask it; "I want her to come, and see my money. She never saw so much before."

"Alas!" said mother, with a heavy sigh; "she will see a great deal more, I fear; and a deal more than is good for her. Whether you ever see her again will depend upon her nature, John."

"What do you mean, mother? Have you quarrelled? Why does not Lorna come to me? Am I never to know?"

"Now, John, be not so impatient," my mother replied, quite calmly, for in truth she was jealous of Lorna; "you could wait now very well, John, if it were till this day week, for the coming of your mother, John. And yet your mother is your best friend. Who can ever fill her place?"

Thinking of her future absence, mother turned away and cried; and the box-iron singed the blanket.

"Now," said I, being wild by this time; "Lizzie, you have a little sense; will you tell me where is Lorna?"

"The Lady Lorna Dugal," said Lizzie, screwing up her lips, as if the title were too grand, "is gone to London, brother John; and not likely to come back again. We must try to get on without her."

"You little" — [something] I cried, which I dare not write down here, as all you are too good for such language; but Lizzie's lips provoked me so — "my Lorna gone, my Lorna gone! And without good-bye to me even! It is your spite has sickened her."

"You are quite mistaken there," she replied; "how can folk of low degree have either spite or liking towards the people so far above them? The Lady Lorna Dugal is gone, because she could not help herself; and she wept enough to break ten hearts — if hearts are ever broken, John."

"Darling Lizzie, how good you are!" I cried, without noticing her sneer: "tell me all about it, dear; tell me every word she said."

"That will not take long," said Lizzie, quite as unmoved by soft coaxing as by urgent cursing: "the lady spoke very little to anyone except indeed to mother, and to Gwenny Carfax; and Gwenny is gone with her, so that the benefit of that is lost. But she left a letter for 'poor John,' as in charity she called him. How grand she looked, to be sure, with the fine clothes on that were come for her!"

"Where is the letter, you utter vixen? Oh, may you have a husband!"

"Who will thrash it out of you, and starve it, and swear it out of you;" was the meaning of my imprecation: but Lizzie, not dreaming as yet of such things, could not understand me, and was rather thankful; therefore she answered quietly:

"The letter is in the little cupboard, near the head of Lady Lorna's bed, where she used to keep the diamond necklace, which we contrived to get stolen."

Without another word, I rushed (so that every board in the house shook) up to my lost Lorna's room, and tore the little wall-niche open, and espied my treasure. It was as simple, and as homely, and loving, as even I could wish. Part of it ran as follows — the other parts it behoves me not to open out to strangers: "My own love, and sometime lord, — Take it not amiss of me, that even without farewell, I go; for I cannot persuade the men to wait, your return being doubtful. My great uncle, some grand lord, is awaiting me at Dunster, having fear of venturing too near this Exmoor country. I, who have been so lawless always, and the child of outlaws, am now to atone for this, it seems, by living in a court of law, and under special surveillance (as they call it, I believe) of His Majesty's Court of Chancery. My uncle is appointed my guardian and master; and I must live beneath his care, until I am twenty-one years old. To me this appears a dreadful thing, and very unjust, and cruel; for why should

I lose my freedom, through heritage of land and gold? I offered to abandon all, if they would only let me go: I went down on my knees to them, and said I wanted titles not, neither land, nor money; only to stay where I was, where first I had known happiness. But they only laughed, and called me 'child,' and said I must talk of that to the King's High Chancellor. Their orders they had, and must obey them; and Master Stickles was ordered too to help, as the King's Commissioner. And then, although it pierced my heart not to say one 'Good-bye, John,' I was glad upon the whole that you were not here to dispute it. For I am almost certain that you would not, without force to yourself, have let your Lorna go to people who never, never can care for her."

Here my darling had wept again, by the tokens on the paper; and then there followed some sweet words, too sweet for me to chatter them. But she finished with these noble lines, which (being common to all humanity, in a case of steadfast love) I do not harm, but rather help all true love, by repeating: "Of one thing rest you well assured — and I do hope that it may prove of service to your rest, love, else would my own be broken — no difference of rank, or fortune, or of life itself, shall ever make me swerve from truth to you. We have passed through many troubles, dangers, and dispartments, but never yet was doubt between us; neither ever shall be. Each has trusted well the other; and still each must do so. Though they tell you I am false, though your own mind harbours it, from the sense of things around, and your own under-valuing, yet take counsel of your heart, and cast such thoughts away from you; being unworthy of itself, they must be unworthy also of the one who dwells there: and that one is, and ever shall be, your own Lorna Dugal."

Some people cannot understand that tears should come from pleasure; but whether from pleasure or from sorrow (mixed as they are in the twisted strings of a man's heart, or a woman's), great tears fell from my stupid eyes, even on the blots of Lorna's.

"No doubt it is all over!" my mind said to me bitterly: "Trust me, all shall yet be right!" my heart replied very sweetly.

CHAPTER LX

Annie Luckier Than John

Some people may look down upon us for our slavish ways (as they may choose to call them), but in our part of the country, we do love to mention title, and to roll it on our tongues, with a conscience and a comfort. Even if a man knows not, through fault of education, who the Duke of this is, or the Earl of that, it will never do for him to say so, lest the room look down on him. Therefore he must nod his head, and say, "Ah, to be sure! I know him as well as ever I know my own good woman's brother. He married Lord Flipflap's second daughter, and a precious life she led him." Whereupon the room looks up at him. But I, being quite unable to carry all this in my head, as I ought, was speedily put down by people of a noble tendency, apt at Lords, and pat with Dukes, and knowing more about the King than His Majesty would have requested. Therefore, I fell back in thought, not daring in words to do so, upon the titles of our horses. And all these horses deserved their names, not having merely inherited, but by their own doing earned them. Smiler, for instance, had been so called, not so much from a habit of smiling, as from his general geniality, white nose, and white ankle. This worthy horse was now in years, but hale and gay as ever; and when you let him out of the stable, he could neigh and whinny, and make men and horses know it. On the other hand, Kickums was a horse of morose and surly order; harbouring up revenge, and leading a rider to false confidence. Very smoothly he would go, and as gentle as a turtle-dove; until his rider fully believed that a packthread was enough for him, and a pat of approval upon his neck the aim and crown of his worthy life. Then suddenly up went his hind feet to heaven, and the rider for the most part flew over his nose: whereupon good Kickums would take advantage of his favourable position, to come and bite a piece out of his back. Now in my present state of mind; being understood of nobody, having none to bear me company, neither wishing to have any, an indefinite kind of attraction drew me into Kickums' society. A bond of mutual sympathy was soon established between us: I would ride no other horse, neither Kickums be ridden by any other man. And this good horse became as jealous about me as a dog might be; and would lash out, or run teeth foremost, at anyone who came near him when I was on his back. This season, the reaping of the corn, which had been, but a year ago, so pleasant and so lightsome, was become a heavy labour, and a thing for grumbling rather than for gladness. However, for the sake of all, it must be attended to, and with as fair a show of spirit, and alacrity, as might be. For otherwise the rest would drag, and drop their hands and idle, being quicker to take infection of dulness than of diligence. And the harvest was a heavy one, even heavier than the year before, although of poorer quality. Therefore was I forced to work as hard as any horse could, during all the daylight hours, and defer all night the brooding upon my misfortune. But the darkness always found me stiff with work, and weary, and less able to think than to dream, may be, of Lorna. But now the house was so dull and lonesome, wanting Annie's pretty presence, and the light of Lorna's eyes, that a man had no temptation, after supper-time, even to sit and smoke a pipe.

For Lizzie, though so learned, and pleasant when it suited her, never had taken very kindly to my love for Lorna, and being of a proud and slightly upstart nature, could not bear to be eclipsed, in bearing, looks, and breeding, and even in clothes, by the stranger. For one thing I will say of the Doones, that whether by purchase or plunder, they had always dressed my darling well, with her own sweet taste to help them. And though Lizzie's natural hate of the maid (as a Doone, and burdened with father's death) should have been changed to remorse, when she learned of Lorna's real parentage, it was only altered to sullenness, and discontent with herself, for frequent rudeness to an innocent person, and one of such high descent. Moreover the child had imbibed strange ideas as to our aristocracy, partly perhaps from her own way of thinking, and partly from reading of history. For while from one point of view she looked up at them very demurely, as commissioned by God for the country's good; from another sight she disliked them as ready to sacrifice their best, and follow their worst members.

Yet why should this wench dare to judge upon a matter so far beyond her, and form opinions which she knew better than to declare before mother? But with me she had no such scruple, for

I had no authority over her; and my intellect she looked down upon, because I praised her own so. Thus she made herself very unpleasant to me; by little jags and jerks of sneering, sped as though unwittingly; which I (who now considered myself allied to the aristocracy, and perhaps took airs on that account) had not wit enough to parry, yet had wound enough to feel.

Now anyone who does not know exactly how mothers feel and think, would have expected mother (than whom could be no better one) to pet me, and make much of me, under my sad trouble; to hang with anxiety on my looks, and shed her tears with mine (if any), and season every dish of meat put by for her John's return. And if the whole truth must be told, I did expect that sort of thing, and thought what a plague it would be to me; yet not getting it, was vexed, as if by some new injury. For mother was a special creature (as I suppose we all are), being the warmest of the warm, when fired at the proper corner; and yet, if taken at the wrong point, you would say she was incombustible.

Hence it came to pass that I had no one even to speak to about Lorna and my grievances; for Captain Stickles was now gone southward; and John Fry, of course, was too low for it, although a married man, and well under his wife's management. But finding myself unable at last to bear this any longer, upon the first day when all the wheat was cut, and the stooks set up in every field, yet none quite fit for carrying, I saddled good Kickums at five in the morning, and without a word to mother (for a little anxiety might do her good) off I set for Molland parish, to have the counsel and the comfort of my darling Annie.

The horse took me over the ground so fast (there being few better to go, when he liked), that by nine o'clock Annie was in my arms, and blushing to the colour of Winnie's cheeks, with sudden delight and young happiness.

"You precious little soul!" I cried: "how does Tom behave to you?"

"Hush!" said Annie: "how dare you ask? He is the kindest, and the best and the noblest of all men, John: not even setting yourself aside. Now look not jealous, John: so it is. We all have special gifts, you know. You are as good as you can be, John; but my husband's special gift is nobility of character." Here she looked at me, as one who has discovered something quite unknown.

"I am devilish glad to hear it," said I, being touched at going down so: "keep him to that mark, my dear; and cork the whiskey bottle."

"Yes, darling John," she answered quickly, not desiring to open that subject, and being too sweet to resent it: "and how is lovely Lorna? What an age it is since I have seen you! I suppose we must thank her for that."

"You may thank her for seeing me now," said I; "or rather," seeing how hurt she looked, "you may thank my knowledge of your kindness, and my desire to speak of her to a soft-hearted dear little soul like you. I think all the women are gone mad. Even mother treats me shamefully. And as for Lizzie ——— " Here I stopped, knowing no words strong enough, without shocking Annie.

"Do you mean to say that Lorna is gone?" asked Annie, in great amazement; yet leaping at the truth, as women do, with nothing at all to leap from.

"Gone. And I never shall see her again. It serves me right for aspiring so."

Being grieved at my manner, she led me in where none could interrupt us; and in spite of all my dejection, I could not help noticing how very pretty, and even elegant all things were around. For we upon Exmoor have little taste; all we care for is warm comfort, and plenty to eat, and to give away, and a hearty smack in everything. But Squire Faggus had seen the world, and kept company with great people; and the taste he had first displayed in the shoeing of farmers' horses (which led almost to his ruin, by bringing him into jealousy, and flattery, and dashing ways) had now been cultivated in London, and by moonlight, so that none could help admiring it.

"Well!" I cried, for the moment dropping care and woe in astonishment: "we have nothing like this at Plover's Barrows; nor even Uncle Reuben. I do hope it is honest, Annie?"

"Would I sit in a chair that was not my own?" asked Annie, turning crimson, and dropping defiantly, and with a whisk of her dress which I never had seen before, into the very grandest one: "would I lie on a couch, brother John, do you think, unless good money was paid for it? Because other people are clever, John, you need not grudge them their earnings."

"A couch?" I replied: "why what can you want with a couch in the day-time, Annie? A couch is a small bed, set up in a room without space for a good four-poster. What can you want with a couch downstairs? I never heard of such nonsense. And you ought to be in the dairy."

"I won't cry, brother John, I won't; because you want to make me cry;" and all the time she was crying; you always were so nasty, John, sometimes. Ah, you have no nobility of character, like my husband. And I have not seen you for two months, John: and now you come to scold me!"

"You little darling," I said, for Annie's tears always conquered me; "if all the rest ill-use me, I will not quarrel with you, dear. You have always been true to me; and I can forgive your vanity. Your things are very pretty, dear; and you may couch ten times a day, without my interference. No doubt your husband has paid for all this with the ponies he stole from Exmoor. Nobility of character is a thing beyond my understanding; but when my sister loves a man, and he does well and flourishes, who am I to find fault with him? Mother ought to see these things: they would turn her head almost: look at the pimples on the chairs!"

"They are nothing," Annie answered, after kissing me for my kindness; "they are only put in for the time indeed: and we are to have much better, with gold all round the bindings, and double plush at the corners; so soon as ever the King repays the debt he owes to my poor Tom."

I thought to myself that our present King had been most unlucky in one thing — debts all over the kingdom. Not a man who had struck a blow for the King, or for his poor father, or even said a good word for him, in the time of his adversity, but expected at least a baronetcy, and a grant of estates to support it. Many have called King Charles ungrateful: and he may have been so. But some indulgence is due to a man, with entries few on the credit side, and a terrible column of debits.

"Have no fear for the chair," I said, for it creaked under me very fearfully, having legs not so large as my finger; "if the chair breaks, Annie, your fear should be, lest the tortoise-shell run into me. Why it is striped like a viper's loins! I saw some hundreds in London; and very cheap they are. They are made to be sold to the country people, such as you and me, dear; and carefully kept they will last for almost half a year. Now will you come back from your furniture, and listen to my story?"

Annie was a hearty dear, and she knew that half my talk was joke, to make light of my worrying. Therefore she took it in good part, as I well knew that she would do; and she led me to a good honest chair; and she sat in my lap, and kissed me.

"All this is not like you, John. All this is not one bit like you: and your cheeks are not as they ought to be. I shall have to come home again, if the women worry my brother so. We always held together, John; and we always will, you know."

"You dear!" I cried, "there is nobody who understands me as you do. Lorna makes too much of me, and the rest make too little."

"Not mother; oh, not mother, John!"

"No, mother makes too much, no doubt; but wants it all for herself alone; and reckons it as a part of her. She makes me more wroth than anyone: as if not only my life, but all my head and heart must seek from hers, and have no other thought or care."

Being sped of my grumbling thus, and eased into better temper, I told Annie all the strange history about Lorna, and her departure, and the small chance that now remained to me of ever seeing my love again. To this Annie would not hearken twice, but judging women by her faithful self, was quite vexed with me for thinking so. And then, to my surprise and sorrow, she would deliver no opinion as to what I ought to do, until she had consulted darling Tom.

Dear Tom knew much of the world, no doubt, especially the dark side of it. But to me it scarcely seemed becoming that my course of action with regard to the Lady Lorna Dugal should be referred to Tom Faggus, and depend upon his decision. However, I would not grieve Annie again by making light of her husband; and so when he came in to dinner, the matter was laid before him.

Now this man never confessed himself surprised, under any circumstances; his knowledge of life being so profound, and his charity universal. And in the present case he vowed that he had suspected it all along, and could have thrown light upon Lorna's history, if we had seen fit to apply to him. Upon further inquiry I found that this light was a very dim one, flowing only from the fact that he had stopped her mother's coach, at the village of Bolham, on the Bampton road, the day before I saw them. Finding only women therein, and these in a sad condition, Tom with his usual chivalry (as he had no scent of the necklace) allowed them to pass; with nothing more than a pleasant exchange of courtesies, and a testimonial forced upon him, in the shape of a bottle of Burgundy wine. This the poor countess handed him; and he twisted the cork out with his teeth, and drank her health with his hat off.

"A lady she was, and a true one: and I am a pretty good judge," said Tom: "ah, I do like a high lady!"

Our Annie looked rather queer at this, having no pretensions to be one: but she conquered herself, and said, "Yes, Tom; and many of them liked you."

With this, Tom went on the brag at once, being but a shallow fellow, and not of settled principles, though steadier than he used to be; until I felt myself almost bound to fetch him back a little; for of all things I do hate brag the most, as any reader of this tale must by this time know. Therefore I said to Squire Faggus, "Come back from your highway days. You have married the daughter of an honest man; and such talk is not fit for her. If you were right in robbing people, I am right in robbing you. I could bind you to your own mantelpiece, as you know thoroughly well, Tom; and drive away with your own horses, and all your goods behind them, but for the sense of honesty. And should I not do as fine a thing as any you did on the highway? If everything is of public right, how does this chair belong to you? Clever as you are, Tom Faggus, you are nothing but a fool to mix your felony with your farmership. Drop the one, or drop the other; you cannot maintain them both."

As I finished very sternly a speech which had exhausted me more than ten rounds of wrestling — but I was carried away by the truth, as sometimes happens to all of us — Tom had not a word to say; albeit his mind was so much more nimble and rapid than ever mine was. He leaned against the mantelpiece (a newly-invented affair in his house) as if I had corded him to it, even as I spoke of doing. And he laid one hand on his breast, in a way which made Annie creep softly to him, and look at me not like a sister.

"You have done me good, John," he said at last, and the hand he gave me was trembling; "there is no other man on God's earth would have dared to speak to me as you have done. From no other would I have taken it. Nevertheless every word is true; and I shall dwell on it when you are gone. If you never did good in your life before, John, my brother, you have done it now."

He turned away in bitter pain, that none might see his trouble: and Annie going along with him, looked as if I had killed our mother. For my part, I was so upset, for fear of having gone too far, that without a word to either of them, but a message on the title-page of King James his Prayer-book, I saddled Kickums, and was off, and glad of the moorland air again.

CHAPTER LXI

Therefore He seeks Comfort

It was for poor Annie's sake that I had spoken my mind to her husband so freely, and even harshly. For we all knew she would break her heart, if Tom took to evil ways again. And the right mode of preventing this was not to coax, and flatter, and make a hero of him (which he did for himself, quite sufficiently), but to set before him the folly of the thing, and the ruin to his own interests.

They would both be vexed with me, of course, for having left them so hastily, and especially just before dinner-time; but that would soon wear off; and most likely they would come to see mother, and tell her that I was hard to manage, and they could feel for her about it.

Now with a certain yearning, I know not what, for softness, and for one who could understand me — for simple as a child though being, I found few to do that last, at any rate in my love-time — I relied upon Kickums' strength to take me round by Dulverton. It would make the journey some eight miles longer, but what was that to a brisk young horse, even with my weight upon him? And having left Squire Faggus, and Annie, much sooner than had been intended, I had plenty of time before me, and too much, ere ever a prospect of dinner. Therefore I struck to the right, across the hills, for Dulverton.

Pretty Ruth was in the main street of the town, with a basket in her hand, going home from the market.

"Why, Cousin Ruth, you are grown," I exclaimed; "I do believe you are, Ruth. And you were almost too tall, already."

At this the little thing was so pleased, that she smiled through her blushes beautifully, and must needs come to shake hands with me; though I signed to her not to do it, because of my horse's temper. But scarcely was her hand in mine, when Kickums turned like an eel upon her, and caught her by the left arm with his teeth, so that she screamed with agony. I saw the white of his vicious eye, and struck him there with all my force, with my left hand over her right arm, and he never used that eye again; none the less he kept his hold on her. Then I smote him again on the jaw, and caught the little maid up by her right hand, and laid her on the saddle in front of me; while the horse being giddy and staggered with blows, and foiled of his spite, ran backwards. Ruth's wits were gone: and she lay before me in such a helpless and senseless way, that I could have killed vile Kickums. I struck the spurs into him past the rowels, and away he went at full gallop; while I had enough to do to hold on, with the little girl lying in front of me. But I called to the men who were flocking around, to send up a surgeon, as quick as could be, to Master Reuben Huckaback's.

The moment I brought my right arm to bear, the vicious horse had no chance with me; and if ever a horse was well paid for spite, Kickums had his change that day. The bridle would almost have held a whale, and I drew on it so that his lower jaw was well-nigh broken from him; while with both spurs I tore his flanks, and he learned a little lesson. There are times when a man is more vicious than any horse may vie with. Therefore by the time we had reached Uncle Reuben's house at the top of the hill, the bad horse was only too happy to stop; every string of his body was trembling, and his head hanging down with impotence. I leaped from his back at once, and carried the maiden into her own sweet room.

Now Cousin Ruth was recovering softly from her fright and faintness; and the volley of the wind from galloping so had made her little ears quite pink, and shaken her locks all round her. But anyone who might wish to see a comely sight, and a moving one, need only have looked at Ruth Huckaback, when she learned (and imagined yet more than it was) the manner of her little ride with me. Her hair was of hazel-brown, and full of waving readiness; and with no concealment of the trick, she spread it over her eyes and face. Being so delighted with her, and so glad to see her safe, I kissed her through the thick of it, as a cousin has a right to do; yea, and ought to do with gravity.

"Darling," I said; "he has bitten you dreadfully: show me your poor arm, dear."

She pulled up her sleeve in the simplest manner, rather to look at it herself, than to show me where the wound was. Her sleeve was of dark blue Taunton staple; and her white arm shone, coming out of it, as round and plump and velvety, as a stalk of asparagus, newly fetched out of ground. But above the curved soft elbow, where no room was for one cross word (according to our proverb[3]), three sad gashes, edged with crimson, spoiled the flow of the pearly flesh. My presence of mind was lost altogether; and I raised the poor sore arm to my lips, both to stop the bleeding and to take the venom out, having heard how wise it was, and thinking of my mother. But Ruth, to my great amazement, drew away from me in bitter haste, as if I had been inserting, instead of extracting poison. For the bite of a horse is most venomous; especially when he sheds his teeth; and far more to be feared than the bite of a dog, or even of a cat. And in my haste, I had forgotten that Ruth might not know a word about this, and might doubt about my meaning, and the warmth of my osculation. But knowing the danger, I durst not heed her childishness, or her feelings.

"Don't be a fool, Cousin Ruth," I said, catching her so that she could not move; "the poison is soaking into you. Do you think that I do it for pleasure?"

The spread of shame on her face was such, when she saw her own misunderstanding, that I was ashamed to look at her: and occupied myself with drawing all the risk of glanders forth from the white limb, hanging helpless now, and left entirely to my will. Before I was quite sure of having wholly exhausted suction, and when I had made the holes in her arm like the gills of a lamprey, in came the doctor, partly drunk, and in haste to get through his business.

"Ha, ha! I see," he cried; "bite of a horse, they tell me. Very poisonous; must be burned away. Sally, the iron in the fire. If you have a fire, this weather."

"Crave your pardon, good sir," I said; for poor little Ruth was fainting again at his savage orders; "but my cousin's arm shall not be burned; it is a great deal too pretty, and I have sucked all the poison out. Look, sir, how clean and fresh it is."

"Bless my heart! And so it is! No need at all for cauterizing. The epidermis will close over, and the cutis and the pellis. John Ridd, you ought to have studied medicine, with your healing powers. Half my virtue lies in touch. A clean and wholesome body, sir; I have taught you the Latin grammar. I leave you in

---

[3] "A maid with an elbow sharp, or knee,
Hath cross words two, out of every three."

excellent hands, my dear, and they wait for me at shovel-board. Bread and water poultice cold, to be renewed, *tribus horis.* John Ridd, I was at school with you, and you beat me very lamentably, when I tried to fight with you. You remember me not? It is likely enough: I am forced to take strong waters, John, from infirmity of the liver. Attend to my directions; and I will call again in the morning."

And in that melancholy plight, caring nothing for business, went one of the cleverest fellows ever known at Tiverton. He could write Latin verses a great deal faster than I could ever write English prose, and nothing seemed too great for him. We thought that he would go to Oxford, and astonish every one, and write in the style of Buchanan; but he fell all abroad very lamentably; and now, when I met him again, was come down to push-pin and shovel-board, with a wager of spirits pending.

When Master Huckaback came home, he looked at me very sulkily; not only because of my refusal to become a slave to the gold-digging, but also because he regarded me as the cause of a savage broil, between Simon Carfax and the men who had cheated him as to his Gwenny. However, when Uncle Ben saw Ruth, and knew what had befallen her, and she with tears in her eyes declared that she owed her life to Cousin Ridd, the old man became very gracious to me; for if he loved anyone on earth, it was his little granddaughter.

I could not stay very long, because, my horse being quite unfit to travel (from the injuries, which his violence and vice had brought upon him), there was nothing for me but to go on foot, as none of Uncle Ben's horses could take me to Plover's Barrows, without downright cruelty: and though there would be a harvest-moon, Ruth agreed with me that I must not keep my mother waiting, with no idea where I might be, until a late hour of the night. I told Ruth all about our Annie, and her noble furniture; and the little maid was very lively (although her wounds were paining her so, that half her laughter came "on the wrong side of her mouth," as we rather coarsely express it); especially she laughed about Annie's new-fangled closet for clothes, or standing-press, as she called it. This had frightened me, so that I would not come without my stick to look at it; for the front was inlaid with two fiery dragons, and a glass which distorted everything, making even Annie look hideous; and when it was opened, a woman's skeleton, all in white, revealed itself, in the midst of three standing women. "It is only to keep my best frocks in shape," Annie had explained to me; "hanging them up does ruin them so. But I own that I was afraid of it, John, until I had got all my best clothes there, and then I became very fond of it. But even now it frightens me sometimes in the moonlight."

Having made poor Ruth a little cheerful, with a full account of all Annie's frocks, material, pattern, and fashion (of which I had taken a list for my mother, and for Lizzie, lest they should cry out at man's stupidity about anything of real interest), I proceeded to tell her about my own troubles, and the sudden departure of Lorna; concluding, with all the show of indifference which my pride could muster, that now I never should see her again, and must do my best to forget her, as being so far above me. I had not intended to speak of this, but Ruth's face was so kind and earnest, that I could not stop myself.

"You must not talk like that, Cousin Ridd," she said, in a low and gentle tone, and turning her eyes away from me; "no lady can be above a man, who is pure, and brave, and gentle. And if her heart be worth having, she will never let you give her up, for her grandeur, and her nobility."

She pronounced those last few words, as I thought, with a little bitterness unperceived by herself perhaps, for it was not in her appearance. But I, attaching great importance to a maiden's opinion about a maiden (because she might judge from experience), would have led her further into that subject. But she declined to follow, having now no more to say in a matter so removed from her. Then I asked her full and straight, and looking at her, in such a manner, that she could not look away, without appearing vanquished by feelings of her own — which thing was very vile of me; but all men are so selfish:

"Dear cousin, tell me once for all, what is your advice to me?"

"My advice to you," she answered bravely, with her dark eyes full of pride, and instead of flinching, foiling me — "is to do what every man must do, if he would win fair maiden. Since she cannot send you token, neither is free to return to you, follow her, pay court to her; show that you will not be forgotten; and perhaps she will look down — I mean she will relent to you."

"She has nothing to relent about. I have never vexed nor injured her. My thoughts have never strayed from her. There is no one to compare with her."

"Then keep her in that same mind about you. See now, I can advise no more. My arm is swelling painfully, in spite of all your goodness, and bitter task of surgeonship. I shall have another poultice on, and go to bed, I think, Cousin Ridd, if you will not hold me ungrateful. I am so sorry for your long walk. Surely it might be avoided. Give my love to dear Lizzie: oh, the room is going round so!"

And she fainted into the arms of Sally, who was come just in time to fetch her: no doubt she had been suffering agony, all the time she talked to me. Leaving word that I would come again to inquire for her, and fetch Kickums home, so soon as the harvest permitted me, I gave directions about the horse, and striding away from the ancient town, was soon upon the moorlands.

Now, through the whole of that long walk — the latter part of which was led by starlight, till the moon arose — I dwelt, in my young and foolish way, upon the ordering of our steps by a Power beyond us. But as I could not bring my mind to any clearness upon this matter, and the stars shed no light upon it, but rather confused me with wondering how their Lord could attend to all of them, and yet to a puny fool like me, it came to pass that my thoughts on the subject were not worth ink, if I knew them.

But it is perhaps worth ink to relate, so far as I can do so, mother's delight at my return, when she had almost abandoned hope, and concluded that I was gone to London, in disgust at her behaviour. And now she was looking up the lane, at the rise of the harvest-moon, in despair, as she said afterwards. But if she had despaired in truth, what use to look at all? Yet, according to the epigram made by a good Blundellite:

> Despair was never yet so deep
>   In sinking, as in seeming;
> Despair is hope just dropp'd asleep,
>   For better chance of dreaming.

And mother's dream was a happy one, when she knew my step at a furlong distant; for the night was of those that carry sounds, thrice as far as day can. She recovered herself, when she was sure, and even made up her mind to scold me, and felt as if she could do it. But when she was in my arms, into which she threw herself, and I by the light of the moon descried the silver gleam on one side of her head (now spreading since Annie's departure), bless my heart, and yours therewith, no room was left for scolding. She hugged me, and she clung to me; and I looked at her, with duty made tenfold, and discharged by love. We said nothing to one another; but all was right between us.

Even Lizzie behaved very well, so far as her nature admitted; not even saying a nasty thing, all the time she was getting my supper ready, with a weak imitation of Annie. She knew that the gift of cooking was not vouchsafed by God to her; but sometimes she would do her best, by intellect, to win it. Whereas it is no more to be won by intellect, than is divine poetry. An amount of strong quick heart is needful, and the understanding must second it, in the one art as in the other. Now my fare was very choice for the next three days or more; yet not turned out like Annie's. They could do a thing well enough on the fire; but they could not put it on table so; nor even have plates all piping hot. This was Annie's special gift; born in her, and ready to cool with her; like a plate borne away from the fire-place. I sighed sometimes about Lorna; and they thought it was about the plates. And mother would stand and look at me, as much as to say, "No pleasing him;" and Lizzie would jerk up one shoulder, and cry, "He had better have Lorna to cook for him:" while the whole truth was that I wanted not to be plagued about any cookery; but just to have something good and quiet, and then smoke, and think about Lorna.

Nevertheless the time went on, with one change and another; and we gathered all our harvest in; and Parson Bowden thanked God for it, both in church and out of it; for his tithes would be very goodly. The unmatched cold of the previous winter, and general fear of scarcity, and our own talk about our ruin, had sent prices up to a grand high pitch; and we did our best to keep them there. For nine Englishmen out of every ten believe that a bitter winter must breed a sour summer, and explain away topmost prices. While according to my experience, more often it would be otherwise, except for the public thinking so. However, I have said too much; and if any farmer reads my book, he will vow that I wrote it for nothing else except to rob his family.

CHAPTER LXII

The King must not be prayed for

All our neighbourhood was surprised that the Doones had not ere now attacked, and probably made an end of us. For we lay almost at their mercy now, having only Serjeant Bloxham, and three men, to protect us. Captain Stickles having been ordered southwards with all his force, except such as might be needful for collecting toll, and watching the imports at Lynmouth, and thence to Porlock. The Serjeant, having now imbibed a taste for writing reports (though his first great effort had done him no good, and only offended Stickles), reported weekly from Plover's Barrows, whenever he could find a messenger. And though we fed not Serjeant Bloxham at our own table, with the best we had (as in the case of Stickles, who represented His Majesty), yet we treated him so well, that he reported very highly of us, as loyal and true-hearted lieges, and most devoted to our lord the King. And indeed he could scarcely have done less, when Lizzie wrote great part of his reports, and furbished up the rest to such a pitch of lustre, that Lord Clarendon himself need scarce have been ashamed of them. And though this cost a great deal of ale, and even of strong waters (for Lizzie would have it the duty of a critic to stand treat to the author), and though it was otherwise a plague, as giving the maid such airs of patronage, and such pretence to politics; yet there was no stopping it, without the risk of mortal offence to both writer and reviewer. Our mother also, while disapproving Lizzie's long stay in the saddle-room on a Friday night and a Saturday, and insisting that Betty should be there, was nevertheless as proud as need be, that the King should read our Eliza's writing — at least so the innocent soul believed — and we all looked forward to something great, as the fruit of all this history. And something great did come of it, though not as we expected; for these reports, or as many of them as were ever opened, stood us in good stead the next year, when we were accused of harbouring and comforting guilty rebels.

Now the reason why the Doones did not attack us was that they were preparing to meet another, and more powerful assault, upon their fortress; being assured that their repulse of King's troops could not be looked over when brought before the authorities. And no doubt they were right; for although the conflicts in the government during that summer, and autumn, had delayed the matter, yet positive orders had been issued, that these outlaws and malefactors should at any price be brought to justice; when the sudden death of King Charles the Second threw all things into confusion, and all minds into a panic.

We heard of it first in church, on Sunday, the eighth day of February, 1684 — 5, from a cousin of John Fry, who had ridden over on purpose from Porlock. He came in just before the anthem, splashed and heated from his ride, so that every one turned and looked at him. He wanted to create a stir (knowing how much would be made of him), and he took the best way to do it. For he let the anthem go by very quietly — or rather I should say very pleasingly, for our choir was exceedingly proud of itself, and I sang bass twice as loud as a bull, to beat the clerk with the clarionet — and then just as Parson Bowden, with a look of pride at his minstrels, was kneeling down to begin the prayer for the King's Most Excellent Majesty (for he never read the Litany except upon Easter Sunday), up jumps young Sam Fry, and shouts:

"I forbid that there prai-er."

"What!" cried the parson, rising slowly, and looking for some one to shut the door: "have we a rebel in the congregation?" For the parson was growing short-sighted now, and knew not Sam Fry at that distance.

"No," replied Sam, not a whit abashed by the staring of all the parish; "no rebel, parson; but a man who mislaiketh popery and murder. That there prai-er be a prai-er for the dead."

"Nay," cried the parson, now recognizing and knowing him to be our John's first cousin, "you do not mean to say, Sam, that His Gracious Majesty is dead?"

"Dead as a sto-un; poisoned by they Papishers." And Sam rubbed his hands with enjoyment, at the effect he had produced.

"Remember where you are, Sam," said Parson Bowden, solemnly; "when did this most sad thing happen? The King is the head of the Church, Sam Fry; when did His Majesty leave her?"

"Day afore yesterday. Twelve o'clock. Warn't us quick to hear of 'un?"

"Can't be," said the minister; "the tidings can never have come so soon. Anyhow, he will want it all the more. Let us pray for His Gracious Majesty."

And with that he proceeded as usual; but nobody cried "Amen," for fear of being entangled with popery. But after giving forth his text, our parson said a few words out of a book, about the many virtues of His Majesty, and self-denial, and devotion, comparing his pious mirth to the dancing of the patriarch David before the ark of the covenant; and he added, with some severity, that if his flock would not join their pastor (who was much more likely to judge aright) in praying for the King, the least they could do, on returning home, was to pray that the King might not be dead, as his enemies had asserted.

Now when the service was over, we killed the King, and we brought him to life, at least fifty times in the churchyard: and Sam Fry was mounted on a high gravestone, to tell every one all he knew of it. But he knew no more than he had told us in the church, as before repeated; upon which we were much disappointed with him, and inclined to disbelieve him: until he happily remembered that His Majesty had died in great pain, with blue spots on his breast, and black spots all across his back, and these in the form of a cross, by reason of papists having poisoned him. When Sam called this to his remembrance (or to his imagination) he was overwhelmed, at once, with so many invitations to dinner, that he scarce knew which of them to accept; but decided in our favour.

Grieving much for the loss of the King, however greatly it might be (as the parson had declared it was, while telling us to pray against it) for the royal benefit, I resolved to ride to Porlock myself, directly after dinner, and make sure whether he were dead or not. For it was not by any means hard to suppose that Sam Fry, being John's first cousin, might have inherited (either from grandfather or grandmother) some of those gifts which had made our John so famous for mendacity. At Porlock, I found that it was too true; and the women of the town were in great distress, for the King had always been popular with them: the men, on the other hand, were forecasting what would be likely to ensue.

And I myself was of this number, riding sadly home again; although bound to the King, as churchwarden now; which dignity, next to the parson's in rank, is with us (as it ought to be in every good parish) hereditary. For who can stick to the church like the man whose father stuck to it before him; and who knows all the little ins, and great outs, which must in these troublous times come across?

But though appointed at last, by virtue of being best farmer in the parish (as well as by vice of mismanagement, on the part of my mother, and Nicholas Snowe, who had thoroughly muxed up everything, being too quick-headed), yet, while I dwelled with pride upon the fact that I stood in the King's shoes, as the manager and promoter of the Church of England — and I knew that we must miss His Majesty (whose arms were above the Commandments), as the leader of our thoughts in church, and handsome upon a guinea — nevertheless, I kept on thinking how his death would act on me.

And here I saw it, many ways. In the first place, troubles must break out; and we had eight-and-twenty ricks; counting grain, and straw, and hay. Moreover mother was growing weak about riots, and shooting, and burning; and she gathered the bed-clothes around her ears every night, when her feet were tucked up; and prayed not to awake until morning. In the next place, much rebellion (though we would not own it, in either sense of the verb, to "own") was whispering, and plucking skirts, and making signs, among us. And the terror of the Doones helped greatly; as a fruitful tree of lawlessness, and a good excuse for everybody. And after this — or rather before it, and first of all indeed (if I must state the true order) — arose upon me the thought of Lorna, and how these things would affect her fate.

And indeed I must admit that it had occurred to me some-times, or been suggested by others, that the Lady Lorna had not behaved altogether kindly, since her departure from among us. For although in those days the post (as we call the service of let-ter-carrying, which now comes within twenty miles of us) did not extend to our part of the world, yet it might have been possi-ble to procure for hire a man who would ride post, if Lorna feared to trust the pack-horses, or the troopers, who went to and fro. Yet no message whatever had reached us, neither any token even of her safety in London. As to this last, however, we had no misgivings, having learned from the orderlies, more than once, that the wealth, and beauty, and adventures of young Lady Lorna

Dugal were greatly talked of both at court and among the common people.

Now riding sadly homewards, in the sunset of the early spring, I was more than ever touched with sorrow, and a sense of being, as it were, abandoned. And the weather growing quite beautiful, and so mild that the trees were budding, and the cattle full of happiness, I could not but think of the difference between the world of to-day and the world of this day twelvemonth. Then all was howling desolation, all the earth blocked up with snow, and all the air with barbs of ice as small as splintered needles, yet glittering, in and out, like stars, and gathering so upon a man (if long he stayed among them) that they began to weigh him down to sleepiness and frozen death. Not a sign of life was moving, nor was any change of view; unless the wild wind struck the crest of some cold drift, and bowed it.

Now, on the other hand, all was good. The open palm of spring was laid upon the yielding of the hills; and each particular valley seemed to be the glove for a finger. And although the sun was low, and dipping in the western clouds, the grey light of the sea came up, and took, and taking, told the special tone of everything. All this lay upon my heart, without a word of thinking, spreading light and shadow there, and the soft delight of sadness. Nevertheless, I would it were the savage snow around me, and the piping of the restless winds, and the death of everything. For in those days I had Lorna.

Then I thought of promise fair; such as glowed around me, where the red rocks held the sun, when he was departed: and the distant crags endeavoured to retain his memory. But as evening spread across them, shading with a silent fold, all the colour stole away; all remembrance waned, and died.

"So has it been with love," I thought, "and with simple truth and warmth. The maid has chosen the glittering stars, instead of the plain daylight."

Nevertheless I would not give in, although in deep despondency (especially when I passed the place where my dear father had fought in vain), and I tried to see things right, and then judge aright about them. This, however, was more easy to attempt than to achieve; and by the time I came down the hill, I was none the wiser. Only I could tell my mother that the King was dead for sure; and she would have tried to cry, but for thought of her mourning.

There was not a moment for lamenting. All the mourning must be ready (if we cared to beat the Snowes) in eight-and-forty hours: and although it was Sunday night, mother now feeling sure of the thing, sat up with Lizzie, cutting patterns, and stitching things on brown paper, and snipping, and laying the fashions down, and requesting all opinions, yet when given scorning them; insomuch that I grew weary even of tobacco (which had comforted me since Lorna), and prayed her to go on, until the King should be alive again.

The thought of that so flurried her — for she never yet could see a joke — that she laid her scissors on the table, and said, "The Lord forbid, John! after what I have cut up!"

"It would be just like him," I answered, with a knowing smile. "Mother, you had better stop. Patterns may do very well; but don't cut up any more good stuff."

"Well, good lack, I am a fool! Three tables pegged with needles! The Lord in His mercy keep His Majesty, if ever He hath gotten him!"

By this device we went to bed; and not another stitch was struck, until the troopers had office-tidings that the King was truly dead. Hence the Snowes beat us by a day; and both old Betty and Lizzie laid the blame upon me, as usual.

Almost before we had put off the mourning, which as loyal subjects we kept for the King, three months and a week; rumours of disturbances, of plottings, and of outbreak began to stir among us. We heard of fighting in Scotland, and buying of ships on the Continent, and of arms in Dorset and Somerset; and we kept our beacon in readiness to give signals of a landing; or rather the soldiers did so. For we, having trustworthy reports that the new King had been to high mass himself in the Abbey of Westminster, making all the bishops go with him, and all the guards in London, and then tortured all the Protestants who dared to wait outside, moreover had received from the Pope a flower grown in the Virgin Mary's garden, and warranted to last for ever, we of the moderate party, hearing all this and ten times as much, and having no love for this sour James, such as we had for the lively Charles, were ready to wait for what might happen, rather than care about stopping it. Therefore we listened to rumours gladly, and shook our heads with gravity, and predicted, every man something, but scarce any two the same. Nevertheless, in our part, things went on as usual, until the middle of June was nigh. We ploughed the ground, and sowed the corn, and tended the cattle, and heeded every one his neighbour's business, as carefully as heretofore; and the only thing that moved us much was that Annie had a baby. This being a very fine child with blue eyes, and christened "John" in compliment to me, and with me for his godfather, it is natural to suppose that I thought a good deal about him; and when mother or Lizzie would ask me, all of a sudden, and treacherously, when the fire flared up at supper-time (for we always kept a little wood just alight in summer-time, and enough to make the pot boil), then when they would say to me, "John, what are you thinking of? At a word, speak!" I would always answer, "Little John Faggus;" and so they made no more of me.

But when I was down, on Saturday the thirteenth of June, at the blacksmith's forge by Brendon town, where the Lynn-stream runs so close that he dips his horse-shoes in it, and where the news is apt to come first of all our neighbourhood (except upon a Sunday), while we were talking of the hay-crop, and of a great sheep-stealer, round the corner came a man upon a piebald horse, looking flagged and weary. But seeing half a dozen of us, young, and brisk, and hearty, he made a flourish with his horse, and waved a blue flag vehemently, shouting with great glory:

"Monmouth, and the Protestant faith! Monmouth, and no Popery! Monmouth, the good King's eldest son! Down with the poisoning murderer! Down with the black usurper, and to the devil with all papists!"

"Why so, thou little varlet?" I asked very quietly; for the man was too small to quarrel with: yet knowing Lorna to be a "papist," as we choose to call them — though they might as welt call us "kingists," after the head of our Church — I thought that this scurvy scampish knave might show them the way to the place he mentioned, unless his courage failed him.

"Papist yourself, be you?" said the fellow, not daring to answer much: "then take this, and read it."

And he handed me a long rigmarole, which he called a "Declaration": I saw that it was but a heap of lies, and thrust it into the blacksmith's fire, and blew the bellows thrice at it. No one dared attempt to stop me, for my mood had not been sweet of late; and of course they knew my strength.

The man rode on with a muttering noise, having won no recruits from us, by force of my example; and he stopped at the alehouse further down, where the road goes away from the Lynn-stream. Some of us went thither after a time, when our horses were shodden and rasped, for although we might not like the man, we might be glad of his tidings, which seemed to be something wonderful. He had set up his blue flag in the tap-room, and was teaching every one.

"Here coom'th Maister Jan Ridd," said the landlady, being well pleased with the call for beer and cider; "her hath been to Lunnon-town, and live within a maile of me. Arl the news coom from them nowadays, instead of from here, as her ought to do. If Jan Ridd say it be true, I will try a'most to belave it. Hath the good Duke landed, sir?" And she looked at me over a foaming cup, and blew the froth off, and put more in.

"I have no doubt it is true enough," I answered, before drinking; "and too true, Mistress Pugsley. Many a poor man will die; but none shall die from our parish, nor from Brendon, if I can help it."

And I knew that I could help it: for every one in those little places would abide by my advice; not only from the fame of my schooling, and long sojourn in London, but also because I had earned repute for being very "slow and sure": and with nine people out of ten this is the very best recommendation. For they think themselves much before you in wit, and under no obligation, but rather conferring a favour, by doing the thing that you do. Hence, if I cared for influence — which means, for the most part, making people do one's will, without knowing it — my first step towards it would be to be called, in common parlance, "slow but sure."

For the next fortnight, we were daily troubled with con-flicting rumours, each man relating what he desired, rather than what he had right, to believe. We were told that the Duke had been proclaimed King of England, in every town of Dorset and of Somerset; that he had won a great battle at Axminster, and another at Bridport, and another somewhere else; that all the western counties had risen as one man for him, and all the militia joined his ranks; that Taunton, and Bridgwater, and Bristowe, were all mad with delight, the two former being in his hands, and the latter craving to be so. And then, on the other hand, we heard that the Duke had been vanquished, and put to flight, and upon being apprehended had confessed himself an impostor, and a papist, as bad as the King was.

We longed for Colonel Stickles (as he always became in time of war, though he fell back to Captain, and even Lieutenant, directly the fight was over), for then we should have won trusty news, as well as good consideration. But even Serjeant Bloxham, much against his will, was gone, having left his heart with our Lizzie, and a collection of all his writings. All the soldiers had been ordered away at full speed for Exeter, to join the Duke of Albemarle, or if he were gone, to follow him. As for us, who had fed them so long (although not quite for nothing), we must take our chance of Doones, or any other enemies.

Now all these tidings moved me a little; not enough to spoil appetite, but enough to make things lively, and to teach me that look of wisdom, which is bred of practice only, and the hearing of many lies. Therefore I withheld my judgment, fearing to be triumphed over, if it should happen to miss the mark. But mother, and Lizzie, ten times in a day, predicted all they could imagine; and their prophecies increased in strength, according to contradiction. Yet this was not in the proper style for a house like ours, which knew the news, or at least had known it; and still was famous, all around, for the last advices. Even from Lynmouth, people sent up to Plover's Barrows, to ask how things were going on; and it was very grievous to answer, that in truth we knew not, neither had heard for days and days; and our reputation was so great, especially since the death of the King had gone abroad from Oare parish, that many inquirers would only wink, and lay a finger on the lip, as if to say, "You know well enough, but see not fit to tell me." And before the end arrived, those people believed that they had been right all along, and that we had concealed the truth from them.

For I myself became involved (God knows how much against my will and my proper judgment) in the troubles, and the conflict, and the cruel work coming afterwards. If ever I had made up my mind to anything in all my life, it was at this particular time, and as stern and strong as could be. I had resolved to let things pass — to hear about them gladly, to encourage all my friends to talk, and myself to express opinion upon each particular point, when in the fulness of time no further doubt could be. But all my policy went for nothing, through a few touches of feeling.

One day at the beginning of July, I came home from mowing about noon, or a little later, to fetch some cider for all of us, and to eat a morsel of bacon. For mowing was no joke that year, the summer being wonderfully wet (even for our wet country), and the swathe falling heavier over the scythe than ever I could remember it. We were drenched with rain almost every day; but the mowing must be done somehow; and we must trust to God for the hay-making.

In the court-yard I saw a little cart, with iron breaks underneath it, such as fastidious people use to deaden the jolting of the road; but few men under a lord or baronet would be so particular. Therefore I wondered who our noble visitor could be. But when I entered the kitchen-place, brushing up my hair for somebody, behold it was no one greater than our Annie, with my godson in her arms, and looking pale and tear-begone. And at first she could not speak to me. But presently having sat down a little, and received much praise for her baby, she smiled, and blushed, and found her tongue, as if she had never gone from us.

"How natural it all looks again! Oh, I love this old kitchen so! Baby dear, only look at it, wid him pitty, pitty eyes, and him tongue out of his mousy! But who put the flour riddle up there? And look at the pestle and mortar, and rust I declare in the patty pans! And a book, positively a dirty book, where the clean skewers ought to hang! Oh, Lizzie, Lizzie, Lizzie!"

"You may just as well cease lamenting," I said, "for you can't alter Lizzie's nature, and you will only make mother uncomfortable, and perhaps have a quarrel with Lizzie, who is proud as Punch of her housekeeping."

"She!" cried Annie, with all the contempt that could be compressed in a syllable. "Well, John, no doubt you are right about it. I will try not to notice things. But it is a hard thing, after all my care, to see everything going to ruin. But what can be expected of a girl who knows all the kings of Carthage?"

"There were no kings of Carthage, Annie. They were called, why let me see — they were called — oh, something else."

"Never mind what they were called," said Annie; "will they cook our dinner for us? But now, John, I am in such trouble. All this talk is make-believe."

"Don't you cry, my dear: don't cry, my darling sister," I answered, as she dropped into the worn place of the settle, and bent above her infant, rocking as if both their hearts were one: "don't you know, Annie, I cannot tell, but I know, or at least I mean, I have heard the men of experience say, it is so bad for the baby."

"Perhaps I know that as well as you do, John," said Annie, looking up at me with a gleam of her old laughing: "but how can I help crying? I am in such trouble."

"Tell me what it is, my dear. Any grief of yours will vex me greatly; but I will try to bear it."

"Then, John, it is just this. Tom has gone off with the rebels; and you must, oh, you must go after him."

CHAPTER LXIII

John is worsted by the Women

Moved as I was by Annie's tears, and gentle style of coaxing, and most of all by my love for her, I yet declared that I could not go, and leave our house and homestead, far less my dear mother and Lizzie, at the mercy of the merciless Doones.

"Is that all your objection, John?" asked Annie, in her quick panting way: "would you go but for that, John?"

"Now," I said, "be in no such hurry;" for while I was gradually yielding, I liked to pass it through my fingers, as if my fingers shaped it: "there are many things to be thought about, and many ways of viewing it."

"Oh, you never can have loved Lorna! No wonder you gave her up so! John, you can love nobody, but your oat-ricks, and your hay-ricks."

"Sister mine, because I rant not, neither rave of what I feel, can you be so shallow as to dream that I feel nothing? What is your love for Tom Faggus? What is your love for your baby (pretty darling as he is) to compare with such a love as for ever dwells with me? Because I do not prate of it; because it is beyond me, not only to express, but even form to my own heart in thoughts; because I do not shape my face, and would scorn to play to it, as a thing of acting, and lay it out before you, are you fools enough to think —— " but here I stopped, having said more than was usual with me.

"I am very sorry, John. Dear John, I am so sorry. What a shallow fool I am!"

"I will go seek your husband," I said, to change the subject, for even to Annie I would not lay open all my heart about Lorna: "but only upon condition that you ensure this house, and people, from the Doones meanwhile. Even for the sake of Tom, I cannot leave all helpless. The oak-ricks and the hay-ricks, which are my only love, they are welcome to make cinders of. But I will not have mother treated so; nor even little Lizzie, although you scorn your sister so."

"Oh, John, I do think you art the hardest, as well as the softest, of all the men I know. Not even a woman's bitter word but what you pay her out for. Will you never understand that we are not like you, John? We say all sorts of spiteful things, without a bit of meaning. John, for God's sake, fetch Tom home; and then revile me as you please, and I will kneel and thank you."

"I will not promise to fetch him home," I answered, being ashamed of myself, for having lost command so: "but I will promise to do my best, if we can only hit on a plan for leaving mother harmless."

Annie thought for a little while, trying to gather her smooth clear brow into maternal wrinkles, and then she looked at her child, and said, "I will risk it, for daddy's sake, darling; you precious soul, for daddy's sake." I asked her what she was going to risk. She would not tell me; but took upper hand, and saw to my cider-cans and bacon, and went from corner to cupboard, exactly as if she had never been married; only without an apron on. And then she said, "Now to your mowers, John; and make the most of this fine afternoon: kiss your godson, before you go." And I, being used to obey her, in little things of that sort, kissed the baby, and took my cans, and went back to my scythe again.

By the time I came home it was dark night, and pouring again with a foggy rain, such as we have in July, even more than in January. Being soaked all through and through, and with water quelching in my boots, like a pump with a bad bucket, I was only too glad to find Annie's bright face, and quick figure, flitting in and out the firelight, instead of Lizzie sitting grandly, with a feast of literature, and not a drop of gravy. Mother was in the corner also, with her cherry-coloured ribbons glistening very nice by candle light, looking at Annie now and then, with memories of her babyhood; and then at her having a baby; yet half afraid of praising her much, for fear of that young Lizzie. But Lizzie showed no jealousy: she truly loved our Annie (now that she was gone from us), and she wanted to know all sorts of things, and she adored the baby. Therefore Annie was allowed to attend to me, as she used to do.

"Now, John, you must start the first thing in the morning," she said, when the others had left the room, but somehow she stuck to the baby, "to fetch me back my rebel, according to your promise."

234

"Not so," I replied, misliking the job; "all I promised was to go, if this house were assured against any onslaught of the Doones."

"Just so; and here is that assurance." With these words she drew forth a paper, and laid it on my knee with triumph, enjoying my amazement. This, as you may suppose, was great; not only at the document, but also at her possession of it. For in truth it was no less than a formal undertaking, on the part of the Doones, not to attack Plover's Barrows farm, or molest any of the inmates, or carry off any chattels, during the absence of John Ridd upon a special errand. This document was signed not only by the Counsellor, but by many other Doones: whether Carver's name were there, I could not say for certain; as of course he would not sign it under his name of "Carver," and I had never heard Lorna say to what (if any) he had been baptized.

In the face of such a deed as this, I could no longer refuse to go; and having received my promise, Annie told me (as was only fair) how she had procured that paper. It was both a clever and courageous act; and would have seemed to me, at first sight, far beyond Annie's power. But none may gauge a woman's power, when her love and faith are moved.

The first thing Annie had done was this: she made herself look ugly. This was not an easy thing; but she had learned a great deal from her husband, upon the subject of disguises. It hurt her feelings not a little to make so sad a fright of herself; but what could it matter? — if she lost Tom, she must be a far greater fright in earnest, than now she was in seeming. And then she left her child asleep under Betty Muxworthy's tendance — for Betty took to that child, as if there never had been a child before — and away she went in her own "spring-cart" (as the name of that engine proved to be), without a word to anyone, except the old man who had driven her from Molland parish that morning; and who coolly took one of our best horses, without "by your leave" to anyone.

Annie made the old man drive her within easy reach of the Doone-gate, whose position she knew well enough, from all our talk about it. And there she bade the old man stay, until she should return to him. Then with her comely figure hidden by a dirty old woman's cloak, and her fair young face defaced by patches and by liniments, so that none might covet her, she addressed the young men at the gate in a cracked and trembling voice; and they were scarcely civil to the "old hag," as they called her. She said that she bore important tidings for Sir Counsellor himself, and must be conducted to him. To him accordingly she was led, without even any hood-winking; for she had spectacles over her eyes, and made believe not to see ten yards.

She found Sir Counsellor at home, and when the rest were out of sight, threw off all disguise to him, flashing forth as a lovely young woman, from all her wraps and disfigurements. She flung her patches on the floor, amid the old man's laughter, and let her tucked-up hair come down; and then went up and kissed him.

"Worthy and reverend Counsellor, I have a favour to ask," she began.

"So I should think from your proceedings," the old man interrupted; "ah, if I were half my age ——— "

"If you were, I would not sue so. But, most excellent Counsellor, you owe me some amends, you know, for the way in which you robbed me."

"Beyond a doubt I do, my dear. You have put it rather strongly; and it might offend some people. Nevertheless I own my debt, having so fair a creditor."

"And do you remember how you slept, and how much we made of you, and would have seen you home, sir; only you did not wish it?"

"And for excellent reasons, child. My best escort was in my cloak, after we made the cream to rise. Ha ha! The unholy spell. My pretty child, has it injured you?"

"Yes, I fear it has," said Annie; "or whence can all my ill luck come?" And here she showed some signs of crying, knowing that the Counsellor hated it.

"You shall not have ill luck, my dear. I have heard all about your marriage to a very noble highwayman. Ah, you made a mistake in that; you were worthy of a Doone, my child; your frying was a blessing meant for those who can appreciate."

"My husband can appreciate," she answered very proudly; "but what I wish to know is this, will you try to help me?"

The Counsellor answered that he would do so, if her needs were moderate; whereupon she opened her meaning to him, and told of all her anxieties. Considering that Lorna was gone, and her necklace in his possession, and that I (against whom alone of us the Doones could bear any malice) would be out of the way all the while, the old man readily undertook that our house should not be assaulted, nor our property molested, until my return. And to the promptitude of his pledge, two things perhaps contributed, namely, that he knew not how we were stripped of all defenders, and that some of his own forces were away in the rebel camp. For (as I learned thereafter) the Doones being now in direct feud with the present Government, and sure to be crushed if that prevailed, had resolved to drop all religious questions, and cast in their lot with Monmouth. And the turbulent youths, being long restrained from their wonted outlet for vehemence, by the troopers in the neighbourhood, were only too glad to rush forth upon any promise of blows and excitement.

However, Annie knew little of this, but took the Counsellor's pledge as a mark of especial favour in her behalf (which it may have been, to some extent), and thanked him for it most heartily, and felt that he had earned the necklace; while he, like an ancient gentleman, disclaimed all obligation, and sent her under an escort safe to her own cart again. But Annie, repassing the sentinels, with her youth restored, and blooming with the flush of triumph, went up to them very gravely, and said, "The old hag wishes you good evening, gentlemen;" and so made her best courtesy.

Now look at it as I would, there was no excuse left for me, after the promise given. Dear Annie had not only cheated the Doones, but also had gotten the best of me by a pledge to a thing impossible. And I bitterly said, "I am not like Lorna: a pledge once given, I keep it."

"I will not have a word against Lorna," cried Annie: "I will answer for her truth, as surely as I would for my own, or yours, John." And with that she vanquished me.

But when my poor mother heard that I was committed, by word of honour, to a wild-goose chase, among the rebels, after that runagate Tom Faggus, she simply stared, and would not believe it. For lately I had joked with her, in a little style of jerks, as people do when out of sorts; and she not understanding this, and knowing jokes to be out of my power, would only look, and sigh, and toss, and hope that I meant nothing. At last, however, we convinced her that I was in earnest, and must be off in the early morning, and leave John Fry with the hay crop.

Then mother was ready to fall upon Annie, as not content with disgracing us, by wedding a man of new honesty (if indeed of any), but laying traps to catch her brother, and entangle him perhaps to his death, for the sake of a worthless fellow; and "felon" — she was going to say, as by the shape of her lips I knew. But I laid my hand upon dear mother's lips; because what must be, must be; and if mother and daughter stayed at home, better in love than in quarrelling.

Right early in the morning I was off, without word to any-one; knowing that mother, and sister mine, had cried each her good self to sleep; relenting when the light was out, and sorry for hard words and thoughts; and yet too much alike in nature to understand each other. Therefore I took good Kickums, who (although with one eye spoiled) was worth ten sweet-tempered horses, to a man who knew how to manage him; and being well charged both with bacon and powder, forth I set on my wild-goose chase.

For this I claim no bravery. I cared but little what came of it; save for mother's sake, and Annie's, and the keeping of the farm, and discomfiture of the Snowes, and lamenting of Lorna at my death, if die I must in a lonesome manner, not found out till afterwards, and bleaching bones left to weep over. However, I had a little kettle, and a pound and a half of tobacco, and two dirty pipes and a clean one; also a bit of clothes for change, also a brisket of hung venison, and four loaves of farm-house bread, and of the upper side of bacon a stone and a half it might be, not to mention divers small things for campaigning, which may come in handily, when no one else has gotten them.

We went away in merry style; my horse being ready for anything, and I only glad of a bit of change, after months of working, and brooding; with no content to crown the work; no hope to hatch the brooding, or without hatching to reckon it. Who could tell but what Lorna might be discovered, or at any rate heard of, before the end of this campaign; if campaign it could be called of a man who went to fight nobody, only to re-deem a runagate? And vexed as I was about the hay, and the hunch-backed ricks John was sure to make (which spoil the look of a farm-yard), still even this was better than to have the mows and houses fired, as I had nightly expected, and been worn out with the worry of it.

Yet there was one thing rather unfavourable to my present enterprise, namely, that I knew nothing of the country I was bound to, nor even in what part of it my business might be supposed to lie. For beside the uncertainty caused by the conflict of reports, it was likely that King Monmouth's army would be moving from place to place, according to the prospect of supplies and of reinforcements. However there would arise more chance of getting news as I went on: and my road being towards the east and south, Dulverton would not lie so very far aside of it, but what it might be worth a visit, both to collect the latest tidings, and to consult the maps and plans in Uncle Reuben's parlour. Therefore I drew the off-hand rein, at the cross-road on the hills, and made for the town; expecting perhaps to have breakfast with Master Huckaback, and Ruth to help and encourage us. This little maiden was now become a very great favourite with me, having long outgrown, no doubt, her childish fancies and follies, such as my mother and Annie had planted under her soft brown hair. It had been my duty, as well as my true interest (for Uncle Ben was more and more testy, as he went on gold-digging), to ride thither, now and again, to inquire what the doctor thought of her. Not that her wounds were long in healing, but that people can scarcely be too careful and too inquisitive, after a great horse-bite. And she always let me look at the arm, as I had been first doctor, and she held it up in a graceful manner, curving at the elbow, and with a sweep of white roundness going to a wrist the size of my thumb or so, and without any thimble-top standing forth, such as even our Annie had. But gradually all I could see, above the elbow, where the bite had been, was very clear transparent skin, with very firm sweet flesh below, and three little blue marks as far asunder as the prongs of a toasting-fork, and no deeper than where a twig has chafed the peel of a waxen apple. And then I used to say in fun, as the children do, "Shall I kiss it, to make it well, dear?"

Now Ruth looked very grave indeed, upon hearing of this my enterprise; and crying, said she could almost cry, for the sake of my dear mother. Did I know the risks and chances, not of the battle-field alone, but of the havoc afterwards; the swearing away of innocent lives, and the hurdle, and the hanging? And if I would please not to laugh (which was so unkind of me), had I never heard of imprisonments, and torturing with the cruel boot, and selling into slavery, where the sun and the lash outvied one another in cutting a man to pieces? I replied that of all these things I had heard, and would take especial care to steer me free of all of them. My duty was all that I wished to do; and none could harm me for doing that. And I begged my cousin to give me good-speed, instead of talking dolefully. Upon this she changed her manner wholly, becoming so lively and cheerful that I was convinced of her indifference, and surprised even more than gratified.

"Go and earn your spurs, Cousin Ridd," she said; "you are strong enough for anything. Which side is to have the benefit of your doughty arm?"

"Have I not told you, Ruth," I answered, not being fond of this kind of talk, more suitable for Lizzie, "that I do not mean to join either side, that is to say, until —— "

"Until, as the common proverb goes, you know which way the cat will jump. Oh, John Ridd! Oh, John Ridd!"

"Nothing of the sort," said I: "what a hurry you are in! I am for the King, of course."

"But not enough to fight for him. Only enough to vote, I suppose, or drink his health, or shout for him, as soon as you are sure who is the King."

"I can't make you out to-day, Cousin Ruth; you are nearly as bad as Lizzie. You do not say any bitter things, but you seem to mean them."

"No, cousin, think not so of me. It is far more likely that I say them, without meaning them."

"Anyhow, it is not like you. And I know not what I can have done in any way, to vex you."

"Dear me, nothing, Cousin Ridd; you never do anything to vex me."

"Then I hope I shall do something now, Ruth, when I say good-bye. God knows if we ever shall meet again, Ruth; but I hope we may."

"To be sure we shall," she answered in her brightest manner. "Try not to look wretched, John; you are as happy as a Maypole."

"And you as a rose in May," I said; "and pretty nearly as pretty. Give my love to Uncle Ben; and I trust him to keep on the winning side."

"Of that you need have no misgiving. Never yet has he failed of it. Now, Cousin Ridd, why go you not? You hurried me so at breakfast time."

"My only reason for waiting, Ruth, is that you have not kissed me, as you are almost bound to do, for the last time perhaps of seeing me."

"Oh, if that is all, just fetch the stool; and I will do my best, cousin."

"I pray you be not so vexatious; you always used to do it nicely, without any stool, Ruth."

"Ah, but you are grown since then, and become a famous man, John Ridd, and a member of the nobility. Go your way, and win your spurs. I want no lip-service."

Being at the end of my wits, I did even as she ordered me. At least I had no spurs to win, because there were big ones on my boots, paid for in the Easter bill, and made by a famous saddler, so as never to clog with marsh-weed, but prick as hard as any horse, in reason, could desire. And Kickums never wanted spurs; but always went tail-foremost, if anybody offered them for his consideration.

CHAPTER LXIV

Slaughter in the Marshes

We rattled away, at a merry pace, out of the town of Dulverton; my horse being gaily fed, and myself quite fit again for going. Of course I was puzzled about Cousin Ruth; for her behaviour was not at all such as I had expected; and indeed I had hoped for a far more loving and moving farewell than I got from her. But I said to myself, "It is useless ever to count upon what a woman will do; and I think that I must have vexed her, almost as much as she vexed me. And now to see what comes of it." So I put my horse across the moorland; and he threw his chest out bravely.

Now if I tried to set down at length all the things that happened to me, upon this adventure, every in and out, and up and down, and to and fro, that occupied me, together with the things I saw, and the things I heard of — however much the wiser people might applaud my narrative, it is likely enough that idle readers might exclaim, "What ails this man? Knows he not that men of parts, and of real understanding, have told us all we care to hear of that miserable business? Let him keep to his farm, and bacon, his wrestling, and constant feeding."

Fearing to meet with such rebuffs (which after my death would vex me), I will try to set down only what is needful for my story, and the clearing of my character, and the good name of our parish. But the manner in which I was bandied about, by false information, from pillar to post, or at other times driven quite out of my way by the presence of the King's soldiers, may be known by the names of the following towns, to which I was sent in succession, Bath, Frome, Wells, Wincanton, Glastonbury, Shepton, Bradford, Axbridge, Somerton, and Bridgwater.

This last place I reached on a Sunday night, the fourth or fifth of July, I think — or it might be the sixth, for that matter; inasmuch as I had been too much worried to get the day of the month at church. Only I know that my horse and myself were glad to come to a decent place, where meat, and corn, could be had for money; and being quite weary of wandering about, we hoped to rest there a little.

Of this, however, we found no chance, for the town was full of the good Duke's soldiers; if men may be called so, the half of whom had never been drilled, nor had fired a gun. And it was rumoured among them, that the "popish army," as they called it, was to be attacked that very night, and with God's assistance beaten. However, by this time I had been taught to pay little attention to rumours; and having sought vainly for Tom Faggus, among these poor rustic warriors, I took to my hostel, and went to bed, being as weary as weary can be.

Falling asleep immediately, I took heed of nothing; although the town was all alive, and lights had come glancing, as I lay down, and shouts making echo all round my room. But all I did was to hug my pillow; not an inch would I budge, unless the house, and even my bed, were on fire. And so for several hours I lay, in the depth of the deepest slumber, without even a dream on its surface; until I was roused and awakened at last, by a pushing, and pulling, and pinching, and a plucking of hair out by the roots. And at length, being able to open mine eyes, I saw the old landlady, with a candle, heavily wondering at me.

"Can't you let me alone?" I grumbled: "I have paid for my bed, mistress; and I won't get up, for anyone."

"Would to God, young man," she answered, shaking me as hard as ever, "that the popish soldiers may sleep this night, only half as strong as thou dost! Fie on thee, fie on thee! Get up, and go fight; we can hear the battle already; and a man of thy size mought stop a cannon."

"I would rather stop a-bed," said I; "what have I to do with fighting? I am for King James, if any."

"Then thou mayest even stop a-bed," the old woman muttered sulkily. "A' would never have laboured half an hour to awake a Papisher. But hearken you one thing, young man; Zummerzett thou art, by thy brogue; or at least by thy understanding of it; no Zummerzett maid will look at thee, in spite of thy size and stature, unless thou strikest a blow this night."

"I lack no Zummerzett maid, mistress; I have a fairer than your brown things; and for her alone would I strike a blow."

At this the old woman gave me up as being beyond correction; and it vexed me a little that my great fame had not reached so far as Bridgwater, when I thought that it went to Bristowe. But those people in East Somerset know nothing about wrestling. Devon is the headquarters of the art; and Devon is the county of my chief love. Howbeit, my vanity was moved by this slur upon it — for I had told her my name was "John Ridd," when I had a gallon of ale with her, ere ever I came upstairs; and she had nodded, in such a manner, that I thought she knew both name and fame — and here was I, not only shaken, pinched, and with many hairs pulled out, in the midst of my first good sleep for a week, but also abused, and taken amiss, and (which vexed me most of all) unknown.

Now there is nothing like vanity to keep a man awake at night, however he be weary; and most of all, when he believes that he is doing something great — this time, if never done before — yet other people will not see, except what they may laugh at; and so be far above him, and sleep themselves the happier. Therefore their sleep robs his own: for all things play so, in and out (with the godly and ungodly ever swaying in a balance, as they have done in my time, almost every year or two), all things have such nice reply of produce to the call for it, and such a spread across the world, giving here and taking there, yet on the whole pretty even, that haply sleep itself has but a certain stock, and keeps in hand, and sells to flattered (which can pay) that which flattened vanity cannot pay, and will not sue for.

Be that as it may, I was by this time wide awake, though much aggrieved at feeling so, and through the open window heard the distant roll of musketry, and the beating of drums, with a quick rub-a-dub, and the "come round the corner," or trumpet-call. And perhaps Tom Faggus might be there, and shot at any moment, and my dear Annie left a poor widow, and my godson Jack an orphan, without a tooth to help him.

Therefore I reviled myself for all my heavy laziness; and partly through good honest will, and partly through the stings of pride, and yet a little perhaps by virtue of a young man's love of riot, up I arose, and dressed myself, and woke Kickums (who was snoring), and set out to see the worst of it. The sleepy hostler scratched his poll, and could not tell me which way to take; what odds to him who was King, or Pope, so long as he paid his way; and got a bit of bacon on Sunday? And would I please to remember that I had roused him up at night, and the quality always made a point of paying four times over for a man's loss of his beauty-sleep. I replied that his loss of beauty-sleep was rather improving to a man of so high complexion; and that I, being none of the quality, must pay half-quality prices: and so I gave him double fee, as became a good farmer; and he was glad to be quit of Kickums; as I saw by the turn of his eye, while going out at the archway.

All this was done by lanthorn light, although the moon was high and bold; and in the northern heaven, flags and ribbons of a jostling pattern; such as we often have in autumn, but in July very rarely. Of these Master Dryden has spoken somewhere, in his courtly manner; but of him I think so little — because by fashion preferred to Shakespeare — that I cannot remember the passage; neither is it a credit to him.

Therefore I was guided mainly by the sound of guns and trumpets, in riding out of the narrow ways, and into the open marshes. And thus I might have found my road, in spite of all the spread of water, and the glaze of moonshine; but that, as I followed sound (far from hedge or causeway), fog (like a chestnut-tree in blossom, touched with moonlight) met me. Now fog is a thing that I understand, and can do with well enough, where I know the country; but here I had never been before. It was nothing to our Exmoor fogs; not to be compared with them; and all the time one could see the moon; which we cannot do in our fogs; nor even the sun, for a week together. Yet the gleam of water always makes a fog more difficult: like a curtain on a mirror; none can tell the boundaries.

And here we had broad-water patches, in and out, inlaid on land, like mother-of-pearl in brown Shittim wood. To a wild duck, born and bred there, it would almost be a puzzle to find her own nest amongst them; what chance then had I and Kickums, both unused to marsh and mere? Each time when we thought that we must be right, now at last, by track or passage, and approaching the conflict, with the sounds of it waxing nearer, suddenly a break of water would be laid before us, with the moon looking mildly over it, and the northern lights behind us, dancing down the lines of fog.

It was an awful thing, I say (and to this day I remember it), to hear the sounds of raging fight, and the yells of raving slayers, and the howls of poor men stricken hard, and shattered from wrath to wailing; then suddenly the dead low hush, as of a soul departing, and spirits kneeling over it. Through the vapour of the earth, and white breath of the water, and beneath the pale round moon (bowing as the drift went by), all this rush and pause of fear passed, or lingered, on my path.

At last, when I almost despaired of escaping from this tangle of spongy banks, and of hazy creeks, and reed-fringe, my horse heard the neigh of a fellow-horse, and was only too glad to answer it; upon which the other, having lost his rider, came up, and pricked his ears at us, and gazed through the fog very steadfastly. Therefore I encouraged him with a soft and genial whistle, and Kickums did his best to tempt him with a snort of inquiry. However, nothing would suit that nag, except to enjoy his new freedom; and he capered away with his tail set on high, and the stirrup-irons clashing under him. Therefore as he might know the way, and appeared to have been in the battle, we followed him very carefully: and he led us to a little hamlet, called (as I found afterwards) West Zuyland, or Zealand, so named perhaps from its situation amid this inland sea.

Here the King's troops had been quite lately, and their fires were still burning; but the men themselves had been summoned away by the night attack of the rebels. Hence I procured for my guide a young man who knew the district thoroughly, and who led me by many intricate ways to the rear of the rebel army. We came upon a broad open moor, striped with sullen watercourses, shagged with sedge, and yellow iris, and in the drier part with bilberries. For by this time it was four o'clock, and the summer sun, arising wanly, showed us all the ghastly scene.

Would that I had never been there! Often in the lonely hours, even now it haunts me: would, far more, that the piteous thing had never been done in England! Flying men, flung back from dreams of victory and honour, only glad to have the luck of life and limbs to fly with, mud-bedraggled, foul with slime, reeking both with sweat and blood, which they could not stop to wipe, cursing, with their pumped-out lungs, every stick that hindered them, or gory puddle that slipped the step, scarcely able to leap over the corses that had dragged to die. And to see how the corses lay; some, as fair as death in sleep; with the smile of placid valour, and of noble manhood, hovering yet on the silent lips. These had bloodless hands put upwards, white as wax, and firm as death, clasped (as on a monument) in prayer for dear ones left behind, or in high thanksgiving. And of these men there was nothing in their broad blue eyes to fear. But others were of different sort; simple fellows unused to pain, accustomed to the billhook, perhaps, or rasp of the knuckles in a quick-set hedge, or making some to-do, at breakfast, over a thumb cut in sharpening a scythe, and expecting their wives to make more to-do. Yet here lay these poor chaps, dead; dead, after a deal of pain, with little mind to bear it, and a soul they had never thought of; gone, their God alone knows whither; but to mercy we may trust. Upon these things I cannot dwell; and none, I trow, would ask me; only if a plain man saw what I saw that morning, he (if God had blessed him with the heart that is in most of us) must have sickened of all desire to be great among mankind.

Seeing me riding to the front (where the work of death went on, among the men of true English pluck; which, when moved, no further moves), the fugitives called out to me, in half a dozen dialects, to make no utter fool of myself; for the great guns were come, and the fight was over; all the rest was slaughter.

"Arl oop wi' Moonmo'," shouted one big fellow, a miner of the Mendip hills, whose weapon was a pick-axe: "na oose to vaight na moor. Wend thee hame, young mon, agin."

Upon this I stopped my horse, desiring not to be shot for nothing; and eager to aid some poor sick people, who tried to lift their arms to me. And this I did to the best of my power, though void of skill in the business; and more inclined to weep with them than to check their weeping. While I was giving a drop of cordial from my flask to one poor fellow, who sat up, while his life was ebbing, and with slow insistence urged me when his broken voice would come, to tell his wife (whose name I knew not) something about an apple-tree, and a golden guinea stored in it, to divide among six children — in the midst of this, I felt warm lips laid against my cheek quite softly, and then a little push; and behold it was a horse leaning over me! I arose in haste, and there stood Winnie, looking at me with beseeching eyes, enough to melt a heart of stone. Then seeing my attention fixed, she turned her head, and glanced back sadly towards the place of battle, and gave a little wistful neigh; and then looked me full in the face again, as much as to say, "Do you understand?" while she scraped with one hoof impatiently. If ever a horse tried hard to speak, it was Winnie at that moment. I went to her side and patted her; but that was not what she wanted. Then I offered to leap into the empty saddle; but neither did that seem good to her; for the ran away toward the part of the field at which she had been glancing back, and then turned round, and shook her mane, entreating me to follow her.

Upon this I learned from the dying man where to find his apple-tree, and promised to add another guinea to the one in store for his children; and so, commending him to God, I mounted my own horse again, and to Winnie's great delight, professed myself at her service. With her ringing silvery neigh, such as no other horse of all I ever knew could equal, she at once proclaimed her triumph, and told her master (or meant to tell, if death should not have closed his ears), that she was coming to his aid, and bringing one who might be trusted, of the higher race that kill.

A cannon-bullet fired low, and ploughing the marsh slowly, met poor Winnie front to front; and she, being as quick as thought, lowered her nose to sniff at it. It might be a message from her master; for it made a mournful noise. But luckily for Winnie's life, a rise of wet ground took the ball, even under her very nose; and there it cut a splashy groove, missing her off hind-foot by an inch, and scattering black mud over her. It frightened me much more than Winnie; of that I am quite certain; because, though I am firm enough, when it comes to a real tussle, and the heart of a fellow warms up, and tells him that he must go through with it; yet I never did approve of making a cold pie of death.

Therefore, with those reckless cannons, brazen-mouthed and bellowing, two furlongs off, or it might be more (and the more the merrier), I would have given that year's hay-crop, for a bit of a hill, or a thicket of oaks, or almost even a badger's earth. People will call me a coward for this (especially when I had made up my mind, that life was not worth having without any sign of Lorna); nevertheless, I cannot help it: those were my feelings; and I set them down, because they made a mark on me. At Glen Doone I had fought, even against cannon, with some spirit and fury; but now I saw nothing to fight about; but rather in every poor doubled corpse, a good reason for not fighting. So, in cold blood riding on, and yet ashamed that a man should shrink where a horse went bravely, I cast a bitter blame upon the reckless ways of Winnie.

Nearly all were scattered now. Of the noble countrymen (armed with scythe, or pick-axe, blacksmith's hammer, or fold-pitcher), who had stood their ground for hours against blazing musketry, from men whom they could not get at, by reason of the water-dyke, and then against the deadly cannon, dragged by the Bishop's horses to slaughter his own sheep; of these sturdy Englishmen, noble in their want of sense, scarce one out of four remained for the cowards to shoot down. "Cross the rhaine," they shouted out, "cross the rhaine, and coom within rache:" but the other mongrel Britons, with a mongrel at their head, found it pleasanter to shoot men, who could not shoot in answer, than to meet the chance of mischief, from strong arms and stronger hearts.

The last scene of this piteous play was acting, just as I rode up. Broad daylight, and upstanding sun, winnowing fog from the eastern hills, and spreading the moors with freshness; all along the dykes they shone, glistened on the willow-trunks, and touched the banks with a hoary grey. But alas! those banks were touched more deeply with a gory red, and strewn with fallen trunks, more woeful than the wreck of trees; while howling, cursing, yelling, and the loathsome reek of carnage, drowned the scent of new-mown hay, and the carol of the lark.

Then the cavalry of the King, with their horses at full speed, dashed from either side upon the helpless mob of countrymen. A few pikes feebly levelled met them; but they shot the pike-men, drew swords, and helter-skelter leaped into the shattered and scattering mass. Right and left, they hacked and hewed; I could hear the snapping of scythes beneath them, and see the flash of their sweeping swords. How it must end was plain enough, even to one like myself, who had never beheld such a battle before. But Winnie led me away to the left; and as I could not help the people, neither stop the slaughter, but found the cannon-bullets coming very rudely nigh me, I was only too glad to follow her.

CHAPTER LXV
Falling among Lambs

That faithful creature, whom I began to admire as if she were my own (which is no little thing for a man to say of another man's horse), stopped in front of a low black shed, such as we call a "linhay." And here she uttered a little greeting, in a subdued and softened voice, hoping to obtain an answer, such as her master was wont to give in a cheery manner. Receiving no reply, she entered; and I (who could scarce keep up with her, poor Kickums being weary) leaped from his back, and followed. There I found her sniffing gently, but with great emotion, at the body of Tom Faggus. A corpse poor Tom appeared to be, if ever there was one in this world; and I turned away, and felt unable to keep altogether from weeping. But the mare either could not understand, or else would not believe it. She reached her long neck forth, and felt him with her under lip, passing it over his skin as softly as a mother would do to an infant; and then she looked up at me again; as much as to say, "He is all right."

Upon this I took courage, and handled poor Tom, which being young I had feared at first to do. He groaned very feebly, as I raised him up; and there was the wound, a great savage one (whether from pike-thrust or musket-ball), gaping and welling in his right side, from which a piece seemed to be torn away. I bound it up with some of my linen, so far as I knew how; just to stanch the flow of blood, until we could get a doctor. Then I gave him a little weak brandy and water, which he drank with the greatest eagerness, and made sign to me for more of it. But not knowing how far it was right to give cordial under the circumstances, I handed him unmixed water that time; thinking that he was too far gone to perceive the difference. But herein I wronged Tom Faggus; for he shook his head, and frowned at me. Even at the door of death, he would not drink what Adam drank, by whom came death into the world. So I gave him a little more eau-de-vie, and he took it most submissively.

After that he seemed better, and a little colour came into his cheeks; and he looked at Winnie and knew her; and would have her nose in his clammy hand, though I thought it not good for either of them. With the stay of my arm he sat upright, and faintly looked about him; as if at the end of a violent dream, too much for his power of mind. Then he managed to whisper, "Is Winnie hurt?"

"As sound as a roach," I answered. "Then so am I," said he: "put me upon her back, John; she and I die together."

Surprised as I was at this fatalism (for so it appeared to me), of which he had often shown symptoms before (but I took them for mere levity), now I knew not what to do; for it seemed to me a murderous thing to set such a man on horseback; where he must surely bleed to death, even if he could keep the saddle. But he told me, with many breaks and pauses, that unless I obeyed his orders, he would tear off all my bandages, and accept no further aid from me.

While I was yet hesitating, a storm of horse at full gallop went by, tearing, swearing, bearing away all the country before them. Only a little pollard hedge kept us from their blood-shot eyes. "Now is the time," said my cousin Tom, so far as I could make out his words; "on their heels, I am safe, John, if I only have Winnie under me. Winnie and I die together."

Seeing this strong bent of his mind, stronger than any pains of death, I even did what his feeble eyes sometimes implored, and sometimes commanded. With a strong sash, from his own hot neck, bound and twisted, tight as wax, around his damaged waist, I set him upon Winnie's back, and placed his trembling feet in stirrups, with a band from one to other, under the good mare's body; so that no swerve could throw him out: and then I said, "Lean forward, Tom; it will stop your hurt from bleeding." He leaned almost on the neck of the mare, which, as I knew, must close the wound; and the light of his eyes was quite different, and the pain of his forehead unstrung itself, as he felt the undulous readiness of her volatile paces under him.

"God bless you, John; I am safe," he whispered, fearing to open his lungs much: "who can come near my Winnie mare? A mile of her gallop is ten years of life. Look out for yourself, John Ridd." He sucked his lips, and the mare went off, as easy and swift as a swallow.

"Well," thought I, as I looked at Kickums, ignobly cropping a bit of grass, "I have done a very good thing, no doubt, and ought to be thankful to God for the chance. But as for getting away unharmed, with all these scoundrels about me, and only a foundered horse to trust in — good and spiteful as he is — upon the whole, I begin to think that I have made a fool of myself, according to my habit. No wonder Tom said, 'Look out for yourself!' I shall look out from a prison window, or perhaps even out of a halter. And then, what will Lorna think of me?"

Being in this wistful mood, I resolved to abide awhile, even where fate had thrown me; for my horse required good rest, no doubt, and was taking it even while he cropped, with his hind-legs far away stretched out, and his forelegs gathered under him, and his muzzle on the mole-hills; so that he had five supportings from his mother earth. Moreover the linhay itself was full of very ancient cow-dung; than which there is no balmier and more maiden soporific. Hence I resolved, upon the whole, though grieving about breakfast, to light a pipe and go to sleep; or at least until the hot sun should arouse the flies.

I may have slept three hours, or four, or it might be even five — for I never count time, while sleeping — when a shaking, more rude than the old landlady's, brought me back to the world again. I looked up with a mighty yawn; and saw twenty, or so, of foot-soldiers.

"This linhay is not yours," I said, when they had quite aroused me, with tongue, and hand, and even sword-prick: "what business have you here, good fellows?"

"Business bad for you," said one, "and will lead you to the gallows."

"Do you wish to know the way out again?" I asked, very quietly, as being no braggadocio.

"We will show thee the way out," said one, "and the way out of the world," said another: "But not the way to heaven," said one chap, most unlikely to know it: and thereupon they all fell wagging, like a bed of clover leaves in the morning, at their own choice humour.

"Will you pile your arms outside," I said, "and try a bit of fair play with me?"

For I disliked these men sincerely, and was fain to teach them a lesson; they were so unchristian in appearance, having faces of a coffee colour, and dirty beards half over them. Moreover their dress was outrageous, and their address still worse. However I had wiser let them alone, as will appear afterwards.

These savage-looking fellows laughed at the idea of my having any chance against some twenty of them: but I knew that the place was in my favour; for my part of it had been fenced off (for weaning a calf most likely), so that only two could come at me at once; and I must be very much out of training, if I could not manage two of them. Therefore I laid aside my carbine, and the two horse-pistols; and they with many coarse jokes at me went a little way outside, and set their weapons against the wall, and turned up their coat-sleeves jauntily; and then began to hesitate.

"Go you first, Bob," I heard them say; "you are the biggest man of us; and Dick the wrestler along of you. Us will back you up, boy."

"I'll warrant I'll draw the badger," said Bob; "and not a tooth will I leave him. But mind, for the honour of Kirke's lambs, every man stands me a glass of gin." Then he, and another man, made a rush, and the others came double-quick-march on their heels. But as Bob ran at me most stupidly, not even knowing how to place his hands, I caught him with my knuckles at the back of his neck, and with all the sway of my right arm sent him over the heads of his comrades. Meanwhile Dick the wrestler had grappled me, expecting to show off his art, of which indeed he had some small knowledge; but being quite of the light weights, in a second he was flying after his companion Bob.

Now these two men were hurt so badly, the light one having knocked his head against the lintel of the outer gate, that the rest had no desire to encounter the like misfortune. So they hung back whispering; and before they had made up their minds, I rushed into the midst of them. The suddenness and the weight of my onset took them wholly by surprise; and for once in their lives, perhaps, Kirke's lambs were worthy of their name. Like a flock of sheep at a dog's attack, they fell away, hustling one another, and my only difficulty was not to tumble over them.

I had taken my carbine out with me, having a fondness for it; but the two horse-pistols I left behind; and therefore felt good title to take two from the magazine of the lambs. And with these, and my carbine, I leaped upon Kickums, who was now quite glad of a gallop again; and I bade adieu to that mongrel lot; yet they had the meanness to shoot at me. Thanking God for my deliverance (inasmuch as those men would have strung me up, from a pollard ash without trial, as I heard them tell one another, and saw the tree they had settled upon), I ventured to go rather fast on my way, with doubt and uneasiness urging me. And now my way was home again. Nobody could say but what I had done my duty, and rescued Tom (if he could be rescued) from the mischief into which his own perverseness and love of change (rather than deep religious convictions, to which our Annie ascribed his outbreak) had led, or seemed likely to lead him. And how proud would my mother be; and — ah well, there was nobody else to be proud of me now.

But while thinking these things, and desiring my breakfast, beyond any power of describing, and even beyond my remembrance, I fell into another fold of lambs, from which there was no exit. These, like true crusaders, met me, swaggering very heartily, and with their barrels of cider set, like so many cannon, across the road, over against a small hostel.

"We have won the victory, my lord King, and we mean to enjoy it. Down from thy horse, and have a stoop of cider, thou big rebel."

"No rebel am I. My name is John Ridd. I belong to the side of the King; and I want some breakfast."

These fellows were truly hospitable; that much I will say for them. Being accustomed to Arab ways, they could toss a grill, or fritter, or the inner meaning of an egg, into any form they pleased, comely and very good to eat; and it led me to think of Annie. So I made the rarest breakfast any man might hope for, after all his troubles; and getting on with these brown fellows better than could be expected, I craved permission to light a pipe, if not disagreeable. Hearing this, they roared at me, with a superior laughter, and asked me, whether or not, I knew the tobacco-leaf from the chickweed; and when I was forced to answer no, not having gone into the subject, but being content with anything brown, they clapped me on the back, and swore they had never seen anyone like me. Upon the whole, this pleased me much; for I do not wish to be taken always as of the common pattern: and so we smoked admirable tobacco — for they would not have any of mine, though very courteous concerning it — and I was beginning to understand a little of what they told me; when up came those confounded lambs, who had shown more tail than head to me, in the linhay, as I mentioned.

Now these men upset everything. Having been among wrestlers so much as my duty compelled me to be, and having learned the necessity of the rest which follows the conflict, and the right of discussion which all people have who pay their sixpence to enter; and how they obtrude this right, and their wisdom, upon the man who has laboured until he forgets all the work he did, and begins to think that they did it; having some knowledge of this sort of thing, and the flux of minds swimming in liquor, I foresaw a brawl, as plainly as if it were Bear Street in Barnstaple.

And a brawl there was, without any error, except of the men who hit their friends, and those who defended their enemies. My partners in beer-can, and tobacco, swore that I was no prisoner, but the best and most loyal subject, and the finest-hearted fellow they had ever the luck to meet with. Whereas the men from the linhay swore that I was a rebel miscreant; and have me they would, with a rope's-end ready, in spite of every [violent language] who had got drunk at my expense, and been misled by my [strong word] lies.

While this fight was going on (and its mere occurrence shows, perhaps, that my conversation in those days was not entirely despicable — else why should my new friends fight for me, when I had paid for the ale, and therefore won the wrong tense of gratitude?) it was in my power at any moment to take horse and go. And this would have been my wisest plan, and a very great saving of money; but somehow I felt as if it would be a mean thing; to slip off so. Even while I was hesitating, and the men were breaking each other's heads, a superior officer rode up, with his sword drawn, and his face on fire.

"What, my lambs, my lambs!" he cried, smiting with the flat of his sword; "is this how you waste my time, and my purse, when you ought to be catching a hundred prisoners, worth ten pounds apiece to me? Who is this young fellow we have here? Speak up, sirrah; what art thou, and how much will thy good mother pay for thee?"

"My mother will pay naught for me," I answered; while the lambs fell back and glowered at one another: "so please your worship, I am no rebel; but an honest farmer, and well-proved of loyalty."

"Ha, ha! a farmer art thou? Those fellows always pay the best. Good farmer, come to yon barren tree; thou shalt make it fruitful."

Colonel Kirke made a sign to his men, and before I could think of resistance, stout new ropes were flung around me; and with three men on either side, I was led along very painfully. And now I saw, and repented deeply of my careless folly, in stopping with those boon-companions, instead of being far away. But the newness of their manners to me, and their mode of regarding the world (differing so much from mine own), as well as the flavour of their tobacco, had made me quite forget my duty to the farm and to myself. Yet me-thought they would be tender to me, after all our speeches: how then was I disappointed, when the men who had drunk my beer, drew on those grievous ropes, twice as hard as the men I had been at strife with! Yet this may have been from no ill will; but simply that having fallen under suspicion of laxity, they were compelled, in self-defence, now to be over-zealous. Nevertheless, however pure and godly might be their motives, I beheld myself in a grievous case, and likely to get the worst of it. For the face of the Colonel was hard and stern as a block of bogwood oak; and though the men might pity me, and think me unjustly executed, yet they must obey their orders, or themselves be put to death. Therefore I addressed myself to the Colonel, in a most ingratiating manner; begging him not to sully the glory of his victory, and dwelling upon my pure innocence, and even good service to our lord the King. But Colonel Kirke only gave command that I should be smitten in the mouth; which office Bob, whom I had flung so hard out of the linhay, performed with great zeal and efficiency. But being aware of the coming smack, I thrust forth a pair of teeth; upon which the knuckles of my good friend made a melancholy shipwreck.

It is not in my power to tell half the thoughts that moved me, when we came to the fatal tree, and saw two men hanging there already, as innocent perhaps as I was, and henceforth entirely harmless. Though ordered by the Colonel to look steadfastly upon them, I could not bear to do so: upon which he called me a paltry coward, and promised my breeches to any man who would spit upon my countenance. This vile thing Bob, being angered perhaps by the smarting wound of his knuckles, bravely stepped forward to do for me, trusting no doubt to the rope I was led with. But, unluckily as it proved for him, my right arm was free for a moment; and therewith I dealt him such a blow, that he never spoke again. For this thing I have often grieved; but the provocation was very sore to the pride of a young man; and I trust that God has forgiven me. At the sound and sight of that bitter stroke, the other men drew back; and Colonel Kirke, now black in the face with fury and vexation, gave orders for to shoot me, and cast me into the ditch hard by. The men raised their pieces, and pointed at me, waiting for the word to fire; and I, being quite overcome by the hurry of these events, and quite unprepared to die yet, could only think all upside down about Lorna, and my mother, and wonder what each would say to it. I spread my hands before my eyes, not being so brave as some men; and hoping, in some foolish way, to cover my heart with my elbows. I heard the breath of all around, as if my skull were a sounding-board; and knew even how the different men were fingering their triggers. And a cold sweat broke all over me, as the Colonel, prolonging his enjoyment, began slowly to say, "Fire."

But while he was yet dwelling on the "F," the hoofs of a horse dashed out on the road, and horse and horseman flung themselves betwixt me and the gun-muzzles. So narrowly was I saved, that one man could not check his trigger: his musket went off, and the ball struck the horse on the withers, and scared him exceedingly. He began to lash out with his heels all around, and the Colonel was glad to keep clear of him; and the men made excuse to lower their guns, not really wishing to shoot me.

"How now, Captain Stickles?" cried Kirke, the more angry because he had shown his cowardice; "dare you, sir, to come betwixt me and my lawful prisoner?"

"Nay, hearken one moment, Colonel," replied my old friend Jeremy; and his damaged voice was the sweetest sound I had heard for many a day; "for your own sake hearken." He looked so full of momentous tidings, that Colonel Kirke made a sign to his men, not to shoot me till further orders; and then he went aside with Stickles, so that in spite of all my anxiety I could not catch what passed between them. But I fancied that the name of the Lord Chief-Justice Jeffreys was spoken more than once, and with emphasis, and deference.

"Then I leave him in your hands, Captain Stickles," said Kirke at last, so that all might hear him; and though the news was so good for me, the smile of baffled malice made his dark face look most hideous; "and I shall hold you answerable for the custody of this prisoner."

"Colonel Kirke, I will answer for him," Master Stickles replied, with a grave bow, and one hand on his breast. "John Ridd, you are my prisoner. Follow me, John Ridd."

Upon that, those precious lambs flocked away, leaving the rope still around me; and some were glad, and some were sorry, not to see me swinging. Being free of my arms again, I touched my hat to Colonel Kirke, as became his rank and experience; but he did not condescend to return my short salutation, having espied in the distance a prisoner, out of whom he might make money.

I wrung the hand of Jeremy Stickles, for his truth and goodness; and he almost wept (for since his wound, he had been a weakened man) as he answered, "Turn for turn, John. You saved my life from the Doones; and by the mercy of God, I have saved you from a far worse company. Let your sister Annie know it."

CHAPTER LXVI

Suitable Devotion

Now Kickums was not like Winnie, any more than a man is like a woman; and go he had not followed my fortunes, except at his own distance. No doubt but what he felt a certain interest in me; but his interest was not devotion; and man might go his way and be hanged, rather than horse would meet hardship. Therefore seeing things to be bad, and his master involved in trouble, what did the horse do but start for the ease and comfort of Plover's Barrows, and the plentiful ration of oats abiding in his own manger. For that I do not blame him. It is the manner of mankind.

But I could not help being very uneasy at the thought of my mother's discomfort and worry, when she should spy this good horse coming home, without any master, or rider, and I almost hoped that he might be caught (although he was worth at least twenty pounds) by some of the King's troopers, rather than find his way home, and spread distress among our people. Yet knowing his nature, I doubted if any could catch, or catching, would keep him.

Jeremy Stickles assured me, as we took the road to Bridgwater, that the only chance for my life (if I still refused to fly) was to obtain an order forthwith for my despatch to London, as a suspected person indeed, but not found in open rebellion, and believed to be under the patronage of the great Lord Jeffreys. "For," said he, "in a few hours' time, you would fall into the hands of Lord Feversham, who has won this fight, without seeing it, and who has returned to bed again, to have his breakfast more comfortably. Now he may not be quite so savage perhaps as Colonel Kirke, nor find so much sport in gibbeting; but he is equally pitiless, and his price no doubt would be higher."

"I will pay no price whatever," I answered, "neither will I fly. An hour agone I would have fled, for the sake of my mother, and the farm. But now that I have been taken prisoner, and my name is known, if I fly, the farm is forfeited; and my mother and sister must starve. Moreover, I have done no harm; I have borne no weapons against the King, nor desired the success of his enemies. I like not that the son of a bona-roba should be King of England; neither do I count the papists any worse than we are. If they have aught to try me for, I will stand my trial."

"Then to London thou must go, my son. There is no such thing as trial here: we hang the good folk without it, which saves them much anxiety. But quicken thy step, good John; I have influence with Lord Churchill, and we must contrive to see him, ere the foreigner falls to work again. Lord Churchill is a man of sense, and imprisons nothing but his money."

We were lucky enough to find this nobleman, who has since become so famous by his foreign victories. He received us with great civility; and looked at me with much interest, being a tall and fine young man himself, but not to compare with me in size, although far better favoured. I liked his face well enough, but thought there was something false about it. He put me a few keen questions, such as a man not assured of honesty might have found hard to answer; and he stood in a very upright attitude, making the most of his figure.

I saw nothing to be proud of, at the moment, in this interview; but since the great Duke of Marlborough rose to the top of glory, I have tried to remember more about him than my conscience quite backs up. How should I know that this man would be foremost in our kingdom in five-and-twenty years or so; and not knowing, why should I heed him, except for my own pocket? Nevertheless I have been so cross-questioned — far worse than by young Lord Churchill — about His Grace the Duke of Marlborough, and what he said to me, and what I said then, and how His Grace replied to that, and whether he smiled like another man, or screwed up his lips like a button (as our parish tailor said of him), and whether I knew from the turn of his nose that no Frenchman could stand before him; all these inquiries have worried me so, ever since the battle of Blenheim, that if tailors would only print upon waistcoats, I would give double price for a vest bearing this inscription, "No information can be given about the Duke of Marlborough."

Now this good Lord Churchill — for one might call him good, by comparison with the very bad people around him — granted, without any long hesitation, the order for my safe deliverance to the Court of King's Bench at Westminster; and Stickles, who had to report in London, was empowered to convey me, and made answerable for producing me. This arrangement would have been entirely to my liking, although the time of year was bad for leaving Plover's Barrows so; but no man may quite choose his times, and on the whole I would have been quite content to visit London, if my mother could be warned that nothing was amiss with me, only a mild, and as one might say, nominal captivity. And to prevent her anxiety, I did my best to send a letter through good Serjeant Bloxham, of whom I heard as quartered with Dumbarton's regiment at Chedzuy. But that regiment was away in pursuit; and I was forced to entrust my letter to a man who said that he knew him, and accepted a shilling to see to it.

For fear of any unpleasant change, we set forth at once for London; and truly thankful may I be that God in His mercy spared me the sight of the cruel and bloody work, with which the whole country reeked and howled, during the next fortnight. I have heard things that set my hair on end, and made me loathe good meat for days; but I make a point of setting down only the things which I saw done; and in this particular case, not many will quarrel with my decision. Enough, therefore, that we rode on (for Stickles had found me a horse at last) as far as Wells, where we slept that night; and being joined in the morning by several troopers and orderlies, we made a slow but safe journey to London, by way of Bath, and Reading.

The sight of London warmed my heart with various emotions, such as a cordial man must draw from the heart of all humanity. Here there are quick ways and manners, and the rapid sense of knowledge, and the power of understanding, ere a word be spoken. Whereas at Oare, you may say a thing three times, very slowly, before it gets inside of the skull of the good man you are addressing. And yet we are far more clever there, than in any parish for fifteen miles.

But what moved me most, when I saw again the noble oil and tallow of the London lights, and the dripping torches at almost every corner, and the handsome signboards, was the thought that here my Lorna lived, and walked, and took the air, and perhaps thought, now and then, of the old days in the good farm-house. Although I would make no approach to her, any more than she had done to me (upon which grief I have not dwelt, for fear of seeming selfish), yet there must be some large chance, or the little chance might be enlarged, of falling in with the maiden somehow, and learning how her mind was set. If against me, all should be over. I was not the man to sigh and cry for love, like a hot-brained Romeo; none should even guess my grief, except my sister Annie.

But if Lorna loved me still — as in my heart of hearts I hoped — then would I for no one care, except her own delicious self. Rank and title, wealth and grandeur, all should go to the winds, before they scared me from my own true love.

Thinking thus, I went to bed in the centre of London town, and was bitten so grievously, by creatures whose name is "Legion," mad with the delight of getting a wholesome farmer among them, that verily I was ashamed to walk in the courtly parts of the town next day, having lumps upon my face the size of a pickling walnut. The landlord said that this was nothing; and that he expected, in two days at the utmost, a very fresh young Irishman, for whom they would all forsake me. Nevertheless, I declined to wait, unless he could find me a hay-rick to sleep in; for the insects of grass only tickle. He assured me that no hay-rick could now be found in London; upon which I was forced to leave him, and with mutual esteem we parted.

The next night I had better luck, being introduced to a decent widow, of very high Scotch origin. That house was swept and garnished so, that not a bit was left to eat, for either man or insect. The change of air having made me hungry, I wanted something after supper; being quite ready to pay for it, and showing my purse as a symptom. But the face of Widow MacAlister, when I proposed to have some more food, was a thing to be drawn (if it could be drawn further) by our new caricaturist.

Therefore I left her also; for liefer would I be eaten myself than have nothing to eat; and so I came back to my old furrier; the which was a thoroughly hearty man, and welcomed me to my room again, with two shillings added to the rent in the joy of his heart at seeing me. Being under parole to Master Stickles, I only went out betwixt certain hours; because I was accounted as liable to be called upon; for what purpose I knew not, but hoped it might be a good one. I felt it a loss, and a hindrance to me, that I was so bound to remain at home, during the session of the courts of law; for thereby the chance of ever beholding Lorna was greatly damaged, if not altogether done away with. For these were the very hours in which the people of fashion, and the high world, were wont to appear to the rest of mankind, so as to encourage them. And of course by this time, the Lady Lorna was high among people of fashion, and was not likely to be seen out of fashionable hours. It is true that there were some places of expensive entertainment, at which the better sort of mankind might be seen and studied, in their hours of relaxation, by those of the lower order, who could pay sufficiently. But alas, my money was getting low; and the privilege of seeing my betters was more and more denied to me, as my cash drew shorter. For a man must have a good coat at least, and the pockets not wholly empty, before he can look at those whom God has created for his ensample.

Hence, and from many other causes — part of which was my own pride — it happened that I abode in London, betwixt a month and five weeks' time, ere ever I saw Lorna. It seemed unfit that I should go, and waylay her, and spy on her, and say (or mean to say), "Lo, here is your poor faithful farmer, a man who is unworthy of you, by means of his common birth; and yet who dares to crawl across your path, that you may pity him. For God's sake show a little pity, though you may not feel it." Such behaviour might be comely in a lovelorn boy, a page to some grand princess; but I, John Ridd, would never stoop to the lowering of love so.

Nevertheless I heard of Lorna, from my worthy furrier, almost every day, and with a fine exaggeration. This honest man was one of those who, in virtue of their trade, and nicety of behaviour, are admitted into noble life, to take measurements, and show patterns. And while so doing, they contrive to acquire what is to the English mind at once the most important, and most interesting of all knowledge — the science of being able to talk about the titled people. So my furrier (whose name was Ramsack), having to make robes for peers, and cloaks for their wives and otherwise, knew the great folk, sham or real, as well as he knew a fox, or skunk, from a wolverine skin.

And when, with some fencing and foils of inquiry, I hinted about Lady Lorna Dugal, the old man's face became so pleasant, that I knew her birth must be wondrous high. At this my own countenance fell, I suppose — for the better she was born, the harder she would be to marry — and, mistaking my object, he took me up:

"Perhaps you think, Master Ridd, that because her ladyship, Lady Lorna Dugal, is of Scottish origin, therefore her birth is not as high as of our English nobility. If you think so, you are wrong, sir. She comes not of the sandy Scotch race, with high cheek-bones, and raw shoulder-blades, who set up pillars in their court-yards. But she comes of the very best Scotch blood, descended from the Norsemen. Her mother was of the very noblest race, the Lords of Lorne; higher even than the great Argyle, who has lately made a sad mistake, and paid for it most sadly. And her father was descended from the King Dugal, who fought against Alexander the Great. No, no, Master Ridd; none of your promiscuous blood, such as runs in the veins of half our modern peerage."

"Why should you trouble yourself about it, Master Ramsack?" I replied; "let them all go their own ways; and let us all look up to them, whether they come by hook or crook."

"Not at all, not at all, my lad. That is not the way to regard it. We look up at the well-born folk, and sideways at the base-born."

"Then we are all base-born ourselves. I will look up to no man, except for what himself has done."

"Come, Master Ridd, you might be lashed, from Newgate to Tyburn, and back again, once a week, for a twelvemonth, if some people heard you. Keep your tongue more close, young man; or here you lodge no longer; albeit I love your company, which smells to me of the hay-field. Ah, I have not seen a hay-field for nine-and-twenty years, John Ridd. The cursed moths keep me at home every day of the summer."

"Spread your furs on the haycocks," I answered very boldly; "the indoor moth cannot abide the presence of the outdoor ones."

"Is it so?" he answered; "I never thought of that before. And yet I have known such strange things happen in the way of fur, that I can well believe it. If you only knew, John Ridd, the way in which they lay their eggs, and how they work tail-foremost —— "

"Tell me nothing of the kind," I replied, with equal confidence; "they cannot work tail foremost; and they have no tails to work with." For I knew a little about grubs, and the ignorance concerning them, which we have no right to put up with. However, not to go into that (for the argument lasted a fortnight; and then was only come so far as to begin again), Master Ramsack soon convinced me of the things I knew already; the excellence of Lorna's birth, as well as her lofty place at Court, and beauty, and wealth, and elegance. But all these only made me sigh, and wish that I were born to them.

From Master Ramsack I discovered that the nobleman to whose charge Lady Lorna had been committed by the Court of Chancery, was Earl Brandir of Lochawe, her poor mother's uncle. For the Countess of Dugal was daughter, and only child, of the last Lord Lorne whose sister had married Sir Ensor Doone; while he himself had married the sister of Earl Brandir. This nobleman had a country house near the village of Kensington; and here his niece dwelled with him, when she was not in attendance on Her Majesty the Queen, who had taken a liking to her. Now since the King had begun to attend the celebration of mass in the chapel at Whitehall — and not at Westminster Abbey, as our gossips had averred — he had given order that the doors should be thrown open, so that all who could make interest to get into the antechamber, might see this form of worship. Master Ramsack told me that Lorna was there almost every Sunday; their Majesties being most anxious to have the presence of all the nobility of the Catholic persuasion, so as to make a goodly show. And the worthy furrier, having influence with the door-keepers, kindly obtained admittance for me, one Sunday, into the antechamber.

Here I took care to be in waiting, before the Royal procession entered; but being unknown, and of no high rank, I was not allowed to stand forward among the better people, but ordered back into a corner very dark and dismal; the verger remarking, with a grin, that I could see over all other heads, and must not set my own so high. Being frightened to find myself among so many people, of great rank and gorgeous apparel, I blushed at the notice drawn upon me by this uncourteous fellow, and silently fell back into the corner by the hangings.

You may suppose that my heart beat high when the King and Queen appeared, and entered, followed by the Duke of Norfolk, bearing the sword of state, and by several other noblemen, and people of repute. Then the doors of the chapel were thrown wide open; and though I could only see a little, being in the corner so, I thought that it was beautiful. Bowers of rich silk were there, and plenty of metal shining, and polished wood with lovely carving, flowers too of the noblest kind, and candles made by somebody who had learned how to clarify tallow. This last thing amazed me more than all, for our dips never will come clear, melt the mutton fat how you will. And methought that this hanging of flowers about was a very pretty thing, for if a man can worship God best of all beneath a tree, as the natural instinct is, surely when by fault of climate the tree would be too apt to drip, the very best make-believe is to have enough and to spare of flowers; which to the dwellers in London seem to have grown on the tree denied them.

Be that as it may, when the King and Queen crossed the threshold, a mighty flourish of trumpets arose, and a waving of banners. The Knights of the Garter (whoever they be) were to attend that day in state; and some went in, and some stayed out, and it made me think of the difference betwixt the ewes and the wethers. For the ewes will go wherever you lead them; but the wethers will not, having strong opinions, and meaning to abide by them. And one man I noticed was of the wethers, to wit the Duke of Norfolk; who stopped outside with the sword of state, like a beadle with a rapping-rod. This has taken more time to tell than the time it happened in. For after all the men were gone, some to this side, some to that, according to their feelings, a number of ladies, beautifully dressed, being of the Queen's retinue, began to enter, and were stared at three times as much as the men had been. And indeed they were worth looking at (which men never are to my ideas, when they trick themselves with gewgaws), but none was so well worth eye-service as my own beloved Lorna. She entered modestly and shyly, with her eyes upon the ground, knowing the rudeness of the gallants, and the large sum she was priced at. Her dress was of the purest white, very sweet and simple, without a line of ornament, for she herself adorned it. The way she walked, and touched her skirt (rather than seemed to hold it up), with a white hand bearing one red rose, this, and her stately supple neck, and the flowing of her hair would show, at a distance of a hundred yards, that she could be none but Lorna Doone — Lorna Doone of my early love; in the days when she blushed for her name before me, by reason of dishonesty; but now the Lady Lorna Dugal; as far beyond reproach as above my poor affection. All my heart, and all my mind, gathered themselves upon her. Would she see me, or would she pass? Was there instinct in our love?

By some strange chance she saw me. Or was it through our destiny? While with eyes kept sedulously on the marble floor, to shun the weight of admiration thrust too boldly on them, while with shy quick steps she passed, some one (perhaps with purpose) trod on the skirt other clear white dress — with the quickness taught her by many a scene of danger, she looked up, and her eyes met mine.

As I gazed upon her, steadfastly, yearningly, yet with some reproach, and more of pride than humility, she made me one of the courtly bows which I do so much detest; yet even that was sweet and graceful, when my Lorna did it. But the colour of her pure clear cheeks was nearly as deep as that of my own, when she went on for the religious work. And the shining of her eyes was owing to an unpaid debt of tears.

Upon the whole I was satisfied. Lorna had seen me, and had not (according to the phrase of the high world then) even tried to "cut" me. Whether this low phrase is born of their own stupid meanness, or whether it comes of necessity exercised on a man without money, I know not, and I care not. But one thing I know right well; any man who "cuts" a man (except for vice, or meanness) should be quartered without quarter.

All these proud thoughts arose within me, as the lovely form of Lorna went inside, and was no more seen. And then I felt how coarse I was; how apt to think strong thoughts, and so on; without brains to bear me out: even as a hen's egg laid, without enough of life, and looking only a poor jelly.

Nevertheless, I waited on; as my usual manner is. For to be beaten, while running away, is ten times worse than to face it out, and take it, and have done with it. So at least I have always found, because of reproach of conscience: and all the things those clever people carried on inside, at large, made me long for our Parson Bowden, that he might know how to act.

While I stored up in my memory enough to keep our parson going through six pipes on a Saturday night — to have it as right as could be next day — a lean man with a yellow beard, too thin for a good Catholic (which religion always fattens), came up to me, working sideways in the manner of a female crab.

"This is not to my liking," I said; "if aught thou hast, speak plainly; while they make that musical roar inside."

Nothing had this man to say; but with many sighs, because I was not of the proper faith, he took my reprobate hand to save me; and with several religious tears, looked up at me, and winked with one eye. Although the skin of my palms was thick, I felt a little suggestion there, as of a gentle leaf in spring, fearing to seem too forward. I paid the man, and he went happy; for the standard of heretical silver is purer than that of the Catholics.

Then I lifted up my little billet, and in that dark corner read it, with a strong rainbow of colours coming from the angled light. And in mine eyes there was enough to make rainbow of strongest sun, as my anger clouded off.

Not that it began so well; but that in my heart I knew (ere three lines were through me) that I was with all heart loved — and beyond that, who may need? The darling of my life went on, as if I were of her own rank, or even better than she was; and she dotted her "i's" and crossed her "t's" as if I were at least a schoolmaster. All of it was done in pencil; but as plain as plain could be. In my coffin it shall lie, with my ring, and something else. Therefore will I not expose it to every man who buys this book, and haply thinks that he has bought me to the bottom of my heart. Enough for men of gentle birth (who never are inquisitive) that my love told me, in her letter, just to come and see her.

I ran away, and could not stop. To behold even her, at the moment, would have dashed my fancy's joy. Yet my brain was so amiss, that I must do something. Therefore unto the river Thames, with all speed, I hurried: and keeping all my best clothes on (indeed for sake of Lorna), into the quiet stream I leaped, and swam as far as London Bridge, and ate noble dinner afterwards.

CHAPTER LXVII

Lorna Still is Lorna

Although a man may be as simple as the flowers of the field; knowing when, but scarcely why, he closes to the bitter wind; and feeling why, but scarcely when, he opens to the genial sun; yet without his questing much into the capsule of himself — to do which is a misery — he may have a general notion how he happens to be getting on.

I felt myself to be getting on better than at any time since the last wheat-harvest, as I took the lane to Kensington upon the Monday evening. For although no time was given in my Lorna's letter, I was not inclined to wait any more than decency required. And though I went and watched the house, decency would not allow me to knock on the Sunday evening, especially when I found at the corner that his lordship was at home.

The lanes and fields between Charing Cross and the village of Kensington are, or were at that time, more than reasonably infested with footpads, and with highwaymen. However, my stature and holly club kept these fellows from doing more than casting sheep's eyes at me. For it was still broad daylight, and the view of the distant villages, Chelsea, Battersea, Tyburn, and others, as well as a few large houses, among the hams, and towards the river, made it seem less lonely. Therefore I sang a song in the broadest Exmoor dialect, which caused no little amazement in the minds of all who met me.

When I came to Earl Brandir's house, my natural modesty forbade me to appear at the door for guests; therefore I went to the entrance for servants and retainers. Here, to my great surprise, who should come and let me in but little Gwenny Carfax, whose very existence had almost escaped my recollection. Her mistress, no doubt, had seen me coming, and sent her to save trouble. But when I offered to kiss Gwenny, in my joy and comfort to see a farm-house face again, she looked ashamed, and turned away and would hardly speak to me.

I followed her to a little room, furnished very daintily; and there she ordered me to wait, in a most ungracious manner. "Well," thought I, "if the mistress and the maid are alike in temper, better it had been for me to abide at Master Ramsack's." But almost ere my thought was done, I heard the light quick step which I knew as well as "Watch," my dog, knew mine; and my breast began to tremble, like the trembling of an arch ere the keystone is put in.

Almost ere I hoped — for fear and hope were so entangled, that they hindered one another — the velvet hangings of the doorway parted, with a little doubt, and then a good face put on it. Lorna, in her perfect beauty, stood before the crimson folds, and her dress was all pure white, and her cheeks were rosy pink, and her lips were scarlet.

Like a maiden, with skill and sense checking violent impulse, she stayed there for one moment only, just to be admired: and then like a woman, she came to me, seeing how alarmed I was. The hand she offered me I took, and raised it to my lips with fear, as a thing too good for me. "Is that all?" she whispered; and then her eyes gleamed up at me; and in another instant she was weeping on my breast.

"Darling Lorna, Lady Lorna," I cried, in astonishment, yet unable but to keep her closer to me, and closer; "surely, though I love you so, this is not as it should be."

"Yes, it is, John. Yes, it is. Nothing else should ever be. Oh, why have you behaved so?"

"I am behaving," I replied, "to the very best of my ability. There is no other man in the world could hold you so without kissing you."

"Then why don't you do it, John?" asked Lorna, looking up at me with a flash of her old fun.

Now this matter, proverbially, is not so meet for discussion as it is for repetition. Enough that we said nothing more than, "Oh, John, how glad I am!" and, "Lorna, Lorna, Lorna!" for about five minutes. Then my darling drew back proudly; with blushing cheeks and tear-bright eyes she began to cross-examine me.

"Master John Ridd, you shall tell the truth, the whole truth, and nothing but the truth. I have been in Chancery, sir; and can detect a story. Now why have you never, for more than a twelvemonth, taken the smallest notice of your old friend, Mistress Lorna Doone?" Although she spoke in this lightsome manner, as if it made no difference, I saw that her quick heart was moving, and the flash of her eyes controlled.

"Simply for this cause," I answered, "that my old friend, and true love, took not the smallest heed of me. Nor knew I where to find her."

"What!" cried Lorna; and nothing more; being overcome with wondering; and much inclined to fall away, but for my assistance. I told her over and over again that not a single syllable of any message from her, or tidings of her welfare, had reached me, or any one of us, since the letter she left behind; except by soldiers' gossip.

"Oh, you poor dear John!" said Lorna, sighing at thought of my misery, "how wonderfully good of you, thinking of me as you must have done, not to marry that little plain thing (or perhaps I should say that lovely creature, for I have never seen her). Mistress Ruth — I forget her name; but something like a towel."

"Ruth Huckaback is a worthy maid," I answered with some dignity, "and she alone of all our world, except, indeed, poor Annie, has kept her confidence in you, and told me not to dread your rank, but trust your heart, Lady Lorna."

"Then Ruth is my best friend," she answered, "and is worthy of you, John. And now remember one thing, dear; if God should part us, as may be by nothing short of death, try to marry that little Ruth, when you cease to remember me. And now for the head-traitor. I have often suspected it, but she looks me in the face and wishes — fearful things, which I cannot repeat."

With these words, she moved an implement such as I had not seen before, and which made a ringing noise at a serious distance. And before I had ceased wondering — for if such things go on, we might ring the church bells, while sitting in our back-kitchen — little Gwenny Carfax came, with a grave and sullen face.

"Gwenny," began my Lorna, in a tone of high rank and dignity, "go and fetch the letters, which I gave you at various times for despatch to Mistress Ridd."

"How can I fetch them, when they are gone? It be no use for him to tell no lies —— "

"Now, Gwenny, can you look at me?" I asked very sternly; for the matter was no joke to me, after a year's unhappiness.

"I don't want to look at 'ee. What should I look at a young man for, although he did offer to kiss me?"

I saw the spite and impudence of this last remark; and so did Lorna, although she could not quite refrain from smiling.

"Now, Gwenny, not to speak of that," said Lorna very demurely, "if you thought it honest to keep the letters, was it honest to keep the money?"

At this the Cornish maiden broke into a rage of honesty: "A' putt the money by for 'ee. 'Ee shall have every farden of it." And so she flung out of the room.

"And, Gwenny," said Lorna very softly, following under the door-hangings; "if it is not honest to keep the money, it is not honest to keep the letters, which would have been worth more than any gold, to those who were so kind to you. Your father shall know the whole, Gwenny, unless you tell the truth."

"Now, a' will tell all the truth," this strange maiden answered, talking to herself at least as much as to her mistress, while she went out of sight and hearing. And then I was so glad at having my own Lorna once again, cleared of all contempt for us, and true to me through all of it, that I would have forgiven Gwenny for treason, or even forgery.

"I trusted her so much," said Lorna, in her old ill-fortuned way; "and look how she has deceived me! That is why I love you, John (setting other things aside), because you never told me falsehood; and you never could, you know."

"Well, I am not so sure of that. I think I could tell any lie, to have you, darling, all my own."

"Yes. And perhaps it might be right. To other people besides us two. But you could not do it to me, John. You never could do it to me, you know."

Before I quite perceived my way to the bottom of this distinction — although beyond doubt a valid one — Gwenny came back with a leathern bag, and tossed it upon the table. Not a word did she vouchsafe to us; but stood there, looking injured.

"Go, and get your letters, John," said Lorna very gravely; "or at least your mother's letters, made of messages to you. As for Gwenny, she shall go before Lord Justice Jeffreys." I knew that Lorna meant it not; but thought that the girl deserved a frightening; as indeed she did. But we both mistook the courage of this child of Cornwall. She stepped upon a little round thing, in the nature of a stool, such as I never had seen before, and thus delivered her sentiments.

"And you may take me, if you please, before the great Lord Jefferays. I have done no more than duty, though I did it crookedly, and told a heap of lies, for your sake. And pretty gratitude I gets."

"Much gratitude you have shown," replied Lorna, "to Master Ridd, for all his kindness, and his goodness to you. Who was it that went down, at the peril of his life, and brought your father to you, when you had lost him for months and months? Who was it? Answer me, Gwenny.''

"Girt Jan Ridd," said the handmaid, very sulkily.

"What made you treat me so, little Gwenny?" I asked, for Lorna would not ask, lest the reply should vex me.

"Because 'ee be'est below her so. Her shanna' have a poor farmering chap, not even if her were a Carnishman. All her land, and all her birth — and who be you, I'd like to know?"

"Gwenny, you may go," said Lorna, reddening with quiet anger; "and remember that you come not near me for the next three days. It is the only way to punish her," she continued to me, when the maid was gone, in a storm of sobbing and weeping. "Now, for the next three days, she will scarcely touch a morsel of food, and scarcely do a thing but cry. Make up your mind to one thing, John; if you mean to take me, for better for worse, you will have to take Gwenny with me."

"I would take you with fifty Gwennies," said I, "although every one of them hated me; which I do not believe this little maid does, in the bottom of her heart."

"No one can possibly hate you, John," she answered very softly; and I was better pleased with this, than if she had called me the most noble and glorious man in the kingdom.

After this, we spoke of ourselves, and the way people would regard us, supposing that when Lorna came to be her own free mistress (as she must do in the course of time) she were to throw her rank aside, and refuse her title, and caring not a fig for folk who cared less than a fig-stalk for her, should shape her mind to its native bent, and to my perfect happiness. It was not my place to say much, lest I should appear to use an improper and selfish influence. And of course to all men of common sense, and to everybody of middle age (who must know best what is good for youth), the thoughts which my Lorna entertained would be enough to prove her madness.

Not that we could not keep her well, comfortably, and with nice clothes, and plenty of flowers and fruit, and landscape, and the knowledge of our neighbours' affairs, and their kind interest in our own. Still this would not be as if she were the owner of a county, and a haughty title; and able to lead the first men of the age, by her mind, and face, and money.

Therefore was I quite resolved not to have a word to say, while this young queen of wealth and beauty, and of nobleman's desire, made her mind up how to act for her purest happiness. But to do her justice, this was not the first thing she was thinking of: the test of her judgment, was only this, "How will my love be happiest?"

"Now, John," she cried; for she was so quick that she always had my thoughts beforehand; "why will you be backward, as if you cared not for me? Do you dream, that I am doubting? My mind has been made up, good John, that you must be my husband, for — well, I will not say how long, lest you should laugh at my folly. But I believe it was ever since you came, with your stockings off, and the loaches. Right early for me to make up my mind; but you know that you made up yours, John; and, of course, I knew it; and that had a great effect on me. Now, after all this age of loving, shall a trifle sever us?"

I told her that it was no trifle, but a most important thing, to abandon wealth and honour, and the brilliance of high life, and be despised by every one for such abundant folly. Moreover that I should appear a knave for taking advantage of her youth, and boundless generosity, and ruining (as men would say) a noble maid by my selfishness. And I told her outright, having worked myself up by my own conversation, that she was bound to consult her guardian, and that without his knowledge, I would come no more to see her. Her flash of pride at these last words made her look like an Empress; and I was about to explain myself better, but she put forth her hand, and stopped me.

"I think that condition should rather have proceeded from me. You are mistaken, Master Ridd, in supposing that I would think of receiving you, in secret. It was a different thing in Glen Doone, where all except yourself were thieves, and when I was but a simple child, and oppressed with constant fear. You are quite right in threatening to visit me thus no more; but I think you might have waited for an invitation, sir."

"And you are quite right, Lady Lorna, in pointing out my presumption. It is a fault that must ever be found in any speech of mine to you."

This I said so humbly, and not with any bitterness — for I knew that I had gone too far — and made her so polite a bow, that she forgave me in a moment, and we begged each other's pardon.

"Now, will you allow me just to explain my own view of this matter, John?" said she, once more my darling. "It may be a very foolish view, but I shall never change it. Please not to interrupt me, dear, until you have heard me to the end. In the first place, it is quite certain, that neither you nor I can be happy without the other. Then what stands between us? Worldly position, and nothing else. I have no more education than you have, John Ridd; nay, and not so much. My birth and ancestry are not one whit more pure than yours, although they may be better known. Your descent from ancient freeholders, for five-and-twenty generations of good, honest men, although you bear no coat of arms, is better than the lineage of nine proud English noblemen out of every ten I meet with. In manners, though your mighty strength, and hatred of any meanness, sometimes break out in violence — of which I must try to cure you, dear — in manners, if kindness, and gentleness, and modesty are the true things wanted, you are immeasurably above any of our Court gallants; who, indeed, have very little. As for difference of religion, we allow for one another, neither having been brought up in a bitterly pious manner."

Here, though the tears were in my eyes, at the loving things love said of me, I could not help a little laugh, at the notion of any bitter piety being found among the Doones, or even in mother, for that matter. Lorna smiled, in her slyest manner, and went on again:

"Now, you see, I have proved my point; there is nothing between us but worldly position — if you can defend me against the Doones, for which, I trow, I may trust you. And worldly position means wealth, and title, and the right to be in great houses, and the pleasure of being envied. I have not been here for a year, John, without learning something. Oh, I hate it; how I hate it! Of all the people I know, there are but two, besides my uncle, who do not either covet or detest me. And who are those two, think you?"

"Gwenny, for one," I answered.

"Yes, Gwenny, for one. And the Queen, for the other. The one is too far below me (I mean, in her own opinion), and the other too high above. As for the women who dislike me, without having even heard my voice, I simply have nothing to do with them. As for the men who covet me, for my land and money, I merely compare them with you, John Ridd; and all thought of them is over. Oh, John, you must never forsake me, however cross I am to you. I thought you would have gone, just now; and though I would not move to stop you, my heart would have broken."

"You don't catch me go in a hurry," I answered very sensibly, "when the loveliest maiden in the world, and the best, and the dearest loves me. All my fear of you is gone, darling Lorna, all my fear —— "

"Is it possible you could fear me, John, after all we have been through together? Now you promised not to interrupt me; is this fair behaviour? Well, let me see where I left off: — oh, that my heart would have broken. Upon that point I will say no more, lest you should grow conceited, John; if anything could make you so. But I do assure you that half London — however, upon that point also I will check my power of speech, lest you think me conceited. And now to put aside all nonsense; though I have talked none for a year, John, having been so unhappy; and now it is such a relief to me —— "

"Then talk it for an hour," said I; "and let me sit and watch you. To me it is the very sweetest of all sweetest wisdom."

"Nay, there is no time," she answered, glancing at a jewelled timepiece, scarcely larger than an oyster, which she drew from near her waist-band; and then she pushed it away, in confusion, lest its wealth should startle me. "My uncle will come home in less than half an hour, dear: and you are not the one to take a side-passage, and avoid him. I shall tell him that you have been here: and that I mean you to come again."

As Lorna said this, with a manner as confident as need be, I saw that she had learned in town the power of her beauty, and knew that she could do with most men aught she set her mind upon. And as she stood there, flushed with pride and faith in her own loveliness, and radiant with the love itself, I felt that she must do exactly as she pleased with every one. For now, in turn, and elegance, and richness, and variety, there was nothing to compare with her face, unless it were her figure. Therefore I gave in and said:

"Darling, do just what you please. Only make no rogue of me."

For that she gave me the simplest, kindest, and sweetest of all kisses; and I went down the great stairs grandly, thinking of nothing else but that.

CHAPTER LXVIII

John is John No Longer

It would be hard for me to tell the state of mind in which I lived for a long time after this. I put away from me all torment, and the thought of future cares, and the sight of difficulty; and to myself appeared, which means that I became, the luckiest of lucky fellows, since the world itself began. I thought not of the harvest even, nor of the men who would get their wages without having earned them, nor of my mother's anxiety, and worry about John Fry's great fatness (which was growing upon him), and how she would cry fifty times in a day, "Ah, if our John would only come home, how different everything would look!"

Although there were no soldiers now quartered at Plover's Barrows, all being busied in harassing the country, and hanging the people, where the rebellion had thriven most, my mother, having received from me a message containing my place of abode, contrived to send me, by the pack-horses, as fine a maund as need be of provisions, and money, and other comfort. Therein I found addressed to Colonel Jeremiah Stickles, in Lizzie's best handwriting, half a side of the dried deer's flesh, in which he rejoiced so greatly. Also, for Lorna, a fine green goose, with a little salt towards the tail, and new-laid eggs inside it, as well as a bottle of brandied cherries, and seven, or it may have been eight pounds of fresh home-made butter. Moreover to myself there was a letter full of good advice, excellently well expressed, and would have been of the greatest value, if I had cared to read it. But I read all about the farm affairs, and the man who had offered himself to our Betty for the five pounds in her stocking — as well as the antics of Sally Snowe, and how she had almost thrown herself at Parson Bowden's head (old enough to be her grandfather), because on the Sunday after the hanging of a Countisbury man, he had preached a beautiful sermon about Christian love; which Lizzie, with her sharp eyes, found to be the work of good Bishop Ken. Also I read that the Doones were quiet; the parishes round about having united to feed them well through the harvest time, so that after the day's hard work, the farmers might go to bed at night. And this plan had been found to answer well, and to save much trouble on both sides, so that everybody wondered it had not been done before. But Lizzie thought that the Doones could hardly be expected much longer to put up with it, and probably would not have done so now, but for a little adversity; to wit, that the famous Colonel Kirke had, in the most outrageous manner hanged no less than six of them, who were captured among the rebels; for he said that men of their rank and breeding, and above all of their religion, should have known better than to join plough-boys, and carters, and pickaxe-men, against our Lord the King, and his holy Holiness the Pope. This hanging of so many Doones caused some indignation, among people who were used to them; and it seemed for a while to check the rest from any spirit of enterprise.

Moreover, I found from this same letter (which was pinned upon the knuckle of a leg of mutton, for fear of being lost in straw) that good Tom Faggus was at home again, and nearly cured of his dreadful wound; but intended to go to war no more, only to mind his family. And it grieved him, more than anything he ever could have imagined, that his duty to his family, and the strong power of his conscience, so totally forbade him to come up and see after me. For now his design was to lead a new life, and be in charity with all men. Many better men than he had been hanged, he saw no cause to doubt; but by the grace of God, he hoped himself to cheat the gallows.

There was no further news of moment in this very clever letter, except that the price of horses' shoes was gone up again, though already twopence-farthing each; and that Betty had broken her lover's head, with the stocking full of money; and then in the corner it was written, that the distinguished man of war, and worshipful scholar Master Bloxham, was now promoted to take the tolls, and catch all the rebels around our part.

Lorna was greatly pleased with the goose, and the butter, and the brandied cherries; and the Earl Brandir himself declared that he never tasted better than those last, and would beg the young man from the country to procure him instructions for making them. This nobleman, being as deaf as a post, and of a very solid mind, could never be brought to understand the nature of my thoughts towards Lorna. He looked upon me as an excellent youth, who had rescued the maiden from the Doones, whom he cordially detested; and learning that I had thrown two of them out of window (as the story was told him), he patted me on the back, and declared that his doors would ever be open to me, and that I could not come too often.

I thought this very kind of his lordship, especially as it enabled me to see my darling Lorna, not indeed as often as I wished, but at any rate very frequently, and as many times as modesty (ever my leading principle) would in common conscience approve of. And I made up my mind, that if ever I could help Earl Brandir, it would be — as we say, when with brandy and water — the "proudest moment of my life," when I could fulfil the pledge.

And I soon was able to help Lord Brandir, as I think, in two different ways; first of all, as regarded his mind, and then as concerned his body: and the latter perhaps was the greatest service, at his time of life. But not to be too nice about that; let me tell how these things were.

Lorna said to me one day, being in a state of excitement — whereto she was over prone, when reft of my slowness to steady her:

"I will tell him, John; I must tell him, John. It is mean of me to conceal it."

I thought that she meant all about our love, which we had endeavoured thrice to drill into his fine old ears; but could not make him comprehend, without the risk of bringing the house down: and so I said, "By all means, darling: have another try at it."

Lorna, however, looked at me — for her eyes told more than tongue — as much as to say, "Well, you are a stupid! We agreed to let that subject rest." And then she saw that I was vexed at my own want of quickness; and so she spoke very kindly:

"I meant about his poor son, dearest; the son of his old age almost; whose loss threw him into that dreadful cold — for he went, without hat, to look for him — which ended in his losing the use of his dear old ears. I believe if we could only get him to Plover's Barrows for a month, he would be able to hear again. And look at his age! he is not much over seventy, John, you know; and I hope that you will be able to hear me long after you are seventy, John."

"Well," said I, "God settles that. Or at any rate. He leaves us time to think about those questions, when we are over fifty. Now let me know what you want, Lorna. The idea of my being seventy! But you would still be beautiful."

"To the one who loves me," she answered, trying to make wrinkles in her pure bright forehead: "but if you will have common sense, as you always will, John, whether I wish it or otherwise, I want to know whether I am bound, in honour, and in conscience, to tell my dear and good old uncle what I know about his son."

"First let me understand quite clearly," said I, never being in a hurry, except when passion moves me, "what his lordship thinks at present; and how far his mind is urged with sorrow and anxiety." This was not the first time we had spoken of the matter.

"Why, you know, John, well enough," she answered, wondering at my coolness, "that my poor uncle still believes that his one beloved son will come to light and life again. He has made all arrangements accordingly: all his property is settled on that supposition. He knows that young Alan always was what he calls a 'feckless ne'er-do-weel'; but he loves him all the more for that. He cannot believe that he will die, without his son coming back to him; and he always has a bedroom ready, and a bottle of Alan's favourite wine cool from out the cellar; he has made me work him a pair of slippers, from the size of a mouldy boot; and if he hears of a new tobacco — much as he hates the smell of it — he will go to the other end of London, to get some for Alan. Now you know how deaf he is; but if anyone say 'Alan,' even in the place outside the door, he will make his courteous bow to the very highest visitor, and be out here in a moment, and search the entire passage, and yet let no one know it."

"It is a piteous thing," I said; for Lorna's eyes were full of tears.

"And he means me to marry him. It is the pet scheme of his life. I am to grow more beautiful, and more highly taught, and graceful, until it pleases Alan to come back, and demand me. Can you understand this matter, John? Or do you think my uncle mad?"

"Lorna, I should be mad myself, to call any man mad, for hoping."

"Then will you tell me what to do? It makes me very sorrowful. For I know that Alan Brandir lies below the sod in Doone-valley."

"And if you tell his father," I answered softly, but clearly, "in a few weeks he will lie below the sod in London; at least if there is any."

"Perhaps you are right, John," she replied: "to lose hope must be a dreadful thing, when one is turned of seventy. Therefore I will never tell him."

The other way in which I managed to help the good Earl Brandir was of less true moment to him; but as he could not know of the first, this was the one which moved him. And it happened pretty much as follows — though I hardly like to tell, because it advanced me to such a height as I myself was giddy at; and which all my friends resented greatly (save those of my own family), and even now are sometimes bitter, in spite of all my humility. Now this is a matter of history, because the King was concerned in it; and being so strongly misunderstood, especially in my own neighbourhood, I will overcome (so far as I can) my diffidence in telling it.

The good Earl Brandir was a man of the noblest charity. True charity begins at home, and so did his; and was afraid of losing the way, if it went abroad. So this good nobleman kept his money in a handsome pewter box, with his coat of arms upon it, and a double lid, and locks. Moreover, there was a heavy chain, fixed to a staple in the wall, so that none might carry off the pewter with the gold inside of it. Lorna told me the box was full, for she had seen him go to it, and she often thought that it would be nice for us to begin the world with. I told her that she must not allow her mind to dwell upon things of this sort; being wholly against the last commandment set up in our church at Oare.

Now one evening towards September, when the days were drawing in, looking back at the house, to see whether Lorna were looking after me, I espied (by a little glimpse, as it were) a pair of villainous fellows (about whom there could be no mistake) watching from the thicket-corner, some hundred yards or so behind the good Earl's dwelling. "There is mischief a-foot," thought I to myself, being thoroughly conversant with theft, from my knowledge of the Doones; "how will be the moon to-night, and when may we expect the watch?"

I found that neither moon, nor watch, could be looked for until the morning; the moon, of course, before the watch, and more likely to be punctual. Therefore I resolved to wait, and see what those two villains did, and save (if it were possible) the Earl of Brandir's pewter box. But, inasmuch as those bad men were almost sure to have seen me leaving the house, and looking back, and striking out on the London road, I marched along at a merry pace, until they could not discern me; and then I fetched a compass round, and refreshed myself at a certain inn, entitled "The Cross-bones, and Buttons."

Here I remained until it was very nearly as dark as pitch; and the house being full of foot-pads and cut-throats, I thought it right to leave them. One or two came after me, in the hope of designing a stratagem; but I dropped them in the darkness; and knowing all the neighbourhood well, I took up my position, two hours before midnight, among the shrubs at the eastern end of Lord Brandir's mansion. Hence, although I might not see, I could scarcely fail to hear, if any unlawful entrance, either at back or front, were made.

From my own observation, I thought it likely that the attack would be in the rear; and so indeed it came to pass. For when all the lights were quenched, and all the house was quiet, I heard a low and wily whistle from a clump of trees close by; and then three figures passed between me and a whitewashed wall, and came to a window which opened into a part of the servants' basement. This window was carefully raised by some one inside the house: and after a little whispering, and something which sounded like a kiss, all the three men entered.

"Oh, you villains!" I said to myself; "this is worse than any Doone job: because there is treachery in it." But without waiting to consider the subject from a moral point of view, I crept along the wall, and entered very quietly after them; being rather uneasy about my life, because I bore no firearms, and had nothing more than my holly staff, for even a violent combat.

To me this was matter of deep regret, as I followed these vile men inward. Nevertheless I was resolved that my Lorna should not be robbed again. Through us (or at least through our Annie) she had lost that brilliant necklace; which then was her only birthright: therefore it behoved me doubly to preserve the pewter box; which must belong to her in the end, unless the thieves got hold of it.

I went along very delicately (as a man who has learned to wrestle can do, although he may weigh twenty stone), following carefully the light, brought by the traitorous maid, and shaking in her loose dishonest hand. I saw her lead the men into a little place called a pantry; and there she gave them cordials, and I could hear them boasting.

Not to be too long over it — which they were much inclined to be — I followed them from this drinking-bout, by the aid of the light they bore, as far as Earl Brandir's bedroom, which I knew, because Lorna had shown it to me, that I might admire the tapestry. But I had said that no horse could ever be shod as the horses were shod therein, unless he had the foot of a frog, as well as a frog to his foot. And Lorna had been vexed at this (as taste and high art always are, at any small accurate knowledge), and so she had brought me out again, before I had time to admire things.

Now, keeping well away in the dark, yet nearer than was necessary to my own dear Lorna's room, I saw these fellows try the door of the good Earl Brandir, knowing from the maid, of course, that his lordship could hear nothing, except the name of Alan. They tried the lock, and pushed at it, and even set their knees upright; but a Scottish nobleman may be trusted to secure his door at night. So they were forced to break it open; and at this the guilty maid, or woman, ran away. These three rogues — for rogues they were, and no charity may deny it — burst into Earl Brandir's room, with a light, and a crowbar, and fire-arms. I thought to myself that this was hard upon an honest nobleman; and if further mischief could be saved, I would try to save it.

When I came to the door of the room, being myself in shadow, I beheld two bad men trying vainly to break open the pewter box, and the third with a pistol muzzle laid to the night-cap of his lordship. With foul face, and yet fouler words, this man was demanding the key of the box, which the other men could by no means open, neither drag it from the chain. "I tell you," said this aged Earl, beginning to understand at last what these rogues were up for; "I will give no key to you. It all belongs to my boy, Alan. No one else shall have a farthing."

"Then you may count your moments, lord. The key is in your old cramped hand. One, two; and at three, I shoot you."

I saw that the old man was abroad; not with fear, but with great wonder, and the regret of deafness. And I saw that rather would he be shot, than let these men go rob his son, buried now, or laid to bleach in the tangles of the wood, three or it might be four years agone, but still alive to his father. Hereupon my heart was moved; and I resolved to interfere. The thief with the pistol began to count, as I crossed the floor very quietly, while the old Earl fearfully gazed at the muzzle, but clenched still tighter his wrinkled hand. The villain, with hair all over his eyes, and the great horse-pistol levelled, cried, "three," and pulled the trigger; but luckily, at that very moment, I struck up the barrel with my staff, so that the shot pierced the tester, and then with a spin and a thwack, I brought the good holly down upon the rascal's head, in a manner which stretched him upon the floor.

Meanwhile the other two robbers had taken the alarm, and rushed at me, one with a pistol, and one with a hanger; which forced me to be very lively. Fearing the pistol most, I flung the heavy velvet curtain of the bed across, that he might not see where to aim at me, and then stooping very quickly, I caught up the senseless robber, and set him up for a shield and target; whereupon he was shot immediately, without having the pain of knowing it; and a happy thing it was for him. Now the other two were at my mercy, being men below the average strength; and no hanger, except in most skilful hands, as well as firm and strong ones, has any chance to a powerful man armed with a stout cudgel, and thoroughly practised in singlestick.

So I took these two rogues, and bound them together; and leaving them under charge of the butler (a worthy and shrewd Scotchman), I myself went in search of the constables, whom, after some few hours, I found; neither were they so drunk but what they could take roped men to prison. In the morning, these two men were brought before the Justices of the Peace: and now my wonderful luck appeared; for the merit of having defeated, and caught them, would never have raised me one step in the State, or in public consideration, if they had only been common robbers, or even notorious murderers. But when these fellows were recognized, by some one in the court, as Protestant witnesses out of employment, companions and understrappers to

Oates, and Bedloe, and Carstairs, and hand in glove with Dangerfield, Turberville, and Dugdale — in a word, the very men against whom His Majesty the King bore the bitterest rancour, but whom he had hitherto failed to catch — when this was laid before the public (with emphasis, and admiration), at least a dozen men came up, whom I had never seen before, and prayed me to accept their congratulations, and to be sure to remember them; for all were of neglected merit, and required no more than a piece of luck.

I answered them very modestly, and each according to his worth, as stated by himself, who of course could judge the best. The magistrate made me many compliments, ten times more than I deserved, and took good care to have them copied, that His Majesty might see them. And ere the case was thoroughly heard, and those poor fellows were committed, more than a score of generous men had offered to lend me a hundred pounds, wherewith to buy a new Court suit, when called before His Majesty.

Now this may seem very strange to us, who live in a better and purer age — or say at least that we do so — and yet who are we to condemn our fathers, for teaching us better manners, and at their own expense? With these points any virtuous man is bound to deal quite tenderly, making allowance for corruption, and not being too sure of himself. And to tell the truth, although I had seen so little of the world as yet, that which astonished me, in the matter, was not so much that they paid me court, as that they found out so soon the expediency of doing it.

In the course of that same afternoon, I was sent for by His Majesty. He had summoned first the good Earl Brandir, and received the tale from him, not without exaggeration, although my lord was a Scotchman. But the chief thing His Majesty cared to know was that, beyond all possible doubt, these were the very precious fellows from perjury turned to robbery.

Being fully assured at last of this, His Majesty had rubbed his hands, and ordered the boots of a stricter pattern, which he himself had invented, to be brought at once, that he might have them in the best possible order. And he oiled them himself, and expressed his fear that there was no man in London quite competent to work them. Nevertheless he would try one or two, rather than wait for his pleasure, till the torturer came from Edinburgh.

The next thing he did was to send for me; and in great alarm and flurry, I put on my best clothes, and hired a fashionable hairdresser, and drank half a gallon of ale, because both my hands were shaking. Then forth I set, with my holly staff, wishing myself well out of it. I was shown at once, and before I desired it, into His Majesty's presence, and there I stood most humbly, and made the best bow I could think of.

As I could not advance any further — for I saw that the Queen was present, which frightened me tenfold — His Majesty, in the most gracious manner, came down the room to encourage me. And as I remained with my head bent down, he told me to stand up, and look at him.

"I have seen thee before, young man," he said; "thy form is not one to be forgotten. Where was it? Thou an most likely to know."

"May it please Your Most Gracious Majesty the King," I answered, finding my voice in a manner which surprised myself; "it was in the Royal Chapel."

Now I meant no harm whatever by this. I ought to have said the "Ante-Chapel," but I could not remember the word, and feared to keep the King looking at me.

"I am well pleased," said His Majesty, with a smile which almost made his dark and stubborn face look pleasant, "to find that our greatest subject, greatest I mean in the bodily form, is a good Catholic. Thou needest not say otherwise. The time shall be, and that right soon, when men shall be proud of the one true faith." Here he stopped, having gone rather far; but the gleam of his heavy eyes was such, that I durst not contradict.

"This is that great Johann Reed," said Her Majesty, coming forward because the King was in meditation; "for whom I have so much heard, from the dear, dear Lorna. Ah, she is not of this black countree, she of the breet Italie."

I have tried to write it, as she said it: but it wants a better scholar to express her mode of speech.

"Now, John Ridd," said the King, recovering from his thoughts about the true Church, and thinking that his wife was not to take the lead upon me; "thou hast done great service to the realm, and to religion. It was good to save Earl Brandir, a loyal and Catholic nobleman; but it was great service to catch two of the vilest bloodhounds ever laid on by heretics. And to make them shoot another: it was rare; it was rare, my lad. Now ask us anything in reason; thou canst carry any honours, on thy club, like Hercules. What is thy chief ambition, lad?"

"Well," said I, after thinking a little, and meaning to make the most of it, for so the Queen's eyes conveyed to me; "my mother always used to think that having been schooled at Tiverton, with thirty marks a year to pay, I was worthy of a coat of arms. And that is what she longs for."

"A good lad! A very good lad!" said the King, and he looked at the Queen, as if almost in joke; "but what is thy condition in life?"

"I am a freeholder," I answered in my confusion, "ever since the time of King Alfred. A Ridd was with him in the isle of Athelney, and we hold our farm by gift from him; or at least people say so. We have had three very good harvests running, and might support a coat of arms; but for myself I want it not."

"Thou shalt have a coat, my lad," said the King, smiling at his own humour; "but it must be a large one to fit thee. And more than that shalt thou have, John Ridd, being of such loyal breed, and having done such service."

And while I wondered what he meant, he called to some of the people in waiting at the farther end of the room, and they brought him a little sword, such as Annie would skewer a turkey with. Then he signified to me to kneel, which I did (after dusting the board, for the sake of my best breeches), and then he gave me a little tap very nicely upon my shoulder, before I knew what he was up to; and said, "Arise, Sir John Ridd!"

This astonished and amazed me to such extent of loss of mind, that when I got up I looked about, and thought what the Snowes would think of it. And I said to the King, without forms of speech:

"Sir, I am very much obliged. But what be I to do with it?"

CHAPTER LXIX
Not to be put up with

The coat of arms, devised for me by the Royal heralds, was of great size, and rich colours, and full of bright imaginings. They did me the honour to consult me first, and to take no notice of my advice. For I begged that there might be a good-sized cow on it, so as to stamp our pats of butter before they went to market: also a horse on the other side, and a flock snowed up at the bottom. But the gentlemen would not hear of this; and to find something more appropriate, they inquired strictly into the annals of our family. I told them, of course, all about King Alfred; upon which they settled that one quarter should be, three cakes on a bar, with a lion regardant, done upon a field of gold. Also I told them that very likely there had been a Ridd in the battle fought not very far from Plover's Barrows, by the Earl of Devon against the Danes, when Hubba their chief was killed, and the sacred standard taken. As some of the Danes are said to be buried, even upon land of ours, and we call their graves (if such they be) even to this day "barrows," the heralds quite agreed with me that a Ridd might have been there, or thereabouts; and if he was there, he was almost certain to have done his best, being in sight of hearth and home; and it was plain that he must have had good legs, to be at the same time both there and in Athelney; but good legs are an argument for good arms, and supposing a man of this sort to have done his utmost (as the manner of the Ridds is), it was next to certain that he himself must have captured the standard. Moreover the name of our farm was pure proof; a plover being a wild bird, just the same as a raven is. Upon this chain of reasoning, and without any weak misgiving, they charged my growing escutcheon with a black raven on a ground of red. And the next thing which I mentioned possessing absolute certainty, to wit, that a pig with two heads had been born upon our farm, not more than two hundred years agone (although he died within a week), my third quarter was made at once, by a two-headed boar with noble tusks, sable upon silver. All this was very fierce and fine; and so I pressed for a peaceful corner in the lower dexter, and obtained a wheat-sheaf set upright, gold upon a field of green.

Here I was inclined to pause, and admire the effect; for even De Whichehalse could not show a bearing so magnificent. But the heralds said that it looked a mere sign-board, without a good motto under it; and the motto must have my name in it. They offered me first, "Ridd non ridendus;" but I said, "for God's sake, gentlemen, let me forget my Latin." Then they proposed, "Ridd readeth riddles:" but I begged them not to set down such a lie; for no Ridd ever had made, or made out, such a thing as a riddle, since Exmoor itself began. Thirdly, they gave me, "Ridd never be ridden," and fearing to make any further objections, I let them inscribe it in bronze upon blue. The heralds thought that the King would pay for this noble achievement; but His Majesty, although graciously pleased with their ingenuity, declined in the most decided manner to pay a farthing towards it; and as I had no money left, the heralds became as blue as azure, and as red as gules; until Her Majesty the Queen came forward very kindly, and said that if His Majesty gave me a coat of arms, I was not to pay for it; therefore she herself did so quite handsomely, and felt good will towards me in consequence.

Now being in a hurry — so far at least as it is in my nature to hurry — to get to the end of this narrative, is it likely that I would have dwelled so long upon my coat of arms, but for some good reason? And this good reason is that Lorna took the greatest pride in it, and thought (or at any rate said), that it quite threw into the shade, and eclipsed, all her own ancient glories. And half in fun, and half in earnest, she called me "Sir John" so continually, that at last I was almost angry with her; until her eyes were bedewed with tears; and then I was angry with myself.

Beginning to be short of money, and growing anxious about the farm, longing also to show myself and my noble escutcheon to mother, I took advantage of Lady Lorna's interest with the Queen, to obtain my acquittance and full discharge from even nominal custody. It had been intended to keep me in waiting, until the return of Lord Jeffreys from that awful circuit of shambles, through which his name is still used by mothers to frighten their children into bed. And right glad was I — for even London shrank with horror at the news — to escape a man so blood-thirsty, savage, and even to his friends (among whom I was reckoned) malignant.

Earl Brandir was greatly pleased with me, not only for having saved his life, but for saving that which he valued more, the wealth laid by for Lord Alan. And he introduced me to many great people, who quite kindly encouraged me, and promised to help me in every way, when they heard how the King had spoken. As for the furrier, he could never have enough of my society; and this worthy man, praying my commendation, demanded of me one thing only — to speak of him as I found him. As I had found him, many a Sunday, furbishing up old furs for new, with a glaze to conceal the moth's ravages, I begged him to reconsider the point, and not to demand such accuracy. He said, "Well, well; all trades had tricks; especially the trick of business; and I must take him — if I were his true friend — according to his own description." This I was glad enough to do; because it saved so much trouble, and I had no money to spend with him. But still he requested the use of my name; and I begged him to do the best with it, as I never had kept a banker. And the "John Ridd cuffs," and the "Sir John mantles," and the "Holly-staff capes" he put into his window, as the winter was coming on, ay and sold (for everybody was burning with gossip about me), must have made this good man's fortune; since the excess of price over value is the true test of success in life.

To come away from all this stuff, which grieves a man in London — when the brisk air of the autumn cleared its way to Ludgate Hill, and clever 'prentices ran out and sniffed at it, and fed upon it (having little else to eat); and when the horses from the country were a goodly sight to see, with the rasp of winter bristles rising through and among the soft summer-coat; and when the new straw began to come in, golden with the harvest-gloss, and smelling most divinely, at those strange livery-stables where the nags are put quite tail to tail, and when all the London folk themselves were asking about white frost (from recollections of childhood); then, I say, such a yearning seized me for moory crag, and for dewy blade, and even the grunting of our sheep (when the sun goes down), that nothing but the new wisps of Samson could have held me in London town.

Lorna was moved with equal longing towards the country, and country ways; and she spoke quite as much of the glistening dew, as she did of the smell of our oven. And here let me mention — although the two are quite distinct and different — that both the dew, and the bread, of Exmoor may be sought, whether high or low, but never found elsewhere. The dew is so crisp, and pure, and pearly, and in such abundance; and the bread is so sweet, so kind, and homely, you can eat a loaf, and then another.

Now, while I was walking daily in and out great crowds of men (few of whom had any freedom from the cares of money, and many of whom were even morbid with a worse pest, called "politics"), I could not be quit of thinking how we jostle one another. God has made the earth quite large, with a spread of land enough for all to live on, without fighting. Also a mighty spread of water, laying hands on sand and cliff, with a solemn voice in storm-time; and in the gentle weather moving men to thoughts of equity. This, as well, is full of food; being two-thirds of the world, and reserved for devouring knowledge, by the time the sons of men have fed away the dry land. Yet before the land itself has acknowledged touch of man, upon one in a hundred acres; and before one mile in ten thousand of the exhaustless ocean has ever felt the plunge of hook, or combing of the haulnets; lo, we crawl, in flocks together, upon the hot ground that stings us, even as the black grubs crowd upon the harried nettle! Surely we are too much given to follow the tracks of each other.

However, for a moralist I never set up, and never shall, while common sense abides with me. Such a man must be truly wretched, in this pure dearth of morality; like a fisherman where no fish be; and most of us have enough to do, to attend to our own morals. Enough that I resolved to go; and as Lorna could not come with me, it was even worse than stopping. Nearly everybody vowed that I was a great fool indeed, to neglect so rudely — which was the proper word, they said — the pushing of my fortunes. But I answered that to push was rude, and I left it to people who had no room; and thought that my fortune must be heavy, if it would not move without pushing.

Lorna cried, when I came away (which gave me great satisfaction), and she sent a whole trunkful of things for mother, and Annie, and even Lizzie. And she seemed to think, though she said it not, that I made my own occasion for going, and might have stayed on till the winter. Whereas I knew well that my mother would think (and every one on the farm the same) that here I had been in London, lagging, and taking my pleasure, and looking at shops, upon pretence of King's business, and leaving the harvest to reap itself, not to mention the spending of money; while all the time there was nothing whatever, except my own love of adventure and sport, to keep me from coming home again. But I knew that my coat of arms, and title, would turn every bit of this grumbling into fine admiration.

And so it fell out, to a greater extent than even I desired: for all the parishes round about united in a sumptuous dinner, at the Mother Melldrum inn — for now that good lady was dead, and her name and face set on a sign-post — to which I was invited, so that it was as good as a summons. And if my health was no better next day, it was not from want of good wishes, any more than from stint of the liquor.

It is needless to say that the real gentry for a long time treated my new honours with contempt and ridicule; but gradually as they found that I was not such a fool as to claim any equality with them, but went about my farm-work, and threw another man at wrestling, and touched my hat to the magistrates, just the same as ever: some gentlemen of the highest blood — of which we think a great deal more than of gold, around our neighbourhood — actually expressed a desire to make my acquaintance. And when, in a manner quite straightforward, and wholly free from bitterness, I thanked them for this (which appeared to me the highest honour yet offered me), but declined to go into their company, because it would make me uncomfortable, and themselves as well, in a different way — they did what nearly all Englishmen do, when a thing is right and sensible. They shook hands with me; and said that they could not deny but that there was reason in my view of the matter. And although they themselves must be the losers — which was a handsome thing to say — they would wait until I was a little older, and more aware of my own value.

Now this reminds me how it is that an English gentleman is so far in front of foreign noblemen and princes. I have seen, at times, a little, both of one and of the other; and making more than due allowance for the difficulties of language, and the difference of training, upon the whole the balance is in favour of our people. And this, because we have two weights, solid and (even in scale of manners) outweighing all light complaisance; to wit, the inborn love of justice, and the power of abiding.

Yet some people may be surprised, that men with any love of justice, whether inborn or otherwise, could continue to abide the arrogance, and rapacity, and tyranny of the Doones.

For now as the winter passed, the Doones were not keeping themselves at home, as in honour they were bound to do. Twenty sheep a week, and one fat ox, and two stout red deer (for wholesome change of diet), as well as threescore bushels of flour, and two hogsheads and a half of cider, and a hundredweight of candles, not to mention other things of almost every variety, which they got by insisting upon it — surely these might have sufficed to keep the robbers happy in their place, with no outburst of wantonness. Nevertheless, it was not so; they had made complaint about something — too much ewe-mutton, I think it was — and in spite of all the pledges given, they had ridden forth, and carried away two maidens of our neighbourhood.

Now these two maidens were known, because they had served the beer at an ale-house; and many men who had looked at them, over a pint or quart vessel (especially as they were comely girls), thought that it was very hard for them to go in that way, and perhaps themselves unwilling. And their mother (although she had taken some money, which the Doones were always full of) declared that it was a robbery; and though it increased for a while the custom, that must soon fall off again. And who would have her two girls now, clever as they were and good?

Before we had finished meditating upon this loose outrage — for so I at least would call it, though people accustomed to the law may take a different view of it — we had news of a thing far worse, which turned the hearts of our women sick. This I will tell in most careful language, so as to give offence to none, if skill of words may help it.

Mistress Margery Badcock, a healthy and upright young woman, with a good rich colour, and one of the finest hen-roosts anywhere round our neighbourhood, was nursing her child about six of the clock, and looking out for her husband. Now this child was too old to be nursed, as everybody told her; for he could run say two yards alone, and perhaps four or five, by holding two handles. And he had a way of looking round, and spreading his legs, and laughing, with his brave little body well fetched up, after a desperate journey to the end of the table, which his mother said nothing could equal. Nevertheless he would come to be nursed, as regular as a clock almost; and inasmuch as he was the first, both father and mother made much of him; for God only knew whether they could ever compass such another one.

Christopher Badcock was a tenant farmer, in the parish of Martinhoe, renting some fifty acres of land, with a right of common attached to them; and at this particular time, being now the month of February, and fine open weather, he was hard at work ploughing, and preparing for spring corn. Therefore his wife was not surprised, although the dusk was falling, that Farmer Christopher should be at work in "blind man's holiday," as we call it.

But she was surprised, nay astonished, when by the light of the kitchen fire (brightened up for her husband) she saw six or seven great armed men burst into the room upon her; and she screamed so that the maid in the back kitchen heard her, but was afraid to come to help. Two of the strongest and fiercest men at once seized poor young Margery; and though she fought for her child and home, she was but an infant herself in their hands. In spite of tears and shrieks and struggles, they tore the babe from the mother's arms, and cast it on the lime-ash floor; then they bore her away to their horses (for by this time she was senseless), and telling the others to sack the house, rode off with their prize to the valley. And from the description of one of those two, who carried off the poor woman, I knew beyond all doubt that it was Carver Doone himself.

The other Doones being left behind, and grieved perhaps in some respects, set to with a will to scour the house, and to bring away all that was good to eat. And being a little vexed herein (for the Badcocks were not a rich couple), and finding no more than bacon, and eggs, and cheese, and little items, and nothing to drink but water; in a word, their taste being offended, they came back to the kitchen, and stamped; and there was the baby lying.

By evil luck, this child began to squeal about his mother, having been petted hitherto, and wont to get all he wanted, by raising his voice but a little. Now the mark of the floor was upon his head; as the maid (who had stolen to look at him, when the rough men were swearing upstairs) gave evidence. And she put a dish-cloth under his head, and kissed him, and ran away again. Her name was Honour Jose, and she meant what was right by her master and mistress; but could not help being frightened. And many women have blamed her, and as I think unduly, for her mode of forsaking baby so. If it had been her own baby, instinct rather than reason might have had the day with her; but the child being born of her mistress, she wished him good luck, and left him, as the fierce men came downstairs. And being alarmed by their power of language (because they had found no silver), she crept away in breathless hurry, and afraid how her breath might come back to her. For oftentimes she had hiccoughs.

While this good maid was in the oven, by side of back kitchen fire-place, with a faggot of wood drawn over her, and lying so that her own heart beat worse than if she were baking; the men (as I said before) came downstairs, and stamped around the baby.

"Rowland, is the bacon good?" one of them asked, with an oath or two: "it is too bad of Carver to go off with the only prize, and leave us in a starving cottage; and not enough to eat for two of us. Fetch down the staves of the rack, my boy. What was farmer to have for supper?"

"Nought but an onion or two, and a loaf, and a rasher of rusty bacon. These poor devils live so badly, they are not worth robbing."

"No game! Then let us have a game of loriot with the baby! It will be the best thing that could befall a lusty infant heretic. Ride a cock-horse to Banbury Cross. Bye, bye, baby Bunting; toss him up, and let me see if my wrist be steady."

The cruelty of this man is a thing it makes me sick to speak of; enough that when the poor baby fell (without attempt at cry or scream, thinking it part of his usual play, when they tossed him up, to come down again), the maid in the oven of the back-kitchen, not being any door between, heard them say as follows:

"If any man asketh who killed thee,
Say 'twas the Doones of Bagworthy."[4]

---

[4] Always pronounced " Badgery."

Now I think that when we heard this story, and poor Kit Badcock came all around, in a sort of half-crazy manner, not looking up at anyone, but dropping his eyes, and asking whether we thought he had been well treated, and seeming void of regard for life, if this were all the style of it; then, having known him a lusty man, and a fine singer in an ale-house, and much inclined to lay down the law, and show a high hand about women, I really think that it moved us more than if he had gone about ranting, and raving, and vowing revenge upon every one.

CHAPTER LXX
Compelled to Volunteer

There had been some trouble in our own home, during the previous autumn, while yet I was in London. For certain noted fugitives from the army of King Monmouth (which he himself had deserted, in a low and currish manner), having failed to obtain free shipment from the coast near Waters-mouth, had returned into the wilds of Exmoor, trusting to lurk, and be comforted, among the common people. Neither were they disappointed, for a certain length of time; nor in the end was their disappointment caused by fault on our part. Major Wade was one of them; an active and well-meaning man; but prone to fail in courage, upon lasting trial, although in a moment ready. Squire John Whichehalse (not the Baron) and Parson Powell[5] caught him, two or three months before my return, in Farley farm-house, near Brendon. He had been up at our house several times; and Lizzie thought a great deal of him. And well I know that if at that time I had been in the neighbourhood, he should not have been taken so easily.

John Birch, the farmer who had sheltered him, was so fearful of punishment that he hanged himself in a few days' time, and even before he was apprehended. But nothing was done to Grace Howe, of Bridgeball, who had been Wade's greatest comforter; neither was anything done to us; although Eliza added greatly to mother's alarm and danger, by falling upon Rector Powell, and most soundly rating him for his meanness, and his cruelty, and cowardice, as she called it, in setting men with fire-arms upon a poor helpless fugitive, and robbing all our neighbourhood of its fame for hospitality. However, by means of Serjeant Bloxham, and his good report of us, as well as by virtue of Wade's confession (which proved of use to the Government) my mother escaped all penalties.

---

[5] Not our Parson Bowden, nor any more a friend of his. Our Parson Bowden never had nought whatever to do with it; and never smoked a pipe with Parson Powell after it. — J. R.

It is likely enough that good folk will think it hard upon our neighbourhood to be threatened, and sometimes heavily punished, for kindness and humanity; and yet to be left to help ourselves against tyranny and base rapine. And new at last our gorge was risen, and our hearts in tumult. We had borne our troubles long, as a wise and wholesome chastisement; quite content to have some few things of our own unmeddled with. But what could a man dare to call his own, or what right could he have to wish for it, while he left his wife and children at the pleasure of any stranger?

The people came flocking all around me, at the black-smith's forge, and the Brendon ale-house; and I could scarce come out of church, but they got me among the tombstones. They all agreed that I was bound to take command and manage-ment. I bade them go to the magistrates, but they said they had been too often. Then I told them that I had no wits for ordering of an armament, although I could find fault enough with the one which had not succeeded. But they would hearken to none of this. All they said was, "Try to lead us; and we will try not to run away."

This seemed to me to be common sense, and good stuff, instead of mere bragging: moreover, I myself was moved by the bitter wrongs of Margery, having known her at our old Dame's School, ere ever I went to Tiverton; and having, in those days, serious thoughts of making her my sweetheart; although she was three years my elder. But now I felt this difficulty — the Doones had behaved very well to our farm, and to mother, and all of us, while I was away in London. Therefore would it not be shabby, and mean, for me to attack them now?

Yet being pressed still harder and harder, as day by day the excitement grew (with more and more talking over it), and no one else coming forward to undertake, the business, I agreed at last to this; that if the Doones, upon fair challenge, would not endeavour to make amends, by giving up Mistress Margery, as well as the man who had slain the babe, then I would lead the expedition, and do my best to subdue them. All our men were content with this, being thoroughly well assured from experi-ence, that the haughty robbers would only shoot any man who durst approach them with such proposal.

And then arose a difficult question — who was to take the risk of making overtures so unpleasant? I waited for the rest to offer; and as none was ready, the burden fell on me, and seemed to be of my own inviting. Hence I undertook the task, sooner than reason about it; for to give the cause of everything is worse than to go through with it.

It may have been three of the afternoon, when leaving my witnesses behind (for they preferred the background) I appeared with our Lizzie's white handkerchief upon a kidney-bean stick, at the entrance to the robbers' dwelling. Scarce knowing what might come of it, I had taken the wise precaution of fastening a Bible over my heart, and another across my spinal column, in case of having to run away, with rude men shooting after me. For my mother said that the Word of God would stop a two-inch bullet with three ounces of powder behind it. Now I took no weapons save those of the Spirit, for fear of being misunderstood. But I could not bring myself to think that any of honourable birth would take advantage of an unarmed man coming in guise of peace to them.

And this conclusion of mine held good, at least for a certain length of time; inasmuch as two decent Doones appeared, and hearing of my purpose, offered, without violence, to go and fetch the Captain; if I would stop where I was, and not begin to spy about anything. To this, of course, I agreed at once; for I wanted no more spying, because I had thorough knowledge of all ins and outs already. Therefore, I stood waiting steadily, with one hand in my pocket feeling a sample of corn for market; and the other against the rock, while I wondered to see it so brown already.

Those men came back in a little while, with a sharp short message that Captain Carver would come out and speak to me, by and by, when his pipe was finished. Accordingly, I waited long, and we talked about the signs of bloom for the coming apple season, and the rain that had fallen last Wednesday night, and the principal dearth of Devonshire, that it will not grow many cowslips — which we quite agreed to be the prettiest of spring flowers; and all the time I was wondering how many black and deadly deeds these two innocent youths had committed, even since last Christmas.

At length, a heavy and haughty step sounded along the stone roof of the way; and then the great Carver Doone drew up, and looked at me rather scornfully. Not with any spoken scorn, nor flash of strong contumely; but with that air of thinking little, and praying not to be troubled, which always vexes a man who feels that he ought not to be despised so, and yet knows not how to help it.

"What is it you want, young man?" he asked, as if he had never seen me before.

In spite of that strong loathing, which I always felt at sight of him, I commanded my temper moderately, and told him that I was come for his good, and that of his worshipful company, far more than for my own. That a general feeling of indignation had arisen among us, at the recent behaviour of certain young men, for which he might not be answerable, and for which we would not condemn him, without knowing the rights of the question. But I begged him clearly to understand, that a vile and inhuman wrong had been done, and such as we could not put up with; but that if he would make what amends he could by restoring the poor-woman, and giving up that odious brute who had slain the harmless infant, we would take no further motion; and things should go on as usual. As I put this in the fewest words that would meet my purpose, I was grieved to see a disdainful smile spread on his sallow countenance. Then he made me a bow of mock courtesy, and replied as follows:

"Sir John, your new honours have turned your poor head, as might have been expected. We are not in the habit of deserting anything that belongs to us; far less our sacred relatives. The insolence of your demands well-nigh outdoes the ingratitude. If there be a man upon Exmoor, who has grossly ill-used us, kidnapped our young women, and slain half a dozen of our young men, you are that outrageous rogue, Sir John. And after all this, how have we behaved? We have laid no hand upon your farm, we have not carried off your women, we have even allowed you to take our Queen, by creeping and crawling treachery; and we have given you leave of absence to help your cousin the highwayman, and to come home with a title. And now, how do you requite us? By inflaming the boorish indignation at a little frolic of our young men; and by coming with insolent demands, to yield to which would ruin us. Ah, you ungrateful viper!"

As he turned away in sorrow from me, shaking his head at my badness, I became so overcome (never having been quite assured, even by people's praises, about my own goodness), moreover the light which he threw upon things differed so greatly from my own, that, in a word — not to be too long — I feared that I was a villain. And with many bitter pangs — for I have had things to repent of — I began at my leisure to ask myself, whether or not this bill of indictment against John Ridd was true. Some of it I knew to be (however much I condemned myself) altogether out of reason; for instance, about my going away with Lorna very quietly, over the snow, and to save my love from being starved away from me. In this there was no creeping, neither crawling treachery; for all was done with sliding: and yet I was so out of training for being charged by other people beyond mine own conscience, that Carver Doone's harsh words came on me like prickly spinach sown with raking. Therefore I replied, and said:

"It is true that I owe you gratitude, sir, for a certain time of forbearance; and it is to prove my gratitude that I am come here now. I do not think that my evil deeds can be set against your own; although I cannot speak flowingly upon my good deeds, as you can. I took your Queen because you starved her, having stolen her long before, and killed her mother and brother. This is not for me to dwell upon now; any more than I would say much about your murdering of my father. But how the balance hangs between us. God knows better than thou or I, thou low miscreant, Carver Doone."

I had worked myself up, as I always do, in the manner of heavy men; growing hot like an ill-washered wheel revolving, though I start with a cool axle; and I felt ashamed of myself for heat, and ready to ask pardon. But Carver Doone regarded me with a noble and fearless grandeur.

"I have given thee thy choice, John Ridd," he said, in a lofty manner, which made me drop away under him: "I always wish to do my best with the worst people who come near me. And of all I have ever met with, thou art the very worst, Sir John, and the most dishonest."

Now after all my labouring to pay every man to a penny, and to allow the women over, when among the couch-grass (which is a sad thing for their gowns), to be charged like this, I say, so amazed me, that I stood with my legs quite open, and ready for an earthquake. And the scornful way in which he said "Sir John," went to my very heart, reminding me of my littleness. But seeing no use in bandying words, nay, rather the chance of mischief, I did my best to look calmly at him, and to say with a quiet voice, "Farewell, Carver Doone, this time; our day of reckoning is nigh."

"Thou fool, it is come," he cried, leaping aside into the niche of rock by the doorway: "Fire!"

Save for the quickness of spring, and readiness, learned in many a wrestling bout, that knavish trick must have ended me: but scarce was the word "Fire!" out of his mouth ere I was out of fire, by a single bound behind the rocky pillar of the opening. In this jump I was so brisk, at impulse of the love of life (for I saw the muzzles set upon me from the darkness of the cavern), that the men who had trained their guns upon me with good will and daintiness, could not check their fingers crooked upon the heavy triggers; and the valley sang with a roar behind it, down the avenue of crags.

With one thing and another, and most of all the treachery of this dastard scheme, I was so amazed that I turned and ran, at the very top of my speed, away from these vile fellows; and luckily for me, they had not another charge to send after me. And thus by good fortune, I escaped; but with a bitter heart, and mind, at their treacherous usage.

Without any further hesitation, I agreed to take command of the honest men, who were burning to punish, ay and destroy, those outlaws, as now beyond all bearing. One condition however I made, namely, that the Counsellor should be spared, if possible: not because he was less a villain than any of the others, but that he seemed less violent: and above all, had been good to Annie. And I found hard work to make them listen to my wish upon this point; for of all the Doones, Sir Counsellor had made himself most hated, by his love of law and reason.

We arranged that all our men should come, and fall into order with pike and musket, over against our dung-hill; and we settled, early in the day, that their wives might come and look at them. For most of these men had good wives; quite different from sweethearts, such as the militia had; women indeed who could hold to a man, and see to him, and bury him — if his luck were evil — and perhaps have no one afterwards. And all these women pressed their rights upon their precious husbands, and brought so many children with them, and made such a fuss, and hugging, and racing after little legs, that our farm-yard might be taken for an out-door school for babies, rather than a review-ground.

I myself was to and fro among the children continually: for if I love anything in the world, foremost I love children. They warm, and yet they cool our hearts, as we think of what we were, and what in young clothes we hoped to be; and how many things have come across. And to see our motives moving in the little things, that know not what their aim or object is, must almost, or ought at least, to lead us home, and soften us. For either end of life is home; both source, and issue, being God.

Nevertheless, I must confess that the children were a plague sometimes. They never could have enough of me — being a hundred to one, you might say — but I had more than enough of them; and yet was not contented. For they had so many ways of talking, and of tugging at my hair, and of sitting upon my neck (not even two with their legs alike), and they forced me to jump so vehemently, seeming to court the peril of my coming down neck-and-crop with them, and urging me still to go faster, however fast I might go with them; I assure you that they were sometimes so hard and tyrannical over me, that I might almost as well have been among the very Doones themselves.

Nevertheless the way in which the children made me use-ful proved also of some use to me; for their mothers were so pleased, by the exertions of the "great Gee-gee" — as all the small ones entitled me — that they gave me unlimited power and authority over their husbands; moreover, they did their utmost among their relatives round about, to fetch recruits for our little band. And by such means, several of the yeomanry from Barn-staple, and from Tiverton, were added to our number; and inas-much as these were armed with heavy swords, and short car-bines, their appearance was truly formidable.

Tom Faggus also joined us heartily, being now quite healed of his wound, except at times when the wind was easterly. He was made second in command to me; and I would gladly have had him first, as more fertile in expedients; but he declined such rank on the plea that I knew most of the seat of war; besides, that I might be held in some measure to draw authority from the King. Also Uncle Ben came over to help us with his advice and presence, as well as with a band of stout warehousemen, whom he brought from Dulverton. For he had never forgiven the old outrage put upon him; and though it had been to his interest to keep quiet during the last attack, under Commander Stickles — for the sake of his secret gold mine — yet now he was in a position to give full vent to his feelings. For he, and his partners, when fully assured of the value of their diggings, had obtained from the Crown a licence to adventure in search of minerals, by payment of a heavy fine and a yearly royalty. Therefore they had now no longer any cause for secrecy, neither for dread of the outlaws, having so added to their force as to be a match for them. And although Uncle Ben was not the man to keep his miners idle, one hour more than might be helped, he promised that when we had fixed the moment for an assault on the valley, a score of them should come to aid us, headed by Simon Carfax, and armed with the guns which they always kept for the protection of their gold.

Now whether it were Uncle Ben, or whether it were Tom Faggus, or even my own self — for all three of us claimed the sole honour — is more than I think fair to settle, without allowing them a voice. But at any rate, a clever thing was devised amongst us; and perhaps it would be the fairest thing to say that this bright stratagem (worthy of the great Duke himself) was contributed, little by little, among the entire three of us, all having pipes, and schnapps-and-water, in the chimney-corner. However, the world, which always judges according to reputation, vowed that so fine a stroke of war could only come from a highwayman: and so Tom Faggus got all the honour, at less perhaps than a third of the cost.

Not to attempt to rob him of it — for robbers, more than any other, contend for rights of property — let me try to describe this grand artifice. It was known that the Doones were fond of money, as well as strong drink, and other things; and more especially fond of gold, when they could get it pure and fine. Therefore it was agreed, that in this way we should tempt them; for we knew that they looked with ridicule upon our rustic preparations: after repulsing King's troopers, and the militia of two counties, was it likely that they should yield their fortress to a set of ploughboys? We, for our part, felt, of course, the power of this reasoning, and that where regular troops had failed, half-armed countrymen must fail, except by superior judgment and harmony of action. Though perhaps the militia would have sufficed, if they had only fought against the foe, instead of against each other. From these things we took warning: having failed through over-confidence, was it not possible now to make the enemy fail, through the self-same cause?

Hence, what we devised was this: to delude from home a part of the robbers, and fall by surprise on the other part. We caused it to be spread abroad that a large heap of gold was now collected at the mine of the Wizard's Slough. And when this rumour must have reached them, through women who came to and fro, as some entirely faithful to them were allowed to do, we sent Captain Simon Carfax, the father of little Gwenny, to demand an interview with the Counsellor by night, and as it were secretly. Then he was to set forth a list of imaginary grievances against the owners of the mine; and to offer, partly through resentment, partly through the hope of gain, to betray into their hands, upon the Friday night, by far the greatest weight of gold as yet sent up for refining. He was to have one quarter part, and they to take the residue. But inasmuch as the convoy across the moors under his command would be strong, and strongly armed, the Doones must be sure to send not less than a score of men if possible. He himself, at a place agreed upon, and fit for an ambuscade, would call a halt, and contrive in the darkness to pour a little water into the priming of his company's guns.

It cost us some trouble, and a great deal of money, to bring the sturdy Cornishman into this deceitful part; and perhaps he never would have consented but for his obligation to me, and the wrongs (as he said) of his daughter. However, as he was the man for the task, both from his coolness and courage, and being known to have charge of the mine, I pressed him, until he undertook to tell all the lies we required. And right well he did it too, having once made up his mind to it; and perceiving that his own interests called for the total destruction of the robbers.

CHAPTER LXXI

A Long Account settled

Having resolved on a night assault (as our undisciplined men, three-fourths of whom had never been shot at, could not fairly be expected to march up to visible musket-mouths), we cared not much about drilling our forces, only to teach them to hold a musket, so far as we could supply that weapon to those with the cleverest eyes; and to give them familiarity with the noise it made in exploding. And we fixed upon Friday night for our venture, because the moon would be at the full, and our powder was coming from Dulverton, on the Friday afternoon.

Uncle Reuben did not mean to expose himself to shooting, his time of life for risk of life being now well over, and the residue too valuable. But his counsels and his influence, and above all his warehousemen, well practised in beating carpets, were of true service to us. His miners also did great wonders, having a grudge against the Doones; as indeed who had not for thirty miles round their valley?

It was settled that the yeomen, having good horses under them, should give account with the miners' help of as many Doones as might be despatched to plunder the pretended gold. And as soon as we knew that this party of robbers, be it more or less, was out of hearing from the valley, we were to fall to, ostensibly at the Doone gate (which was impregnable now), but in reality upon their rear, by means of my old water-slide. For I had chosen twenty young fellows, partly miners, and partly warehousemen, and sheep-farmers, and some of other vocations, but all to be relied upon for spirit and power of climbing. And with proper tools to aid us, and myself to lead the way, I felt no doubt whatever but that we could all attain the crest, where first I had met with Lorna.

Upon the whole I rejoiced that Lorna was not present now. It must have been irksome to her feelings to have all her kindred and old associates (much as she kept aloof from them) put to death without ceremony, or else putting all of us to death. For all of us were resolved this time to have no more shilly-shallying, but to go through with a nasty business, in the style of honest Englishmen, when the question comes to "Your life or mine."

There was hardly a man among us who had not suffered bitterly from the miscreants now before us. One had lost his wife perhaps, another had lost a daughter — according to their ages, another had lost his favourite cow; in a word, there was scarcely anyone who had not to complain of a hay-rick; and what surprised me then, not now, was that the men least injured made the greatest push concerning it. But be the wrong too great to speak of, or too small to swear about, from poor Kit Badcock to rich Master Huckaback, there was not one but went heart and soul for stamping out these firebrands.

The moon was lifting well above the shoulder of the uplands, when we, the chosen band, set forth, having the shortcut along the valleys to foot of the Bagworthy water; and therefore, having allowed the rest an hour to fetch round the moors and hills, we were not to begin our climbing until we heard a musket fired from the heights, on the left-hand side, where John Fry himself was stationed, upon his own and his wife's request, to keep him out of combat. And that was the place where I had been used to sit, and to watch for Lorna. And John Fry was to fire his gun, with a ball of wool inside it, so soon as he heard the hurly-burly at the Doone gate beginning; which we, by reason of waterfall, could not hear, down in the meadows there.

We waited a very long time, with the moon marching up heaven steadfastly, and the white fog trembling in chords and quavers, like a silver harp of the meadows. And then the moon drew up the fogs, and scarfed herself in white with them; and so being proud, gleamed upon the water, like a bride at her looking-glass; and yet there was no sound of either John Fry or his blunderbuss.

I began to think that the worthy John, being out of all danger, and having brought a counterpane (according to his wife's directions, because one of the children had a cold), must veritably have gone to sleep; leaving other people to kill, or be killed, as might be the will of God; so that he were comfortable. But herein I did wrong to John, and am ready to acknowledge it; for suddenly the most awful noise that anything short of thunder could make, came down among the rocks, and went and hung upon the corners.

"The signal, my lads!" I cried, leaping up, and rubbing my eyes; for even now, while condemning John unjustly, I was giving him right to be hard upon me. "Now hold on by the rope, and lay your quarter-staffs across, my lads; and keep your guns pointing to heaven, lest haply we shoot one another."

"Us shan't never shutt one anoother, wi' our goons at that mark, I reckon," said an oldish chap, but as tough as leather, and esteemed a wit for his dryness.

"You come next to me, old Ike; you be enough to dry up the waters; now, remember, all lean well forward. If any man throws his weight back, down he goes, and perhaps he may never get up again, and most likely he will shoot himself."

I was still more afraid of their shooting me; for my chief alarm in this steep ascent was neither of the water, nor of the rocks, but of the loaded guns we bore. If any man slipped, off might go his gun; and however good his meaning, I being first was most likely to take far more than I fain would apprehend.

For this cause, I had debated with Uncle Ben and with Cousin Tom as to the expediency of our climbing with guns unloaded. But they, not being in the way themselves, assured me that there was nothing to fear, except through uncommon clumsiness, and that as for charging our guns at the top, even veteran troops could scarce be trusted to perform it properly in the hurry and the darkness and the noise of fighting before them.

However, thank God, though a gun went off, no one was any the worse for it, neither did the Doones notice it, in the thick of the firing in front of them. For the order to those of the sham attack, conducted by Tom Faggus, was to make the greatest possible noise, without exposure of themselves; until we in the rear had fallen to; which John Fry was again to give signal of.

Therefore we of the chosen band stole up the meadow quietly, keeping in the blots of shade, and hollow of the watercourse. And the earliest notice the Counsellor had, or anyone else, of our presence, was the blazing of the log-wood house, where lived that villain Carver. It was my especial privilege to set this house on fire; upon which I had insisted, exclusively and conclusively. No other hand but mine should lay a brand, or strike steel on flint for it; I had made all preparations carefully for a good blaze. And I must confess that I rubbed my hands with a strong delight and comfort when I saw the home of that man, who had fired so many houses, having its turn of smoke, and blaze, and of crackling fury.

We took good care, however, to burn no innocent women or children in that most righteous destruction. For we brought them all out beforehand; some were glad, and some were sorry; according to their dispositions. For Carver had ten or a dozen wives; and perhaps that had something to do with his taking the loss of Lorna so easily. One child I noticed, as I saved him; a fair and handsome little fellow, beloved by Carver Doone, as much as anything beyond himself could be. The boy climbed on my back, and rode, and much as I hated his father, it was not in my heart to say or do a thing to vex him.

Leaving these poor injured people to behold their burning home, we drew aside, by my directions, into the covert beneath the cliff. But not before we had laid our brands to three other houses, after calling the women forth, and bidding them go for their husbands, to come and fight a hundred of us. In the smoke and rush and fire they believed that we were a hundred, and away they ran, in consternation, to the battle at the Doone gate.

"All Doone town is on fire, on fire!" we heard them shrieking as they went; "a hundred soldiers are burning it, with a dreadful great man at the head of them!"

Presently, just as I expected, back came the warriors of the Doones; leaving but two or three at the gate, and burning with wrath to crush under foot the presumptuous clowns in their valley. Just then the waxing fire leaped above the red crest of the cliffs, and danced on the pillars of the forest, and lapped like a tide on the stones of the slope. All the valley flowed with light, and the limpid waters reddened, and the fair young women shone, and the naked children glistened.

But the finest sight of all was to see those haughty men striding down the causeway darkly, reckless of their end, but resolute to have two lives for every one. A finer dozen of young men could not have been found in the world perhaps, nor a braver, nor a viler one.

Seeing how few there were of them, I was very loth to fire, although I covered the leader, who appeared to be dashing Charley; for they were at easy distance now, brightly shown by the firelight, yet ignorant where to look for us. I thought that we might take them prisoners — though what good that could be.

God knows, as they must have been hanged thereafter — anyhow I was loth to shoot, or to give the word to my followers.

But my followers waited for no word: they saw a fair shot at the men they abhorred, the men who had robbed them of home or of love, and the chance was too much for their charity. At a signal from old Ikey, who levelled his own gun first, a dozen muskets were discharged, and half of the Doones dropped lifeless, like so many logs of firewood, or chopping-blocks rolled over.

Although I had seen a great battle before, and a hundred times the carnage, this appeared to me to be horrible, and I was at first inclined to fall upon our men, for behaving so. But one instant showed me that they were right; for while the valley was filled with howling, and with shrieks of women, and the beams of blazing houses fell, and hissed in the bubbling river, all the rest of the Doones leaped at us like so many demons. They fired wildly, not seeing us well among the hazel bushes; and then they clubbed their muskets or drew their swords, as might be, and furiously drove at us.

For a moment, although we were twice their number, we fell back before their valorous fame, and the power of their onset. For my part, admiring their courage greatly, and counting it slur upon manliness that two should be down upon one so, I withheld my hand awhile; for I cared to meet none but Carver, and he was not among them. The whirl and hurry of this fight, and the hard blows raining down — for now all guns were empty — took away my power of seeing, or reasoning, upon anything. Yet one thing I saw, which dwelled long with me, and that was Christopher Badcock spending his life to get Charley's.

How he had found out none may tell, both being dead so long ago; but at any rate he had found out that Charley was the man who had robbed him of his wife and honour. It was Carver Doone who took her away, but Charlesworth Doone was beside him, and according to cast of dice, she fell to Charley's share. All this Kit Badcock (who was mad, according to our measures) had discovered and treasured up, and now was his revenge-time.

He had come into the conflict without a weapon of any kind; only begging me to let him be in the very thick of it. For him, he said, life was no matter, after the loss of his wife and child; but death was matter to him, and he meant to make the most of it. Such a face I never saw, and never hope to see again, as when poor Kit Badcock spied Charley coming towards us.

We had thought this man a patient fool, a philosopher of a little sort, or one who could feel nothing. And his quiet manner of going about, and the gentleness of his answers (when some brutes asked him where his wife was, and whether his baby had been well trussed), these had misled us to think that the man would turn the mild cheek to everything. But I, in the loneliness of our barn, had listened, and had wept with him.

Therefore was I not surprised so much as all the rest of us, when, in the foremost of red light, Kit went up to Charlesworth Doone, as if to some inheritance, and took his seisin of right upon him, being himself a powerful man, and begged a word aside with him. What they said aside I know not; all I know is that without weapon each man killed the other. And Margery Badcock came and wept, and hung upon her dead husband, and died that summer of heart-disease.

Now for these and other things (whereof I could tell a thousand) was the reckoning come that night, and not a line we missed of it; soon as our bad blood was up. I like not to tell of slaughter, though it might be of wolves and tigers: and that was a night of fire and slaughter, and of very long-harboured revenge. Enough that ere the daylight broke, upon that wan March morning, the only Doones still left alive were the Counsellor and Carver. And of all the dwellings of the Doones (inhabited with luxury and luscious taste and licentiousness) not even one was left, but all made potash in the river.

This may seem a violent and unholy revenge upon them. And I (who led the heart of it) have in these my latter years doubted how I shall be judged, not of men — for God only knows the errors of man's judgments — but by that great God Himself, the front of whose forehead is mercy.

CHAPTER LXXII

The Counsellor and the Carver

From that great confusion — for nothing can be broken up, whether lawful or unlawful, without a vast amount of dust, and many people grumbling and mourning for the good old times, when all the world was happiness, and every man a gentleman, and the sun himself far brighter than since the brassy idol upon which he shone was broken — from all this loss of ancient landmarks (as unrobbed men began to call our clearance of those murderers) we returned on the following day, almost as full of anxiety as we were of triumph. In the first place, what could we frugally do with all these women and children, thrown on our hands, as one might say, with none to protect and care for them? Again, how should we answer to the Justices of the Peace, or perhaps even to Lord Jeffreys, for having without even a warrant taken the law into our own hands, and abated our nuisance so forcibly? And then, what was to be done with the spoil, which was of great value; though the diamond necklace came not to public light? For we saw a mighty host of claimants already leaping up for booty. Every man who had ever been robbed expected usury on his loss; the lords of the manors demanded the whole; and so did the King's Commissioner of Revenue at Porlock, and so did the men who had fought our battle; while even the parsons, both Bowden and Powell, and another who had no parish in it, threatened us with the just wrath of the Church, unless each had tithes of the whole of it.

Now this was not as it ought to be; and it seemed as if by burning the nest of robbers, we had but hatched their eggs; until being made sole guardian of the captured treasure (by reason of my known honesty) I hit upon a plan, which gave very little satisfaction; yet carried this advantage, that the grumblers argued against one another, and for the most part came to blows; which renewed their good-will to me, as being abused by the adversary.

And my plan was no more than this — not to pay a farthing to lord of manor, parson, or even King's Commissioner, but after making good some of the recent and proven losses — where the men could not afford to lose — to pay the residue (which might be worth some fifty thousand pounds) into the Exchequer at Westminster, and then let all the claimants file what bills they pleased in Chancery.

Now this was a very noble device; for the mere name of Chancery, and the high repute of the fees therein, and the low repute of the lawyers, and the comfortable knowledge that the woolsack itself is the golden fleece, absorbing gold for ever, if the standard be but pure; consideration of these things staved off at once the lords of the manors, and all the little farmers, and even those whom most I feared; videlicet, the parsons. And the King's Commissioner was compelled to confess himself contented, although of all he was most aggrieved; for his pickings would have been goodly.

Moreover, by this plan I made — although I never thought of that — a mighty friend, worth all the enemies whom the toss of money moved. The first man now in the kingdom (by virtue perhaps of energy, rather than of excellence) was the great Lord Jeffreys, appointed the head of the Equity, as well as of the larger law, for his kindness in hanging five hundred people, without the mere grief of trial. Nine out of ten of these people were innocent, it is true, but that proved the merit of the Lord Chief-Justice so much the greater for hanging them, as showing what might be expected of him when he truly got hold of a guilty man. Now the King had seen the force of this argument; and not being without gratitude for a high-seasoned dish of cruelty, had promoted the only man in England, combining the gifts both of butcher and cook.

Nevertheless, I do beg you all to believe of me — and I think that, after following me so long, you must believe it — that I did not even know at the time of Lord Jeffreys' high promotion. Not that my knowledge of this would have led me to act otherwise in the matter; for my object was to pay into an office, and not to any official; neither, if I had known the fact, could I have seen its bearing upon the receipt of my money. For the King's Exchequer is, meseemeth, of the Common Law; while Chancery is of Equity, and well named for its many chances. But the true result of the thing was this — Lord Jeffreys being now head of the law, and almost head of the kingdom, got possession of that money, and was kindly pleased with it.

And this met our second difficulty; for the law having won and laughed over the spoil, must have injured its own title by impugning our legality.

Next, with regard to the women and children, we were long in a state of perplexity. We did our very best at the farm, and so did many others, to provide for them, until they should manage about their own subsistence. And after a while this trouble went, as nearly all troubles go, with time. Some of the women were taken back by their parents, or their husbands, or it may be their old sweethearts; and those who failed of this, went forth, some upon their own account to the New World plantations, where the fairer sex is valuable, and some to English cities, and the plainer ones to field-work. And most of the children went with their mothers, or were bound apprentices; only Carver Doone's handsome child had lost his mother, and stayed with me.

This boy went about with me everywhere. He had taken as much of liking to me — first shown in his eyes by the firelight — as his father had of hatred; and I, perceiving his noble courage, scorn of lies, and high spirit, became almost as fond of Ensie as he was of me. He told us that his name was "Ensie," meant for "Ensor," I suppose, from his father's grandfather, the old Sir Ensor Doone. And this boy appeared to be Carver's heir, having been born in wedlock, contrary to the general manner and custom of the Doones.

However, although I loved the poor child, I could not help feeling very uneasy about the escape of his father, the savage and brutal Carver. This man was left to roam the country, homeless, foodless, and desperate, with his giant strength, and great skill in arms, and the whole world to be revenged upon. For his escape the miners, as I shall show, were answerable; but of the Counsellor's safe departure the burden lay on myself alone. And inasmuch as there are people who consider themselves ill-used unless one tells them everything, straitened though I am for space, I will glance at this transaction.

After the desperate charge of young Doones had been met by us, and broken, and just as poor Kit Badcock died in the arms of the dead Charley, I happened to descry a patch or white on the grass of the meadow, like the head of a sheep after washing-day. Observing, with some curiosity, how carefully this white thing moved, along the bars of darkness betwixt the panels of firelight, I ran up to intercept it before it reached the little postern which we used to call Gwenny's door. Perceiving me, the white thing stopped, and was for making back again; but I ran up at full speed, and lo, it was the flowing silvery hair of that sage the Counsellor, who was scuttling away upon all fours; but now rose, and confronted me.

"John," he said, "Sir John, you will not play falsely with your ancient friend, among these violent fellows. I look to you to protect me, John."

"Honoured sir, you are right," I replied; "but surely that posture was unworthy of yourself and your many resources. It is my intention to let you go free."

"I knew it. I could have sworn to it. You are a noble fellow, John; I said so, from the very first; you are a noble fellow, and an ornament to any rank."

"But upon two conditions," I added, gently taking him by the arm; for instead of displaying any desire for commune with my nobility, he was edging away towards the postern: "the first is that you tell me truly (for now it can matter to none of you) who it was that slew my father."

"I will tell you truly and frankly, John; however painful to me to confess it. It was my son, Carver."

"I thought as much, or I felt as much, all along," I answered; "but the fault was none of yours, sir; for you were not even present."

"If I had been there it would not have happened. I am always opposed to violence. Therefore, let me haste away; this scene is against my nature."

"You shall go directly, Sir Counsellor, after meeting my other condition; which is, that you place in my hands Lady Lorna's diamond necklace."

"Ah, how often I have wished," said the old man, with a heavy sigh, "that it might yet be in my power to ease my mind in that respect, and to do a thoroughly good deed, by lawful restitution."

"Then try to have it in your power, sir. Surely, with my encouragement, you might summon resolution."

"Alas, John, the resolution has been ready long ago. But the thing is not in my possession. Carver, my son, who slew your father, upon him you will find the necklace. What are jewels to me, young man, at my time of life? Baubles and trash — I detest them, from the sins they have led me to answer for. When you come to my age, good Sir John, you will scorn all jewels, and care only for a pure and bright conscience. Ah! ah! Let me go. I have made my peace with God."

He looked so hoary and so silvery, and serene in the moonlight, that verily I must have believed him, if he had not drawn in his breast. But I happened to have noticed that when an honest man gives vent to noble and great sentiments, he spreads his breast, and throws it out, as if his heart were swelling, whereas I had seen this old gentleman draw his breast in, more than once, as it happened to contain better goods than sentiment.

"Will you applaud me, kind sir," I said, keeping him very tight all the while, "if I place it in your power to ratify your peace with God? The pledge is upon your heart, no doubt, for there it lies at this moment."

With these words, and some apology for having recourse to strong measures, I thrust my hand inside his waistcoat, and drew forth Lorna's necklace, purely sparkling in the moonlight, like the dancing of new stars. The old man made a stab at me with a knife which I had not espied; but the vicious onset failed, and then he knelt and clasped his hands.

"Oh, for God's sake, John, my son, rob me not in that manner. They belong to me, and I love them so; I would give almost my life for them. There is one jewel there I can look at for hours, and see all the lights of heaven in it, which I never shall see elsewhere. All my wretched wicked life — Oh, John, I am a sad hypocrite — but give me back my jewels. Or else kill me here: I am a babe in your hands; but I must have back my jewels."

As his beautiful white hair fell away from his noble forehead, like a silver wreath of glory, and his powerful face for once was moved with real emotion, I was so amazed and overcome by the grand contradictions of nature, that verily I was on the point of giving him back the necklace. But honesty, which is said to be the first instinct of all Ridds (though I myself never found it so), happened here to occur to me; and so I said, without more haste than might be expected:

"Sir Counsellor, I cannot give you what does not belong to me. But if you will show me that particular diamond, which is heaven to you, I will take upon myself the risk and the folly of cutting it out for you. And with that you must go contented; and I beseech you not to starve, with that jewel upon your lips."

Seeing no hope of better terms, he showed me his pet love of a jewel, and I thought of what Lorna was to me as I cut it out (with the hinge of my knife severing the snakes of gold) and placed it in his careful hand. Another moment, and he was gone, and away through Gwenny's postern, and God knows what became of him.

Now as to Carver, the thing was this — so far as I could ascertain from the valiant miners, no two of whom told the same story, any more than one of them told it twice. The band of Doones which sallied forth for the robbery of the pretended convoy, was met by Simon Carfax, according to arrangement, at the ruined house called the "Warren," in that part of Bagworthy Forest where the river Exe (as yet a very small stream) runs through it. The Warren, as all our people know, had belonged to a fine old gentleman, whom every one called "The Squire," who had retreated from active life to pass the rest of his days in fishing, and shooting, and helping his neighbours. For he was a man of some substance, and no poor man ever left the Warren without a bag of good victuals and a few shillings put in his pocket. However, this poor Squire never made a greater mistake than in hoping to end his life peacefully upon the banks of a trout-stream, and in the green forest of Bagworthy. For as he came home from the brook at dusk, with his fly-rod over his shoulder, the Doones fell upon him, and murdered him, and then sacked his house and burned it.

Now this had made honest people timid about going past the Warren at night; for of course it was said that the old Squire "walked" upon certain nights of the moon in and out the trunks of trees, on the green path from the river. On his shoulder he bore a fishing-rod, and his book of trout-flies in one hand, and on his back a wicker-creel, and now and then he would burst out laughing, to think of the way he was caught by the Doones.

And now that one turns to consider it, this seems a strangely righteous thing, that the scene of one of the greatest crimes even by Doones committed should, after twenty years, become the scene of vengeance falling (like hail from heaven) upon them. For (although the Warren lies well away to the westward of the mine, and the gold, under escort to Bristowe or London, would have gone in the other direction) Captain Carfax, finding this place best suited for working of his design, had persuaded the Doones that for reasons of Government the ore must go first to Barnstaple for inspection, or something of that sort. And as every one knows that our Government sends all things westward when eastward bound, this had won the more faith for Simon, as being according to nature.

Now Simon, having met these flowers of the flock of villainy, where the rising moonlight flowed through the weir-work of the wood, begged them to dismount, and led them, with an air of mystery, into the Squire's ruined hall, black with fire, and green with weeds.

"Captain, I have found a thing," he said to Carver Doone himself, "which may help to pass the hour ere the lump of gold comes by. The smugglers are a noble race, but a miner's eyes are a match for them. There lies a puncheon of rare spirit, with the Dutchman's brand upon it, hidden behind the broken hearth. Set a man to watch outside, and let us see what this be like."

With one accord they agreed to this, and Carver pledged Master Carfax, and all the Doones grew merry. But Simon being bound, as he said, to see to their strict sobriety, drew a bucket of water from the well, into which they had thrown the dead owner, and begged them to mingle it with their drink, which some of them did, and some refused.

But the water from that well was poured, while they were carousing, into the priming-pan of every gun of theirs; even as Simon had promised to do with the guns of the men they were come to kill. Then just as the giant Carver arose, with a glass of pure hollands in his hand, and by the light of the torch they had struck, proposed the good health of the Squire's ghost — in the broken doorway stood a press of men, with pointed muskets, covering every drunken Doone. How it fared upon that I know not, having none to tell me; for each man wrought, neither thought of telling nor whether he might be alive to tell. The Doones rushed to their guns at once, and pointed them, and pulled at them; but the Squire's well had drowned their fire; and then they knew that they were betrayed, but resolved to fight like men for it. Upon fighting I can never dwell; it breeds such savage delight in me; of which I would fain have less. Enough that all the Doones fought bravely, and like men (though bad ones) died in the hall of the man they had murdered. And with them died poor young De Whichehalse, who, in spite of all his good father's prayers, had cast in his lot with the robbers. Carver Doone alone escaped. Partly through his fearful strength, and yet his more fearful face, but mainly perhaps through his perfect coolness and his mode of taking things.

I am happy to say that no more than eight of the gallant miners were killed in that combat, or died of their wounds afterwards; and adding to these the eight we had lost in our assault on the valley (and two of them excellent warehousemen), it cost no more than sixteen lives to be rid of nearly forty Doones, each of whom would most likely have killed three men in the course of a year or two. Therefore, as I said at the time, a great work was done very reasonably; here were nigh upon forty Doones destroyed (in the valley, and up at the Warren), despite their extraordinary strength and high skill in gunnery; whereas of us ignorant rustics there were only sixteen to be counted dead — though others might be lamed or so — and of those sixteen, only two had left wives, and their wives had no trouble to marry again.

Yet for Lorna's sake I was vexed at the bold escape of Carver. Not that I sought for Carver's life any more than I did for the Counsellor's; but that for us it was no light thing to have a man of such power, and resource, and desperation left at large and furious, like a famished wolf round the sheep-fold. Yet greatly as I blamed the yeomen who were posted on their horses, just out of shot from the Doone-gate, for the very purpose of intercepting those who escaped the miners, I could not get them to admit that any blame attached to them.

But lo, he had dashed through the whole of them, with his horse at full gallop, and was out of range ere ever they began to think of shooting him. Then it appears from what a boy said — for boys manage to be everywhere — that Captain Carver rode through the Doone-gate, and so to the head of the valley. There he discovered all the houses, and his own among the number, flaming with a handsome blaze, and throwing a fine light around, such as he often had revelled in, when of other people's property. Now he swore the deadliest of all oaths, and seeing himself to be vanquished (so far as the luck of the moment went), spurred his great black horse away, and passed into the darkness.

CHAPTER LXXIII

How to get out of Chancery

Things at this time so befell me that I cannot tell one half; but am like a boy who has left his lesson (to the master's very footfall) unready, except with false excuses. And as this makes no good work, so I lament upon my lingering, in the times when I might have got through a good page, but went astray after trifles. However, every man must do according to his intellect; and looking at the easy manner of my constitution, I think that most men will regard me with pity and good will for trying, more than with contempt and wrath, for having tried unworthily. Even as in the wrestling ring, whatever man did his very best, and made an honest conflict, I always laid him down with softness, easing off his dusty fall.

But the thing which next betided me was not a fall of any sort, but rather a most glorious rise to the summit of all fortune. For in good truth it was no less than the return of Lorna — my Lorna, my own darling, in wonderful health and spirits, and as glad as a bird to get back again. It would have done anyone good for a twelvemonth to behold her face and doings, and her beaming eyes and smile (not to mention blushes also at my salutation), when this Queen of every heart ran about our rooms again. She did love this, and she must see that, and where was her old friend the cat? All the house was full of brightness, as if the sun had come over the hill, and Lorna were his looking-glass.

My mother sat in an ancient chair, and wiped her cheeks, and gazed at her; and even Lizzie's eyes must dance to the freshness and joy of her beauty. As for me, you might call me mad; for I ran out, and flung my best hat on the barn, and kissed mother Fry, till she made at me with the clacker of the churn.

What a quantity of things Lorna had to tell us! And yet how often we stopped her mouth — at least mother, I mean, and Lizzie — and she quite as often would stop her own, running up in her joy to some one of us! And then there arose the eating business — which people now call "refreshments," in these dandyfied days of our language — for how was it possible that our

Lorna could have come all that way, and to her own Exmoor, without being terribly hungry?

"Oh, I do love it all so much," said Lorna, now for the fiftieth time, and not meaning only the victuals; "the scent of the gorse on the moors drove me wild and the primroses under the hedges. I am sure I was meant for a farmer's — I mean for a farm-house life, dear Lizzie" — for Lizzie was looking saucily — "just as you were meant for a soldier's bride, and for writing despatches of victory. And now, since you will not ask me, dear mother, in the excellence of your manners, and even John has not the impudence, in spite of all his coat of arms — I must tell you a thing, which I vowed to keep until to-morrow morning; but my resolution fails me. I am my own mistress; what think you of that, mother? I am my own mistress!"

"Then you shall not be so long," cried I; for mother seemed not to understand her, and sought about for her glasses: "darling, you shall be mistress of me, and I will be your master."

"A frank announcement of your intent, and beyond doubt a true one; but surely unusual at this stage, and a little premature, John. However, what must be, must be." And with tears springing out of smiles, she fell on my breast, and cried a bit.

When I came to smoke a pipe over it (after the rest were gone to bed), I could hardly believe in my good luck. For here was I, without any merit except of bodily power, and the absence of any falsehood (which surely is no commendation), so placed that the noblest men in England might envy me, and be vexed with me. For the noblest lady in all the land, and the purest, and the sweetest, hung upon my heart, as if there was none to equal it.

I dwelled upon this matter, long and very severely, while I smoked a new tobacco, brought by my own Lorna for me, and next to herself most delicious, and as the smoke curled away, I thought, "Surely this is too fine to last, for a man who never deserved it!"

Seeing no way out of this, I resolved to place my faith in God, and so went to bed, and dreamed of it. For having no presence of mind to pray for anything, under the circumstances, I thought it best to fall asleep, and trust myself to the future. Yet ere I fell asleep, the roof above me swarmed with angels, having Lorna under it.

In the morning Lorna was ready to tell her story, and we to hearken; and she wore a dress of most simple stuff; and yet perfectly wonderful, by means of the shape and her figure. Lizzie was wild with jealousy, as might be expected (though never would Annie have been so, but have praised it, and craved for the pattern), and mother, not understanding it, looked forth, to be taught about it. For it was strange to note that lately my dear mother had lost her quickness, and was never quite brisk, unless the question were about myself. She had seen a great deal of trouble; and grief begins to close on people, as their power of life declines. We said that she was hard of hearing; but my opinion was, that seeing me inclined for marriage made her think of my father, and so perhaps a little too much to dwell upon the courting of thirty years agone. Anyhow, she was the very best of mothers, and would smile and command herself, and be (or try to believe herself) as happy as could be, in the doings of the younger folk, and her own skill in detecting them. Yet, with the wisdom of age, renouncing any opinion upon the matter; since none could see the end of it.

But Lorna, in her bright young beauty, and her knowledge of my heart, was not to be checked by any thoughts of haply coming evil. In the morning she was up, even sooner than I was, and through all the corners of the hens, remembering every one of them. I caught her, and saluted her with such warmth (being now none to look at us), that she vowed she would never come out again, and yet she came the next morning!

These things ought not to be chronicled. Yet I am of such nature that finding many parts of life adverse to our wishes, I must now and then draw pleasure from the blessed portions. And what portion can be more blessed than with youth, and health, and strength, to be loved by a virtuous maid, and to love her with all one's heart? Neither was my pride diminished, when I found what she had done, only from her love of me.

Earl Brandir's ancient steward, in whose charge she had travelled, with a proper escort, looked upon her as a lovely maniac; and the mixture of pity, and admiration, wherewith he regarded her was a strange thing to observe; especially after he had seen our simple house and manners. On the other hand, Lorna considered him a worthy but foolish old gentleman; to whom true happiness meant no more than money and high position.

These two last she had been ready to abandon wholly, and had in part escaped from them, as the enemies of her happiness. And she took advantage of the times in a truly clever manner. For that happened to be a time — as indeed all times hitherto (so far as my knowledge extends) have, somehow or other, happened to be — when everybody was only too glad to take money for doing anything. And the greatest money-taker in the kingdom (next to the King and Queen, of course, who had due pre-eminence, and had taught the maids of honour) was generally acknowledged to be the Lord Chief-Justice Jeffreys.

Upon his return from the Bloody Assizes, with triumph and great glory, after hanging every man who was too poor to help it, he pleased His Gracious Majesty so purely with the description of their delightful agonies, that the King exclaimed, "This man alone is worthy to be at the head of the law." Accordingly in his hand was placed the Great Seal of England.

So it came to pass that Lorna's destiny hung upon Lord Jeffreys; for at this time Earl Brandir died, being taken with gout in the heart, soon after I left London. Lorna was very sorry for him; but as he had never been able to hear one tone of her sweet silvery voice, it is not to be supposed that she wept without consolation. She grieved for him, as we ought to grieve for any good man going, and yet with a comforting sense of the benefit which the blessed exchange must bring to him.

Now the Lady Lorna Dugal appeared to Lord Chancellor Jeffreys so exceeding wealthy a ward, that the lock would pay for turning. Therefore he came of his own accord to visit her, and to treat with her; having heard (for the man was as big a gossip as never cared for anybody, yet loved to know all about everybody) that this wealthy and beautiful maiden would not listen to any young lord, having pledged her faith to the plain John Ridd.

Thereupon, our Lorna managed so to hold out golden hopes to the Lord High Chancellor, that he, being not more than three parts drunk, saw his way to a heap of money. And there and then (for he was not the man to dally long about anything) upon surety of a certain round sum — the amount of which I will not mention, because of his kindness towards me — he gave to his fair ward permission, under sign and seal, to marry that loyal knight, John Ridd; upon condition only that the King's consent should be obtained.

His Majesty, well disposed towards me for my previous service; and regarding me as a good Catholic, being moved moreover by the Queen, who desired to please Lorna, consented, without much hesitation, upon the understanding that Lorna, when she became of full age, and the mistress of her property (which was still under guardianship), should pay a heavy fine to the Crown, and devote a fixed portion of her estate to the promotion of the holy Catholic faith, in a manner to be dictated by the King himself. Inasmuch, however, as King James was driven out of his kingdom before this arrangement could take effect, and another king succeeded, who desired not the promotion of the Catholic religion, neither hankered after subsidies (whether French or English), that agreement was pronounced invalid, improper, and contemptible. However, there was no getting back the money once paid to Lord Chancellor Jeffreys.

But what thought we of money, at this present moment, or of position, or anything else, except indeed one another? Lorna told me, with the sweetest smile, that if I were minded to take her at all, I must take her without anything; inasmuch as she meant, upon coming of age, to make over the residue of her estate to the next of kin, as being unfit for a farmer's wife. And I replied, with the greatest warmth, and a readiness to worship her, that this was exactly what I longed for, but had never dared to propose it. But dear mother looked most exceeding grave, and said that to be sure her opinion could not be expected to count for much, but she really hoped that in three years' time we should both be a little wiser, and have more regard for our interests, and perhaps those of others by that time; and Master Snowe having daughters only, and nobody coming to marry them, if anything happened to the good old man — and who could tell in three years' time what might happen to all, or any of us? — why, perhaps his farm would be for sale, and perhaps Lady Lorna's estates in Scotland would fetch enough money to buy it, and so throw the two farms into one, and save all the trouble about the brook, as my poor father had longed to do many and many a time, but not having a title could not do all quite as he wanted. And then if we young people grew tired of the old mother, as seemed only too likely, and was according to nature, why, we could send her over there, and Lizzie to keep her company.

When mother had finished, and wiped her eyes, Lorna, who had been blushing rosily at some portions of this great speech, flung her fair arms around mother's neck, and kissed her very heartily, and scolded her (as she well deserved) for her want of confidence in us. My mother replied, that if anybody could deserve her John, it was Lorna; but that she could not hold with the rashness of giving up money so easily; while her next of kin would be John himself, and who could tell what others, by the time she was one-and-twenty?

Hereupon I felt that after all my mother had common sense on her side; for if Master Snowe's farm should be for sale, it would be far more to the purpose than my coat of arms, to get it; for there was a different pasture there, just suited for change of diet to our sheep, as well as large cattle. And beside this, even with all Annie's skill (and of course yet more now she was gone), their butter would always command in the market from one to three farthings a pound more than we could get for ours. And few things vexed us more than this. Whereas, if we got possession of the farm, we might, without breach of the market laws, or any harm done to anyone (the price being but a prejudice), sell all our butter as Snowe butter, and do good to all our customers.

Thinking thus, yet remembering that Farmer Nicholas might hold out for another score of years — as I heartily hoped he might — or that one, if not all, of his comely daughters might marry a good young farmer (or farmers, if the case were so) — or that, even without that, the farm might never be put up for sale; I begged my Lorna to do as she liked; or rather to wait and think of it; for as yet she could do nothing.

CHAPTER LXXIV
Blood upon the Altar

Everything was settled smoothly, and without any fear or fuss, that Lorna might find end of troubles, and myself of eager waiting, with the help of Parson Bowden, and the good wishes of two counties. I could scarce believe my fortune, when I looked upon her beauty, gentleness, and sweetness, mingled with enough of humour, and warm woman's feeling, never to be dull or tiring; never themselves to be weary.

For she might be called woman now; although a very young one, and as full of playful ways, or perhaps I may say ten times as full, as if she had known no trouble. To wit, the spirit of bright childhood, having been so curbed and straitened, ere its time was over, now broke forth, enriched and varied with the garb of conscious maidenhood. And the sense of steadfast love, and eager love enfolding her, coloured with so many tinges all her looks, and words, and thoughts, that to me it was the noblest vision even to think about her.

But this was far too bright to last, without bitter break, and the plunging of happiness in horror, and of passionate joy in agony. My darling, in her softest moments, when she was alone with me, when the spark of defiant eyes was veiled beneath dark lashes, and the challenge of gay beauty passed into sweetest invitation; at such times of her purest love and warmest faith in me, a deep abiding fear would flutter in her bounding heart, as of deadly fate's approach. She would cling to me, and nestle to me, being scared of coyishness, and lay one arm around my neck, and ask if I could do without her.

Hence, as all emotions haply, of those who are more to us than ourselves, find within us stronger echo, and more perfect answer, so I could not be regardless of some hidden evil; and my dark misgivings deepened as the time drew nearer. I kept a steadfast watch on Lorna, neglecting a field of beans entirely, as well as a litter of young pigs, and a cow somewhat given to jaundice. And I let Jem Slocombe go to sleep in the tallat, all one afternoon, and Bill Dadds draw off a bucket of cider, without so much as a "by your leave." For these men knew that my knighthood, and my coat of arms, and (most of all) my love, were greatly against good farming; the sense of our country being — and perhaps it may be sensible — that a man who sticks up to be anything, must allow himself to be cheated.

But I never did stick up, nor would, though all the parish bade me; and I whistled the same tunes to my horses, and held my plough-tree just the same, as if no King, nor Queen, had ever come to spoil my tune or hand. For this thing, nearly all the men around our part upbraided me, but the women praised me; and for the most part these are right, when themselves are not concerned.

However humble I might be, no one, knowing anything of our part of the country, would for a moment doubt that now here was a great to-do, and talk of John Ridd and his wedding. The fierce fight with the Doones so lately, and my leading of the combat (though I fought not more than need be), and the vanishing of Sir Counsellor, and the galloping madness of Carver, and the religious fear of the women that this last was gone to hell — for he himself had declared that his aim, while he cut through our yeomanry; also their remorse, that he should have been made to go thither, with all his children left behind — these things, I say (if ever I can again contrive to say anything), had led to the broadest excitement about my wedding of Lorna. We heard that people meant to come from more than thirty miles around, upon excuse of seeing my stature and Lorna's beauty; but in good truth out of sheer curiosity, and the love of meddling.

Our clerk had given notice, that not a man should come inside the door of his church without shilling-fee; and women (as sure to see twice as much) must every one pay two shillings. I thought this wrong; and, as churchwarden, begged that the money might be paid into mine own hands, when taken. But the clerk said that was against all law; and he had orders from the parson to pay it to him without any delay. So as I always obey the parson, when I care not much about a thing, I let them have it their own way; though feeling inclined to believe, sometimes, that I ought to have some of the money.

Dear mother arranged all the ins and outs of the way in which it was to be done; and Annie, and Lizzie, and all the Snowes, and even Ruth Huckaback (who was there, after great persuasion), made such a sweeping of dresses, that I scarcely knew where to place my feet, and longed for a staff, to put by their gowns. Then Lorna came out of a pew half-way, in a manner which quite astonished me, and took my left hand in her right, and I prayed God that it were done with.

My darling looked so glorious, that I was afraid of glancing at her, yet took in all her beauty. She was in a fright, no doubt; but nobody should see it; whereas I said (to myself at least), "I will go through it like a gravedigger."

Lorna's dress was of pure white, clouded with faint lavender (for the sake of the old Earl Brandir), and as simple as need be, except for perfect loveliness. I was afraid to look at her, as I said before, except when each of us said, "I will;" and then each dwelled upon the other.

It is impossible for any, who have not loved as I have, to conceive my joy and pride, when after ring and all was done, and the parson had blessed us, Lorna turned to look at me, with her playful glance subdued, and deepened by this solemn act.

Her eyes, which none on earth may ever equal, or compare with, told me such a tale of hope, and faith, and heart's devotion, that I was almost amazed, thoroughly as I knew them. Darling eyes, the dearest eyes, the loveliest, the most loving eyes — the sound of a shot rang through the church, and those eyes were dim with death.

Lorna fell across my knees, when I was going to kiss her, as the bridegroom is allowed to do, and encouraged, if he needs it; a flood of blood came out upon the yellow wood of the altar steps; and at my feet lay Lorna, trying to tell me some last message out of her faithful eyes. I lifted her up, and petted her, and coaxed her, but it was no good; the only sign of life remaining was a drip of bright red blood.

Some men know what things befall them in the supreme time of their life — far above the time of death — but to me comes back as a hazy dream without any knowledge in it, what I did, or felt, or thought, with my wife's arms flagging, flagging, around my neck, as I raised her up, and softly put them there. She sighed a long sigh on my breast, for her last farewell to life, and then she grew so cold, and cold, that I asked the time of year.

It was now Whit-Tuesday, and the lilacs all in blossom; and why I thought of the time of year, with the young death in my arms, God, or His angels, may decide, having so strangely given us. Enough that so I did, and looked; and our white lilacs were beautiful. Then I laid my wife in my mother's arms, and begging that no one would make a noise, went forth for my revenge.

Of course, I knew who had done it. There was but one man upon earth, or under it, where the devil dwells, who could have done such a thing — such a thing. I used no harsher word about it, while I leaped upon our best horse, with bridle but no saddle, and set the head of Kickums towards the course now pointed out to me. Who showed me the course, I cannot tell. I only know that I took it. And the men fell back before me.

Weapon of no sort had I. Unarmed, and wondering at my strange attire (with a bridal vest, wrought by our Annie, and red with the blood of the bride), I went forth just to find out this; whether in this world there be, or be not, God of justice.

With my vicious horse at a furious speed, I came upon Black Barrow Down, directed by some shout of men, which seemed to me but a whisper. And there, about a furlong before me, rode a man on a great black horse; and I knew that the man was Carver Doone.

"Thy life, or mine," I said to myself; "as the will of God may be. But we two live not upon this earth, one more hour, together."

I knew the strength of this great man; and I knew that he was armed with a gun — if he had time to load again, after shooting my Lorna — or at any rate with pistols, and a horseman's sword as well. Nevertheless, I had no more doubt of killing the man before me, than a cook has of spitting a headless fowl.

Sometimes seeing no ground beneath me, and sometimes heeding every leaf, and the crossing of the grass blades, I followed over the long moor, reckless whether seen or not. But only once, the other man turned round, and looked back again; and then I was beside a rock, with a reedy swamp behind me.

Although he was so far before me, and riding as hard as ride he might, I saw that he had something on the horse in front of him; something which needed care, and stopped him from looking backward. In the whirling of my wits, I fancied first that this was Lorna; until the scene I had been through fell, across hot brain, and heart, like a drop at the close of a tragedy. Rushing there, through crag and quag, at utmost speed of a maddened horse, I saw, as of another's fate, calmly (as on canvas laid), the brutal deed, the piteous anguish, and the cold despair.

The man turned up the gully leading from the moor to Cloven Rocks, through which John Fry had tracked Uncle Ben, as of old related. But as Carver entered it, he turned round and beheld me not a hundred yards behind; and I saw that he was bearing his child, little Ensie, before him. Ensie also descried me, and stretched his hands, and cried to me; for the face of his father frightened him.

Carver Doone, with a vile oath, thrust spurs into his flagging horse, and laid one hand on a pistol-stock, whence I knew that his slung carbine had received no bullet, since the one that had pierced Lorna. And a cry of triumph rose from the black depths of my heart. What cared I for pistols? I had no spurs, neither was my horse one to need the rowel; I rather held him in than urged him, for he was fresh as ever; and I knew that the black steed in front, if he breasted the steep ascent, where the track divided, must be in our reach at once.

His rider knew this; and, having no room in the rocky channel to turn and fire, drew rein at the crossways sharply, and plunged into the black ravine leading to the Wizard's Slough. "Is it so?" I said to myself, with brain and head cold as iron: "though the foul fiend come from the slough to save thee, thou shalt carve it, Carver."

I followed my enemy carefully, steadily, even leisurely: for I had him, as in a pitfall, whence no escape might be. He thought that I feared to approach him, for he knew not where he was: and his low disdainful laugh came back. "Laugh he who wins," thought I.

A gnarled and half-starved oak, as stubborn as my own resolve, and smitten by some storm of old, hung from the crag above me. Rising from my horse's back, although I had no stirrups, I caught a limb, and tore it (like a wheat-awn) from the socket. Men show the rent even now, with wonder; none with more wonder than myself.

Carver Doone turned the corner suddenly, on the black and bottomless bog; with a start of fear he reined back his horse, and I thought he would have rushed upon me. But instead of that he again rode on; hoping to find a way round the side.

Now there is a way between cliff and slough, for those who know the ground thoroughly, or have time enough to search it; but for him there was no road, and he lost some time in seeking it. Upon this he made up his mind, and wheeling, fired, and then rode at me.

His bullet struck me somewhere, but I took no heed of that. Fearing only his escape, I laid my horse across the way, and with the limb of the oak struck full on the forehead his charging steed. Ere the slash of the sword came nigh me, man and horse rolled over, and well-nigh bore my own horse down, with the power of their onset.

Carver Doone was somewhat stunned, and could not arise for a moment. Meanwhile I leaped on the ground, and waited, smoothing my hair back, and baring my arms, as though in the ring for wrestling. Then the little boy ran to me, clasped my leg, and looked up at me: and the terror in his eyes made me almost fear myself.

"Ensie, dear," I said, quite gently, grieving that he should see his wicked father killed, "run up yonder round the corner, and try to find a bunch of bluebells for the pretty lady." The child obeyed me, hanging back, and looking back, and then laughing, while I prepared for business. There and then, I might have killed mine enemy, with a single blow, while he lay unconscious; but it would have been foul play.

With a sullen and black scowl, the Carver gathered his mighty limbs, and arose, and looked round for his weapons; but I had put them well away. Then he came to me, and gazed, being wont to frighten thus young men.

"I would not harm you, lad," he said, with a lofty style of sneering: "I have punished you enough, for most of your impertinence. For the rest I forgive you; because you have been good, and gracious, to my little son. Go, and be contented."

For answer, I smote him on the cheek, lightly, and not to hurt him: but to make his blood leap up. I would not sully my tongue, by speaking to a man like this.

There was a level space of sward, between us and the slough. With the courtesy derived from London, and the processions I had seen, to this place I led him. And that he might breathe himself, and have every fibre cool, and every muscle ready, my hold upon his coat I loosed, and left him to begin with me, whenever he thought proper.

I think he felt that his time was come. I think he knew from my knitted muscles, and the firm arch of my breast, and the way in which I stood; but most of all from my stern blue eyes; that he had found his master. At any rate, a paleness came, an ashy paleness on his cheeks, and the vast calves of his legs bowed in, as if he were out of training.

Seeing this, villain as he was, I offered him first chance. I stretched forth my left hand, as I do to a weaker antagonist, and I let him have the hug of me. But in this I was too generous; having forgotten my pistol-wound, and the cracking of one of my short lower ribs. Carver Doone caught me round the waist, with such a grip as never yet had been laid upon me.

I heard my rib go; I grasped his arm, and tore the muscle out of it (as the going comes out of an orange); then I took him by the throat, which is not allowed in wrestling; but he had snatched at mine; and now was no time of dalliance. In vain he tugged, and strained, and writhed, dashed his bleeding fist into my face, and flung himself on me, with gnashing jaws. Beneath the iron of my strength — for God that day was with me — I had him helpless in two minutes, and his blazing eyes lolled out.

"I will not harm thee any more," I cried, so far as I could for panting, the work being very furious; "Carver Doone, thou art beaten: own it, and thank God for it; and go thy way, and repent thyself."

It was all too late. Even if he had yielded in his ravening frenzy, for his beard was frothy as a mad dog's jowl; even if he would have owned that, for the first time in his life, he had found his master; it was all too late.

The black bog had him by the feet; the sucking of the ground drew on him, like the thirsty lips of death. In our fury, we had heeded neither wet nor dry, nor thought of earth beneath us. I myself might scarcely leap, with the last spring of o'erlaboured legs, from the engulfing grave of slime. He fell back, with his swarthy breast (from which my gripe had rent all clothing), like a hummock of bog-oak, standing out the quagmire; and then he tossed his arms to heaven, and they were black to the elbow, and the glare of his eyes was ghastly. I could only gaze and pant: for my strength was no more than an infant's, from the fury and the horror. Scarcely could I turn away, while, joint by joint, he sank from sight.

CHAPTER LXXV
Give away the Grandeur

When the little boy came back with the bluebells, which he had managed to find — as children always do find flowers, when older eyes see none — the only sign of his father left was a dark brown bubble, with a new-formed patch of blackness. But to the centre of its pulpy gorge, the greedy slough was heaving, and sullenly grinding its weltering jaws, among the flags, and the sedges.

With pain, and ache, both of mind and body, and shame at my own fury, I heavily mounted my horse again, and looked down at the innocent Ensie. Would this playful, loving child grow up like his cruel father, and end a godless life of hatred with a death of violence? He lifted his noble forehead towards me, as if to answer, "Nay, I will not:" but the words he spoke were these:

"Don" — for he never could say "John" — "oh, Don, I am so glad, that nasty naughty man is gone away. Take me home, Don. Take me home."

It has been said of the wicked, "Not even their own children love them." And I could easily believe that Carver Doone's cold-hearted ways had scared from him even his favourite child. No man would I call truly wicked, unless his heart be cold.

It hurt me, more than I can tell, even through all other grief, to take into my arms the child of the man just slain by me. The feeling was a foolish one, and a wrong one, as the thing had been — for I would fain have saved that man, after he was conquered — nevertheless my arms went coldly round that little fellow; neither would they have gone at all, if there had been any help for it. But I could not leave him there, till some one else might fetch him; on account of the cruel slough, and the ravens which had come hovering over the dead horse; neither could I, with my wound, tie him on my horse, and walk.

For now I had spent a great deal of blood, and was rather faint and weary. And it was lucky for me that Kickums had lost spirit, like his master, and went home as mildly as a lamb. For, when we came towards the farm, I seemed to be riding in a dream almost; and the voices both of men and women (who had hurried forth upon my track), as they met me, seemed to wander from a distant muffling cloud. Only the thought of Lorna's death, like a heavy knell, was tolling in the belfry of my brain.

When we came to the stable door, I rather fell from my horse than got off; and John Fry, with a look of wonder, took Kickums' head, and led him in. Into the old farm-house I tottered, like a weanling child, with mother in her common clothes, helping me along, yet fearing, except by stealth, to look at me.

"I have killed him," was all I said; "even as he killed Lorna. Now let me see my wife, mother. She belongs to me none the less, though dead."

"You cannot see her now, dear John," said Ruth Huckaback, coming forward; since no one else had the courage. "Annie is with her now, John."

"What has that to do with it? Let me see my dead one; and then die."

All the women fell away, and whispered, and looked at me, with side-glances, and some sobbing; for my face was hard as flint. Ruth alone stood by me, and dropped her eyes, and trembled. Then one little hand of hers stole into my great shaking palm, and the other was laid on my tattered coat; yet with her clothes she shunned my blood, while she whispered gently:

"John, she is not your dead one. She may even be your living one yet, your wife, your home, and your happiness. But you must not see her now."

"Is there any chance for her? For me, I mean; for me, I mean?"

"God in heaven knows, dear John. But the sight of you, and in this sad plight, would be certain death to her. Now come first, and be healed yourself."

I obeyed her, like a child, whispering only as I went, for none but myself knew her goodness — "Almighty God will bless you, darling, for the good you are doing now."

Tenfold, ay and a thousandfold, I prayed and I believed it, when I came to know the truth. If it had not been for this little maid, Lorna must have died at once, as in my arms she lay for dead, from the dastard and murderous cruelty. But the moment I left her Ruth came forward, and took the command of every one, in right of her firmness and readiness.

She made them bear her home at once upon the door of the pulpit, with the cushion under the drooping head. With her own little hands she cut off, as tenderly as a pear is peeled, the bridal-dress so steeped and stained, and then with her dainty transparent fingers (no larger than a pencil) she probed the vile wound in the side, and fetched the reeking bullet forth; and then with the coldest water stanched the flowing of the life-blood. All this while, my darling lay insensible, and white as death; and the rest declared that she was dead, and needed nothing but her maiden shroud.

But Ruth still sponged the poor side and forehead, and watched the long eyelashes flat upon the marble cheek; and laid her pure face on the faint heart, and bade them fetch her Spanish wine. Then she parted the pearly teeth (feebly clenched on the hovering breath), and poured in wine from a christening spoon, and raised the graceful neck and breast, and stroked the delicate throat, and waited; and then poured in a little more.

Annie all the while looked on, with horror and amazement, counting herself no second-rate nurse, and this as against all theory. But the quiet lifting of Ruth's hand, and one glance from her dark bright eyes, told Annie just to stand away, and not intercept the air so. And at the very moment, when all the rest had settled that Ruth was a simple idiot, but could not harm the dead much, a little flutter in the throat, followed by a short low sigh, made them pause, and look, and hope.

For hours, however, and days, she lay at the very verge of death, kept alive by nothing but the care, the skill, the tenderness, and perpetual watchfulness of Ruth. Luckily Annie was not there very often, so as to meddle; for kind and clever nurse as she was, she must have done more harm than good. But my broken rib, which was set by a doctor, who chanced to be at the wedding, was allotted to Annie's care; and great inflammation ensuing, it was quite enough to content her. This doctor had pronounced poor Lorna dead; wherefore Ruth refused most firmly to have aught to do with him. She took the whole case on herself; and with God's help, she bore it through.

Now whether it were the light, and brightness of my Lorna's nature, or the freedom from anxiety — for she knew not of my hurt — or, as some people said, her birthright among wounds and violence, or her manner of not drinking beer — I leave that doctor to determine, who pronounced her dead. But anyhow, one thing is certain; sure as the stars of hope above us, Lorna recovered long ere I did.

On me lay overwhelming sorrow, having lost my love and lover, at the moment she was mine. With the power of fate upon me, and the black cauldron of the wizard's death boiling in my heated brain, I had no faith in the tales they told. I believed that Lorna was in the churchyard, while these rogues were lying to me. For with strength of blood like mine, and power of heart behind it, a broken bone must burn himself.

Mine went hard with fires of pain, being of such size and thickness; and I was ashamed of him for breaking by reason of a pistol-ball, and the mere hug of a man. And it fetched me down in conceit of strength; so that I was careful afterwards.

All this was a lesson to me. All this made me very humble; illness being a thing, as yet, altogether unknown to me. Not that I cried small, or skulked, or feared the death which some foretold: shaking their heads about mortification, and a green appearance. Only that I seemed quite fit to go to heaven, and Lorna. For in my sick distracted mind (stirred with many tossings), like the bead in a wisp of frog-spawn drifted by the current, hung the black and worthless burden of the life before me. A life without Lorna; a tadpole life. All stupid head; and no body.

Many men may like such life; anchorites, fakirs, high-priests, and so on; but to my mind, it is not the native thing God meant for us. My dearest mother was a show, with crying, and with fretting. The Doones, as she thought, were born to destroy us. Scarce had she come to some liveliness (though sprinkled with tears, every now and then) after her great bereavement, and ten years' time to dwell on it — when lo, here was her husband's son, the pet child of her own good John, murdered like his father! Well, the ways of God were wonderful!

So they were, and so they are, and so they ever will be. Let us debate them as we will, our ways are His, and much the same; only second-hand from Him. And I expected something from Him, even in my worst of times, knowing that I had done my best.

This is not edifying talk — as the Puritans used to remind my father, when there was no more to drink therefore let me only tell what became of Lorna. One day, I was sitting in my bed-room, for I could not get downstairs, and there was no one strong enough to carry me, even if I would have borne it.

Though it cost me sore trouble and weariness, I had put on all my Sunday clothes, out of respect for the doctor, who was coming to bleed me again (as he always did, twice a week); and it struck me, that he had seemed hurt in his mind, because I wore my worst clothes to be bled in — for lie in bed I would not, after six o'clock; and even that was great laziness.

I looked at my right hand, whose grasp had been like that of a blacksmith's vice; and it seemed to myself impossible, that this could be John Ridd's. The great frame of the hand was there, as well as the muscles, standing forth like the guttering of a can-dle, and the broad blue veins, going up the back, and crossing every finger. But as for colour, even Lorna's could scarcely have been whiter; and as for strength, little Ensie Doone might have come and held it fast. I laughed, as I tried in vain to lift the basin set for bleeding me.

Then I thought of all the lovely things going on out of doors just now, concerning which the drowsy song of the bees came to me. These must be among the thyme, by the sound of their great content. Therefore the roses must be in blossom, and the woodbine, and clove-gillyflower; the cherries on the wall must be turning red, and the first brood of thrushes come to watch them do it; wheat must be callow with a tufted quivering, and the early meadows swathed with hay.

Yet here was I, a helpless creature, quite unfit to stir among them, gifted with no sight, no scent of all the changes that move our love, and lead our hearts, from month to month, along the quiet path of life. And what was worse, I had no hope of caring ever for them more.

Presently a little knock sounded through my gloomy room, and supposing it to be the doctor, I tried to rise, and make my bow. But to my surprise, it was little Ruth, who had never once come to visit me, since I was placed under the doctor's hands. Ruth was dressed so gaily, with rosettes, and flowers, and what not, that I was sorry for her bad manners; and thought she was come to conquer me, now that Lorna was done with.

Ruth ran towards me, with sparkling eyes, being rather short of sight; then suddenly she stopped, and I saw entire amazement in her face.

"Can you receive visitors, Cousin Ridd? — why, they never told me of this!" she cried: "I knew that you were weak, dear John; but not that you were dying. Whatever is that basin for?"

"I have no intention of dying, Ruth; and I like not to talk about it. But that basin, if you must know, is for the doctor's purpose."

"What, do you mean bleeding you? You poor weak cousin! Is it possible that he does that still?"

"Twice a week for the last six weeks, dear. Nothing else has kept me alive."

"Nothing else has killed you, nearly. There!" and she set her little boot across the basin, and crushed it. "Not another drop shall they have from you. Is Annie such a fool as that? And Lizzie, like a zany, at her books! And killing their brother, between them!"

I was surprised to see Ruth excited; her character being so calm and quiet. And I tried to soothe her with my feeble hand, as now she knelt before me.

"Dear cousin, the doctor must know best. Annie says so, every day. Else what has he been brought up for?"

"Brought up for slaying and murdering. Twenty doctors killed King Charles, in spite of all the women. Will you leave it to me, John? I have a little will of my own; and I am not afraid of doctors. Will you leave it to me, dear John? I have saved your Lorna's life. And now I will save yours; which is a far, far easier business."

"You have saved my Lorna's life! What do you mean by talking so?"

"Only what I say, Cousin John. Though perhaps I over-prize my work. But at any rate she says so"

"I do not understand," I said, falling back with bewilderment, "all women are such liars."

"Have you ever known me tell a lie?" cried Ruth in great indignation — more feigned, I doubt, than real — "your mother may tell a story, now and then, when she feels it right; and so may both your sisters. But so you cannot do, John Ridd; and no more than you, can I do it."

If ever there was virtuous truth in the eyes of any woman, it was now in the eyes of Ruth Huckaback: and my brain began very slowly to move, the heart being almost torpid from perpetual loss of blood.

"I do not understand," was all I could say, for a very long time.

"Will you understand, if I show you Lorna? I have feared to do it, for the sake of you both. But now Lorna is well enough, if you think that you are, Cousin John. Surely you will understand, when you see your wife."

Following her, to the very utmost of my mind and heart, I felt that all she said was truth; and yet I could not make it out. And in her last few words, there was such a power of sadness, rising through the cover of gaiety, that I said to myself, half in a dream, "Ruth is very beautiful."

Before I had time to listen much for the approach of footsteps, Ruth came back, and behind her Lorna; coy as if of her bridegroom; and hanging back with her beauty. Ruth banged the door, and ran away; and Lorna stood before me.

But she did not stand for an instant, when she saw what I was like. At the risk of all thick bandages, and upsetting a dozen medicine bottles, and scattering leeches right and left, she managed to get into my arms, although they could not hold her. She laid her panting warm young breast on the place where they meant to bleed me, and she set my pale face up; and she would not look at me, having greater faith in kissing.

I felt my life come back, and glow; I felt my trust in God revive; I felt the joy of living and of loving dearer things than life. It is not a moment to describe; who feels can never tell of it. But the compassion of my sweetheart's tears, and the caressing of my bride's lips, and the throbbing of my wife's heart (now at last at home on mine) made me feel that the world was good, and not a thing to be weary of.

Little more have I to tell. The doctor was turned out at once; and slowly came back my former strength, with a darling wife, and good victuals. As for Lorna, she never tired of sitting and watching me eat and eat. And such is her heart, that she never tires of being with me here and there, among the beautiful places, and talking with her arm around me — so far at least as it can go, though half of mine may go round her — of the many fears, and troubles, dangers and discouragements, and worst of all the bitter partings, which we used to undergo.

There is no need for my farming harder than becomes a man of weight. Lorna has great stores of money, though we never draw it out, except for some poor neighbour; unless I find her a sumptuous dress, out of her own perquisites. And this she always looks upon as a wondrous gift from me; and kisses me much when she puts it on, and walks like the noble woman she is. And yet I may never behold it again; for she gets back to her simple clothes, and I love her the better in them. I believe that she gives half the grandeur away, and keeps the other half for the children.

As for poor Tom Faggus, every one knows his bitter adventures, when his pardon was recalled, because of his sally to Sedgemoor. Not a child in the county, I doubt, but knows far more than I do of Tom's most desperate doings. The law had ruined him once, he said; and then he had been too much for the law: and now that a quiet life was his object, here the base thing came after him. And such was his dread of this evil spirit, that being caught upon Barnstaple Bridge, with soldiers at either end of it (yet doubtful about approaching him), he set his strawberry mare, sweet Winnie, at the left-hand parapet, with a whisper into her dove-coloured ear. Without a moment's doubt she leaped it, into the foaming tide, and swam, and landed according to orders. Also his flight from a public-house (where a trap was set for him, but Winnie came, and broke down the door, and put two men under, and trod on them), is as well known as any ballad. It was reported for awhile that poor Tom had been caught at last, by means of his fondness for liquor, and was hanged before Taunton Gaol; but luckily we knew better. With a good wife, and a wonderful horse, and all the country attached to him, he kept the law at a wholesome distance, until it became too much for its master; and a new king arose. Upon this, Tom sued his pardon afresh; and Jeremy Stickles, who suited the times, was glad to help him in getting it, as well as a compensation. Thereafter, the good and respectable Tom lived a godly and righteous (though not always sober) life; and brought up his children to honesty, as the first of all qualifications.

My dear mother was as happy as possibly need be with us; having no cause for jealousy, as others arose around her. And everybody was well pleased, when Lizzie came in one day and tossed her book-shelf over, and declared that she would have Captain Bloxham, and nobody should prevent her. For that he alone, of all the men she had ever met with, knew good writing when he saw it, and could spell a word when told. As he had now succeeded to Captain Stickles' position (Stickles going up the tree), and had the power of collecting, and of keeping, what he liked, there was nothing to be said against it; and we hoped that he would pay her out.

I sent little Ensie to Blundell's school, at my own cost and charges, having changed his name, for fear of what anyone might do to him. I called him "Ensie Jones"; and I hope that he will be a credit to us. For the bold adventurous nature of the Doones broke out on him, and we got him a commission, and after many scrapes of spirit, he did great things in the Low Countries. He looks upon me as his father; and without my leave will not lay claim to the heritage, and title of the Doones, which clearly belong to him.

Ruth Huckaback is not married yet: although upon Uncle Reuben's death she came into all his property; except, indeed, £2000, which Uncle Ben, in his driest manner, bequeathed "to Sir John Ridd, the worshipful knight, for greasing of the testator's boots." And he left almost a mint of money, not from the mine, but from the shop, and the good use of usury. For the mine had brought in just what it cost, when the vein of gold ended suddenly; leaving all concerned much older, and some, I fear, much poorer; but no one utterly ruined, as is the case with most of them. Ruth herself was his true mine, as upon death-bed he found. I know a man even worthy of her: and though she is not very young, he loves her, as I love Lorna. More and more I hope, and think, that in the end he will win her; and I do not mean to dance again, except at dear Ruth's wedding; if a floor can be found strong enough.

Of Lorna, of my lifelong darling, of my more and more loved wife, I will not talk; for it is not seemly, that a man should exalt his pride. Year by year, her beauty grows, with the growth of goodness, kindness, and true happiness — above all with loving. For change, she makes a joke of this, and plays with it, and laughs at it; and then, when my slow nature marvels, back she comes to the earnest thing. And if I wish to pay her out for something very dreadful — as may happen once or twice, when we become too gladsome — I bring her to forgotten sadness, and to me for cure of it, by the two words, "Lorna Doone."

983729

Printed in Great Britain by
Amazon.co.uk, Ltd.,
Marston Gate.